Praise for the novels of Anne Bishop

The Invisible Ring

"Entertaining otherworlds fantasy adventure. Fresh and interesting." —*Science Fiction Chronicle*

"A weird, but highly diverting and oddly heartwarming mix." —*Locus*

"A formidable talent, Ms. Bishop weaves another intense, emotional tale that sparkles with powerful and imaginative magic." —*Romantic Times*

"Plenty of adventure, romance, dazzling wizardly pyrotechnics, and [a] unique and fascinating hierarchical magic system . . . all set in a thoroughly detailed, invented world of cultures in conflict. . . . It and its predecessors are genuine gems of fantasy much to be prized." —The SF Site

Queen of the Darkness

"As engaging, as strongly characterized, and as fully conceived as its predecessors . . . a perfect—and very moving—conclusion." —The SF Site

"A storyteller of stunning intensity, Ms. Bishop has a knack for appealing but complex characterization realized in a richly drawn, imaginative ambiance." —*Romance Times*

"A powerful finale for this fascinating uniquely dark trilogy." —*Locus*

continued . . .

THE PILLARS OF THE WORLD

Anne Bishop

A ROC BOOK

ROC

Published by New American Library, a division of
Penguin Group (USA) Inc., 375 Hudson Street,
New York, New York 10014, USA
Penguin Group (Canada), 90 Eglinton Avenue East, Suite 700, Toronto,
Ontario M4P 2Y3, Canada (a division of Pearson Penguin Canada Inc.)
Penguin Books Ltd., 80 Strand, London WC2R 0RL, England
Penguin Ireland, 25 St. Stephen's Green, Dublin 2,
Ireland (a division of Penguin Books Ltd.)
Penguin Group (Australia), 250 Camberwell Road, Camberwell, Victoria 3124,
Australia (a division of Pearson Australia Group Pty. Ltd.)
Penguin Books India Pvt. Ltd., 11 Community Centre, Panchsheel Park,
New Delhi - 110 017, India
Penguin Group (NZ), 67 Apollo Drive, Rosedale, North Shore 0632,
New Zealand (a division of Pearson New Zealand Ltd.)
Penguin Books (South Africa) (Pty.) Ltd., 24 Sturdee Avenue,
Rosebank, Johannesburg 2196, South Africa

Penguin Books Ltd., Registered Offices:
80 Strand, London WC2R 0RL, England

First published by Roc, an imprint of New American Library,
a division of Penguin Group (USA) Inc.

First Printing, October 2001
20 19 18 17 16 15 14 13 12

For
Pat York
and
Lynn Flewelling

and
in memory of
Alan Mietlowski

ACKNOWLEDGMENTS

My thanks to Blair Boone for being an encouraging first reader; to Mari Anderson for giving voice to "Love's Jewels"; to Deb Coates, Linda Antonnsen, Mindy Klasky, Doranna Durgin, Vonda McIntire, Deborah Wheeler, Julie Czerneda, and Jennifer Roberson for information and observations about things equine and canine; to Nadine Fallacaro for reviewing things medical; to Kandra for her continued time and energy on the Web site; to Michelle Zymowski, Rick Kohler, Cortney Heitzman, and Hal Leader for their help with the map; and to Pat and Bill Feidner for being there.

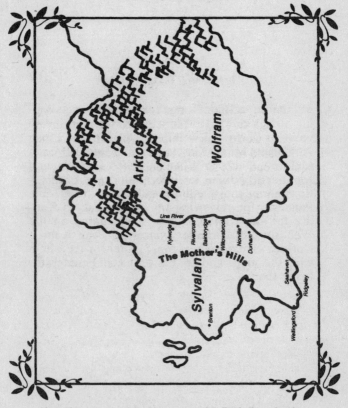

Note: This map was created by a geographically challenged author.
All distances are whimsical and subject to change without notice.

Chapter One

Another road was closing. It would take a little time, but not that long. For a few more days, that road through the Veil that separated Tir Alainn from the human world would shine, as it had for as long as the Fae could remember. Then the Veil would thicken and the road would disappear, and any of the Fae Lords or Ladies who tried to travel that road out of Tir Alainn wouldn't come home again.

And once the road closed, the part of Tir Alainn that was connected to that road would disappear as well—another piece of what had been the Fae's most glorious act of magic mysteriously devoured.

We do not ask what becomes of the Fae who lived in those lost pieces, Dianna thought as she stared at the garden beyond the open window. *We do not ask if they are somehow surviving in their Clan houses, cut off from the rest of us, or if they've become lost souls who will never reach the Summerland when the flesh gives itself back to the Mother.*

Turning away from the window, she faced the man and woman who had been patiently waiting for her attention.

They had the feral beauty that was common to the Fae. The woman had dark red hair and woodland eyes—a brown-flecked green. Some of the Fae said eyes that color harkened back to the House of Gaian, a Clan that had disappeared so long ago it was barely even a legend anymore. Whether that was truth or wishful thinking, no one could say any more than they could remember why the House of Gaian had been special—or why it had disappeared.

The man had black hair and blue eyes that were usually filled with sharp amusement. She saw storms in his eyes now, and sadness in the woman's.

"You found nothing," she said, not bothering to make it a question since their eyes had already answered.

"We found nothing," Lyrra replied. "Inspira, Cariden, and I have asked every storyteller and poet we could find. None remember anything that would help us understand why the roads are closing or how to stop it from happening." She hesitated. "I don't know if this is related to the information we've been seeking, but there was an old poet from another Clan who remembered hearing a fragment of an ancient poem that spoke of the Pillars of the World. But he had been a child when he heard it and could recall nothing else about it."

"The Pillars of the World," Dianna said, forcing herself to remain calm. "Do you know what it means?"

Lyrra shook her head. "It's as if we had once known so well what they were, there was no need to explain them, no need to hold onto them with words."

Dianna swallowed hope turned bitter. "Then it's unlikely they have anything to do with what's happening to us now." She looked at the man.

"I found nothing," Aiden said flatly. "The bards know songs enough about riding the roads and the delights that might be encountered on the other side of the Veil, but nothing that will help us."

If the Muse and the Bard can find nothing, who else can we ask? Dianna wondered. *Where else can we look for the answers?*

None of them mentioned what might have been known to the Clans who had used the shining roads that had connected to the Old Places in the human countries called Arktos and Wolfram—the Clans who had been disappearing, one by one, since she was a little girl.

Now, the only roads through the Veil were the ones connected to Sylvalan, and those, too, were beginning to close.

Had warnings gone unheeded all those years, or had they never been sent? Had the Fae whose territories had been connected to the Old Places in those countries been willfully blind to the danger, so sure that whatever had happened to another Clan couldn't possibly happen to them—or had they kept to their own Clan houses and their own territories because they'd been afraid that it *would* happen to them? Or had it been that those Clans had always seemed so distant anyway that no one in this part of their world had paid much attention?

Now the danger was no longer distant, no longer happening to someone else. Now it was devouring *their* Clans, and they hadn't been able to find out why—and they hadn't been able to stop it.

"I am sorry, Dianna," Lyrra said softly.

"My thanks for trying," Dianna said, turning back to the window.

A rustle of fabric. Quiet footsteps walking away.

Only one set of footsteps.

Looking over her shoulder, she could almost see the swelling anger in Aiden. "Something else?"

He joined her at the window. "Before coming to the Clan house here, I went down one of the other roads." His expression was bland, but his eyes . . . "I traveled through a couple of villages in the northeastern part of Sylvalan."

"And no doubt stopped at the taverns to hear a minstrel or two," she said, working to give him an indulgent smile that might ease his mood.

He didn't smile back. "I listened," he said curtly.

And hadn't liked what he'd heard.

"The minstrels are singing songs about beings they call wiccanfae."

Dianna stiffened at the arrogance of *anything* else referring to itself as Fae. "And they are?"

"Wicked fairies. Witches. Creatures who, out of spite, will make a cow dry or a woman barren, who will creep into a house and devour a newborn's soul so that the mother finds the babe dead in its cradle with no mark upon it. They sometimes steal babies to sacrifice to their master, the Evil One, so that he will come and indulge in carnal acts with them. They use their love charms on chaste young women of good name and family, causing them to become so overcome with lust that they fornicate with men, without the honorable bond of marriage. They are the vessels of dark magic." He paused. "And they control the Small Folk, who are soulless creatures full of mischief magic. Creatures that must be cleansed from the land so that honest men can take the land's bounty without coming to harm. Do you want to hear more?"

"No," Dianna said, feeling a winter wind brush past her face even though spring would soon give way to summer. But what she wanted and what duty required were two different things. "Do you think these . . . wiccanfae . . . are the reason the roads are closing? Could they be using their magic to keep us out of the human world?"

"It is fact that the shining roads close in the human world before we lose a piece of Tir Alainn."

Dianna saw something shift in his eyes. "What happened at those taverns?"

"Just as the Muse can still a tongue or open an inner door inside a person that allows the words to flow, so I can give the gift of music—or take it away."

Dianna hesitated. Even for the Lady of the Moon—a title that made her the most influential female among the Fae—it was the better part of wisdom not to antagonize the Bard. Provoked, he wouldn't hesitate to shape a song that would diminish a person into a fool. "If the witches are our enemies, why stop the minstrels' songs?"

"I cannot stop what already exists, but I can stop any more from being created."

She placed a hand on his arm, felt the tight muscles. "Why stop them?" she asked, wondering how much he hadn't told her.

"One doesn't need to drink from a cup to know that it contains a poison," Aiden said harshly. "There's something wrong with those songs. Music that hasn't flowed through the heart on its journey to the hands offers little and can take much." He smiled bitterly. "And those who play those songs have sold their hearts for a bag of gold coins."

"Minstrels have to eat," Dianna said cautiously.

"There is warm gold and cold gold, and *I* know which has been taken by the end of the first turn. These minstrels play songs that create an ugliness in the hearts of those who hear them. And they've put new words to old tunes—tunes *we* created—that once spoke gently of magic and the gifts that magic gives. *That* is too deep an insult, Dianna, because that is an offense against *us*. The decision to take back the gift of music is mine, and only mine, to make."

"Has Lyrra decided to take back the Muse's gift as well?"

His eyes darkened until they were almost black.

Oh, yes, Dianna thought. *The Bard heard far more than he has said.*

"I have asked her to take back her gift from any minstrel who sings those songs," he said quietly. "But that is her choice."

Which meant that, unless she had a strong reason to oppose him, the Muse *would* honor his request. She and the Bard weren't exclusive lovers, but they were lovers nonetheless and often gave—or withheld—their gifts in tandem.

"And there is another reason to silence the music that would smear all magic with the offal of the witches' deeds." Aiden crossed his arms, leaned against the wall next to the window. "We travel through the Veil and use our gifts to hinder or help the humans."

"We do that because it amuses us, not because we need to," Dianna said impatiently.

"We do that because it amuses us," Aiden agreed, "and because it's . . . invigorating."

Dianna let out a delicate snort. She knew quite well what "invigoration" Fae men found in the human world. Fae women seldom found a similar kind of "invigoration."

Aiden's blue eyes twinkled, a sure sign that he knew exactly what she was thinking. Then the twinkle faded, leaving him serious again. "That isn't exactly what I meant. Living in Tir Alainn is like floating in the sun-warmed water of a quiet pond. Dealing with humans and their world is like riding the rapids of a fast river. One brings peace, the other stirs the blood."

"There's nothing wrong with peace," Dianna insisted. *Especially when it might be taken away at any moment.*

"Tell me something, Dianna," Aiden said. "When you ride with your shadow hounds for the Wild Hunt, do you gallop over the perfect, rolling hills of Tir Alainn or the rough imperfection of the human world?"

She didn't want to answer that, didn't want to acknowledge the truth in what he was saying—that the Fae traveled to the human world because the peace and perfection of Tir Alainn became boring after a while—so she said nothing.

After a moment, Aiden said, "I'll see if I can find any other references to the Pillars of the World. It may have been nothing more than a bard's way of referring to the roads at one time or other, but even knowing that much is more than we know now."

She nodded in agreement. Then there was nothing more to say.

"Dianna," Aiden said, bowing slightly.

"Aiden," she replied.

After he left, she remained at the window. If they

didn't find the reason behind the roads closing, the day would come when she would look out and see . . . what? What had any of the lost Fae seen before their piece of Tir Alainn disappeared?

Wiccanfae.

Her mouth shaped the word without giving it voice.

If they were the reason her beloved Tir Alainn was dying, they would soon discover what it was like to have the Lady of the Moon, who was also called the Huntress, for an enemy.

Chapter Two

Adolfo, the Master Inquisitor, stood near the wide, open grave, his hands lightly clasped at his waist. A spring wind, too cold for this late in the season, tugged at his long, fur-lined, austerely cut brown coat. He paid no more heed to the wind than he did to the baron, Hirstun, standing beside him, or the common men who had gathered at this place to watch; his attention was focused on the men dragging the bound, struggling woman from the cart.

"Take care," he said in that quietly stern voice that the countries of Arktos and Wolfram had already learned to fear. "Do let her wickedness incite you to less than honorable behavior. Her remaining time should be spent in reflection and repentance on the harm she has done the good people of Kylwode and not on any harsh treatment that may come from your hands."

The men holding the woman hesitated, then nodded.

She fought against their hands, making it impossible to lead her forward without dragging her.

Adolfo fixed his brown eyes on her. "Do not make this more difficult. Accept the fate your own actions have brought you to." He paused, then added very gently, "Unless you have other things to confess?"

The woman stiffened, her eyes wide and fearful. A moment later, she sagged in her captors' hands.

They led her to the open grave, keeping their steps small as she shuffled between them as well as the hobbles permitted. When they turned her to face Baron Hirstun and Adolfo, her eyes were filled with loathing for the men who had condemned her. She straightened, a last gesture of defiance that made her look like one of the gentry instead of a frightened, bedraggled woman who was about to die.

Adolfo felt fear creep down his spine, felt it collide with the hatred that had shaped his life until it settled into a dull ache in his lower back. That war within himself didn't show on his face or in the eyes that always remained as soft and gentle-looking as a doe's.

But the other men shifted uneasily as they felt the power rising in her.

It's the last time it will rise, Adolfo reassured himself. *And it can't help her now. I've made sure of that.* "Do you have any last words?" he asked her.

She said nothing.

One of the men holding her glanced at the metal device around her head. "Begging your pardon, Master Adolfo, but I don't think she can be saying much with that thing around her head."

"Get on with it," Hirstun growled.

Adolfo ignored the baron and addressed the man. "I would know her words no matter how garbled. But the metal tongue on the scold's bridle prevents her from clear speech, and, therefore, prevents her from casting a last spell to harm those who bring her to justice."

The other man grinned at the first. "You should get one of those for your Jenny, Sax. Give you a bit of peace."

Sax ducked his head. "Her tongue's got a sharp side to it, and that's the truth, but I couldn't see putting one of those things on my Jenny."

"The scold's bridle is a good man's tool," Adolfo said. "A caring husband and father does not allow his females to stray into unseemly behavior, nor does he allow his females to create discord at home. And it is well known that a woman's sharp words can blight a man's rod and weaken his seed until all he can fill her with are girl babes instead of strong sons."

Sax's face turned bright red. He stared at the ground. "Still, it looks like a harsh thing to do to a woman."

Adolfo smiled indulgently. "Metal is used for witches. For other women, the scold's bridle is made of leather, and a man tends it with the same care he gives the bridle of his favorite mare. It does her no harm. The shame of wearing it is sufficient to teach her modesty and pleasing behavior. Even my own cherished wife must, from time to time, wear the bridle. At first she resented and resisted being disciplined. Now she is grateful for that sign of my deep affection and concern for her well-being." He waited a moment, then added, "But perhaps you do not care quite as much for your Jenny."

After a long pause, Sax mumbled, "Where could I find one of these bridles?"

"I have copies of the pattern," Adolfo said. "I'll see that you get one—when our task is complete."

He kept his eyes on Sax, but he had been watching the witch, had seen the moment when she could no longer maintain her defiant stance and had slumped once more into the resignation of a dumb animal caught in a trap.

"Bind her legs. Be sure to leave enough leather for the spikes."

Sax pulled the length of leather from his belt and hunched down. When he reached under her dress, Adolfo snapped, "Bind it over her dress. We do not want any good man standing witness here to be provoked into lust if she should begin thrashing and expose her limbs. Women are weak vessels, easily corrupted by the Evil One. But even a strong man can be snared through the lascivious actions of a woman who is the Evil One's servant."

Sax quickly finished tying her and stepped back, rubbing his hands against the rough fabric of his trousers, as if even so little exposure to her might put him in danger.

Adolfo made a slight gesture at the grave. "Put her

down. One of you other men get the box from the cart."

When Sax and his friend lowered her into the grave, she began struggling again. Reluctantly, they slid into the hole to force her onto her back.

"Drive the spikes into the ground and tie the leather to them to keep her legs still," Adolfo instructed. He gestured to the man who had retrieved the box that had been built to Adolfo's specifications. "Place the box over her head and shoulders. Fix the other spikes through the straps."

As soon as Sax and his friend were done, the other men helped them out of the grave.

"Fill it in," Adolfo said. "Begin at the feet and work toward the head."

He and the baron watched in silence as the men shoveled dirt into the grave. When the first shovelful of dirt finally hit the wooden box, they heard her scream.

"I wouldn't have thought the Master Inquisitor was a compassionate man," Hirstun said quietly. "What difference does it make if the bitch gets dirt in her eyes?"

"I *am* a compassionate man," Adolfo said just as quietly. "If I were not, I wouldn't have taken up the task of freeing good people from these wicked creatures. The box will hold a little air after the grave is filled in. That will give her time to repent."

Hirstun eyed him warily. "And how will anyone know if she *does* repent?"

Adolfo smiled sadly. "True repentance comes at the moment before death. If she was spared at that moment, she would swear that she had repented, but it would be a lie. Death is the only freedom these creatures know, Baron, and even that isn't freedom since their actions in this world have condemned them to the Fiery Pit that awaits the Evil One's servants."

They said nothing more until the last shovelful of dirt filled the hole.

"Well, it's done," Hirstun said, watching his servant

pass out copper coins to the men who had assisted. "You'll come back to the manor to . . . settle things?"

"I'll be along shortly. I want to maintain watch for another minute."

"You are most diligent in your task." Hirstun walked away, his servant and the common men trailing behind him.

"Yes, I am," Adolfo said softly once there was no one close enough to hear. "I will not suffer a witch to live."

She lay in the dark, feeling the weight of the earth pressing down on her. Not much air left, not much time.

She'd tried to summon the power, had tried to move the earth so that she might somehow escape. But it was water, not earth, that was the branch of the Mother from which she drew her strength, and her efforts had gained her nothing.

Why had things changed? *Why?* For generations, the women in her family and the rest of the people in Kylwode had lived and worked peacefully in each other's company. How many of the common villagers and tenants on the baron's land had been helped by her grandmother's simples when they didn't have the coin to pay the physician, who was really only interested in tending to the gentry and the merchant families in the area? How many had *she* helped by showing them where to dig their wells? And *this* was how they showed their gratitude for all the help that had been given?

She tried to breathe slowly, tried to make the air last, knowing it was useless to hope, and still unable to keep from hoping that some of those men—*any* of those men her family had helped over the years— would defy Baron Hirstun and return to free her.

Why had resentment begun to simmer in Kylwode? Was it because people had looked at the sparse crops they were scraping out of their own overused land and then had turned envious eyes on the rich meadows and forests—and the game that lived there—that belonged to the women of her family since the first witch had walked the boundaries and marked the Old Place that was in her keeping?

How many years had they been telling people, over and over again, that the Mother was bountiful, but one must give as well as take? The people in Kylwode simply didn't want to listen. The Mother gave—and should keep on giving and giving. And lately, the response to any suggestion of giving something back to the land was, "witch words," followed by uneasy, suspicious looks—and the suggestion that the "giving" was some kind of blood sacrifice. And that the bounty of her own garden was payment from the Evil One for carnal pleasures.

She'd never heard of the Evil One until Master Adolfo came to stay with Baron Hirstun. But she knew with absolute certainty that there was such a creature, that the Evil One did, indeed, walk the earth.

And its name was Master Inquisitor Adolfo, the Witch's Hammer.

He was the very breath of Evil with his quietly spoken words and the gentle sadness in his eyes. Those things were the mask that hid a rotted spirit.

Oh, yes, treat the witch gently so that she may repent. Don't look upon her limbs so that you won't be swayed by lust.

The soul-rotted bastard just didn't want those men to see the welts, the cuts, the burns he had inflicted on her to "help" her confess. The hobbles provided a clever excuse for why she couldn't walk well. And *he* certainly hadn't hesitated to indulge his lust. His rod was as much a tool as the heated poker and the thumbscrews.

Three times he had led her to the small writing table in the hated room in Baron Hirstun's cellar that he had changed into his Inquisitor's torture chamber. Three times he had insisted that she must confess her crimes against the good people of Kylwode.

Twice she had refused to sign the confession he had written out, had even demanded the first time to know who had accused her of doing harm. She had done none of the things listed as her "crimes." Harming others was against the creed she and her family lived by.

Twice she had refused. But the third time, he had shown her the other bridle, the one she would force him to use if she continued to resist his attempt to lead her to repentance. That bridle had what he called "witch stingers"—spikes that would pierce the cheeks and tongue. He had shown her the other things that would have to be used to persuade her to "freely" confess.

When she finally signed the confession, he told her he was grateful she had relieved him of the burden of continuing such an onerous task. And by signing, it was she, and not he, who had condemned her to this death.

Bastard!

Tears filled her eyes.

So hard to breathe now. So very hard.

She was glad her mother and grandmother had gone to a neighboring village to help with a birth when the baron's men—and Master Adolfo—had come for her. She hoped one of the Small Folk had warned her family while they were still on the road home so that they could flee.

Not much time now. Her body struggled for air.

Water was her strength and her love. But they had planted her in the middle of a dry field on the other side of the village, too far away from the Old Place that had been her home to give her even that much comfort. If only she could feel water flow over her hand once more, maybe she could accept . . .

She dimly heard her own garbled, anguished cry.

Beyond the field, behind a stand of trees, the brook seemed to hesitate. Its bed shuddered and ripped.

Then ripped deeper. The water poured into that rip, forcing its way between the trees' roots until it found a newly made channel that continued to shiver open before it even as it spread itself beneath the land.

Her hand was wet. Not just damp from the earth, but *wet*.

The water found the open space of the box—and the brook sang to her as it had done so many times.

She closed her eyes and floated on its song.

The water caressed her. She no longer felt her body, no longer felt any pain. Just the water as it continued to rise to the surface—and took her with it.

"This will be enough?" Hirstun said as he studied the confession.

"It has been more than adequate in Arktos and Wolfram," Adolfo replied. "Sylvalan has a similar law: any person convicted of a heinous crime against the community forfeits all property, which then goes to the highest-ranking noble in the community to dispense as he sees fit." It was a law Hirstun knew well; at least three of his tenants had once been freeholders before one of Hirstun's ancestors had found a "crime" against those families that allowed him to confiscate the land and add it to his own holding.

"There's only one copy," Hirstun said.

"I retain the other copy," Adolfo replied. And *that* copy confessed to one other thing, which would only be brought to light if Hirstun proved to be a difficult man to deal with.

"I expect you'll be leaving soon."

That tone, both dismissal and command, infuriated Adolfo, but his voice remained mild when he said, "Unless there are others in Kylwode who are suspected of practicing witchcraft." He made the words almost a question.

"Those three were the only witches in Kylwode," Hirstun said coldly.

Which is not the same thing, Adolfo thought. *Not*

the same thing at all. That was the error the gentry in Arktos and Wolfram had made when they had first started dealing with him. They had treated him like a servant once his duties had given them what they wanted. But they had learned, as the gentry in Sylvalan would learn, just how hard the Witch's Hammer could strike a village, how far the frenzy of accusations could spread with the right incentive, how even a gentry family was not immune.

Hirstun opened a drawer in his desk, pulled out a hand-sized bag of gold coins, and dropped it on the desk.

"When we first discussed the trouble in Kylwode, you agreed to pay two bags of gold for my services," Adolfo said quietly.

"You only had to deal with one of them, not all three," Hirstun said sharply. "And the other two won't be coming back. Half the fee for one-third of the work seems more than fair."

So that's how it would be.

Adolfo sat back in his chair, turning his head just enough to look out the window at the baron's children, who had gathered on the lawn with some of their friends.

"The Evil One is a pernicious adversary," Adolfo said. "Sometimes a person becomes ensnared without realizing it until she—or he—is persuaded to open her soul and confess. Sometimes a person becomes Evil's servant through carnal indiscretion. Pain is the only spiritual purge for someone who has been misled by a witch's lust."

Hirstun looked out the window, stared at his eldest son for a long moment, then swung back to face Adolfo. "Are you accusing *my* son of having carnal acts with a witch?"

"Were we speaking of your son?" Adolfo said mildly.

The way Hirstun paled was confirmation enough about why there was a resemblance between the witch they'd just condemned and Hirstun's daughter.

A long, strained silence hung between them.

Adolfo waited patiently, as he'd done so many times before. He was a middle-aged, balding man who had the lean face of a scholar and the strong body of a common laborer. His clothes, as dull-colored and simply cut as a common man's, were made of the finest wools, the best linens. His voice held the inflections of a gentry education as well as the roughness of a man whose education had been acquired in the alleys. People like the baron were never sure if he had been a younger son of a prominent family who had fallen on hard times or some backstreet brat who had spent years learning to mimic his betters until he could pass for one of them. While their lack of deference infuriated him, he understood the value of letting the gentry think they were dealing with a cur only to discover a wolf had them by the throat.

Finally, reluctantly, Hirstun pulled out another bag of gold.

"My thanks, Baron Hirstun," Adolfo said. "I do what I must because it's the task I have been given, but there are expenses to performing that task."

"You seem to make a good living being the Witch's Hammer," Hirstun said, eyeing the small jewels that completely covered the large medallion Adolfo wore over a brown wool tunic and white linen shirt.

Adolfo brushed a finger over the medallion. "I have spent the last thirty years of my life doing this work. Each of these stones represents a village in my homeland that I cleansed of witches—and all other signs of witchcraft."

"We understand each other well enough," Hirstun said harshly. "I trust that understanding will continue."

"That is my hope as well," Adolfo said, gathering up the bags of gold. "If you will excuse me, Baron, I must send a message to my assistant Inquisitors."

"Why?"

Adolfo smiled slightly. "The work we do is filled with dangers. It is our custom to inform each other of where we are as well as our next destination. That way, if something should happen to one of us, the others would know where to begin the hunt for the Evil One's servant."

"I see," Hirstun said tightly.

You begin to see, Adolfo thought as he made his bow and left the room. *For now, that is enough.*

In the gray, predawn light, Morag let the dark horse pick its way across the sodden field toward the young woman sitting on a small mound of earth.

Seeing the fear and tension in the woman's face, she reined in a few feet away and let a gentle silence build between them.

"You can see me," the woman said.

Morag's lips curved in a hint of a smile. "I am the Gatherer. I see all the ghosts."

The fear and tension drained from the woman, replaced with something close to hope. "You've come to take me to the Summerland?"

She said nothing for a moment, not quite sure what to make of humans who spoke of the Summerland. This was her first extended journey in the human world since she had become the Gatherer less than a year ago—her first journey at all to the northeastern part of Sylvalan. Until recently, none of the humans she had gathered had asked about the Summerland. "I can guide you to the Shadowed Veil. The place beyond it has been called by many names. Perhaps it is many places. Your spirit knows its home. If that is the Summerland, then that is the place you'll find." As she extended her hand, the sleeve of her black gown opened like a raven's wing. "Come."

The woman floated over the ground, floated up behind the Gatherer. Once she was settled, she asked softly, "Do you think I'll see my mother and grandmother in the Summerland one day?"

As she turned the dark horse to go back the way she had come, Morag thought of the two women whose bodies had been left near the road that led to this village, the two women whose spirits she had gathered and taken to the Shadowed Veil. When the mound and field were out of sight, she finally said, "You'll meet them there."

Chapter Three

Ari tried not to sigh out loud as she set her heavy baskets on the floor of Granny Gwynn's shop and sincerely hoped Odella and the other young women from Ridgeley's gentry families would conclude their business quickly.

Seeing the movement, Odella gave Ari a sharp look before turning back to the small, wrinkled woman standing behind the wooden counter at the back of the shop. "Do you have it, Granny?"

Granny Gwynn huffed. "Wicked girl. You wound my heart, indeed you do, to think that I'd forget to make the fancy for my pretty misses. Of course I have it. You wait there." She disappeared behind the heavy curtain that separated the storage rooms from the front of the shop.

Odella and the others girls began whispering and giggling.

Trying to prevend it was as easy to ignore them as it was for them to ignore her, Ari waited. She should have heeded the strange feeling in the air this morning and stayed home. She should have worked in the garden or finished cleaning her cottage. She should have taken her sketchbook and colored chalks into the woods and spent the day quietly making the swift drawings that would be transformed into the woven wall hangings that provided her with some income.

But loneliness had slipped into her dreams last night, making her crave even the illusion of company. So she had rolled up the wall hanging Mistress Brigston had commissioned and the bottles of simples she had made to sell at Granny's shop, packed her baskets into the small handcart, and made the three-mile walk to the village.

Granny Gwynn reappeared, her hands full of small items wrapped in brown waxed paper.

"Here you are, my pretty ladies. A little fancy for a little fun during the Summer Moon."

Odella and the other girls leaned over the counter while Granny Gwynn unwrapped one of the packages. A couple of the girls gasped, then giggled behind their hands.

"Now tuck those safely away until they're needed," Granny Gwynn said after handing a package to each girl. She narrowed her eyes. "Where's the last girl?"

Odella waved an impatient hand. "It doesn't matter. What do we do with the fancy? How does it work?"

"It matters, Miss Odella," Granny Gwynn said darkly. "Seven were asked for. Seven were made. Seven must be taken."

"Then I'll take the other one, too."

Granny Gwynn shook her head. "There's no way to tell what will happen if one is left or if two are taken by the same person."

Odella paled a little. She glanced around the shop. A predatory look came into her eyes. "Then give the last one to Ari." She made a come-forward motion. "Come on, Ari. It's just a bit of fun to celebrate the first moon of summer."

Ari studied the other girls, who were now watching her with avid interest. An inner voice whispered, *Beware. Beware. They do not mean you well.* The loneliness coiled around her heart, and whispered, *It's a chance to belong, even if only for a little while.*

She stepped up to the counter.

"Hold out your left hand," Granny Gwynn said.

When Ari hesitated, Granny grabbed her hand and tipped the package's contents into her palm.

Ari hissed as a small jolt of magic shot up her left arm and stabbed her heart. A moment later, the feel-

ing was gone. Then she looked at the fancy, and uneasiness washed through her.

Two pieces of brown-sugar candy. One was shaped
like a full-bodied woman. The other was shaped like
a phallus.

"Wrap them up now," Granny Gwynn said, smiling
slyly as she handed the brown waxed paper to Ari.

Ari hurriedly wrapped the fancy and would have
left it on the counter if Granny hadn't watched her
closely until she tucked it into her skirt pocket.

"Now," Granny Gwynn said, crossing her hands
over her sagging belly. "The full moon rises in two
days' time. You must go out walking that night.
Choose your path well because you must offer the
female half of the fancy to the first male you see that
night who isn't close kin, and say, 'With this fancy, I
offer the affection of my body from the full moon to
the dark. This I swear by the Lord of the Sun and the
Lady of the Moon. May they never again shine upon
me if I do not fulfill this promise.'"

Ari shivered. Not a bit of summer fun, then. Not if
a promise had to be sworn in the name of *those* two.

"If the male accepts his piece of the fancy," Granny
Gwynn continued, "then the choice has been made.
You *must* eat the male half of the fancy in his presence to complete the magic, and you must give him
as much affection as he wishes until the dark of the
moon." She smiled slyly again. "You'll have no trouble doing that."

"What if we don't want the first male we see?"
Bonnie, a plump blonde, asked.

Granny gave her a hard look. "The *first.* If he refuses, you're free to seek another. If he accepts . . . the
magic is binding, pretty miss. Defy it, deny it, refuse it
at your peril. If you do not use that fancy to draw
the brightness of affection, then you'll draw the dark
feelings to you."

The girls shuffled nervously. Even Odella looked
worried.

Ari felt sick.

Granny patted Odella's hand. "For the next two days, take a few quiet minutes for yourself before you retire and think of what you'd like in a lover. Don't try to draw a specific man," she warned, holding up a finger. "Just the qualities you want in the man who will be your lover from the full moon to the dark—and, perhaps, for much longer if you're clever."

"But—" Odella began to protest.

"The men of Ridgeley aren't the *only* ones who wander the roads the night of the Summer Moon," Granny said, grinning wickedly.

"Oooh." Odella wiggled. Then she smiled maliciously at Ari. "I'm sure my brother Royce will have some business that evening."

Ari felt her throat close until it hurt to swallow.

"Now be off with you," Granny Gwynn said, shooing the other girls out the door. Then she motioned to Ari. "Back here."

Ari picked up her baskets of simples and followed Granny Gwynn behind the curtain.

As soon as she set the baskets on the table in the center of the room, Granny Gwynn waved her aside and began to unpack them. "Good. Good. I sold the last bottle of that yesterday." She continued commenting and muttering while she read each neat label. Finally, she stepped back, crossed her arms over her belly, and narrowed her eyes at Ari. "I'll give you one and a half coppers for each bottle."

Ari stared at Granny for a long moment before she found her voice. "Our agreement was three coppers a bottle."

"That was before Squire Kenton bought a bottle for his delicate wife. Perhaps you added a little ill-wishing when you stirred that brew, eh? Because Mistress Kenton became desperately sick after she took a couple of spoonfuls. Sick enough that the physician had to be called in. And who do you think the squire raved at and threatened to bring in front of the magistrate's court unless I paid the physician's fee?"

"If it was taken properly, there was nothing in that

simple that would have made her ill," Ari said. *Except what you may have added in order to claim it was of your own making,* she added silently. *If, that is, Mistress Kenton had become ill at all.*

Granny Gwynn's face reddened, as if she'd heard the thought. "One and a half coppers. That's all you'll get."

An icy calm filled Ari as she quickly repacked the baskets. "Then I'll sell them elsewhere."

"Elsewhere?" Granny's voice rose. "Who do you think will buy from *you*? No one in Ridgeley will buy a simple if they have to admit it came from *you*."

"Then I'll sell them at Wellingsford or Seahaven."

"A full day's coach journey there and back to reach either one, and more time to peddle your goods. You'd leave your place for so long?"

The touch of malicious knowledge in Granny's voice made Ari look up.

Last spring, she had made arrangements with Ahern, a gruff old man who was her nearest neighbor, to have one of the men who worked in his stables tend her cow and chickens so that she could make the journey to Seahaven to sell a few of her wall hangings. The merchant she'd shown the wall hangings to had been impressed by the quality of her work and had bought them all—and had promised to look at anything else she had. Lighthearted and full of plans to sell her work for the fair price she couldn't get from the gentry in Ridgeley, she had danced up the road after the night coach that traveled the coastal road from Seahaven to Wellingsford had let her off at the crossroads that led to Ridgeley—and to Brightwood, her home.

Then, in the early-morning light, she had found the "welcome" that had been left for her.

Her animals had been slaughtered, hacked to pieces. The cow's head and two of the chickens had been dumped in the home well. Some of the gore had been splashed across the back of her cottage.

Ahern's man arrived shortly after she did, took one

look, and ran back to tell his master. Ahern and all of his men showed up a little while after that. The old man had walked through the cottage with her, but her warding spells had kept the inside of her home protected.

The men cleaned the well, removed the dead animals, even cleaned up the back of her cottage. Still, for weeks afterward, she went to the nearest stream each morning to bring back drinking water.

Later that year, when Ahern asked her if she was going to Seahaven again to sell her weaving, she had made excuses. She had understood the warning. The people in Ridgeley would tolerate her living outside their village on whatever scraps they chose to throw her way, but they wouldn't tolerate her slipping the leash unless she forfeited Brightwood, the land that had been held by the women in her family since the first witch had walked the boundaries.

She couldn't forfeit the land. It was her heritage . . . and her burden.

"All right," Granny Gwynn said, bringing Ari back to the present. "All right. Two coppers. That's the best you'll get."

Ari held out her hand.

Granny's face darkened. Muttering, she pulled a coin pouch out of her skirt pocket. She looked like she wanted to spit on each copper before she dropped it into Ari's hand.

Saying nothing, Ari slipped the coins into her own deep skirt pocket before she again unpacked the baskets.

When she picked up her empty baskets and pulled the curtain aside, Granny Gwynn said spitefully, "I hope that fancy brings you everything you deserve."

Or at least no harm, Ari thought as she left the shop.

Odella and the other girls were still gathered nearby. When none of them even looked at her, Ari breathed a sigh of relief.

"I'm going to try one of the paths through the

woods," Bonnie said. "If any of *them* are about, they won't be on the main road."

Another girl fanned herself with a lace hanky. Her voice quivered with excitement and fear. "Do you really think *they'll* come for the Summer Moon?"

"You'll probably end up with Eddis or Hest," Bonnie said with a touch of malice.

"Not Hest," the hanky waver whined. "He has spots."

"Well," Odella said with a sharp smile, "you know what all the boys say is the best cure for spots, don't you?"

The girls giggled.

Dropping her baskets into the handcart, Ari left as swiftly as she could without seeming to run away.

She should have heeded the strange feel in the air.

Mistress Brigston had tried to cheat her out of the payment for the wall hanging. Having learned the hard lesson that the gentry tended to see nothing dishonorable about trying to cheat anyone but one of their own, Ari had refused to let the woman bring the wall hanging into the house "to check the colors" before she had received payment. Then there was dealing with Granny Gwynn, who was a hedge witch with just enough skill in magic to be dangerous to anyone who trusted her potions and spells, and more than enough greed to never deal fairly if she could get away with it.

So now she was on her way home with a wall hanging no one would buy, a few coppers, and an intense desire to escape before anything else happened.

She didn't escape fast enough.

Royce, Baron Felston's heir, was waiting for her outside the village, just beyond a slight bend in the road.

Most of the girls sighed over Royce's trim figure and the handsome face framed by golden curls, but Ari knew the temper that lurked behind his blue eyes, the meanness of spirit that no amount of flattering words could sweeten.

Ari gave him a cool, civil nod, hoping he'd let her pass.

Wearing a satisfied grin, Royce fell into step beside her. "I hear you got a fancy for the Summer Moon. Let's have a look at it."

She dodged his hands, putting the cart between them. "Stay away from me." She was so intent on watching him, she barely noticed the power beginning to rise inside her—the strength of the earth and the heat of fire.

"Why should I?" Royce sneered. "You've lifted your skirts for me before." His eyes raked over her. "You were better than nothing, but not by much. A cold toss that wasn't worth a second try. But I figure the magic in that fancy will warm you up a bit and make things interesting."

Warm her up? *Warm her up?* If she were any hotter right now, she'd burn.

"Leave. Me. Alone," she said, spacing out her words.

"As the lady wishes," Royce said, giving her a mocking bow. Then his face hardened. "But I'm going to be riding toward the coast road that night, and I expect to meet you along the way." He turned toward the village, then turned back and pointed a finger at her. "And if I find out you lifted your skirts for any other man before I've had my fill of you, you'll regret it."

She waited just long enough to feel sure he was really leaving. Then she grabbed the handle of her cart and hurried down the road in the opposite direction.

She managed half a mile before she had to stop. Feeling shaky and feverish, she stripped off her short cloak. "Don't get sick now," she said as she folded the cloak and put it in one of the baskets. "Don't get—"

She paused, focused, felt the thrum of power waiting to be released.

"Foolish," she muttered, stepping away from the cart. "Foolish, foolish, foolish. How many times did

Mother tell you that drawing power without awareness was as dangerous for the witch as it was for the world around her?"

She closed her eyes, feeling her heart ache as if she had brushed against the bruise that had been left on it by her mother's death two winters ago.

Taking a couple of deep breaths to steady herself, she slowly, carefully, grounded the power she had unthinkingly summoned, giving it back to the Great Mother. When she was done, she felt depleted and fiercely thirsty, but also calmer.

There was a time, her grandmother had told her, when a witch could command the power of all four branches of the Mother—earth, air, water, and fire. But something had happened over the years, and the witches' strength had waned. For the past few generations, the women of her family had been gifted with one primary branch and a trickle of power from another. She was the first in a long, long time who had almost equal strength in the two branches of the Mother that were hers to command—earth and fire.

"But even that much power isn't very useful when it comes to dealing with the likes of Mistress Brigston or Granny Gwynn," she said softly as she dug into her skirt pocket and pulled out the fancy. Just enough magic in it that she didn't dare ignore it. So, if she couldn't ignore it, what kind of lover would she like to draw to her?

"A man who has kindness inside him as well as strength," she told the fancy. "A man who could accept me for what I am. A man who isn't from Ridgeley." *As I will it . . .*

Ari shook her head and stuffed the fancy back into her skirt pocket. Granny Gwynn might be a hedge witch with enough strength to do a bit of mischief magic, but *she,* like all the other women in the family who had come before her, was a witch full and true. And a witch did not send out idle wishing.

Retrieving the handcart, she continued the walk home while thoughts and memories chased her.

Royce had begun "courting" her shortly after her fifteenth birthday. He had been the first man in Ridgeley who had treated her with courtesy, and his sweet words had seduced her into believing that he was as much in love with her as she was with him—until the night she had met him in a meadow and he had pleaded with her to make their love a physical union. Since she had been raised to believe that intimacy was a gift from the Mother, she had been willing to celebrate their love. She had gotten no pleasure from the quick, rough coupling he had seemed to enjoy. And afterward . . . Afterward he had sneeringly thanked her for giving his rod some relief . . . and for helping him win the bet that he could have her on her back within a moon's cycle of beginning his "courtship."

She had crept home, ashamed and brokenhearted. Her mother and grandmother had been understanding—and never spoke aloud the sadness she knew they had felt that her first experience had left her with such bitter memories.

Taking a deep breath, Ari turned aside from those thoughts. It did no good to look back at something that had happened two years before—something that she had never allowed to happen since.

Maybe it was that feel in the air that made a budding summer day have an edge like an approaching winter storm. There was a message there, if only she could understand it. But earth and fire were the branches of the Mother that were her strength, and she couldn't sense what the branches of water and air might have told her.

Think of something else, she told herself sternly. *Your thoughts are your will, and you bring to yourself what you will.*

Loneliness had brought today's events down on her like an earthslide. Well, she would ignore it the next time it crept into her dreams. She'd been alone since her mother died a few months after Grandmother Astra. She would get used to it, wouldn't let herself be ruled by it. She had no choice, since she was all that was left of her family.

We are witches. I'll not deny it, Astra had told her once. *Whether that's a gift or a burden is something each must choose for herself. But, child, it's only a word, and only you can decide what that word will mean. When you let others define you, you give up the greatest power of all.*

Wise words from a strong, wise woman. But even Astra couldn't have foreseen a time when there would be only one of them left, and that one being a seventeen-year-old girl struggling to define herself while an entire village strove to reshape and diminish her.

Willing herself not to cry, Ari looked around and spotted a hawk watching her from a nearby tree. She felt her mood shift, as it always did when she saw one of the Mother's wild children, and she smiled for the first time that day. Raising her hand in greeting, she called out, "Blessings of the day to you, brother hawk."

The hawk chose not to answer. But she noticed that, every time she looked back, it was still watching her.

It's only a hawk, she thought as that feel in the air began to press in on her again. Of course it was only a hawk. Then again, it could have been a Fae Lord or Lady from Tir Alainn. It was said that each of them had another form that could be taken at will.

Tir Alainn. The Fair Land. The Otherland. The land of magic—and the home of the Fae, who were the Mother's most powerful children.

It was better to believe the hawk was only a hawk. Despite what Odella and the other girls might think about a romantic encounter with a Fae Lord on a moonlit road, the Fae were not always kind when they dealt with humans.

Suddenly shivering, Ari hurried toward the safety of her home.

She had two days to understand the magic Granny Gwynn had set into the fancy, two days to see if there was some way to safely counter the spell. If she couldn't she would have to abide by that spell and swear a promise that invoked the two most powerful Fae—the Lady of the Moon and the Lord of the Sun, the Lord of Fire.

The Huntress . . . and the Lightbringer.

Chapter Four

Dianna stood on one of the terraces overlooking the gardens of the Clan house, watching her brother until the path took him out of sight.

"He's has been prowling the gardens all morning," Lyrra said, settling herself on the low terrace wall. "And he's got that look in his eyes that bodes ill for anyone offering him company."

"You mean for anyone offering him a romp," Dianna replied defensively. "Lucian accepts invitations when he chooses and takes his pleasure where he wills." Her voice ripened with impatience. "Besides, men don't *always* think about *that.*"

"Really?" Lyrra said dryly. "Even on this day, when the first moon of summer rises?" She made a rude noise that expressed her opinion quite adequately.

Turning her back on the garden, Dianna sat on the terrace wall near Lyrra. She sighed. As much as she'd tried to pretend she didn't know why the Fae men were acting so restless, Lyrra was right. They viewed the night of the Summer Moon as other men might view a banquet table filled with a variety of dishes to be sampled. And the dishes that were the most familiar had the least appeal.

Which is neither here nor there to me, Dianna thought. *The Wild Hunt also rides tonight, and anyone crossing our path is fair game.*

"Will Aiden be among those traveling the road through the Veil tonight?" Dianna asked.

"I wouldn't know," Lyrra said too casually.

Oh, you know, Dianna thought, seeing the way Lyrra's eyes fixed on the gardens without seeing them. *You know, and the casual way he seeks other lovers hurts you.* "If our paths cross tonight, shall I bring you back his heart?" She said the words lightly, but there was nothing light about the question.

"Haven't you realized it yet, Huntress?" Lyrra said with equal lightness. "Fae men have no hearts."

Not knowing what to say, Dianna remained silent until Lyrra retreated inside the Clan house.

That wasn't true, Dianna thought as she left the terrace and meandered the garden paths. Not exactly. It wasn't in the Fae's nature to be . . . warm . . . with each other. Not that way. Physical coupling was pleasant, but it wasn't *supposed* to involve the heart. Why should it?

And since it didn't, there was no reason why the males shouldn't enjoy females from the human world. It required little of them and meant even less. Besides, it was the women from a handful of extended families who made up each Clan. The woman and their offspring. Fae males tended to make lengthy visits to other Clans to avoid sowing their own meadow. It was a woman's male relatives, her brothers and cousins, who helped raise the child, not its sire. Fae women seldom found a human interesting enough to take as a lover, but if the males took their ease in a human's bed, what difference did it make?

A whine made her look to her left. Her lips softened in the beginning of a smile.

The shadow hounds were her joy—sleek and lethal, with beautiful gray coats streaked with black. When they ran, they were moonlight and shadow in motion, and there was no prey, on four legs or two, that was fast enough or clever enough to elude them when they hunted.

The bitch whined again, wagging her tail hesitantly.

Dianna almost extended her hand to welcome the hound. Then the three puppies from the bitch's last litter joined their mother, and Dianna remembered why this bitch was no longer her favorite, why she could no longer give the petting and praise that had once come so easily.

Two of the puppies were perfect. But the third . . .

The tan forelegs that marred the lovely blend of gray and black were a constant reminder that the bitch had pursued a different kind of hunt the last time Dianna had taken the pack through the Veil.

It was one thing for a Fae male to plant a child in a human woman. After all, the woman was getting a better offspring than she ever could have gotten from a human male, even if the child *wouldn't* have any magical gifts. It was quite another to allow inferior creatures to live in Tir Alainn.

She should have had the pups destroyed the minute she'd seen that one. They couldn't be allowed to breed since the sire's influence could well show up in the next generation, even from the pups who showed no sign of him now. But the bitch had been so fiercely protective, allowing no one to get near her pups until Dianna came into the kennels. The animal had been so pleased to see her, so willing to share her pups with her mistress . . .

She had given the bitch the praise and petting it had wanted, and she'd given no orders that would end the puppies' existence, but she hadn't been able to force herself to touch the bitch since that day.

Dianna turned away, ignoring the bitch's unhappy whine.

There had been times when a Fae woman would find a human male enticing enough to enjoy him. And there had been times when that enjoyment had resulted in a child. But no Fae woman kept such a creature in Tir Alainn. That kind of child was left on the sire's doorstep for him to do with as he chose.

Now that the pups were weaned, perhaps she should do the same with them. Just leave them in the human world the next time she passed through the Veil.

No, that was unacceptable. The shadow hounds belonged to the Fae. If humans were to acquire even mongrel pups, the shadow hounds would no longer belong exclusively to the Fae. They would become . . . diminished, ordinary. And *that* was unthinkable. Which meant she would have to find something else to do with the worthless puppies.

"Shadows surround the moon, sister," a baritone voice said. "Is it your mind or your heart that travels a dark path?"

The voice made her focus on the man standing in front of her.

"I could ask the same of you, Lucian," Dianna replied.

Saying nothing more, he offered his arm. As they strolled the gardens together, Dianna studied him out of the corner of her eye.

He was her twin, her opposite, and her equal. Their mother once said that they must have gotten mixed in the womb because they reflected the opposite of what they were. In a way, that was true. She, who was the Lady of the Moon, was the golden one—fair hair and amber eyes, and skin that warmed to the sun's kiss— while he had black hair, gray eyes, and fair skin the sun couldn't touch. But he was the Lord of the Sun, the Lord of Fire. The Lightbringer.

"Are you going to cross the Veil tonight?" Dianna asked.

"I haven't decided," Lucian replied curtly.

Lyrra was right, Dianna thought. *This mood of his bodes ill for everyone.* "I think you should. You didn't seem to enjoy your last visit to one of the other Clans. It was mentioned that you weren't a receptive guest." Which is why she had felt defensive when Lyrra had pointed out that Lucian was avoiding company. It was unusual for a Fae male to refuse an invitation to a woman's bed when he was guesting at a Clan house. It was, in fact, considered ill mannered for him to repeatedly refuse unless he was already having an affair and had promised a modicum of fidelity. So the veiled complaints that had been entwined in the flowery phrases of the messages she'd received had disturbed her and made her quick to take his side of the argument—even before an argument had actually surfaced. He was her brother. It was second nature to take his side in any disagreement—unless, of course, he was disagreeing with her.

She almost jerked away from him when she felt his temper begin to rise. It took effort to keep her arm lightly linked with his when he turned his head to look at her and she could see his eyes clearly.

"I don't keep track of what you do in your bed, sister," he said with deadly control. "What makes you think you have any right to keep track of what I do in mine?"

Dianna swallowed carefully. "It is less in my nature than it is in yours to seek that kind of company." She knew it had been the wrong thing to say a moment before he pulled away from her. "Lucian—"

"What favors haven't I granted that they should complain to my *sister*?" he snarled. "What is it that they feel they can't get from me by making an honest request instead of tying it to the bed?"

"It isn't like that," Dianna protested.

"Isn't it?" Lucian paced away from her, turned, came back. "Who is it that refused their invitation, Dianna? Lucian . . . or the Lightbringer?"

"You *are* the Lightbringer, so how—"

"Which one?" he demanded. "When they pouted to you, which one did they say failed to accept their lures?"

She didn't answer him. Didn't dare. Not with the mood he was in. What was wrong with a woman wanting the strongest and the best for a lover and, possibly, to be the sire of her child? When had this bitterness in him started? It was rooted too deep to be solely because of that last visit to another Clan. Why hadn't she seen this in him until now? And how could she aim that fury at a target that wasn't his own kind?

"It is customary to grant a boon for the pleasure of the bed," she said carefully. "That is our way."

"Have you considered that the price may no longer equal the pleasure?" he said softly. His face hardened.

"I dance to no one's tune. You can send *that* message back to the Clans."

This time, when he turned away from her, he kept going.

Dianna didn't follow him. There was no argument she could have made that would have softened his mood. And the truth was, she *hadn't* made the distinction that he had. Now, thinking back on the way those messages had been worded, she wondered if he was right. Had the women in the other Clan been disappointed that none of them had enjoyed Lucian as a lover, or had they been disappointed not to have a required favor from the Lightbringer, who could command anything and everything in Tir Alainn except the Lady of the Moon?

Dianna headed back to the Clan house, needing the solitude of her own rooms.

She hoped Lucian *did* take the road through the Veil tonight, but she felt a moment's pity for whatever, or whoever, crossed his path.

Hearing Aiden's harp, Lucian headed in another direction. He wasn't interested in talking to anyone, and certainly wasn't interested in being on the receiving end of the Bard's sometimes-barbed speech. So he headed to the one place in the gardens he had avoided all morning.

He hesitated a moment, then walked down the steps under a stone arch. Stone rose up around him. Above him, the trees formed a canopy, letting in dappled sunlight. He could still hear Aiden's harp, but now it blended with the stir of leaves, a natural song that offered comfort.

Like this place, he thought as he followed the path, his fingers brushing against the stone. He couldn't say why this place felt different from the rest of the gardens, but the silence here was richer, rooted in a peace that could drain the heart of any sorrows.

Maybe his anger wasn't fair. A handful of the roads that led from Tir Alainn to Sylvalan had closed, and many of the ones that were still open were harder to use. The Fae couldn't stop a road from closing, nor could they create a new one. They were the Mother's most powerful children, but that piece of magic had been lost to them. It was even getting harder to travel between Clan territories. They were islands of land connected by bridges that spanned mist. Sometimes, even when a road *wasn't* closing, the mist claimed a bridge, breaking the connection between two Clans.

So he could understand why the Clan women would want the use of any male who wasn't kin while they still had access to him. But fire was too much a part of his nature, and he didn't like the coldness that had crept into the bedding. In the past two years, since he'd become the Lightbringer, the gleam in the eyes of Fae women who invited him to their beds had seemed more calculating than lustful, more shrewd than desiring.

Perhaps it wasn't coldness that crept into the bed with him lately. Perhaps it was simply boredom. He knew what to expect, knew what was given and what was taken, knew it so well it had all become less than what it had been. What he didn't know was *why* it felt that way.

He was twenty-four years old. That was far too young to have become bored with sex. But, perhaps, the number of women he'd enjoyed during his first year as the Lord of the Sun accounted for his waning interest now. Or perhaps his passion had slumbered like the winter sun and had not yet quite reawakened. He felt the waxing and waning of power now more than he had when he was just another young Lord of Fire.

Waxing and waning. Like the sun through the seasons. Like the moon through its cycle. Like the Fae who were the leaders of their respective gifts.

It seemed like every other Clan had a Lord of Fire, but only one might feel his power swell on Harvest Eve as he stood before the man who already held the title. Only one might eclipse the old Lord's waning strength and became *the* Lord of Fire, the Lord of the Sun, the Lightbringer. And while a challenge wasn't issued every year, the young Lords of Fire still gathered on that night wherever the Lightbringer chose to measure their strength against his. And sometimes an impatient fool tried to wrest the title from the one who held it before the old Lord's power had sufficiently waned. A fool could discover that defeat was sometimes brutal—sometimes even fatal. But when the time, and the challenger, was right, the challenge was merely a formality, a ritual that allowed the old to yield to the new.

And so it was with all of the Fae. They didn't meet at the same place or at the same time, but for every magical gift the Fae could claim, there was one of them who commanded all the others who shared that particular gift. And all those who commanded the others followed the Lord of the Sun and the Lady of the Moon.

So it wasn't strange that he was sought after more now than he'd ever been before, but it had surprised him to feel more alone at the same time.

Lucian shook his head. He was brooding again, and if he returned to the Clan house before shaking off this mood, Aiden would haul out some tune about the follies of those who ruled that would prick and sting the ego. The Bard's sharp mind and sharper tongue asked for no mercy and seldom gave it, even to those who could claim kinship.

Besides, there were better reasons to brood.

Aiden and Lyrra had quietly sent messages to the bards and storytellers among the Fae. None of the storytellers had heard of the wiccanfae, and the only songs about witches that were sent back to Aiden were the ones he'd already heard. If the storytellers and bards knew almost nothing about their potential enemy, the rest of the Fae certainly wouldn't have heard of the wiccanfae.

Mother's mercy! How could they protect Tir Alainn when they didn't even know where these creatures had come from? Had they come over the mountains that formed the eastern border of Arktos and Wolfram? Was that why the Clans whose territories had been anchored to the Old Places in those human countries had disappeared first? Could it be as simple, and ugly, a thing as a fight for land? Could these witches have destroyed the roads through the Veil so that *they* could claim the Old Places for themselves?

Questions nested within questions, but neither he nor Aiden nor Lyrra nor Dianna had found any answers. The only bards who had heard the songs about the witches traveled through the eastern part of Sylvalan. The ones who traveled through the midlands had heard nothing at all, and the ones from the western Clans . . . Well, they didn't have much to do with the rest of the Fae anyway. They had to be invited for the challenges, although, thankfully, most of the time none of them came. And when they did . . . It was embarrassing to have to acknowledge them as Fae. There was a roughness about them no veneer of manners could hide. And being around one of them made everyone else . . . uncomfortable.

Shaking his head, Lucian left his private spot in the gardens. Until they had some answers, there was nothing he could do. So he *would* travel the road through the Veil tonight, but not for the reason Dianna thought. He would take a long, hard ride under the full moon and enjoy a different kind of mistress. The Great Mother. The land in the human world. Unlike the other females he was familiar with, she always remained intriguing.

Chapter Five

Adolfo secured the latch on the window, then pulled the draperies across it, closing out the coming night. The meal he'd ordered sat on the table, cooling.

Crossing to the table, he poured a glass of wine but didn't drink.

Tonight was the Summer Moon, a night of magic and loose morals, a night when any decent man stayed inside once the moon rose and kept himself safe behind stout walls and strong locks.

Why *had* one of the carriage horses thrown a shoe late in the afternoon, forcing him to stay at this inn instead of arriving at Squire Westun's house in Bainbrydge as he had planned? And why would the coachman who had worked for him for the past two years suddenly suggest that they could continue on this evening once the horse got a new shoe, that the full moon would light the road almost as well as the sun? Why would a man who should have known his employer better suggest that they'd be safe enough if they bought a few fairy cakes and a couple of bottles of wine to appease anyone they might meet on the road?

Mischance or mischief? Had it been luck that this inn had been a couple of miles down the road? Or had the horse lost the shoe precisely as intended so that he would be forced to spend the night here?

He sensed no magic around this place, and he could sense magic as keenly as a harrier could catch a rabbit's scent. But just because he couldn't sense it didn't mean magic wasn't the cause. Ill-wishing wasn't an immediate spell; it exploited a weakness, turning it into misfortune, great or small.

Had his coachman's eyes looked too bright, too eager when the man had suggested traveling tonight? Fairy cakes and wine. Did the fool actually believe *that* would keep a man safe from the Fae?

That had been the thrust of it. The coachman was hoping to meet a creature he'd only heard of in stories, was hoping for a slightly dangerous encounter with one of the Fae.

Damn fool. The Fae weren't as dangerous as they sounded in the stories—at least, not anymore—but they couldn't be dismissed either. They had magic, and magic equaled power to control the world, even if it was only one small piece that responded to a particular kind of magic. Oh, they all had the magic of persuasion, the ability to cloud a weaker mind to make a person do their bidding, and they had the glamour that could hide their true faces and make them look human. Beyond that, their magic was tied to a particular skill or thing in the world. That *could* make them dangerous, depending on what their magic could command. Still, they were only visitors who rode down their shining roads from the Otherland to amuse themselves in the human world—or seduce foolish young women or lure equally foolish young men to their doom. They were like the Small Folk in that they avoided the strongholds of civilization—the cities, the larger towns and villages. The places where men ruled. And they were like the Small Folk in that, once the land was tamed and scoured clean of its magic, they went away. In Wolfram, there were still new stories of meeting one of the Small Folk in the deepest part of a forest, but it had been many years since anyone had seen one of the Fae.

Adolfo lifted the cover off his plate, then sat down, intending to consume his meal.

The coachman would have to be dealt with. Obviously being in a country that stank of magic for even a few weeks had affected the man to the point where he was no longer trustworthy. And having too much idle time to gossip with Sylvalan coachmen and grooms was changing the unpalatable into the romantically intriguing.

Adolfo sat back, the food untouched.

Men—*human* men—were meant to be the masters of the world, but the land was like a coy mistress who would be bountiful one day and withhold her treasures the next. It had to be conquered, stripped of its wildness.

Rather like women. No man who allowed himself to be captivated by the lures of breasts and thighs could call himself his own master—at least, not until he had torn out everything that needed to be stripped from a woman before she would submit to being a proper helpmate. Then, as with the land, he could enjoy the bounty as a man should. Neither land nor woman was as alluring when tamed, but both were far more useful.

Twenty years ago, in Wolfram, his homeland, the men had been ripe for change, and he had given them the key that had helped change flood the country. Men were the conquerors now, the rulers who held the land, and women's lives, in their hands.

The gentry in Sylvalan were ready for change too. Their land was yielding less and less each year, and many of them resented the bounty they couldn't touch—rich land owned by women whose magic stood in their way.

So he would give them the same key he and the assistants he had carefully trained over the years had given the men in Wolfram . . . and in Arktos. He had his own reasons for feeding gentry greed until it ripened into a desire to exterminate what couldn't be tamed, but, in the end, he and the barons both would achieve their goals. They would have the land they coveted and domination over everything within their grasp. And he would destroy the witches.

Morag studied the faint glimmering in the heart of the old wood. When she had come down that road at the dark of the moon, it had been strong and shining.

True, the Veil between this world and the Fair Land had seemed a little thicker and took longer to cross through, but she hadn't given it much thought. There were many roads that were difficult to use these days.

The dark horse shifted restlessly, then took a step toward the glimmering.

"No," Morag said, resting her hand on the dark horse's neck to soothe him. "We can't get home that way." *Not anymore.*

The dark horse stamped his foot. Took another step forward.

"*No,*" Morag said more firmly. Gathering the reins, she turned him away from the glimmering—and temptation. He was a Fae horse and could sense the roads through the Veil as well as she, but he couldn't tell that the magic that signaled "home" to him wasn't strong enough anymore to get them back safely.

What had changed in the time between the dark of the moon and the full? she wondered as the dark horse picked his way along the game trail, still fretting because they were going in the opposite direction of where he wanted to go. What had changed? And why?

She was tired, and she was troubled by the number of female spirits she had gathered lately to lead to whatever was beyond the Shadowed Veil. Too many of them were young women, and they had died hard deaths.

Because she was tired, she hadn't paid attention when she had crossed the boundaries into the Old Place, had only been focused on reaching the road through the Veil and going to Tir Alainn to rest again. Now she drew in a deep breath and let it out slowly.

The air was slightly sour. It always smelled like that in the human world—except in the Old Places. They were as close as the human world came to the feel of Tir Alainn. But this place was already losing that sweetness. Why? *Why?*

She opened herself to the magic that filled this land, needing to draw some of its strength into herself. A couple of heartbeats later, she closed herself off from it and hunched in the saddle, one fist pressed against her breast.

Watery soup instead of a rich stew. That's how the magic felt. Worse, instead of being able to draw strength from it, the land had tried to drain magic *from her*, as if there was a gaping hole in it that it was trying to fill.

As they entered a clearing where a cottage stood, Morag straightened in the saddle. Even as tired as she was, she could maintain a glamour spell long enough to ask for food and drink. It wasn't that hard to hide the pointed ears and the feral looks behind a more human mask. Many of the Fae didn't bother with such things, and she certainly didn't when she stood as the Gatherer. But the Fae had magic, and the Fae were feared. So it was sensible to approach a human dwelling looking like a human and not frighten the people inside to the point where the door would be barred against her.

Halfway across the clearing, she released the glamour, knowing it wasn't needed. At the new moon, when she had skirted this clearing on her way out to the human world, she had smelled the woodsmoke, had seen the glow of lamps in the windows. Now the cottage was dark and empty. Not the waiting emptiness of a place where the people were away for a little while and were coming back, but the thick, stark emptiness of abandonment.

And all around the cottage, Morag could feel a deep well of magic drying up, withering like a tree whose tap root had been severed.

Turning away from it, she guided the dark horse to the edge of the clearing. She sensed the presence of the Small Folk, knew they were watching her pass by, but none of them came forward to greet a Lady from Tir Alainn. That, too, was something that had changed in recent years.

But it was the sound that was gathering under the rustle of leaves and water flowing over stone that made her urge the dark horse into a canter. She didn't

slow his pace until they reached the human road a
few minutes later. Then she reined in and listened.

It had been nothing more than the wood nymphs
and water sprites. She knew that. But it still sounded
as if the brook and the trees had been weeping, as if
the land itself was grieving the loss of . . . something.

Who had lived in that cottage? Why had they left?
And why would their leaving make so much difference
to an Old Place in so short a time? Was the magic
bleeding out from the land the reason the road
through the Veil was no longer strong enough to carry
her home?

"We'll find a place to rest," Morag said, petting the
dark horse's neck. *But not here.*

Shivering from weariness and from night air that
suddenly seemed colder, she studied the road. She had
been traveling slowly but steadily toward the south of
Sylvalan until she had reached this Old Place and had
used the road through the Veil to return to Tir Alainn
for a brief rest. When she came back down the shining
road at the dark of the moon, she had drifted on the
outskirts of the nearby villages before circling back
here. She had no desire to go back to any of those
places, no desire to see what might have happened to
other women in those villages.

Turning the dark horse, she resumed her journey
south.

Chapter Six

Ari hurriedly filled the small pack with cheese, apples, and two of the fairy cakes she had made to celebrate the Summer Moon. She strapped two canteens of water into their places on the pack, then looked around. A blanket would be nice, but she didn't want to be too burdened down. Her cloak would have to do for bedding. With the moon shining tonight, there was no need for a lantern, even if she would have dared use anything that might help someone locate her.

She wiped her hand on her trousers as she stared at the small package lying on the table and fought the revulsion that had been growing throughout the day. Then she gritted her teeth and stuffed the fancy into her left trouser pocket. Her folding knife went into the right pocket.

Grabbing her dark cloak, Ari took one last look around. She'd let the fire in the main hearth go out and had banked the one in the stove. The windows were all shuttered and locked. She'd put every warding spell she knew on the cottage to keep it safe. She'd even extended one of the wardings to protect the cow shed and her garden.

Nothing left to do.

Taking a deep breath to steady herself, she slipped out of the cottage and paused to listen.

Silence. Not even the usual night sounds.

Would the Huntress be out tonight with her pack of great hounds, riding over the land while her moon banished the hiding places the hunted usually found in the night shadows?

Fool, Ari thought as she closed the door and locked it. The Huntress wasn't the only one who would be roaming the land tonight. And in truth, if she had to choose between Royce and the Wild Hunt, she'd rather take her chances with the hounds. At least with them it would end quickly.

She pressed her hand against the door in farewell and headed toward the sea.

A quick walk turned into a run until the stitch in her side forced her to stop. By then the cottage was out of sight.

Royce wouldn't look for her on this beach. Surely not. Even if he remembered it existed.

She'd thought this out very carefully. Had thought of little else in the past two days. If the Gwynn women had any gift for magic, it was centered in their ability to brew love potions, so she couldn't dismiss Granny Gwynn's warning about the magic turning back on a person if it wasn't properly released. Which meant she couldn't just hide in the cottage. If Royce came to the door, she'd have to offer him the fancy—and herself, since she was sure he would accept it. But if she saw no one tonight, she wouldn't be refusing the spell in the fancy, and since the offer had to be made on this particular night, the magic should fade harmlessly.

She hoped.

Another half a mile and she'd reach the rough path that led to the beach and the shallow cave in the cliff wall. Her mother had loved to come here, alone, on summer nights. Tonight it would provide shelter from the wind and, even more important, hide her from anyone who might look down from the cliff.

Clouds drifted across the moon, cutting the light, at the same moment Ari sensed that she was no longer alone.

Her heart raced as she spun around, straining to see down the road. Great Mother, had Royce been to the cottage already? Had he guessed her intention? Was he riding after her?

The road remained empty, but *something* came closer. She could feel it, even though she heard nothing.

The clouds drifted past.

The moon returned, bright enough to cast a shadow.

Ari forgot to breathe when she saw the black horse racing over the land. This was grace married to strength, an animal so beautiful it made Royce's finest hunter look like a plow horse.

It wasn't running away from anything, she decided as she watched it turn toward the old sea road that followed the coast. Just running for the sheer joy of it, as a celebration of life.

She stood there until it was out of sight.

Where had it come from? she wondered as she continued toward the sea. Old Ahern's farm? He did raise magnificent horses, but even he didn't have anything in his stables that could compare with this one. Unless this was one of his "special" horses that she hadn't seen before.

Or perhaps it had slipped away from Tir Alainn itself. She could imagine the Huntress mounted on such a fine animal.

Remembering that she could well be the hunted one spurred her forward until she reached the cliffs that overlooked the sea. Even knowing what to look for, it took her several minutes to find the break in the cliff. She clattered down the rough path as quickly as she could, slipping a couple of times in her haste, until she reached the empty beach.

Over the years, her mother had gathered small boulders and pieces of driftwood that she'd used to build two low walls, using the cliff itself to form the third side of an open-air room. A few times, as a special treat, Meredith had invited Ari to stay with her overnight, but, for the most part, this had been her mother's private place.

She had never been on this beach without her mother, hadn't been here at all since Meredith's death. Because of that, she could almost pretend that Meredith had simply gone for a walk along the beach and would be back soon. Then, as her hand brushed against the pocket that held the fancy, even that much pretense faded, giving loneliness a keener edge and

reminding her that she was here to hide, not enjoy a
summer evening by the sea.

After making sure the shallow cave wasn't occupied
by anything else, Ari tucked her pack inside. There
was a small stack of dried wood at the back of the
cave. If she'd dared, she could have made a fire.

No matter. The low wall would block a fair amount
of wind, and the night was fairly warm for early summer. Tucked in the cave with her cloak, she would be
comfortable enough.

Ari closed her eyes and took a couple of deep
breaths, letting the rhythm of the sea and the roll of
quiet waves settle her pounding heart.

No one had seen her come here. No one would find
her here.

She opened her eyes and saw the black horse galloping along the water's edge.

It must have found another path down to the beach,
she thought as she watched it. But wasn't it odd that
the horse would even try to find its way down the cliff
on its own? It couldn't drink the water, and there was
nothing on the beach for it to eat. Maybe it just liked
the feel of sand beneath its hooves and sea foam
around its legs? She'd have to ask Ahern the next
time she saw him. His "special" horses tended to act
a bit differently from other animals.

She didn't know if the horse had seen her or had
caught her scent in some shift of the wind, but one
moment it was galloping in the foam and the next it
was charging up the beach straight at her.

Ari took a step back, ready to duck into the cave.

The horse stopped a length away from the wall
and reared.

A wave of heat went through Ari's body, leaving
behind the strange sensation of a heavy lushness com-
bined with the ability to float.

The horse laid its ears back and pawed the sand.

"I have as much right to be here as you do," Ari said.

Rearing again, the horse trumpeted a challenge.

Obviously, it didn't like sharing the beach. Well that

was just too bad. It could just go galloping back to
Ahern's farm—or wherever it came from. Besides, it
was making too much noise, which could draw someone's attention.

Ari put her hands on her hips. "Now see here, my
handsome lad," she said sternly. "Showing off your
fifth leg might make your four-legged ladies roll their
eyes and swish their tails, but it *doesn't* impress me."

A flash of panic swept through her. Why had she
said that? Was this part of the fancy's magic, to make
a woman speak so brazenly?

The stallion's forelegs hit the sand. He snorted
indignantly.

Ari laughed. "There's no need for you to nurse a
bruised ego. I'm sure your ladies are most appreciative
of your . . ." She waved a hand vaguely at his body.

He snorted again.

Ari's chest tightened. Since it already bound her,
she couldn't fight the fancy's magic. It would turn back
on her if she did. So she had to find some harmless
way to channel it. But, Lord and Lady, her body was
becoming a stranger she couldn't trust, and her
thoughts were following unfamiliar paths. Even when
she'd so foolishly believed herself in love with Royce
she hadn't felt like this.

The stallion pawed the sand.

Ari held out her hand and took a few steps toward the
horse. "You *are* a handsome lad, aren't you?" she said
softly.

The stallion regarded her for a moment before coming forward to sniff her hand.

Ari remained still while he sniffed and lipped her
palm, but when he began to lip her long, dark hair,
she leaned back. "That isn't hay."

He snorted softly, almost sounding amused.

She'd never seen a gray-eyed horse before, Ari
thought while the stallion pushed his muzzle under
her cloak and snuffled her hip. In the moonlight, those
eyes reminded her of her grandmother's pewter vase
that sat on the mantel.

The stallion nudged her left pocket. He stiffened, made an angry sound, then leaped away from her. He laid his ears back and pawed the sand while he stared at her.

Confused, Ari slowly reached into her left pocket. She withdrew the fancy wrapped in the brown waxed paper. Swallowing her distaste, she unwrapped it and dumped the two pieces into her hand.

"It's just a fancy, a brown-sugar candy with some love magic added to it," she said quietly while she studied the horse. "I've checked it with every bit of magic I know, and there's nothing in it that would do harm. Except the love magic if it's denied, but the magic's binding on the female, not the male. It won't hurt *you*."

The stallion pricked his ears. He didn't approach her, but at least he didn't bolt.

It won't hurt you.

The thought took root, making her a little dizzy. "I didn't know what it was when Granny Gwynn dropped it into my hand. By then it was too late because, as soon as I touched it, I was bound to the magic. But Granny Gwynn *did* say the first *male* I met on the night of the full moon, *not* the first *man*. Oh, she *meant* the first man, but that wasn't what she *said*." That was the problem with all of Granny Gwynn's spells. They were always phrased in a way that something could go wrong. But that might work to her advantage tonight. If she used the fancy based on what Granny Gwynn *said* rather than what was *meant*. . . . "I don't suppose sugar is all that good for a horse, but old Ahern gives his horses a lump of sugar as a treat now and then, and this isn't much bigger."

Not giving herself time to think about what might happen if she was wrong about the importance of the spell's wording, Ari stuffed the paper back into her pocket, kept the brown-sugar phallus in her left hand and held out the full-bodied woman in her right. She licked her lips, then took a deep breath. "With this fancy, I promise my affection from the full moon to the dark. This I swear by the Lord of the Sun and the

Lady of the Moon. May they never again shine upon me if I do not fulfill my promise."

The stallion froze.

Ari waited. The air seemed to get thicker, making it hard to breathe, making it hard to think clearly. There was something about the horse. Something that wasn't quite right, but . . . He had beautiful gray eyes. And he was so big, so strong. Would he let her pet him, let her feel the ripple of muscles under that warm skin?

She felt strange. Why did she feel so strange? Was the magic in the fancy doing this to her?

Coming forward warily, the horse sniffed the fancy for several long seconds before he took it.

Ari popped the other piece into her mouth and tried not to gag.

It was just a piece of candy, no matter how it was shaped. But it reminded her of Royce's anger when she'd refused to take him into her mouth as a prelude to the coupling. It reminded her of the way he'd laughed at her when he was done and the cruel things he'd called her before he walked away.

The candy melting on her tongue made her queasy so she chewed a couple of times and swallowed.

Pressing her hand to her stomach, she gulped air and waited for the queasiness to pass.

"Well, that's done," Ari sighed a minute later, "and it's a better bargain than I would have made with any of the men in Ridgeley. So, my handsome lad, if your wanderings bring you to my cottage, you'll be welcomed. And you won't even have to wander far since it's the cottage closest to Ahern's farm." She giggled with relief. "The rooms might be bit crowded with you filling them up, and I've not the slightest idea how those great legs of yours would fit into my bed, which is where I'm supposed to give you my affection, but a promise is a promise. Not that that would be of much interest to you."

The stallion snorted delicately.

Ari stroked his cheek. "But that's only one kind of affection, isn't it?" she said softly as her hand traveled down the strong neck. She fingercombed the long mane. "There are other kinds, aren't there? Like friendship. That's something I could give with a willing heart."

Oh, she liked petting him. Liked feeling his warmth under her hand. Liked the way that black mane brushed against her skin.

"I feel strange," she whispered.

He made a sound that might have been agreement or understanding.

She pressed her hands against his cheeks.

He lipped her chin.

For a moment, she couldn't look away from those strange gray eyes. Then she pressed her lips against his muzzle. "There. A kiss to seal the bargain." Suddenly feeling shy, she went to the cave and pulled out her pack. "Since we're friends now, I'll share my meal with you. I don't think cheese is of any interest to you, but horses like apples, don't they?"

The stallion nodded vigorously.

Ari eyed him a moment. "You *are* a horse, aren't you?"

He turned his head as if he needed to check the body behind him. He swished his tail, then gave her such a quizzical look she couldn't help but laugh.

"All right. So it was a foolish question. But I wouldn't want to insult one of the Fae by offering such humble fare."

He shook his head.

It was nothing, Ari assured herself while she cut up the apples with her folding knife. Just moondreams and too many of her grandmother's tales about the Fae and how they could change into another shape. The horse was used to people. And Ahern's "special" horses tended to act as if they understood what was being said, so maybe there was some inflection in her voice that the horse was responding to, some cue she wasn't aware of that made it seem like he was really answering her. He was just a horse that, for some reason, was curious enough about her to stay.

As expected, he wasn't interested in the cheese, but

happily munched his share of the apples. Since he seemed determined to have his share of the fairy cakes as well, she gave him one, hoping it wouldn't make him ill. There was no fresh water nearby, so she kept pouring water from a canteen into her palm until he'd had his fill.

After slaking her own thirst, she tucked her pack back into the cave, then she joined him on the beach.

He arched his neck and pranced in a circle around her.

"Don't you think it's time you headed home?" Ari asked.

He stopped, shook his head. One foreleg stamped the sand.

"You're going to have to make your wishes clearer than that, lad," Ari said primly.

He did. As soon as she turned her back on him, he came up behind her and gave her a firm nudge.

"Do you bully all your ladies like this?" Ari demanded.

He didn't bother to answer. He just kept herding her back toward the rock wall. She tried slipping past him a couple of times, but he was bigger and faster and more experienced in herding than she was at dodging.

"All right. All right," Ari grumbled a minute later. "I'm standing on the wall. Are you pleased now?"

The stallion shook his head. Sidling close to the wall, he presented his left side.

That invitation was plain enough.

"I've only ridden a horse a few times when I was a girl," she said, hesitating. "I'm not sure I remember how." But she wanted to ride him. Tonight. Here. Now. Oh, she wanted to.

He turned his head and looked at her.

She took off her cloak, folded it, and set in on the wall. Gripping a fistful of his mane, she eased one leg over his back, glad that she had chosen to wear the loose trousers and long tunic she usually dressed in except when going to Ridgeley.

He moved away from the wall at a quiet walk, giving her time to get used to the feel of him under her.

An odd sensation, to have her thighs spread this way, to feel the heat of his body where she was pressed against his back.

They walked along the edge of the foam. There was no sound but the sea sending gentle waves to kiss the shore.

Ari breathed deeply, draining one kind of tension from her body.

He lifted into a canter, the change so smooth she didn't have time to tense her muscles. The wind in her face tasted of the sea. She knew they were moving far more slowly than his gallop down the beach, but she felt like she was flying. Here there were no problems, no unhappiness. There was only the sea and the wind and the sand . . . and the powerful body moving beneath hers.

He circled, headed back toward her mother's place, then went past it, taking them farther down the beach. As he circled again, Ari glanced up at the cliff's edge.

Her muscles involuntarily clenched, throwing off her balance. The horse immediately slowed to a walk, his ears flicking back and forth.

"That's enough," Ari said quietly, trying to watch the cliff without appearing too obvious. "That's enough."

The horse snorted softly, sounding disappointed, but he headed back to her mother's place.

Unable to resist, Ari looked over her shoulder and studied the cliff for a moment. *Had* there been a man crouching on the edge of the cliff, watching her? Or had it been nothing more than stone and a trick of the moonlight? It didn't matter. It had scared her enough to remind her of why she should have remained out of sight instead of riding on the beach.

As soon as they were close to the low stone walls, she slid off the horse's back, not waiting for him to stop.

"Quiet," she whispered harshly before he could voice his opinion of having indulged an erratic rider. She scurried to the cliff base, hardly daring to breathe until she was safely hidden.

The horse hesitated a moment, then followed her.

Ari petted his neck. "Thank you for the ride," she whispered, "but you have to go now. Someone might notice you and come down here to find out why you're wandering by yourself. I can't take that chance. There are too many hunters out tonight." She shivered.

His gray eyes studied her for far too long. Then he turned and trotted back down the beach in the direction he'd originally come.

She snatched up her cloak and wrapped herself in it. That didn't stop the shivering. Sitting next to the wall, she pulled her knees up and rested her forehead against them.

Please, Lady. Please don't let anyone find me tonight.

Ari wasn't sure if she was making that plea to the Mother of All Things or the Lady of the Moon. To the Great Mother, she decided as she raised her head to look at the night sky, feeling a little disappointed that she couldn't see the full moon from where she sat. The Lady of the Moon would be wearing another face tonight, and it wasn't a gentle one.

Eventually, she stopped shivering. Leaning back against the wall, she let the sea's endless song lull her into sleep.

And dreamt that a puzzled, gray-eyed horse had quietly returned to watch over her.

Neall leaned against a tree at one edge of the woods that bordered the meadow behind Ari's house.

If you'd had the brains you were born with, you would have stayed in your room tonight . . . with the door bolted. Some men may joke about the Summer Moon being the Bedding Moon, but the ones who bedded a woman they wouldn't have chosen to wed tend to call it the Ensnarer's Moon . . . with good reason.

His heart had overruled his head. He knew Royce was coming here tonight, which was why he'd crept out of his uncle's house and ridden to Brightwood. But when he'd slipped away, his cousin had still been at the table, guzzling ale, so there was a little time to decide what to do.

He knew perfectly well how Royce would react if *he* was the one Ari offered the fancy to. Royce would make his life more of a misery than it already was. But Ari was worth whatever misery might come of it. She was worth far more than that—even if she never seemed to actually see *him*.

So he was here to make sure he was the first man she would see. When he'd heard the whispers about the fancies Odella and some of the other girls had purchased from Granny Gwynn, he'd told himself over and over that he was just acting as a friend. A man could accept the fancy without taking advantage of the physical pleasure that was offered with it. Or, perhaps, accepting that offer just once to seal the bargain—and to assure the girl that she was desirable.

He told himself that he would refrain so that Ari would realize he *wasn't* like Royce, that she mattered to him far too much for him to take advantage of love magic that gave her no choice. He needed to have her make that choice. If she didn't, if she just tolerated him in her bed because she had to . . .

If she gave you the fancy, you'd be spending as much time in her bed as you could before the bargain ended. And if her belly swelled with your child because of it . . .

Neall closed his eyes. Even if he got her with child, she wouldn't necessarily agree to stand with him at Midsummer and say the pledge that would make them husband and wife. And if she didn't agree, she would be facing those months, and the birth that would come after, alone. He couldn't do that to her. And he couldn't stand by and *not* take advantage of anything that *might* bind her to him.

"Prey isn't usually so obliging as to stand waiting for an arrow in the heart," a rusty voice said quietly.

Neall stiffened but made no other movement. As he opened his eyes, he turned his head slowly in the direction of the voice.

The small man was no taller than the length of Neall's arm, a stout little man dressed in the brown and gray clothing that would make him invisible in the woods. An arrow was loosely nocked in the bow he held.

"The Mother's blessings be upon you," Neall said softly. When the man didn't respond to the greeting, Neall's chest tightened. He'd always been courteous and careful not to give offense whenever he and one of the Small Folk crossed paths. They didn't wield the power the Fae did, but their mischief magic could make a person's life difficult, and if they were sufficiently riled, they could be deadly. But he knew this one, had spoken with him any number of times, so he didn't understand the anger filling the air between them now.

"What brings you to Brightwood tonight, young Lord?" the small man asked.

Ah. So *that* was it. "The same thing as you," Neall replied, giving the man a bit of a smile.

"I think not."

Neall's smile faded. "What I do here is none of your business." Then he added angrily, "You're not the only one who cares about Brightwood and the witches who live here."

"Witch," the small man said with a trace of bitterness. "There's only one left now, isn't there?"

Before Neall could reply, they heard a horse cantering down the road. Neall crouched down. His eyes flicked from the piece of the road he could see to the dark cottage.

Royce came into view, reining in hard enough to set his horse on its haunches. He studied the cottage for a long moment before dismounting and striding toward the front door.

"No lights," the small man said, now standing beside Neall. "No smoke rising from the hearth. No reason for anyone to think she's home."

That was what worried him. He'd seen no flicker of a candle or lamp since he'd arrived, and he'd seen no sign of Ari. But she *must* know she couldn't thwart the fancy *that* way. And where else could she be?

The small man said, "If she keeps the door bolted—"

"Love magic doesn't work that way," Neall snapped. "If she tries to defy it, it will turn against her."

"A convenient spell, that," the small man said with deadly softness.

They heard Royce pounding on the front door, watched him circle round the cottage and pound the kitchen door. His curses reached them clearly.

But no light flickered at any of the windows, no shutter moved to indicate someone might be peering out.

"You *bitch*!" Royce shouted. He threw his weight against the door again and again until the lock broke and the door swung inward. "You'll give me what I came for, one way or another."

Royce tried to take a step forward, and ended up taking a step back. He tried several times, but couldn't cross the threshold. *"Bitch!"* He spun around, and every line of his body shouted his intention to vent his rage on something.

Give him a different target, Neall thought, rising from the crouch and glancing at the still-dark cottage. *You can survive a beating.* As he started to step away from the tree, the small man gripped his wrist, holding him back.

"Can't you *feel* it?" the small man whispered harshly, pulling Neall down to a crouch again.

"Feel wh—"

Magic rippled across the land. A moment after that, a howl filled the air.

"Mother's mercy," Neall whispered.

"Best to stay down and stay quiet, young Lord," the small man said. "The Wild Hunt rides through Brightwood."

Neall shivered. He saw Royce freeze, then run to the front of the cottage where he had left his horse. He had one glimpse of Royce whipping the horse into a flat-out gallop before horse and rider vanished from his line of sight.

Twisting around, he stared at his gelding, which hadn't stirred at all.

"Sleeping dust," the small man said softly. "He'll sleep a bit longer. Perhaps long enough," he added under his breath.

The pack of shadow hounds burst from the woods that bordered the back of the meadow, racing silently toward the road.

Neall's breath caught, suspended by fear and awe. The hounds looked like phantoms shifting across the meadow rather than living creatures. As they streaked past his hiding place, he didn't dare move. The traveling minstrels and storytellers had plenty of tales about men who had been invited to participate in the Wild Hunt—as the prey. True, all the men in those tales were scoundrels whose own misdeeds made the Hunt a deserved justice. But it was one thing to listen to those tales while sitting safely by the hearth; it was quite another to be out in the open with the hounds racing by.

It was the small man digging his fingers into Neall's wrist that made him glance away from the hounds in time to see the Huntress and her pale mare canter into the meadow.

When she was abreast of his hiding place, she reined in the mare. She studied Ari's cottage with its broken kitchen door for a long time. Then she turned her head and seemed to look straight at him.

The small man's grip on his wrist grew painful. The Huntress's stare was compelling enough to be painful in another way.

She's ice, Neil thought. *A man would be a fool to put his life in her hands.*

One of the shadow hounds returned, as if wondering why its mistress no longer followed the pack.

She looked at the hound, hesitated . . . and moved on.

When she could no longer easily see him, Neall dared to turn his head toward the road. The pack was gathered there, sniffing the tracks. Some of them were staring in the direction of Ridgeley—the direction Royce had taken.

The Huntress paused there too, then crossed the road. She urged the mare into a canter and headed toward old Ahern's farm, the hounds flowing on either side of her.

"You'd best be gone before she comes back this way," the small man said, finally releasing Neall's wrist.

"What makes you think she'll be back?" Neall asked as he straightened up slowly.

"She'll be back."

Neall walked over to Darcy, placed a hand on the gelding's neck. Startled awake, the animal jerked away from his hand, then turned its head toward him, as if needing the reassurance of a familiar smell and touch.

"You'd best ride, young Lord, before she begins wondering a bit too much about you," the small man insisted.

"What's there to wonder about?" Neall said uneasily as he untied Darcy. "And being a poor relation of Baron Felston doesn't make me a lord."

"Wasn't talking about the likes of *him*," the small man said, annoyed. He studied Neall, his expression grim. "You think the Small Folk talk to every lad that comes looking for us? We watch them the same way we keep watch to make sure the rats don't harm our young. The only difference between most humans and rats is that rats are more honest. But like will recognize like, even when the blood has thinned—and yours isn't as thin as you pretend. *That's* why the Small Folk have made themselves known to you, and *that's* why the Huntress will wonder about you."

Neall stared at the small man. "You're mistaken."

"Am I?" the small man asked softly. "Am I really, young Lord?" He shrugged. "As you will. But the boy you were has grown to be a man, and a lie told by a boy isn't swallowed as easily when it's told by a man. Remember that."

Neall didn't see any movement, but the small man was no longer standing there.

"Let's get home before anything else happens," Neall muttered to Darcy.

He kept to the woods for as long as he could, skirted the tenant farms his uncle controlled, and finally reached Felston's manor house. As he gave Darcy a hurried grooming, he noticed Royce's horse wasn't in its stall yet, which probably meant his cousin had stopped at the tavern in Ridgeley. He imagined the place would be crowded tonight with the younger men who wanted a roomful of witnesses in case a girl pointed a finger in their direction. It didn't matter if the man left early or came late. They would protect each other to keep from getting caught.

Slipping out of the stables, Neall headed for the back of the house. The kitchen door was unlatched, and there was no one sleeping by the hearth. Well, even servants weren't excluded from the delights— and dangers—this night could hold, and he could well imagine what would happen to a young servant who had the misfortune of being the first man a gentry lady saw—especially Odella, if she was still out.

Using the servants' stairway, Neall made it up to his room and gratefully bolted the door. Quickly undressing in the dark, he got into bed, releasing a sigh of relief.

Not that any of the gentry girls would have wanted to make an offer to *him*. He had no more to offer any of them than the servants. At least, nothing he was ready to acknowledge yet.

He had turned twenty-one a few weeks ago. He could own property in his own name now, without "Uncle" Felston claiming control over it as his guardian. He could leave Ridgeley and finally go back to the mistily remembered place that had been his home as a small boy. His mother's house. His mother's land.

"Why do I have to go with them?" Neall asked. *Tears filled his eyes, despite his efforts not to cry, as he watched Ashk calmly fill the trunk with his clothes and the wooden toys his father had made for him. "I don't know them."* His young voice rose to a wail.

Ashk turned to look at him, her woodland eyes filled

with dry grief. "Your father was a good man. If he had lived, he would have taught you what you need to know about the world. But he is gone, so you need to learn those things from his people, his family."

"But I don't know them! Why can't I learn those things from you? Why can't I stay with you?"

She knelt before him, brushed her fingers through his hair. "First you must learn what your father's people can teach you. Then, when you are grown and return here, I will teach you other things about the world."

Neall sniffed, studied the eyes of his mother's closest friend—eyes that reminded him of his mother's. "I can come back?"

"This house and land will be waiting for you. That much I can promise." She hesitated. "But you mustn't tell your father's people about the land. It belongs to the daughters, and no one else has any say here."

So he'd kept the secret about the land from Baron Felston for all these years. One of the many secrets he'd thought he'd kept well since he was brought to the baron's house as a young boy grieving the loss of both parents.

Now that he was grown, and no longer legally Felston's ward, there was only one thing that stopped him from saddling his horse and riding to the western part of Sylvalan: Ari. He wanted her to go with him, but he didn't think she would ever leave Brightwood. And he knew, despite his daydreams of being her lover and husband, that being with her here would be no good for either of them. Even if they married, he would always be considered Baron Felston's poor relation as long as he stayed around Ridgeley. And Felston, claiming a "family" connection, would look with already-greedy eyes on the bounty Brightwood held and expect to make use of it.

Ari was still young, barely more than a girl. Now that her mother and grandmother were gone, maybe she *would* be willing to leave Brightwood, and the cruelty she faced every time she went to Ridgeley, and start a new life somewhere else . . . with him.

He would give it another year . . . and spend another year working from sunup to sunset as the baron's unofficial steward, wearing Royce's castoff clothes while Royce, Odella, and the baron and baroness spent all the profits that could be squeezed from the estate, bitterly complaining all the while that he wasn't trying harder to wring a little bit more out of the land already wrung dry.

He would give it another year. Then, with her or without her, he was going to go home and put his heart and his sweat into his own land.

Placing his hands under his head, Neall stared at the ceiling.

If Ashk had understood what it meant to be a poor relation in a gentry family, would she have still sent him away to live with his father's people? Would she have considered the lessons she'd wanted him to learn worth the misery of knowing he was unwanted and unloved?

It had been made clear to him over the past fifteen years that his father had been an . . . embarrassment . . . a blot on the baron's family tree—one the whole family had been happy to forget as soon as he was old enough to strike out on his own. He had been a child conceived during the Summer Moon, and his mother, Neall's grandmother, had calmly refused to name one of the men in their village as the father, insisting that a Fae Lord had fathered her child. It was a common enough claim that was used if a young woman found herself with child after the Summer Moon and either didn't want to marry the man who had sired it or found herself in the position of having the man deny any responsibility.

Sometimes it was even true.

Thinking about what the small man had said, he wondered if Ari would think of him differently if she knew the truth about him: that his paternal grandfather really had been a Fae Lord . . . and that his mother had been a witch.

Chapter Seven

"Be warned," Lyrra said, pouring another cup of tea when Dianna joined her at the table that held the fruit and cakes. "The mood is rather sour this morning." She glanced toward the windows where Lucian stood, his back to the room. "Or brooding."

Dianna casually looked around the large room. There were several of these gathering places within the Clan house. The women looked bored, but Dianna suspected it was a mask to hide their resentment over the lack of available lovers last night. The men seemed . . . disappointed . . . and were nodding as they listened to Falco. Aiden quietly played his harp, not a song as much as notes flowing together—something he'd been doing lately whenever his thoughts troubled him. And Lucian . . .

"What about you?" Lyrra asked. "Did you enjoy the Wild Hunt?"

"What's Falco puffed up about today?" Dianna asked, abruptly changing the subject. She didn't want to talk about last night, or the cottage with its broken door, or that strange-yet-familiar magic she had sensed at the edge of the woods.

Lyrra gave her a long look, sipped her tea, then shrugged. "Listen for yourself."

Dianna moved until she stood at the edge of the cushioned benches where the Fae sat listening to the Lord of the Hawks.

"What you say is true, Falco," one of the other men said, shaking his head sadly. "I remember the tales about succulent women who gave joy to a man. I saw nothing succulent about the females roaming around last night."

"Predators, that's what they are," Falco said. "Like those female insects that devour the male while he's mating with her." He shuddered. "No wonder the males have taken to hiding."

"Not all the males hide," Aiden said with a smile. He plucked a chord, and sang, "When springtime comes, the maidens bloom. They ripen for the Summer Moon." He pressed his hands against the harp strings to quiet them. "The Summer Moon has been the climax"—he grinned at the word—"for the Courting Moon for generations in Sylvalan. It's a night when the female expresses the power of her sex freely. Often, she *is* choosing a mate that night. Sometimes it's only for that night. Sometimes it's the man who will be her husband. For many, the mating that night just seals a bargain their hearts have already made, and the pledge made at Midsummer is the formal agreement before witnesses."

"If the men were as willing as you say, they wouldn't call it the Ensnarer's Moon," Falco argued.

The humor cooled in Aiden's blue eyes. "A man has the right to say yay or nay. If he says yay, he takes his chances. If nothing more than a mating comes from that night, they can both walk away and simply remember whatever pleasure they'd given each other. If there's a child, then the man has made his choice of wife. That, too, is part of their tradition."

"Unless the man is Fae," another man said a bit maliciously.

"That's another thing," Falco said. "Any time there's a child and a marriage *doesn't* take place, *we* get blamed for the child."

"Of course, the blaming is unjust, isn't it?" Lyrra said, the sweetness in her voice warring with the sharpness in her eyes. "After all, it couldn't be true, could it?"

Out of the corner of her eye, Dianna noticed Lucian stiffen, then watched his shoulders sag. She knew he hadn't filled a human woman with his child. She *knew* it. So why had he reacted that way?

"I think," Aiden said, carefully setting his harp aside, "that it's the custom of gifting that has taken the . . . charm . . . out of these encounters."

"That's it exactly," Falco said, jumping in. "The moment you approach a woman, it's 'give me gold, give me silver, give me jewels, give me beauty, gimme gimme gimme.' Which wouldn't be so bad if what they were offering in return was worth the cost."

"So you take what you want and give nothing but your rod in return?" Dianna asked softly, feeling her temper chill. "I'm surprised you can convince any woman to take that bargain."

Falco's eyes widened. He looked at the Huntress and the Muse, who were now standing side by side. "I didn't mean *Fae* women!"

Aiden winced.

At least there's one male here who isn't going to wonder why he's receiving a cold welcome, Dianna thought.

"As I was saying," Aiden began, giving Falco a warning look, "there was a time when a man would leave a token after spending the night with a woman, a small gift to please her. It was a male custom, not a female expectation. Do you see the difference?" He waited until Lyrra nodded. "Perhaps that was the Bard's failing some time in the past; there's a song about the jewels a lover brings his lady because she won't accept him without them. Now, a song isn't enough unless a bag of gold comes with it. And when you're with that woman, you can tell she's thinking about how to spend the gold, and if she thinks of you at all, it's to wonder how much longer you'll be at it." He reached for his harp. "That doesn't excuse our own failings, but, perhaps, it explains why we so often disappoint—and are disappointed."

An awkward silence filled the room until Falco broke it. "That wasn't what I meant. It's the *way* these humans approach the Fae that offends me. And we're partly to blame." He waved an arm to encompass everyone in the room. "We've been tolerant of these . . . *creatures* . . . for far too long. They don't ask for our help, they *demand* it—as if they have any right to the magic we wield. They don't approach us respectfully anymore. They act as if they're our *equals*. They need some fear in their puny lives. That's what they need. Why, just the other day, one of those females, the one who lives in that cottage near the sea, greeted me. 'Blessings of the day to you, brother hawk,' " he mimicked nastily.

"If you were in your other from, she couldn't have known to greet you any other way," Lyrra said dryly.

Falco waved that comment away. "If she *hadn't* at least suspected, she wouldn't have given me any greeting at all. Humans never recognize any of the Mother's other children."

"If she gave you greeting, it was sincerely meant."

Dianna looked at her brother. It was the first time Lucian had spoken, the first indication that he had been listening at all.

"It was insolent and disrespectful," Falco argued. He paused, then added darkly, "I've a mind to go back to that cottage and rake my talons across that creature's face."

Lucian turned away from the window and faced Falco. *"Leave her alone."*

Silence.

Don't be a fool, Falco, Dianna thought. *Remember to whom you speak . . . and take care.*

Falco looked away. "I beg your pardon, Lucian. It was just talk. I meant nothing by it."

No one moved until Lucian turned back to the window. Then all of them, except Dianna, crept out of the room. Putting her cup on the nearest table, she warily approached her brother.

"It was just talk, Lucian," she said, hesitating a moment before resting a hand on his arm. "You know how Falco can be at times. And if this female really did—"

"She meant no harm," he snapped.

Dianna studied his face. She didn't understand the anger and frustration she saw, but it was the sadness in his eyes that worried her. "You met her?"

"Last night."

It was obvious he was holding something back. And it was equally obvious, to her, that he wanted—*needed*—to talk.

"What happened?" *Besides what you'd expect to have happen at the Summer Moon.*

"She gave me a fancy—a piece of sugar candy with some love magic added to it."

Dianna clenched her teeth. Maybe Falco was right after all.

"After assuring me that the magic wasn't binding on *me,* she promised me the affection of her body from the full moon to the dark, swearing that promise by the Lord of the Sun and the Lady of the Moon." He smiled ruefully. "I was in my other form when she made that promise."

Dianna's mouth fell open. "She promised herself to a horse?"

The sadness in his eyes deepened. "She gave that promise to a horse because she didn't want to give it to a man."

"But . . . But she gave that promise to *you.*" Watching him, she suddenly understood the sadness and decided to push. At another time she would have discouraged any interest he might have in a human female, but not now. There was no certainty they would see another Summer Moon, so why not take whatever pleasure could be wrung from each day? "She gave it to you, Lucian, whatever form you were in."

"She gave it to a horse."

"She made the bargain with *you,*" Dianna insisted. "And if you want—" She choked for a moment. How could *Lucian* want one of those females enough to be distressed like this? "If you want the bargain fulfilled, that is your right."

"What happened to all the feminine anger toward men who offer nothing but their rods?"

That was different. They hadn't been talking about her brother then. But that did explain why the talk had disturbed him.

"If there was love magic involved, *some* man was going to have the use of her, isn't that so?" Seeing him flinch, she regretted saying it that way, but kept pushing. "So why shouldn't it be you?"

She felt his anger rising, and knew from past experience he would become completely stubborn and not give in no matter what he wanted.

"Why are you denying yourself this pleasure?" she demanded.

"Because she has no choice!" he shouted.

"Can't you give her one?" she shouted back.

Lucian stared at her.

"Can't you give her one?" she asked again quietly. She gave him a mischievous smile. "Perhaps she *would* find the man as interesting as the horse if she had the chance to decide. But if she doesn't . . . if she truly doesn't want a lover, you could walk away, couldn't you?"

"I—" His body relaxed a bit. "Yes, I could. But I can't just knock on the door . . ."

That's exactly what you want to do. "A traveler, needing shelter, wouldn't be refused hospitality. And nothing says you have to come empty-handed."

Lucian's eyes narrowed. "Why would I be needing shelter?"

"From the rain, of course."

"I'm going to get wet?"

Dianna smiled sweetly. "Soaked. I suggest you bring an extra set of clothes in your saddlebags."

His smile came slowly, but it was warm and real. He kissed her cheek, then left her.

Alone, Dianna wandered back to the table that held the fruit and cakes, but had no appetite for any of it.

More of the roads through the Veil had closed. More of the Clans had disappeared because of whatever was devouring Tir Alainn. And they were no closer to finding a way to stop it. No other information had been passed on to Lyrra or Aiden about the wiccanfae and their dark magic, and the only scrap of information that a bard had recently passed on to Aiden about the Pillars of the World implied that, at some time, they had been connected somehow to the House of Gaian. Which didn't help at all since the House of Gaian had disappeared so long ago and neither Lyrra nor Aiden had any clue about what the Pillars of the World were, let alone where to find them.

There was nothing she could do about Tir Alainn right now, but there *was* something she could do to help her brother get the pleasure he sought.

Dianna left the room. The Fae had long ago lost the ability to command the elements, but with some effort, she thought they could produce a brief storm around a certain cottage.

Chapter Eight

Ari winced as heavy thunder rolled over the cottage and the first fat drops of rain hit the windows. Hurrying into her bedroom, she finished latching the inside shutters and drawing the winter drapes across them. Normally she enjoyed watching a storm roll in from the sea, but this one seemed ominous, somehow.

"You're getting daft, Ari," she muttered as she stripped off her clothes and pulled on her heaviest nightgown. "First you talk to horses, and now you think storms have moods."

But storms *did* have moods, and this one made her uneasy.

A gust of wind struck the cottage hard enough to make the windows rattle.

Ari froze for a moment, then shook her head. Only a fool would ride out on a night like this.

She put on clean socks, stuffed her feet into slippers, then put the snug on over her nightgown. Running her hand down the heavy wool, she smiled sadly.

The snug was her mother's idea. Tired of shawls that never seemed to stay put, Meredith had taken one of her shawls and sewed up the sides to make loose sleeves. Ari had woven fasteners that could keep it closed with a button. The result was a cross between a shawl and a coat that Meredith, laughing when she tried on the result of their efforts, had said would keep them warm and snug even in the stiffest breeze.

Another gust of wind had Ari moving into the cottage's main room. She stood in front of the hearth, breathing steadily as she focused on the wood. The power of fire swelled inside her, making her right hand tingle a little. She banked that power, gently. Raising her hand, she fed the rest of it into the wood. A bit of smoke rose from the kindling. Then a tiny flame flickered, caught more kindling, and grew stronger. She continued to feed that tiny fire until the last log began to burn easily.

Moving into the kitchen, she sniffed the aroma of rabbit stew and pressed her hand against her growling stomach. She started to smile, but it faded when she looked at the kitchen door with its shiny new bolts and locks.

How had old Ahern known that her kitchen door had been broken last night? Surely he hadn't come around last night because it was the Summer Moon? Surely not. He'd never looked at her *that* way. But in his own gruff way, he'd always been kind.

He'd said he'd come looking for the gray stallion, and she *knew* that one came around in the evenings from time to time to graze in the meadow—had been doing so for as long as she could remember.

But Ahern had never come looking for the gray horse before. In fact, one time when she'd asked him if the horse had strayed, there had been a twinkle in his eyes, shadowed by sadness, when he told her that the gray had strayed a bit too far in its younger years but that time was long past, and that she needn't worry about the horse. Then he'd given her a searching look and asked if it troubled her to have the gray around. It didn't trouble her, and she'd told him so. So why *had* Ahern come looking for the gray last night?

"Don't borrow trouble," Ari told herself firmly, dishing out a bowl of stew. "He was here for the reason he said he was, and *because* he was, he noticed the door and came back this morning to fix it. If you keep thinking this way, you'll end up with the headache as well as a stomachache." She cut two slices of sharp cheese from the wheel, then cut a thick slice of bread from the loaf she'd baked that morning. As an indulgence, she spread what she considered to be an extravagant amount of butter over the bread.

Bringing her dishes to the table in the main room, she lit a couple of candles. Satisfied with the look of things, she hurried back to the kitchen, took the stew pot off the stove, put the teakettle on, then filled a glass with water to have with her meal.

Returning to the table, she gave thanks to the Mother for her bounty, then bit into the bread and almost groaned with pleasure. As she chewed slowly, she looked around the room.

After dinner, she could bring the small loom in from the workroom and sit by the fire and weave for a little while. Or she could sit in the rocking chair that someone had given her grandmother so many years ago and just dream by the fire. Or she could snuggle into bed and get the sleep she needed to deal with whatever tomorrow would bring.

Like whatever damage the storm may do to the young lettuce and the seedlings you planted in the past couple of days. Or having the root cellar flood because you still haven't gotten the spell for keeping out water quite right.

Ari shook her head and picked up her spoon. Borrowing trouble again. She'd never thought about those kinds of spells when her mother was alive because Meredith's strength had been water. When she'd commanded, water had obeyed. But water spells didn't work for a witch whose strengths were earth and fire, so Ari had had to learn earth-based spells to keep water out of places it wasn't supposed to be. Or, more truthfully, was still working on *finding* the right spell since her efforts so far had achieved limited success. Of course, even her mother might have been challenged by a storm like this.

A careful nibble confirmed that the stew was cool enough to eat. She dug her spoon into the bowl and was about to take a mouthful when someone knocked on the door.

The spoon slipped out of her fingers. She stared at the door, her heart pounding.

Mother's mercy! Royce!

Another knock, more impatient this time.

With effort, she regained enough self-control to think instead of panic. Even if it *was* Royce, the warding spells would keep him out unless she welcomed him in. And she had no intention of letting him cross her threshold. But what if it was Ahern, coming to ask for a simple because one of his men was sick?

"You won't know by just standing here," Ari muttered, moving toward the door.

A third knock made her freeze, her eyes fixed on the latch. The fact that whoever it was hadn't tried to force his way in gave her courage to open the door.

It wasn't Royce, and it wasn't Ahern. It was a well-dressed, thoroughly wet stranger who was hunched under the roof as far as he could get.

"Good evening," Ari said.

Thunder rolled. Lightning flashed. The stranger glared balefully at the sky, then gave her a small, woeful smile. "Is it?"

Something about him made Ari hesitate. Despite the rain and the chill wind, seeing him made the cottage feel a bit too warm.

Well, you can't leave him standing there. And he's obviously gentry, so suggesting he bed down in the cow shed wouldn't be something he'd forgive.

"Come in and be welcome," Ari said, using the phrase that quieted the warding spells. She stepped back to give him room to enter.

He hesitated on the threshold, and she wondered if he could feel the warding spells draw back like a curtain that would close again the moment he stepped into the room. Then he entered the room, moving to one side so that Ari could close the door.

"I'm . . . grateful . . . for the shelter, mistress," he said, pushing his black hair away from his face. "It's a hard night."

She could tell gratitude wasn't a common feeling

for him. Not surprising. It wasn't a common emotion for any of the gentry as far as she could tell. At least he had manners enough to say the word, which was more than anyone in Ridgeley would have said.

Noticing the saddlebags he carried in one hand, she said, "What about your horse?"

Surprise—and a hint of amusement—filled his gray eyes. "My horse?"

"Did you put it in the cow shed?" Ari bit her lower lip worriedly. "There's straw for bedding, but I don't keep hay or any feed."

"The horse is fine where he is," the man said, something a little odd in his voice.

Ari nodded. The man seemed filled with a waiting tension she didn't understand. His quick glance at the table was explanation enough.

He's hungry. The thought made her shiver. Suddenly, she didn't want to be in the same room with him—at least for a few minutes. Which brought to mind other problems.

"You should get out of those wet clothes," she said, then pressed her lips tightly shut. She had nothing to offer him, and she didn't think it would be wise to have a man sitting around wearing nothing but a blanket and his small clothes—assuming those weren't wet, too.

"I have a change of clothes," he said, raising the saddlebags slightly. He looked at her expectantly.

There wasn't much choice. Squaring her shoulders, she gestured toward the half-open door of her bedroom. "You can change in there."

Inclining his head slightly, he went into the bedroom and closed the door.

Pressing her hands against her nervous stomach, Ari glanced down. She groaned quietly, then shrugged in resignation. The ankle-length nightgown was heavy enough to cover her, and the shrug came down to her thighs. There was nothing immodest about her dress, and if a gentry male assumed that barging in on a woman dressed for bed was the same as an invitation, then he could just go back out into the rain and be welcome to it.

Grabbing her dish of stew, she hurried into the kitchen. Moving the teakettle to the back of the stove, she put the stew pot back on the heat, dumped the contents of her bowl into it, and gave it a stir. She sliced more bread and buttered it, cut more cheese from the wheel. Then she braced her hands against the worktable and closed her eyes.

Where was she supposed to put him tonight? The upstairs rooms hadn't been cleaned since last summer. Not even a quick dust and sweep. She didn't use those rooms, and there were always too many other chores that needed to be done. Even if she made up one of the beds, a fire would be needed to take the chill out of the room, and she didn't have enough firewood chopped to feed another fire until morning. So she'd have to give him her bed and make up a pallet of blankets by the fire in the main room for herself.

Dishing out two generous bowls of stew made her hesitate again. She hoped he wasn't *too* hungry. She'd counted on that stew providing her with meals for a few days, and the coppers she'd gotten from Granny Gwynn for the simples wouldn't go very far if she had to buy supplies in Ridgeley. She eyed the sweet bread sitting on the worktable, carefully wrapped in a towel. She'd made it as a "thank you" to Ahern for fixing her door, but maybe she could also get a few eggs in exchange for it?

She shook her head as she ferried dishes from the kitchen to the table.

Whatever you do comes back to you threefold. That was part of the witch's creed. Bounty was given, bounty was received, and the Mother was the most bountiful giver of all.

She would give the food and shelter she could give tonight with an easy heart, and let tomorrow take care of itself.

She was putting the dishes of stew on the table when he came out of the bedroom, dressed in nothing more than dark trousers and a white shirt. He carried a bottle in one hand and a small sack in the other.

"I can offer a little something for the table," he said, handing her the sack.

Setting the sack on the table, she took out a small, covered pot and a woven box. Opening both, she studied the contents for a long moment before deciding that they must be some kind of biscuits and a creamed cheese.

When she looked up to thank him, she noticed the way he frowned at what he'd brought, as if he'd just realized that it was the kind of thing someone might pack if he was taking a leisurely afternoon ride . . . or if he knew he didn't have to travel far. He could have bought it at an inn where he'd stopped for a midday meal . . . but she didn't think so. Which made her wonder exactly where he *had* come from. He *could* be one of the gentry from another part of Sylvalan who came to Ahern's to look at the horses he was willing to sell. But Ahern's farm wasn't that far from her cottage, so why hadn't he gone back there?

"Shall I open the wine?" he asked, watching her with a touch of wariness.

Nodding, Ari retreated to the kitchen to find some glasses.

Anyone crossing the road and climbing the first rise beyond it would be able to see Ahern's place. And anyone caught in a storm could reach it easily enough. Unless he'd lost his direction in the dark and the storm, or was just looking for shelter until the storm passed and he could return to the farm. Or continue on to Ridgeley. Perhaps he was one of Baron Felston's guests—or a friend of Royce's.

Ari shivered.

She knew quite well what the people in Ridgeley would say if they found out a strange man had stayed the night. As far as they were concerned, *witch* was just another word for *whore*. If the stranger mentioned where he'd spent the night, she could well imagine men in Ridgeley, married or not, who would come knocking on the door expecting the same kind of "hospitality."

After rummaging in the cupboard for a bit, she found the two remaining crystal wineglasses that had belonged to her great-grandmother. The last time they'd been used was when she and her mother had sat before the fire, drinking a bottle of wine Ahern had given them as a gift for the Winter Solstice. Meredith had died not long after that.

Ari wiped the dust off the wineglasses and returned to the main room.

The wine was on the table, open. He was standing next to one of the chairs.

"I ask your pardon, mistress," he said, sounding as if he'd been mentally rehearsing the phrasing. "I should have introduced myself sooner. I am . . . Lucian."

A tremor went through her at the sound of his name, and she knew how a trout must feel when it fights the hook but gets reeled in anyway.

"I am Ari," she said reluctantly. Names had power, and she hadn't wanted to give him hers, but his offering his own hadn't given her much choice.

Fool, she thought as she set the glasses down and took her place at the table. *He doesn't know you. You could have given him any name but your own. For that matter, how can you be sure that* he *didn't do exactly that?*

Now that she thought of it, there *had* been a moment's hesitation before he'd given his name—as if it wasn't the way he usually introduced himself.

She glanced at him. His fingers rested lightly on the spoon, and he looked at her expectantly. It took her a moment to realize he was waiting for her to begin so that he could eat. Suppressing a sigh, Ari picked up her spoon. More gentry manners she didn't know about. Although . . . old Ahern wasn't gentry, and the few times she'd had so much as a cup of tea with him, he'd waited in the same way.

The stew was too hot for her, so she broke off a

piece of cheese to nibble. As soon as she bit into the cheese, he dug into his meal. There wasn't time to warn him that the stew was hot before he had his mouth full. His eyes widened in surprise, but he didn't grab the wine to cool off his burning mouth. He chewed, swallowed, and smiled at her. "This is delicious." It was the only thing he said for several minutes.

He wolfed down half the bowl of stew, most of the cheese, and a couple slices of buttered bread before she took her first spoonful of stew.

She bit into a piece of potato, then sucked in little puffs of air to cool off the hot center of it. She thought she was being fairly quiet about it, but he lifted his head instantly to observe her. When she managed to swallow, she said, "How did you eat that without burning yourself?"

"I like fire," he said.

Grabbing her glass, she took a large swallow of wine, then looked at the glass to make sure she hadn't mistakenly grabbed the glass of water. "I like fire, too, but I'm not fond of burning my tongue."

"But that is the nature of fire. It burns."

"It warms," she replied sharply. She hadn't intended to sound challenging, but something about the way he'd said "it burns" chilled her.

"You don't think fire can destroy?" he asked softly.

She could tell by the way his fingers curled around his wineglass that he wasn't used to being contradicted and certainly didn't like it. Still, she took her time answering. Fire was a branch of the Mother that was a part of her. She knew its nature, its dark side and its light. But how to explain to a stranger something she'd never needed to put into words before?

"Yes, fire can destroy," she said carefully, "but it's also the heat that bakes the bread, the comfort that warms a cold winter's night, the light that guides you home in the dark." She fiddled with her spoon. "That must sound very simple to you."

"It sounds . . . gentler," Lucian replied, looking

away. "And far more thoughtful than my own remark." Sipping the wine, he frowned. "My apologies, mistress. The wine doesn't do justice to the meal."

"It has a delicate flavor," Ari said. In truth, despite the deep-red color of the wine, it was almost tasteless, as if it contained nothing more than a memory of flavor. Spreading a bit of creamed cheese on a biscuit, she took a bite and tried not to sigh. The cheese and biscuits weren't any better than the wine. She hadn't known gentry preferred food that tasted so . . . pale.

They finished the meal in a silence thickened by tension.

Ari looked at her half-full bowl of stew and gave up. Her appetite had fled, her stomach too full of the growing conviction that her guest was waiting for something.

"What was your destination, Lord?" she asked, hoping it was a sufficient distance so that he would want to retire soon in order to get an early start in the morning.

"Nowhere in particular," he replied evasively, his eyes fixed on the wineglass his fingers restlessly turned.

Ari stared at him. If he wasn't going somewhere, what had he been doing out on a night like this?

"Did you enjoy your ride on the beach last night?" he asked abruptly, still not looking at her.

Ari's body went hot and cold at the same time, making her feel sick . . . and furious. "If *that's* what you came for, my Lord, you're too late. The Summer Moon was last night."

"I know," he said quietly, his gray eyes pinning her to her chair. "You didn't answer the question."

"Nor will I," Ari snapped. "It's none of your business." She was so vexed she looked around for something to throw, but she couldn't afford to waste food or crockery. "I thought I had seen someone watching from the cliff."

"Was there?" The sharpness in his voice made her look at him.

"Yes. *You.* How else could you know?"

Lucian's voice softened. "I was on the beach."

Ari shook her head. "There was no one on the beach except the—"

"You gave me apples and some kind of cake—and a fancy."

Ari kept shaking her head.

"You kissed me, and made a promise."

"I didn't," she whispered. As she stared at him, his face changed abruptly, taking on a feral quality, and his ears grew slightly pointed.

Fae.

She leaped away from the table, knocking over her chair. He just sat there, watching her with that blend of wariness and hunger in his gray eyes.

"Y-you're Fae." Her voice shook.

He inclined his head slightly.

"But . . . you said you were a horse. I *asked* you, and you *said* you were a horse."

A hint of amusement joined the wariness and hunger in his eyes. "When you asked me, I *was* a horse."

Ari closed her eyes. Mother's mercy. She'd given the fancy to a Fae Lord in his other form. Well, maybe that wasn't such a bad thing. After all, she *had* avoided any of the men from Ridgeley. And maybe he was a minor lord, like the Lord of Poultry or something. *Was* there a Lord of Poultry? If that was the case, shouldn't his other form be a cock? A rooster, Ari amended quickly as an image of a penis with legs running around the barnyard popped into her head. She clamped one hand over her mouth to keep from giggling, certain that if she started she would end up in hysterics.

She took a couple of deep breaths to steady herself, laced her fingers tightly together, then opened her eyes. "Which one are you?"

He studied her for a long moment. "The Lightbringer."

She fled into the kitchen. Leaning over the sink, she felt grateful she hadn't eaten much since there would be less to clean up if she got sick.

Fire burns.

Oh, that one would certainly know about fire. Yes, he would.

The Lord of the Sun. The Lord of Fire.

Mother of us all, please help me.

She heard wine being poured into a glass, then the soft scrape of a chair being pushed back. She tensed, waiting for him to come into the kitchen and make his demands. Instead, she heard the rhythmic creak of her grandmother's rocking chair.

Gathering her courage, Ari crept out of the kitchen. The table had to be cleared and the remaining food properly stored. Besides, those chores were safe and familiar. She glanced in his direction, but he was staring at the fire in the hearth and didn't seem to notice that she was in the room. Collecting as much as she could, she carried dishes back into the kitchen. On her second trip, he said softly, "I didn't come here to harm you."

She looked at him, puzzled by the strain in his voice. Not trusting her own voice, she just nodded and returned to the kitchen. Setting the dishes on the worktable near the sink, she clasped her shaking hands together.

Whatever you do comes back to you . . .

Be careful what you wish for . . .

As I will it . . .

Could she, in part, be responsible for this? She hadn't wanted to give herself to a man from Ridgeley, especially Royce. She *hadn't* cast a spell to avoid that, but her thoughts and feelings *had* been focused on avoiding it. Could that have been enough to have drawn him to the beach last night? Having magic himself, he would be more sensitive to its call, wouldn't he? Besides, she had made a solemn promise, and, because of who he was, when she had sworn by the Lord of the Sun and the Lady of the Moon to honor that promise, that vow had even more weight than it might have.

And he seemed so . . . alone.

That thought startled her enough to make her take care of the mundane chores around the kitchen. As she cleaned up and put the food away, she felt steadier and able to think more clearly.

He could have changed form after she gave him the fancy and demanded satisfaction last night. But he didn't. He could have told her who he was and why he had come as soon as he crossed the threshold. But he didn't. He had given her a name that wouldn't frighten her, and he had given her time to talk with him and get used to his presence before he'd mentioned the beach and the fancy.

All of those things had weight. And there was one other thing: Her only experience with a man had been painful and disappointing. How different might it be with someone like Lucian? If she didn't take the chance now, would another chance ever come? Even if it was no better than it had been with Royce, could it be any worse?

And he's alone. I don't know why that's so, but he is alone. Like me.

When there was nothing left to do in the kitchen, she took a deep breath and let it out slowly. *Have courage, Ari, and trust the Mother's wisdom. Sometimes things are meant to be.*

She approached the hearth slowly, then stood there, uncertain, until he finally looked at her.

"There's something you need to understand, Lord," she said, feeling her face heat. "I've only done this once."

"Done what? Offered a fancy?"

"No," she said hurriedly. "I've never done that before. I meant the other part."

He looked puzzled for a moment, then his expression cleared. "Once?"

She swallowed hard and nodded.

He studied her. "And it wasn't pleasant."

She shook her head.

He drained his glass and set it beside the rocker. "It has to be your choice, Ari."

"I made my choice when I offered the fancy."

"You didn't know who you were offering it to."

"I keep my promises, Lord." *A witch does.*

He stood up, approached her slowly. His hands framed her face. "Be sure."

"I'm sure, Lord."

He brushed his lips against hers. "Lucian," he murmured.

"Lucian," she said obediently.

She braced for a hard kiss and an invading tongue, but his mouth and hands remained gentle, producing a fluttering sensation inside her, as if she were being brushed by delicate wings. Soft. So soft.

His hands left her face and traveled down her back lightly enough she could barely feel them through the nightgown and snug.

His lips explored her face and throat. His hands slipped under the snug. More sensation, but the nightgown still made his touch elusive enough to make her crave more. She wanted to raise her arms and explore his body, but they were too heavy to lift, and she couldn't seem to focus on anything except the journey his hands were taking over her body.

She was like wax being softened by a quiet flame.

"Come," he said quietly, leading her into the bedroom. As they reached the door, the candle by the bed began to burn.

Lucian pulled back the bedcovers, then removed her shrug. Unable to resist the light pressure of his hands on her shoulders, she sat on the bed while he removed her slippers and socks.

"Get under the covers," he said. "It's cold tonight."

Shivering a little, she obeyed. Before she was completely settled, he had shed his clothes and was stretching out beside her.

His hands circled her wrists, bringing them up beside her head.

He was warm. So wonderfully warm.

"Shouldn't I—"

He brushed his lips against hers, silencing her. "Shh."

Wherever he touched, she melted. By the time he coaxed her to remove her nightgown, she couldn't raise herself up without his help.

Warm. So warm.

"Ari."

It was so hard to open her eyes. Her body was answering his commands far better than it was answering hers.

"Ari."

When she finally opened her eyes, his face was above hers. He studied her for a moment, then smiled. She felt him shift, felt the pressure of his legs opening hers. He filled her slowly, then seemed content to remain still while he kissed her.

It was his balls that finally changed the melting feeling into something sharper and hungry. They rested against her, brushing sensitive skin every time his muscles flexed. The weight of them where nothing had touched her before made her squirm.

"Lucian," she moaned, trying to find some way to ease that soft torment. Her fingers clamped on his buttocks, urging him to move. *"Lucian."*

His lips curved in a smile against her cheek. Then he moved, and with every stroke, he fed passion's fire until she burned.

Lucian eased himself out of Ari's bed. As quietly as he could, he pushed back the drapes and opened the shutters. The gray light that would soon yield to sunrise was enough to see by, so he dressed in the clothes he could find, then slipped out of the bedroom.

Drawing back the bolts, he opened the front door. The storm had long passed. Had, in fact, barely lasted through the meal, but he doubted Ari had realized that.

Where had she put the rest of his clothes? he wondered as he closed the door and moved to the back of the cottage. He studied the clean kitchen. And where had she put the rest of the food?

When a quick rummage through various cupboards didn't yield a pot of hot tea, bowls of stew, or cheese, he opened the large wooden box sitting on the worktable and found the bread as well as the biscuits he had brought. He took a biscuit and bit into it, then made a face. For some reason, they didn't taste as good here as they did in Tir Alainn. He rummaged a bit more in the box, hoping he'd find something more than was apparently there. Like some of those cakes Ari had brought to the beach.

He could wake her. She would want tea if she was awake, wouldn't she? And if she was awake, she wouldn't mind fixing something for him to eat.

He was standing outside the bedroom door when it occurred to him that he still had the custom of gifting to deal with. A satisfied lover may want something very different from a sleepy, disgruntled woman who was expected to cook breakfast. It would be wiser to settle the gift before mentioning food.

He suspected the rules regarding the fancy gave him every right to ignore the custom of gifting, but he had enjoyed Ari far more than he'd expected to, and a gift would make her more eager for his return. Because he *was* going to return. She was his from the full moon to the dark, and he intended to enjoy her while he could.

And he wanted breakfast.

Entering the bedroom, he sat on the bed. She still slept, snuggled under the covers. He reached out to touch her shoulder and give her a little shake into wakefulness, but his hand kept going until it could stroke her hair.

"Mmmmff," she said sleepily. "Did the birds tell you it was time?"

Time for what? "The birds?"

Her nods pressed her face deeper into the pillows, and he wondered if she'd slip back into a deep sleep before he could talk to her.

"Birds always know when it's time," Ari said after

a minute of silence. "As soon as the light begins to change, you can hear the soft chirps, as if they're encouraging the sun to rise." With a sigh, she snuggled deeper under the covers. "Or maybe they're encouraging you."

"I don't need help from the birds in order to rise," Lucian said dryly. There was too much temptation to get back into bed and show her another kind of sunrise. But what she was saying bothered him. Surely she didn't think . . . "You do know that I don't really lift the sun above the horizon, don't you? It can do that just fine by itself."

"Oh, that's good," Ari mumbled. "I'd always wondered what would happen if you overslept. But the birds would wake you."

Lucian studied her for a moment, then shook his head. Either she was too sleepy or he was too awake for this conversation to make sense.

"Ari?"

"Mmmmff."

"It is the custom that when a man enjoys a woman's company, he gives her a gift to show his appreciation."

"Gift?" She frowned for a moment, then smiled. "A present?"

"Yes," Lucian said, his patience strained. "A present."

Ari sighed. "No one's given me a present since my mother died."

Lucian sat back, no longer sure what to do. He'd intended to suggest a couple of things from the Clan's large trinket box, things that would require no effort for him to provide. He hadn't found human women tempting enough to often yield to their enchantments, but from what other Fae males had said, those women were a bit like crows—they liked shiny objects. Since the gold, silver, and jewelry usually found its way back to a Clan trinket box, even if it wasn't the same trinket box, there was nothing there that hadn't been given before.

He'd known there was no one else in the cottage

last night, but he'd assumed they were simply some-where else for the day. There was so much *presence* in this place that it hadn't occurred to him that she was truly alone here. Knowing that, and knowing how much a gift now would disappoint or delight, he had an obligation to give her what she asked for, no matter how greedy the request might be.

Leaning closer, he said, "What kind of present would you like?"

"I get to choose?"

"Yes, you get to choose."

She smiled. "Sunshine."

He stared at her. Was that a coy way of asking for a necklace of amber or citrine? Or gold? "Sunshine."

She nodded. "I have to work in the garden today. Sunshine would be nice." She frowned. "But not too hot."

He brushed his lips against her cheek. "Sun that warms but doesn't burn." When she nodded again, he said, "What else?"

"More?" After a long pause, she said, "A dragon."

Lucian sighed quietly. A *dragon*? Even if such a creature existed and he could capture one, what did she think she could do with it? "A dragon," he said heavily.

She giggled. "A cloud dragon chasing fluffy cloud sheep."

For the first time, he wondered how old she was. It had been obvious that she was young, but it was a woman's body that he had enjoyed last night, not a girl's. No matter. Since he hadn't been the first, she was surely old enough.

He kissed her cheek again. "I have to go now, but I'll be back tonight."

"Tonight," she mumbled.

Moving quietly, he left the bedroom. The saddle-bags were on one of the dining chairs, but he still didn't know where she had put the rest of his clothes—or his boots. He shrugged. He didn't need them right now, and he'd be back tonight.

It was a man who opened the kitchen door and stepped out of the cottage. But it was a black horse that galloped toward the shining road that led to Tir Alainn.

Che-cheep che-cheep che-cheep.

The birds were celebrating the day with enthusiasm.

Too much enthusiasm, Ari thought as she turtled under the covers to avoid the light streaming in from her bedroom window.

Light?

She poked her head back out and reluctantly opened her eyes. The drapes were drawn back and the shutters were open. Two sparrows and a finch stared at her from the other side of the glass.

Che-cheep che-cheep che-cheep.

Wake up, wake up, wake up and greet the day.

"All right, all right. I'm up," Ari grumbled, making no further effort to greet the day. It was past time to get up, but once she started the tasks of the day, last night would become last night, and she wanted to savor those feelings a little while longer and think about the delightful dream she'd had early this morning. Lucian had offered to give her a present, and she'd named a silly thing that only a Fae Lord could give.

It was all nonsense of course, just a bit of fun her mind had conjured to amuse itself while her body still slept. Because if he really *had* offered her a gift in exchange for sex, that would no longer make last night a joining of two people for their mutual pleasure; that would be like being bought.

Not liking where those thoughts were going, Ari rolled out of bed. After stuffing her feet into slippers, she shuffled into the main room. As she opened the drapes and shutters, the sparrows and finch followed her from window to window.

Che-cheep che-cheep che-cheep.

"Shouldn't you be out catching worms or some other crawly thing?" Ari asked.

Che-cheep.

"Well, just stay away from my lettuce. There are plenty of other things for you to eat without eating *my* greens."

Che-cheep!

Smiling, Ari shook her head, then turned to study the hearth. The fire had burned out. No matter. She could tell that the slight chill in the cottage was left over from last night and would be gone once she opened a few of the windows and the top half of the kitchen door.

As she started toward the kitchen, she saw the saddlebags still sitting on the chair where she'd left them.

She *knew* Lucian was gone. She would have felt his presence if he was still nearby. So why had he left the saddlebags? What had he packed his extra clothing in?

Fully awake now, she hurried down the narrow hallway off the kitchen that led to the pantry and the washroom.

She'd collected the wet clothes and hung them up when she'd gotten up to use the chamber pot. His clothes were hanging in the washroom exactly as she'd left them.

A little troubled, she opened the room's small window to freshen the air, then went back to the kitchen to heat water for her morning tea.

The hand pump felt a bit stiff and sounded squeaky as she pumped the water to fill the kettle. Probably needed to be greased. She couldn't remember the last time it had been done. Ari sighed. Just one more thing to struggle with and fill the day. Just one more thing her mother or grandmother had taken care of when there had been the three of them to share the work.

But she couldn't remember either of them doing that task, so they must have asked someone. Who would a family of witches ask? Certainly no one in Ridgeley. Ahern? But he'd already fixed the door. She couldn't ask him for more help without being able to give something in return. Neall? He was usually willing to help with small things when Baron Felston wasn't filling his days with so many chores he barely had time to breathe. But Neall . . . There were reasons why she was reluctant to ask Neall.

After adding some wood to the coals, Ari put the kettle on the stove to heat. Opening a cupboard, she took down a cup. Her hand hovered in front of the jars beside the cups before she chose the one that contained the special blend of herbs.

She could accurately gauge her fertile days by subtle changes in her body. The day before the Summer Moon should have been the last of them, but there was no reason to take chances. Drinking a cup of tea made from these herbs for another couple of days was a sensible precaution—a precaution she'd been taking every month since her mother died. It wasn't fear that some man might force himself on her that made her diligent about drinking the tea, although the way Royce and some of his friends had been looking at her lately made her uneasy. It was herself she feared, that she might yield to loneliness or her body's own romantic yearnings on a day when the consequences might be more costly than a few minutes of pleasure.

There were times when she thought it would be wonderful to have a daughter to love and share the world with. There were more days, especially lately, when she was glad it was unlikely that she would ever carry a child. Her daughter would be as much of an outsider in Ridgeley as she was and would be just as unwelcome. The joy of caring for Brightwood couldn't mask loneliness, and there were times when even the joy felt like a burden. This land was her heritage and her duty, but someone besides the daughter-who-never-would-be would have to take up the mantle once she was gone.

So it was sensible to drink the herb tea for a couple more days to ensure as much as possible that she wouldn't conceive.

But . . . Perhaps Lucian *would* like a child?

Shaking her head, Ari made her tea. Leaving it on the worktable to steep, she took a pitcher of water and the kettle into the washroom, filled the basin, and took a quick sponge bath.

A child was a dangerous thought because it was appealing. But not appealing enough. Oh, Lucian had been a splendid lover and had proved beyond her hopes that not all men were like Royce. Just the thought of what his hands and mouth had done to her made her feel fluttery inside. But that didn't mean he would welcome a child that had been created with a witch. Besides, he would be gone by the dark of the moon—or even sooner, since her courses might start before then.

"And for all you know, he could already have a wife and children," Ari muttered as she returned to the kitchen to drink her tea. Married men weren't supposed to accept an invitation made during the Summer Moon, but plenty of them did. Why should the Fae be any different?

"Because you don't want him to be so . . . common, so much like Royce or Baron Felston or any of the other gentry in Ridgeley. You want his heart to hold the leash on his loins." Ari cut a slice of bread and spread jam over it. "Even if he *does* have a wife, accepting the fancy and coming here last night was *his* choice." But it would be a bitter discovery if she found out he had a wife he should have been loyal to.

Neall certainly wouldn't approve of her welcoming a married man into her bed, whether the Fae lived by a different moral code or not.

Sighing, Ari drank her tea. Leaving the bread on the worktable, she went to her bedroom to get dressed.

In some ways, Neall was as much of an outsider in Ridgeley as she was. Maybe that's why, as children, they had become friends. Were still friends, even though she didn't see much of him anymore. He seemed more . . . cautious . . . about being around her now.

"Which is neither here nor there," Ari told herself firmly. "He doesn't have any right to tell you what to do with your life or whose company you can or can't enjoy."

Since the words didn't sound indifferent when spoken out loud, Ari clamped her teeth together. She could deny it as much as she liked, but what Neall thought *did* matter. Just as what Ahern thought mattered. Maybe because they were the only people left who cared about her at all.

Well, neither of them was likely to find out that she had a Fae lover for the next few days, so she was just chewing worries into her day, as her grandmother used to say.

After pulling on her oldest trousers and tunic, Ari swiftly braided her hair. There was no point in dressing in better clothes when she was going to be working all day. The only person who would see her was Ahern, and the only thing he would notice was the sweet bread she was bringing. So she'd take a quick walk over to his farm, then spend the day working in the garden.

And she would not—*would not*—let herself diminish the satisfaction she felt when she worked with the land because she was brooding about men. She just wouldn't think about them. She wouldn't think about Neall or Ahern. And, most of all, she wouldn't think about the Lightbringer—or wonder if he was coming back tonight.

Chapter Nine

Even though she sensed they would have preferred no other company but their own, Dianna lingered over the morning meal she had shared with Lyrra and Aiden in one of the Clan house's communal rooms. Lucian had returned early that morning, and she had wanted to meet him casually, when enough time had passed that it wouldn't seem like she had been waiting for his return to find out what had happened last night.

Lyrra put her feet up on the padded bench and wrapped her arms around her knees. "Perhaps today I'll whisper in someone's ear and inspire him to write a great epic," she said, smiling.

"If you do, try to pick someone with at least a little skill for writing," Aiden replied, leaning back in his chair. His voice was bland, but his blue eyes sparkled.

Dropping her feet to the floor, Lyrra sat up straight and stiff. "You can't tell me everyone *you* touch has golden fingers or a silver voice. I've heard some of the braying that passes for singing."

"I'll not deny it, but at least a bad song doesn't have to be endured for long, while a bad epic . . ." He made an exaggerated shudder.

"Oh, I can see what this day will bring," Dianna said. "Someone is going to write a very long, very bad epic, which will be set to music. It will be called *The Battle of the Bard and the Muse*. The music will be played off-key and off-tempo. The words, which were written as prose, will be stuffed into the melody with no regard to any sense of rhythm. Wherever it is performed, there will be much weeping, which will have nothing to do with the story itself."

They just stared at her.

"Perhaps the Lady of the Moon should be the epic's subject," Lyrra said coolly after a long pause.

"Perhaps," Aiden agreed quietly.

There was no sparkle in Aiden's eyes and no friendliness in Lyrra's. Apparently only the Muse and the Bard could tease each other and not pay for the jest.

"I ask your indulgence," Dianna said, feeling annoyed by the necessity to say the words. Especially to Lyrra. The Muse came from a Clan a little farther north, but close enough that the Clans visited each other fairly often, and the two women had been friends for several years. Aiden came from a Midlands Clan and until he had come to her Clan's house to help find a way to stop Tir Alainn's destruction, she'd only met him a few times, despite their being distant kin. But the few weeks he'd been living with her Clan were quite enough to make her wary of his sharp mind and even sharper tongue.

"It was meant to tease, as you were doing," Dianna said. "It would seem I have no skill for such things. And . . . my thoughts are a little preoccupied at the moment."

"Oooh?" Lyrra said.

Before Dianna could decide how much to say, Falco entered the room and strode over to them.

"Have you seen Lucian today?" Falco demanded.

"Not yet," Dianna replied. "Why?"

"He's acting strangely. And you wouldn't believe what he's asked the Cloud Sisters to do."

Noting Lyrra's swift, concerned glance at her, Dianna remained focused on the Lord of the Hawks. "What did he ask?"

Falco shook his head. "You have to talk to him, Dianna. You have to find out why he's . . . different . . . today."

Dianna felt chilled. She had urged Lucian to go to that cottage last night. If there was something wrong with him because of it . . . But what could have happened that would make him different? What kind of creature was this female?

"Perhaps he's in love," Aiden said blandly.

Dianna's head whipped around to face the Bard. Did Aiden know where Lucian had gone last night? Did he know he was talking about a Fae male becoming enamored with a human female? It didn't matter. The barb in that bland comment had found its mark.

Oh, there were Fae who became tangled up with human females and not only lost all sense of what was right and proper but actually developed *feelings* for the creatures. But none of them were Lucian, none of them were the Lightbringer. For *him* to become ensnared . . .

"Dianna?" Lyrra said softly.

Fighting to appear calm, Dianna inclined her head slightly toward Falco. "My thanks for bringing this to my attention, Falco. I'll talk to my brother."

"I would advise you to do it soon," Falco said. "It's disturbing the rest of the Clan to see him acting so strange."

No one spoke until Falco left the room.

"I saw Lucian briefly this morning," Aiden said.

"And?" Dianna prodded. "How did he seem?"

"Pleased." Aiden paused. "He wasn't here last night."

"No."

"And he hadn't gone to visit another Clan."

Dianna shook her head slowly. "But where he was is no concern of anyone but—"

"I am not of this Clan, but Lucian and I are still kin through our fathers," Aiden said sharply. He narrowed his eyes and studied her. "As you and I, therefore, are kin. It is my turn to ask for indulgence. I should have not been so sharp about being teased by you."

"There are different rules for kin?" Dianna said, forcing a smile.

"There are," Aiden said, not returning the smile. "Will you talk to him?"

And say what? Dianna wondered. "Not yet." She raised a hand to prevent the protests Lyrra and Aiden seemed ready to make. "There is something that must be done before Lucian and I talk."

"Don't let it wait too long," Aiden said. Then he hummed a few bars of "The Lover's Lament."

Understanding the warning, Dianna stood up. "We'll talk again this evening."

"Good hunting," Lyrra said softly.

Dianna inclined her head and left the room.

Good hunting, she thought as she hurried to her rooms. Yes. Not the usual kind of hunt, but a hunt nonetheless. Until she actually saw this female creature for herself, she was holding an empty quiver instead of sharp arguments that could find their mark.

If Lucian was truly acting as strangely as Falco indicated, she would need arguments sharp enough to pierce a heart.

Neall didn't need to see the stone marker to know he was now on the part of the road that cut through Brightwood. He could feel a subtle change in the air, and his mood lightened in response to it. Even the gelding, which had been bred and raised on Ahern's farm, could sense the boundaries of Ari's land—and could sense them a little too well.

Shortening the reins just enough to keep Darcy's attention, Neall said, "We'll approach at a dignified trot rather than cantering into the yard like unmannered colts."

Darcy snorted, then tested Neall's sincerity by shifting from an easy trot to a brisk one.

"We aren't doing this," Neall warned. His voice didn't hold the sincerity it should have, but his hands were firm. The result was what he expected—a compromise in speed that obeyed the command from his hands but had listened carefully to the tone of his voice.

Well, they'd just get to the cottage that much sooner, and he couldn't argue with that.

Yesterday had been a misery. At breakfast, it had only taken a glance at Odella's face to know that the man she had met on the Summer Moon had not been to her liking, and that the man's skills as a lover—or his lack of them—had made him even less appealing. The fact that she couldn't refuse him until the dark of the moon without having the magic in the fancy turn on her made it even worse. It would have been bad enough to endure one time with a man who disappointed, but to suffer him again and again . . .

Seeing the unhappiness in his cousin's face had made Neall feel more sympathy for Odella, but it was a small cup of sympathy, and weak. Odella had not only brought this on herself by buying love magic from Granny Gwynn, she had also, with no kind intent, boxed Ari into the same corner.

Royce had been suffering from a rough night with the bottle, an overindulgence that he'd probably hoped would numb the fear of seeing the Wild Hunt, and had been more abrasive than usual.

Then Baron Felston began making barbed comments about how he, Neall, had probably spent the Summer Moon in his own virtuous bed instead of "flexing his muscles" as any other young man would have done. Knowing he would have been roundly condemned for "flexing his muscles," especially if any young woman came forward a few weeks later and accused him of getting her with child, didn't take the sting out of the baron's remarks.

Despite what the baron sometimes implied, he was as hungry as any other young man for the pleasure a woman's body could give, but knowing that Felston wouldn't hesitate to try to force him into a marriage that would trap him here made him even more cautious about accepting an invitation from any woman who was looking for a husband and a household of her own. That fleeting pleasure couldn't compare with the need to go home to his mother's land. Besides, he'd given his heart to Ari so long ago he couldn't remember a time when he didn't love her.

To make a bad start to the day even worse, Royce had decided to go with him to check the tenant farms and see what needed to be done. He'd expected Royce to grow bored with playing lord of the manor and return home or ride into Ridgeley to meet with his friends at the tavern. But Royce, with cutting remarks and steady complaints, had stayed with him throughout the long day.

Which was why he hadn't come to Brightwood yesterday, and had even avoided the tenant farms that bordered Ari's land—especially after the second time Royce suggested going there. He'd wondered why Royce had been pushing to visit the cottage while he was with him, and he'd wondered why his cousin hadn't simply gone alone. It wasn't until they were approaching the home yard and Royce finally relaxed that Neall had understood. Royce had wanted to go to Brightwood, probably to find out where Ari had been on the Summer Moon, but he'd been afraid to ride there alone in case he met up with the Huntress and her shadow hounds. In fact, he'd simply been afraid to ride *anywhere* alone, but he hadn't wanted to remain at home under Baron Felston's critical gaze. So Neall had spent the day silently fretting over Ari's broken kitchen door and that he couldn't ride over and fix it for her while Royce was with him.

But that was yesterday. This was today, the cottage was in sight, and he had an hour he could spare for a visit.

As he trotted past the cottage, intending to tether Darcy by the unused cow shed, something caught his eye. He reined in hard enough to set the gelding on its haunches, then murmured a wordless apology to the animal as he stared at the cottage's front door.

It was open. Not wide open, not obviously open. He wouldn't have even noticed it if a light gust of wind hadn't moved the door just enough to catch his attention, and it was something anyone else wouldn't have thought about twice.

Except he'd been visiting Brightwood since he was a child, and he *knew* the front door was rarely used and was never left open unless someone was working right outside.

Uneasy now, he dismounted and led Darcy to the cow shed as quietly as possible, then came back to the front of the cottage to study the door.

Ari might have opened the door for some reason this morning and then hadn't realized the latch hadn't caught securely when she closed the door. She might have wanted to check the flower beds without walking over sloppy ground. The ground, like the road, was drying quickly from last night's rain, but Ari got up with the sun, and the ground would have been very wet. In the gray light, she could have easily missed the fact that the door hadn't latched properly.

Or something could be very wrong.

Pushing the door open, he remained on the threshold, the warding spells making his skin tingle.

"Ari?" he called.

No answer.

He closed his eyes, felt the power in him stir. Astra, Ari's grandmother, had recognized the power in him. It wasn't as refined as a witch's magic, nor as strong, but it let him feel things that other people couldn't, it gave him an instinctive knowledge of woodland creatures, and it helped him sense magic when it was used around him. If his mother had lived, she might have taught him how to use this gift. Or perhaps his father, being half Fae, could have taught him better since, from what little he could remember, his father's diluted ability with magic had been more like his own. As it was, what little he knew about the power that was his heritage he had learned passively from being around the witches of Brightwood and by working with it on his own.

No matter. He knew enough for this.

Raising his right hand, he pressed it against that

unseen, magical barrier that kept people out unless they were welcomed in.

"You know me," he said softly, feeling the magic of the warding spell pushing against him as he channeled his own power into his hand. "You know me. I've been welcomed in this house before. Let me in. As I will it, so mote it be."

The magic in the warding spell didn't pull back like a curtain the way it would have if Ari had welcomed him, but it thinned from feeling like an invisible stone wall to a barrier of thick cobwebs.

As Neall crossed the threshold, he shuddered at the sensation of wispy strands brushing over his hand and face. He shook off the feeling. It was easy enough with something else pushing at his senses.

Someone had been here. Someone new, different, unknown. He could sense the lingering presence that was layered over the familiar feel of Ari's cottage.

She wasn't there. He could sense that too. Still, he quickly peeked into her bedroom to make sure she wasn't there, then the workroom that held the looms and spinning wheels and baskets of yarns that Ari used for her weaving.

As he headed for the kitchen, he glanced down at a chair pulled back a little from the table . . . and froze. He wasn't sure how long he stared at the saddlebags when Ari said, "Neall?"

She was standing in the open doorway, looking puzzled. She was wearing her oldest clothes, the ones she used when she worked in her garden, and she was holding a small, empty basket in one hand. There was color in her cheeks, and her dark, unbound hair looked like it had danced with the wind. It hurt to look at her, standing there so wild and lovely. Especially now.

Crossing the threshold, Ari looked back at the doorway and then at him.

"Your front door was open, and I was concerned," Neall said, striving to keep his voice calm.

She frowned at the doorway, but the way her shoulders relaxed told him she probably knew why the door had been open.

"But . . . How did you get in?" Ari asked, turning back to him.

One day he would tell her about his parents and his power. But not today. Not now.

He tried to smile. "I've been welcomed many times over the years, Ari. I guess the warding spells recognized me." The smile faded. The saddlebags sat on the chair between them. "Or maybe it was because I was concerned that the warding spells let me in. They didn't feel the way they do when you're here, though."

She tipped her head a little to one side and looked at him thoughtfully. "How did they feel?"

"It was like walking through thick cobwebs."

She made a face, brushed her hand across one cheek as if she could feel the cobwebs herself.

"You were out early," Neall said. *Who do the saddlebags belong to, Ari?*

She set the small basket on the table. "I took a loaf of sweet bread over to Ahern to thank him for fixing my kitchen door."

So he couldn't even do that for her.

His chest hurt. Was this what the songs and stories called heartache?

"You have company," Neall said, glancing at the saddlebags.

"No," Ari said quickly. "That is . . ." She looked away.

"You met him on the Summer Moon?"

Her shoulders went back and her chin went up. Defensive pride. He understood it well.

"And if I did?" she asked, challenging.

"Did you give him the fancy?" When she looked at him warily, hurt gave way to the first stirring of anger. "Royce didn't keep silent about that, Ari. I knew he was coming here, and I knew why."

"It wasn't Royce."

"Then who?"

She leaned against the table, looking weary. "No

one you know. He's not . . . He's not from around here."

Neall closed his eyes for a moment. There was mercy in that. At least he wouldn't look at every man in Ridgeley and the surrounding estates and farms and wonder if that was the man who was using Ari.

"Answer me this. Was he . . ." Impossible to ask. Impossible not to. "Was he kind?"

She relaxed a little, but still watched him too closely. "Yes, he was kind."

"That's good, then. That's good." He was feeling too many things—jealousy and pain . . . and relief that Ari would not dread this stranger's return. Because he would return. The saddlebags that hadn't been taken made that clear. If he continued to return until the dark of the moon . . .

He swallowed hard to ease the constriction in his chest. "Ari, if you should find yourself with child—"

She shook her head quickly.

"If you should find yourself with child," he repeated stubbornly, "and he won't stand with you . . . then I will."

She stared at him as if she'd never seen him before. Or as if something familiar had suddenly turned strange.

"You would do that? You would take a husband's vow for another man's child?"

"Your child," he said fiercely. *"Yours.* And if I was the man who was raising it with you, it would be mine as well no matter who sired it."

"Neall . . ." she whispered.

"Don't answer yet. Just know that I'll stand with you. You don't have to be alone." Needing to escape, he strode to the open door.

"Neall," Ari said, moving toward him. She kissed his cheek. It was the kiss of a friend, and it hurt him because he wanted it to be so much more. "Blessings of the day to you, Neall."

His arms came around her, holding her tightly against him. *Ari, Ari, my heart, my life.* Could he really leave Ridgeley without her? Or would he also be leaving so much of himself that he would be little more than a ghost?

He couldn't think about that. Not now.

He eased back, stepped away. "Blessings of the day to you, Ari."

It took effort, but he kept his stride easy and even as he walked to where Darcy was tied. The outward calm might have fooled Ari, but it didn't fool the gelding. Darcy danced in agitation. He held the gelding to a walk, waved at Ari, who was still standing at the front door, then eased up enough to let Darcy trot.

As soon as he was safely out of sight, Neall turned Darcy and headed back the way he'd come. But not to Brightwood. He needed another reason to be on this road in case he passed someone and the person mentioned seeing him to the baron. He wasn't feeling steady enough to cope with the tenant farmers he had to see that morning, but there was one place he could go where the feelings he couldn't hide yet would be noted but not commented upon.

He sent Darcy galloping over the fields to Ahern's farm.

Chapter Ten

Death called her.

Morag hesitated, then reluctantly signaled the dark horse to stop.

She didn't want to answer. In the two days since the Summer Moon, she had continued traveling south through the eastern part of Sylvalan, even though she was no longer sure she wanted to continue. In those two days, she had led too many souls to the Shadowed Veil so that they could go on to the Summerland. It wasn't sickness that had killed so many in the villages she recently had passed through. At least, not a sickness of the body. But something had crept through those villages to give Death such a bitter feast. Hard deaths. Cruel deaths. Burnings. Hangings. Drownings. And that young girl, that child, who had been . . .

Morag bit her lip, tried to draw a mental curtain across that memory.

There were other deaths in those places as well. Squirrels and sparrows. An owl. A fox. The rotting, partially eaten bodies surrounded clusters of dead trees. Even in warm daylight, there was something about those dead trees that made her shiver.

She had begun this journey in order to see this part of the human world and gain some understanding of the people who lived here. She had seen more than she had bargained for. She had seen too much. Now she needed a quiet place to rest and renew herself.

But there was no rest here, as she'd hoped there would be. This was one of the Old Places. She could feel the difference in the land and knew it was so. But she also felt a heart-deep despair, very much like what she felt in people gathered outside a sick room when a loved one was suffering through the last hours of living.

Death called her.

Morag closed her eyes and opened herself to Death's message.

This was not a gentle dying. This was not a soul contained in a body that had lived a full span of years and was ready to return to the Great Mother. Desperation and pain were coming toward her. And fear.

She urged the dark horse forward through the shadows of the old trees.

Gather your own kind, Morag. Let the human world be.

If none of us who have the gift offer to show them the road to the Shadowed Veil, how do the humans find it?

They don't.

Are you saying they have no souls?

Aye, they have them. Crippled, withered things as hard as stone. You'll only break your own heart if you try to help them. But you're still young, and you don't believe it will be that way. I once felt as you do now. And I broke my heart on stone. You'll do the same. I can see it in your eyes. It's glad I am that you'll show me the road to the Summerland before that day arrives.

That will be a long time from now.

No. Death has become an attentive lover. I won't see the seasons change again, and when I take my last breath, you will become the Gatherer in my place. You're the strongest of the Fae who are Death's Servants, so the name, and the power, will be yours. You will become Death's Mistress. The others who have this gift can take a spirit once the body has breathed its last breath. But you will be able to gather the spirit from living flesh. You will have the power to kill.

The shadows under the trees thickened. Morag shivered.

There were places in the human world that were so

thick with ghosts the land always felt cold. And there were stories the Fae bards sang about human battle-fields.

There was one in particular that, having heard it as a child, still haunted her.

According to the bards, two great forces of men had come together on a battlefield. It was never told why they had come to fight. It didn't matter. They had come to that place, and as the fighting began, the one who had been the Gatherer in that long-ago time had felt Death's summons. Taking the form of a raven, she flew over the battlefield, gathering the souls of those who would not survive their wounds and were crying out in agony. But the war chiefs on both sides knew what she was, and they both decided that if she couldn't gather the souls of their men, Death would not be able to touch them and they would know victory over their enemy. When she flew over them, the war chiefs shouted to their best archers, who loosed their arrows into the sky. A handful of arrows pierced her. As she fell, dying, the souls she had gathered in her wings fell with her to become ghosts on the battle-field. Her own spirit, in raven form, flew away to the Summerland. The war chiefs, now certain that they had cheated Death, threw themselves and their men into the battle. The slaughter was ferocious, and the land turned red from the spilled blood.

The song said that no man walked away from that battlefield, and that no Fae who had the gift to be Death's Servant had ever returned to that place to gather any souls. And it said that the ghosts of those men were still fighting that battle, over and over and over, and if a person stepped onto that land, he would hear the clash of swords and the battle cries and the screams of horses and the desperate pleas of the dying. Over and over. And never would it end.

Why am I thinking of that story now? Morag wondered. Reining in the dark horse, she studied the meadow beyond the last trees. There were no shadowed places there to indicate Death's presence outside of the Great Mother's circle of beginnings and endings. But . . .

There was anger coming toward her. And there was power herding that anger the way dogs herded sheep, driving it toward some completion. That power felt almost Fae, but it wasn't Fae. And it didn't belong to the Small Folk. It wasn't clean magic, whatever it was.

But it *was* familiar. This is what still lingered in those villages she recently had passed through.

Death called her.

She urged the dark horse forward at the same moment a woman burst from the trees on the other side of the meadow. The woman ran as best she could, heading straight across the meadow for the trees that were the border for the Old Place, but there was something wrong with her legs that kept her from taking a full stride.

A moment later, a pack of men burst from the same trees, their faces filled with such ugly emotions they looked like they were wearing twisted, obscene masks. Most of them carried clubs. Some just held a rock that filled his hand. Behind them rode a young man dressed in a fine black coat. *His* face shone with an unbearable ecstasy.

As soon as she saw him, Morag knew he was the source of that other power. He reminded her of a septic wound, full of pus. Rotten.

Before she was out of the trees and galloping across the meadow, the men had caught the woman and pulled her to the ground.

Fae horses had silent hooves, so there was no sound to cover the woman's screams, or the sound of rock and wood against bone.

Morag used no glamour to soften what she was. As she rode toward them, one of the men glanced up. He dropped his club and pushed against the other men, trying to back away.

"It's one of the Fae!" the man cried.

"It doesn't matter!" the young man in the black coat shouted. "There's nothing *she* can do!"

Isn't there? Morag thought as she rode toward the men. Rage flashed through her, flooding her until it was the only thought, the only feeling.

Her own power lashed out, striking the young man in the black coat. She gathered his soul, held it for a moment, then released it. That moment was long enough to sever the link between body and soul. She watched his body fall from his horse. His ghost stood nearby, too intent on trying to retain control of the men to notice.

Seeing the ghost, a man screamed, "She's the Gatherer!"

Dropping their clubs and rocks, the men bolted for the trees.

Morag didn't pursue them. Reining in close to the woman, she dismounted and knelt beside the still body. The woman wore nothing but a torn, sleeveless shift that fell to her knees.

Morag looked at the travesty that, not too many days before, must have been a healthy body. She wondered what had been done to make the woman's legs look that way—and she wondered how much courage it must have taken to try to walk, let alone run, on those legs. She saw burns on the arms. She saw the swollen left hand that was full of broken bones. She saw the holes in the woman's face where something had pierced her cheeks. She sensed the damage that had been done inside the woman—damage that would never heal well enough to make living anything but a prison.

The woman opened pain-glazed eyes. She tried to speak, but her tongue seemed too swollen to form words. Had it also been pierced?

"Who?" It sounded more like air being forced out than a word.

Before Morag could answer, the young man's ghost spoke.

"*They* may have run, but I'm not afraid of you," he said. "*Your* time in the world is done. After we rid the world of *her* kind, we'll also rid the world of yours.

Then men will rule as they were meant to rule, and there's nothing you can do to stop us."

"Nothing?" Morag asked softly.

He smiled at her, and she knew with unshakable certainty that he was a man who reveled in inflicting pain. He was a man who found controlling and manipulating others the most intense form of seduction.

"Nothing," he said.

Her only answer was to look at the ground behind him.

His smile wavered. He glanced down, then cried out as he reached for his body. His hands passed through it.

"You bitch!" he screamed. "What have you done?"

She ignored him. Her rage had come and gone as swiftly as a violent storm, leaving her cold and exhausted. But there was still work to do. She looked down at the dying woman.

"Gath . . . rer?"

"Yes," Morag said, touching the woman's head gently. "I am the Gatherer."

"Sum . . . merland. Please." The words were slurred, the effort to say that much horrific.

"I'll take you to the Shadowed Veil." Her power reached out again, and she quietly gathered the woman's soul. As the link between soul and body unraveled, the woman's breath came out with a relieved sigh. It was the last sound, the last movement she made.

When Morag rose to her feet, the woman's ghost stood beside her.

Feeling awkward, Morag asked a question she had never asked before. "Should the body be taken somewhere?"

The woman shook her head. "The Small Folk will take it home and give it to the Mother."

"Home?"

The woman looked at the trees Morag had been riding through before Death had called her. "The Old Place is . . . was my home."

Morag felt the land darken, as if thick clouds had

formed a shroud around the sun. "Come." She turned toward the dark horse but didn't mount. Not quite looking at the woman, she said, "Why did they do this to you?"

Sorrow filled the woman's ghostly eyes. "Because I'm a witch."

Witch. The word seemed to echo through the meadow.

How many of the young women that I have taken to the Shadowed Veil would have given me the same answer if I had asked?

"Come," Morag said, mounting her horse. The woman's ghost floated up to ride behind her.

"Wait!" the young man's ghost shouted. "What about me? You can't leave me here!"

Morag looked at him. "Yes, I can."

She urged the dark horse forward. It cantered across the meadow, not back toward the Old Place, but toward a break in the trees.

Unlike the roads that crossed the Veil into Tir Alainn, the road to the Shadowed Veil would open anywhere when one of Death's Servants summoned it. She could have opened that road right in the meadow, but she hadn't wanted the young man's ghost to be able to reach it before it closed again. So she rode out of the meadow and continued until she was well out of sight. Unless they were released by someone who had the power to set them on the soul's road, ghosts were held to a place. Since he had died in the meadow, he would be able to wander all through it, but he could never go beyond it.

And she would never return to it. She would take the witch to the Shadowed Veil and then head west, deeper into Sylvalan. She would return to the Midlands, to the part of Tir Alainn where her own Clan dwelled, and there she would finally rest for a while.

You'll only break your own heart if you try to help them.

The one who had been the Gatherer before her had been right about that. Let the humans take care of themselves, if they could. But the witches . . . Ah, the witches. That would require some thought.

When she got home, she would ask the Clan bard what he knew about the witches. And she would ask where the Bard was staying these days. If anyone had the answers she was seeking, it was Aiden.

Chapter Eleven

After coming down the road through the Veil, Dianna skirted the edge of Brightwood, keeping to the game trails, where she was less likely to be seen. It would have been easier to simply cross the meadow to reach the cottage, but she had a stop to make first in order to make her plan work. Her mare was too distinctive for anyone not to notice, and the glamour that successfully masked the Fae when they wanted to appear human never quite worked on the horses. So she would get a horse that wasn't so obvious—and she knew who would give her one. At least, she thought he would.

Her chest tightened at the thought of approaching him.

Crossing the road, she let the mare ease into a slow canter over the same fields she'd ridden through at the Summer Moon.

She didn't understand the Fae Clans in the west of Sylvalan who spent as much time in the human world as they did in Tir Alainn. There was something . . . uncomfortable . . . about being around members of those Clans. They were more feral, and darker in intent, than the rest of the Fae.

No, she didn't understand them. She understood even less a Fae who had forsaken Tir Alainn completely to live out his life among these humans. If he wanted to pretend to be human, he should at least give up the title he had held for three generations so that someone else could stand in his place. Oh, he'd accepted any challenges for the title over the years.

He'd won every one of them—and his challengers didn't always survive.

What made her most uneasy was that she wasn't sure how much deference she could demand from him. She wasn't even sure there *was* anyone who could make demands of him. And because of what he commanded, he could be a dangerous enemy for human and Fae alike.

There really wasn't a choice. She was concerned about Lucian, and pretending to be a human gentry lady really was the simplest way to find out what she needed to know. Which meant getting the loan of a horse. Which meant approaching the Lord of the Horse.

Reining the mare back to a sedate trot, Dianna wove the glamour magic around herself while she was still far enough away from the farmhouse that no one would be able to make out the face behind the human mask. She'd dressed carefully in a riding habit that resembled closely enough the garments worn by gentry ladies. The glamour simply completed the illusion.

A few moments after trotting into the yard, she realized the glamour would fool no one here.

The young man who was the first to notice her took a sharp look at her, than a longer, sharper look at her mare. After the slightest hesitation, he touched his fingers to the brim of his cap as a salute, then strode quickly toward the paddocks nearest the stable where several other men were gathered to watch a couple of young horses being trained.

Distaste rippled through Dianna, a natural enough reaction to meeting a human who had so much Fae blood in him that his eyes remained clear-sighted instead of being clouded by the glamour. She should have considered that children sired by Fae men would seek out a place like this where their mixed heritage would be tolerated, if not accepted outright.

She pushed the thought away when the strongly built, gray-haired man turned away from the paddocks and approached her. There was no welcome in his dark eyes, nor any sign of deference in his manner.

"Lord Ahern," Dianna said courteously.

"Huntress," he replied gruffly.

He knew who she was. Not just that she was Fae, but *who* she was. And it made no difference to him.

"I've come to ask a favor," she said, offering a smile that normally had other men eagerly promising to fulfill her slightest whim.

"You can ask."

She hadn't really expected that smile to work, but she would have felt better if it had softened him just a little. "I need the loan of a horse."

He studied her mare for a long moment. "Why? What's wrong with *her*?"

Dianna's teeth clenched. It took a little effort to get her jaw relaxed enough to answer civilly. "There's nothing wrong with her. I just want a horse that's less likely to attract notice."

"Why?"

"That should be obvious," Dianna said coolly.

"You've a mind to go into Ridgeley?"

Despite the fact that the surrounding land was where she rode the most often when she brought the Wild Hunt to the human world, it still took her a moment to remember that Ridgeley was the name of the nearby village. "No, just a ride through the countryside."

"Where?"

"What difference does it make?"

He studied her too long, and there was a violence in the back of his eyes that threatened to turn ugly at any moment.

"Take care where you ride, Huntress," he said quietly. "Take care what you do here. If you bring harm to those at Brightwood, the only time you'll feel four legs under you again is when you change to your other form."

Dianna's mouth fell open. "Are you threatening me? *Me?*"

"You can take it any way you like," Ahern replied, turning away from her, "as long as you don't forget it. Come along. I've a horse you can use."

A few minutes later, Dianna trotted away from Ahern's farm, relieved to be gone. The bay mare she now rode had a blaze and white socks, but nothing that would make it stand out.

Not a Fae horse, Dianna thought, wincing a little at the loud clopping of hooves on the road. Not even one of the horses Ahern bred from both Fae and human animals. But still a fine animal . . . by human standards.

With Ahern's warning still ringing in her ears, she slowed the mare to a walk when she came within sight of the cottage. From that distance, it seemed . . . pleasant. Sturdy. Except for the broken kitchen door, she hadn't paid much attention to the cottage the other night . . . or any other night when she and her hounds had skirted the meadow on their way to the surrounding countryside. Now she studied the building, trying to determine what was here that Fae males found so attractive.

Was it simply that the cottage was built in one of the Old Places and the Mother's power swelled around it so ripe and rich that it enticed Fae men like pollen enticed bees? Or was it the female herself who was so intriguing? If it *was* the female, what was it about her that could make the Lord of the Horse protective and territorial . . . and infatuate the Lightbringer?

Beside the cottage was a large plot of land surrounded by a waist-high stone wall. The female working there was too involved in her task to hear the horse's hooves. Or, perhaps, she paid no attention to travelers. And since the female hadn't noticed her, Dianna faced her first stumbling block. Would a gentry lady speak to a servant?

Of course she would, Dianna decided, if only to be presented to the cottage's owner.

"Good day to you," Dianna called as she guided the mare close to the wall.

The female's head whipped around. The expression in her eyes, before it turned to just wariness, reminded Dianna of prey scenting a hunter.

Was it possible the female realized she had been addressed by one of the Fae? Dianna wondered.

The female turned away and fumbled with the laces of her tunic before getting to her feet. She brushed her hands on her thighs, with no regard to the dirt she was leaving on the cloth, before approaching the wall.

Dianna breathed out slowly. No, she decided. The creature was simply trying to make herself present-able, and whatever made her wary of visitors had nothing to do with the Fae. *Besides, I sense no magic here except what flows from the Mother.*

"Blessings of the day to you, Mistress."

"Kindly tell your mistress that I am here." There. That was surely more courtesy than a servant would usually receive.

The female frowned, looking puzzled. "There's no one else here, Mistress."

Dianna clenched her teeth, then forced herself to smile. She hadn't gone to this effort just to be thwarted. "Then I'll wait for her."

The female's puzzlement deepened. "I didn't mean she was away, Mistress. I meant there's no one else here. This is my cottage."

Dianna stared. Lucian had spurned the invitations of every Fae Lady over the past few months only to bed *this* grubby creature?

"I'm Ari," the female said with a dignity still touched by wariness. "Is there something I can do for you, Mistress?"

What to say now? Dianna looked up at the sky, and let a sigh turn into a smile. So *that's* what Lucian had been up to.

"Mistress?"

Dianna pointed at the puffy clouds that were taking on the shapes of sheep being chased by a dragon. "It would appear that someone is feeling whimsical." She slanted a glance at Ari to see what her reaction would be to Lucian's gift. She was more than startled when Ari turned deathly pale and sagged against the wall.

"No," Ari said. "Oh, *no*."

"Whatever is the matter?" Dianna asked sharply. When she got no answer, she scrambled out of the sidesaddle and slid off the mare's back.

"I didn't know," Ari whispered, staring at the clouds. "I thought it was a game or a dream. I didn't know."

"Know what?" Dianna said, reaching across the wall to grab Ari's arms. What was wrong with the girl? Dianna looked at the sky again. The clouds were already losing their shape. In a few more seconds, there would be nothing to see. "What's wrong with a bit of whimsy?"

"Nothing," Ari said, sounding miserable.

"Hardly nothing," Dianna snapped.

"It's payment," Ari snapped back. Temper and pride flashed in her eyes for a moment before she sagged again. "I didn't ask for payment. I didn't *want* payment. I thought it was just a game. I never thought he really would—" She looked at the sky, then grabbed Dianna's arms, smearing dirt on the sleeves. "Does the sun feel like this elsewhere?"

Where is elsewhere? Dianna wondered. But now that she considered it . . . "It does seem a bit softer here, not quite as hot."

Ari moaned softly. Dianna, losing all patience, shook her. "Stop sounding so pathetic."

"You don't understand!"

"Then we'll go inside and sit, and you'll explain."

"I can't."

"You will." Dianna all but dragged Ari over the wall. Taking the reins, she led girl and horse toward the front door.

"It's locked. We have to go to the kitchen door."

Around the cottage, stopping just long enough to tie the mare to a post near the cow shed, then into the kitchen, with the girl mumbling, "Come in and be welcome," as they crossed the threshold, and on through to the main room.

"Sit," Dianna ordered, pushing Ari into a chair. Returning to the kitchen, she looked around, frowning. Wine would be good; water would be better than nothing. She didn't see either. "Where do you keep your water?" she called out.

"The pump," was the muttered reply.

Pump. Mother's Mercy, she was the Lady of the Moon. What did she know about pumps . . . whatever they were? Even in Tir Alainn, she never made an effort when it came to food or drink. That was for others to do.

She turned toward the shuffling footsteps. Ari appeared in the kitchen doorway. Dianna didn't appreciate the sympathetic humor she saw in Ari's eyes, but it was better than dealing with a shriveling, sniveling female.

"Pump," Ari said, stepping up beside Dianna. She grasped the handle of an odd-looking metal object, then moved it up and down a couple of times. Water gushed out. Ari took one of the mugs sitting beside the pump, filled it with water, and handed it to Dianna. She filled another, then made an effort to smile. "You probably don't see much of your kitchen."

"No, I don't."

The smile faded. Ari shuffled back to the main room. She sat down in a rocking chair in front of a cold hearth. Dianna took the other chair.

"Why are you troubled?" Dianna asked.

"You wouldn't understand," Ari said, her eyes fixed on the mug in her hands.

Dianna thought she understood at least part of the problem. But how to say enough to get the girl to talk without saying too much? "I may be able to help. I've had . . . dealings . . . with the Fae."

Oh, *that* brought some interest.

"Why do you think this concerns the Fae?" Ari asked cautiously.

Why indeed? "Because you look at some clouds that are shaped like sheep and a dragon and you act like some gentry lady who grows faint when confronted with the least little thing." She had no firsthand knowledge of whether or not gentry ladies did this, but there were plenty of songs and stories whose complications began with a human female growing faint over anything and everything. "So it stands to reason that you're upset because you believe someone did this for your benefit, and the only ones who *could* do this are the Fae."

Ari studied Dianna for a long moment. Then, haltingly, with her face turning pale and flushing in turn, she explained about the Summer Moon and having to offer the fancy to the first male she met.

There were many things Dianna was sure were left unsaid, but what was most striking was that, while Ari finally admitted that the male she'd given the fancy to was a Fae Lord, she didn't boast that it had been the Lightbringer who had come to her bed last night.

"Gifting is a custom among the Fae," Dianna said.

"I made a promise," Ari replied quietly. "I wasn't expecting anything in return."

Not even pleasure for yourself, I'll wager. Which probably explained why Lucian hadn't done the easy thing and given Ari a small trinket as a gift. He would have had one or two in his coat pocket. All Fae men did.

"You made a promise, which is important to you." Dianna waited until Ari nodded agreement. "And he fulfilled the custom of gifting, which is important to him."

"But—"

Dianna waved a hand impatiently. "He asked you what you wanted, did he not? So what's wrong with him keeping *his* promise?"

"Nothing, when you say it like that, but—"

"So he gave you a softer day so that you could enjoy working in your garden. What's wrong with that? It was something that was in his power to give.

And the other gift. Consider the children who had looked up at the sky during those few moments and were delighted." Since Ari still seemed inclined to argue, Dianna cut her off. "You made a promise, and you would have kept it no matter what the man was like. Maybe . . ." Knowing her brother as she did, there was no "maybe" to it. "Maybe he wanted to soften the obligation a bit so that he wouldn't be unwelcome if he came back."

Ari caught her lower lip between her teeth. "Do you mean he'll do this every time . . . if he chooses to come back?"

Sensing there was trouble, but not sure what it was, Dianna answered cautiously. "He's a Fae Lord. He'll follow his own customs, Ari . . . just as you will follow yours. It will please him if you accept what you may be given."

Dianna rose. "I'm glad we met."

Ari escorted her to the kitchen door. "Thank you for listening—and for your advice."

Dianna just smiled.

"Blessings of the day to you, Mistress," Ari said.

An odd farewell, Dianna thought as she headed back to Ahern's farm. An odd young woman. Perhaps that was why Ari appealed to Lucian. She wouldn't say the same things any Fae woman would say to him, or do the same things. There certainly was no harm in her, and hadn't *that* been the question that had needed answering?

There was power around that cottage, and it was strong. But it came from the Old Place, from the Great Mother. She had sensed no magic in the girl—had sensed nothing that might harm or alarm.

Still, if Lucian decided to continue visiting the cottage and the girl for the full time allowed him by the fancy, it wouldn't hurt to make a return visit herself.

Sunset.

Ari opened the top half of the kitchen door and

looked at the meadow that gently rolled to the trees that marked the beginning of Brightwood's forest.

She brushed her hand over her best tunic and skirt, smoothing out nonexistent wrinkles.

Would he come? Did she want him to?

The thought of him and what he'd done with her in bed last night made her feel fluttery inside and produced a soft ache between her legs. She wanted to feel that way again, wanted to feel *him* again. But . . . Was that enough?

Of course it was. What more *could* she want or expect from a man who had come into her life so suddenly and would be gone again in a few days' time?

But what was she supposed to do for those few days?

Looking over her shoulder at the stew simmering on the stove, she winced.

What was she going to feed him after tonight? There was barely enough stew left for the evening meal, and nothing for tomorrow. She could just walk across the meadow and wait for him in the woods. If he took his pleasure there, he wouldn't expect hospitality as well, would he? Wouldn't he simply enjoy himself for an hour and then be on his way?

He might. He could. The stories her mother and grandmother had spun by the fire while they also spun the wool had been a pleasant way for a child to absorb the lessons about dealing with the Fair Ones, but they hadn't told stories about the more . . . earthy . . . subjects. If they had lived, would they have sat by the fire last winter and told her tales that would have helped her now? Perhaps.

The truth was she couldn't open the door and walk across the meadow. She couldn't offer to lift her skirt for him while he pulled her to the ground. That felt too much like her experience with Royce.

"You can't change the turn of the seasons," she said quietly. "You can't lay the bounty of the harvest on the table while you're still planting the seeds from which that bounty will grow. Offer what you can, and let that be enough."

Turning away from the door, she stirred the stew, wondering if she should put it on the back of the stove just to warm. When she turned to look out the door again, she saw him, a black horse silently galloping over the meadow.

He slowed to a trot, turned away from the cottage in the direction of the cow shed.

Ari stayed by the door and waited.

A few moments later, Lucian came around the side of the cottage, his hair tousled, his modestly ruffled shirt open to the waist.

"You came back," Ari said. "Come in and be welcome."

He reached over the half door, captured her face in his hands, and kissed her long and slow and deep. When he finally raised his head, he said, "Yes, I came back."

Propped on one elbow, Lucian watched Ari sleep.

She hadn't been as delighted with her gift as he'd expected her to be. She'd stumbled over her thanks and seemed a bit . . . embarrassed . . . to be thanking him at all. His disappointment in her response had a familiar taste. Wasn't that why he had found it so easy to abstain for so long?

Perhaps she'd expected a traditional gift after all. He had one with him, a small jade pendant that was appropriate for a first or second gifting. He would put it on the dressing table before he left in the morning. She didn't have enough artifice to tie up her thanks in pretty lies, and he didn't need a woman's tepid pleasure in a gift spoiling his pleasure of the bed.

Even there . . . Oh, she'd been warm enough, eager enough, desperate enough for the mating by the time he'd decided to mount her. He hadn't been as kind as he should have been to a woman who had so little experience, but it had annoyed him that she had wanted to fuss with the pot on the stove instead of going straight to bed with him. If it had burned, what difference did it make? There was more. But no. She'd fussed long enough to have him simmering with another kind of heat, and he'd let a bit of his temper burn itself out in the bed along with his lust. Not enough to hurt her, but enough that she wouldn't dismiss him so casually again.

I shouldn't have brought anger to the bed. He pushed the thought away, along with the shimmer of guilt the thought produced. He had no reason to feel guilty. She had given herself to him for this measure of days, hadn't she? She was human; he was the Lightbringer. She should be honored to have him in her bed.

She woke, stirred, looked at him with eyes that were a little fearful. "Are you hungry?" she asked hesitantly.

Her fear scraped at him, added chains to the guilt. But not enough to outweigh the heat in his loins.

He mounted her, sank into her, kissed her in a way that would build the warmth to a slow burn and extinguish the fear. "Yes, I'm hungry."

Chapter Twelve

Adolfo stared at Harro, his nephew Konrad's Assistant Inquisitor. The Master Inquisitor's brown eyes revealed nothing, but there was a storm of rage growing inside him trapped behind a wall of shock. It wouldn't stay trapped for long. He could feel it pushing, looking for a weak spot in the wall from which to burst free.

With cold deliberation, Adolfo locked the feeling of shock behind a prison of self-control. The storm of rage would have a target, but not here, not yet.

"Where did this happen?" he asked in a voice stripped of emotion. "*How* did this happen?"

"It was my fault—" Harro said, tears filling his eyes.

Yes, and you will pay for it.

"—but I was his Assistant, and I obeyed his orders." Harro hesitated. "He was young, Master Adolfo, and . . . sometimes . . . too dedicated."

In other words, Konrad had indulged himself too much while extracting the last confession. Fool of a boy! How many times had he been told that even an animal that appears defenseless will bite if cornered?

"What happened?" Adolfo said, keeping his voice soft and his body still.

"There was only one witch, as we'd been told, but she was stronger than the others we had encountered while doing our great work here in Sylvalan."

I know the rhetoric, old man, Adolfo thought impatiently. *I created it.*

"She could draw power from earth, fire, and water. So Konrad felt he had to be more persuasive with this

one. But . . . I know pain is the only way to cleanse
witches of what they are. With this one, I could see it
wasn't breaking her down as it should have but giving
her a kind of mad strength to resist. When I tried to
tell Konrad what I saw in her eyes, he became angry.
He ordered me to go on to Norville to inform the
baron there that he would be arriving in a day or
two." Harro's eyes pleaded. "I couldn't disobey."

Adolfo just waited.

"She escaped. I don't know how, but she got away
from him. He gathered men from the village and tenant farms and went after her."

*At least Konrad had had sense enough not to hunt
alone for a witch who probably no longer cared about
the creed most of her kind lived by.*

"The men caught up with her in a meadow that
bordered the Old Place there," Harro continued, his
voice breaking. "As they attacked her, a woman on a
dark horse rode out of the trees."

Adolfo frowned. "Another witch?"

Harro shook his head. "The village men said it was
Death's Mistress. They said it was the Gatherer."

The spot in his back that always chilled when fear
raised its head turned icy cold. "One of the Fae," he
said in a barely audible voice. "Nothing had been said
about Fae frequenting the Old Place."

"They come around now and again, but the villagers
swore the Fae rarely bothered themselves with human
concerns."

"This one did," Adolfo snapped, his control crack-
ing enough to let a little of the rage gush through him.

Harro wrung his hands. "It was the Gatherer, Master Adolfo." He closed his eyes. "She killed Konrad,
and the other men ran away."

Young fool. The Fae were no longer as strong as
most people thought, and it was easy enough to thwart
one of them if you knew what gift of magic that particular one commanded. But the one who was called the
Gatherer *had* to be avoided because *her* gift . . .

"She killed him because of a witch," Adolfo said heavily.

Harro opened his eyes. Tears filled them. "Yes."

"And no doubt took his spirit to the horror that awaits men's souls in the Evil One's Fiery Pit."

Harro shook his head. "I don't have much of the Inquisitor's Gift, but even the villagers who have none could see . . ." His voice trailed away.

"See what?" Adolfo demanded. That icy spot in his back grew and grew.

"Konrad's ghost," Harro whispered. "She left him there, in the meadow."

Adolfo sank back in his chair. The rage inside him pounded against his self-control.

"The village men came back, intending to retrieve the body and give Konrad a proper mourning and burial. But when they saw the ghost, they were afraid he might be able to follow and haunt the village so they—" It took effort for Harro to swallow. "They buried him in the meadow to bind his ghost there."

Adolfo covered his face with his hands.

"I am sorry, Master Adolfo," Harro said hoarsely. "Konrad was a fine man and a skilled Inquisitor. He will be missed."

As Adolfo lowered his hands and rose from his chair, the power swelled inside him, fed by the rage smashing through his self-control. Fortunately, the means to relieve the pressure inside him—and salvage this disaster—was standing before him.

Adolfo placed his hands on Harro's shoulders. The power that flowed through his hands flooded the weaker man so fast Harro barely had time to realize what was happening.

"You will return to the village," Adolfo said, his voice soft as his power of persuasion ensnared Harro, leaving the man vulnerable—and obedient—to whatever was said. "You will stay at the inn, not at the baron's estate. You will tell the villagers that it was not Death's Mistress but the Evil One in disguise who attacked the men when they attempted to cleanse

their village of the witch's foul influence. It was the
Evil One who killed Konrad."

"The Evil One," Harro mumbled.

"You will tell them you believe that the Evil One
is still nearby, waiting to devour other good folk as it
devoured Konrad, and you have returned to keep
watch until I, the Master Inquisitor, can arrive and
free them."

Harro's eyes were blank and glassy now. Perfect.

"The second night you are at the inn, you will retire
immediately after the evening meal, and you will sit
before the fire in your room. You will watch the fire
carefully. When it has burned down to embers, you
will take an ember the size of your thumb from tip to
the first joint. You will place this ember on your
tongue. You will make no sound, no sound at all.
When the ember has burned out, you will spit it out
on the hearth and take another, smaller ember. You
will swallow this ember. You will make no sound, no
sound at all. You will continue to swallow embers until
you can swallow no more. Do you understand?"

"Un . . . der . . . stand."

"You will remember reporting to me about Konrad's death. You will remember that you confessed
that you had failed him, and that, when you asked my
forgiveness, it was freely given. You will remember
that we grieved together for the loss of a fine young
man. That is all you will remember, but you will follow
my instructions exactly as I have told you."

"Will . . . follow."

"Good. That is good."

Adolfo stepped back, returned to his chair. He carefully released most of the power that now ensnared
Harro, leaving just enough to ensure his will would be
obeyed but not so much that Harro would notice it.

He waited until Harro blinked, drew in a deep
breath, then looked around as if slightly bewildered.

"I thank you for bringing me the news yourself,
Harro," Adolfo said quietly. "Please leave me now. I

need to be alone with my thoughts—and you must prepare for your journey."

"Journey?" Harro appeared to be thinking hard. Then his face cleared. "Yes, the journey. I must return to the villagers and keep watch. Even in grief, the great work must go on."

"Yes, it must."

Adolfo didn't move until Harro left the room. Then he rose and stood before the hearth. He stared at the fire for a minute before releasing one little burst of power. The fire roared, the flames leaping twice as high as they had a moment before. After a count of ten, they shrank back to normal size.

Adolfo still stared at the flames.

Perhaps it was for the best. Even before they had come to Sylvalan, Konrad had begun showing signs of being a bit too much like his grandmother. The day would have come when Konrad no longer saw him as the uncle who had guided and trained him but as a rival for the title of Master Inquisitor.

He had been fond of his nephew. After all, the boy was the only close family he had left. But he wouldn't have tolerated the boy as a rival. He wouldn't tolerate anyone having command over him ever again. So, perhaps, it was for the best that Konrad had died this way. Still, the villagers had to pay for allowing the Gatherer to kill an Inquisitor.

The last of his family. Oh, there were other relatives—after all, his father had had two older brothers—but it had been so long since he had seen them, he no longer thought of them as family. Nor did he consider his wife in that way. She was just a flawed vessel that had never been able to properly grow his seed.

No, women were not family. They were like the cow that gave milk or the hens that laid eggs. They were a necessary part of a man's life for his comfort and well being, but they should never be thought of as being more valuable than the cow or the hen. Their purpose was to open their legs for a man's pleasure and to birth the children who would be his heirs.

If his father had understood that, the old man might still be alive.

His father had been a younger son who would inherit no property, his mother a beautiful woman who owned a substantial piece of land. He suspected his father had married as much for the land as to satisfy lust, and must have been cruelly disappointed when he discovered that the land wasn't signed over to him but remained in his new wife's control. Still, she had done what she had promised. Whole sections of the forest were cut down and the timber sold. Virgin meadows felt the bite of a plow for the first time, and tenant farmers planted tame crops. The wealth they harvested from the land surpassed what the rest of his family could claim, and he had been well pleased.

But his father never forgot that she had kept the land in her own name, and he never forgot that his own pleasures were dependent on how well he pleased *her*.

Despite that, they had been happy together—until the day when his mother had complained that her bedroom was cold and he, their first-born son and barely six years old, performed the trick he'd just learned and lit the fire for her. He clearly remembered the blank way she had stared at him, and how pale her face had become.

The vicious arguments had started after that. Accusations and denials. His father had lied to her by omission, had failed to admit that there had been a foul union between Fae and human somewhere in his bloodline. The son *must* have inherited this perverse magical power from the father because *her* bloodline was pure.

I'm sorry, I'm sorry. I didn't know it was wrong.

You'll not shame me with these tricks that make your mother doubt me. I'll not be a penniless younger son again because of the likes of you. If I have to beat this mischief out of you, then that's what I'll do.

Yes, her bloodline had been pure in that she was a witch who was descended from witches as far back as her family could remember. But she had never mentioned *that* when she'd let that younger son woo and win her. She never mentioned it at all.

But that was something that Adolfo didn't realize until much later, after he'd been disinherited in favor of a younger brother who had shown no signs of impurity, after he'd run away and had learned, haltingly, to use the power that had destroyed his childhood.

That first display of magical power had been the beginning of his mother's hatred for him, and that hatred had changed a warm, happy home into a pit of horrors for a child who couldn't understand what he'd done wrong and didn't have the self-control to deny something inside him that felt so natural.

He had suffered the beatings, the humiliations. He had learned a great deal from the walking evil his father had become in an effort to placate a wife who hated.

At fourteen, he ran away and lived from hand to mouth for several months before he found his calling. It was in a village that had experienced several incidents of bad luck. Milk going sour within hours of being taken from the cow. Chickens on several farms producing two-headed chicks. Wagon wheels breaking on the way to market. Fields that would begin to grow, only to wither when it was too late to plant again in time to harvest.

At first, he sensed the magic as a feeling of something familiar and frightening. After being in the village for a few days, doing whatever work he could to earn a meal, he saw the woman. He saw the easy way she greeted and spoke with the other villagers. He saw the wariness in the eyes of one handsome man. And he saw *her* eyes when that same man met another young woman outside a shop.

A couple of days later, when a riding party was taking a cross-country run, the young woman's horse stumbled for no apparent reason and went down. The fall crippled the young woman in ways that would make a young man look elsewhere for a wife.

That was when he realized what it was about that woman that had troubled him.

She had felt like his mother. And there had been that same shuttered look in her eyes that his mother had had whenever someone's luck had turned bad.

He went to the young woman's family and told them he believed that the accident had been caused by the witch living nearby. And he told them he had some small skill in gaining a confession from such creatures.

They had doubted his professed skill, with good reason, and they had doubted his assurance that the woman they knew *was* a witch. But they had a crippled daughter, and they were hurting.

The confrontation had taken place on the village's main street. It had been a foolish thing to do, and had almost cost him his life. He had stood in the main street and hurled the accusations at her, listing every one of the ills that had beset the villagers. Her only response had been a mocking smile—until he loudly declared that the reason no decent man would have her was because she fornicated with the Evil One and the stench of the vile union clung to her.

She flung her earth magic at him, opening up the street right under his feet. He threw himself away from the deep pit, landing hard enough to knock the air from his lungs. A moment later, the pit snapped shut. If he'd fallen into it, she would have buried him alive.

One of the villagers hit her over the head with his walking stick before she could strike again. Then they had looked to him to tell them what to do with this enemy. And he had the answer: Burn her.

With his help, how those flames did burn.

He spent two days at the inn there, his food and lodging courtesy of the family whose daughter had been crippled.

When he was ready to move on, one of the farmers

mentioned a cousin who was having a bit of trouble, and if Master Adolfo was heading that way, would he mind having a look to see if he could sense if a witch was causing the trouble.

Of course he could head that way. And of course he found a witch. It didn't matter that the troubles had no other cause than nature's whims, there *was* a witch living quietly in the village. She, too, burned.

In each place, there was always someone who knew someone else who was having a bit of trouble that might be caused by magic. And if he arrived at a village where there was no trouble, it wasn't difficult to create some. He didn't have any of the earth magics except for a bit of fire, but he had the gift of persuasion, which made him suspect that his mother had had Fae blood in her as well as witch, since the magic to open a door into another mind was something that belonged to the Fae. So it wasn't difficult to slip around the borders of one of the Old Places and turn the minds of a few of the Small Folk to mischief magic. He would leave and return a month later when the villagers were ripe to have *someone* pay for their troubles. And there was always someone who could be singled out to pay, whether she was truly a witch or not.

Over time, his fee increased from food and lodging and the occasional piece of clothing to coins in his pockets. And the first time a Wolfram baron had needed help with a bit of trouble in order to confiscate some land he coveted, the fee was more than a few coins.

By the time ten years had passed, he was known as the Witch's Hammer, the Inquisitor from whom witches could not hide. By the time those years had passed, he had visited the handful of universities in Wolfram to talk with the scholars who collected stories about the Fae and the Small Folk. He had puzzled with the other men over the oblique references to something called the House of Gaian that appeared in a few of the oldest stories. Whatever it had been, the House of

Gaian disappeared from the stories around the same time that Tir Alainn was first mentioned, so he dismissed it as something too far in the past to be of use to him.

By the time those ten years passed, he had started gathering other men and training them to be his Inquisitors. They were all as he had been—young men, outcast because they were descended from a mating with one of the Fae. He called their magic the Inquisitor's Gift, and taught them how to use that power in order to hunt the witches whose existence thwarted men's right to rule the land.

By the time those years had passed, he had reshaped some of the stories traveling storytellers and bards passed from village to village until it became common knowledge that witches were the Evil One's whores and offered their bodies to decent men in order to trick them into becoming the Evil One's servants.

When another five years had passed, he slipped back to his home village. It took little effort now to persuade a weaker mind to believe what he wanted that person to believe. No one who had seen him arrive at the inn recognized him as Adolfo, the disinherited son who had run away.

It wasn't difficult to discover that his father made regular visits to a nearby town and had been doing so for years. It wasn't difficult to whisper in the maid's ear when she came to clean his room that the main business that was transacted on those visits took place in a mistress's bed. He planted a few other seeds as well, and then left them to do their work.

It was a hard year for the family who had turned him away. His mother, upon hearing the whispers about her husband's infidelities, took a knife to their bed one night and cut out his adulterous heart. She was hanged and then burned.

A few weeks later, his younger brother, still distraught over his parents' deaths, put his horse to a jump the animal couldn't possibly take, and died of his sustained injuries. His pretty wife, swollen with their second child, went mad with grief, threw herself into the small lake on the estate, and drowned.

A month after that, Adolfo returned to the village, a prosperous man who simply wanted to make peace with his estranged family. It was almost touching to see how the gentry in the neighborhood worried about him as he grieved. When he left a week later, all he took with him was his young nephew and the boy's nurse.

Adolfo still stared at the fire.

"You hated me because I revealed your secret, because I couldn't hide what I had inherited from *you*," he said to the mother who was long dead. "You let my father do monstrous things to me in his attempt to win back your love—and retain the wealth you provided. I have used everything he taught me, Mother. I have refined those crude lessons into something elegant. And I use what I learned against your kind. You could have loved me. Because you chose hate instead, I will not suffer a witch to live. I promise you that before I'm done, there won't be one of your kind left."

Chapter Thirteen

She wasn't being deceitful, Dianna assured herself as she and the borrowed mare left Ahern's farm and trotted toward Brightwood. She just didn't see any reason to tell Lucian she had met Ari—or that she had decided to go back to the cottage today. It had nothing to do with his returning to Ari's bed each night, but he would assume it did, and then they'd quarrel about it and he wouldn't listen, and she didn't want to quarrel with her twin about some . . . *human.*

Besides, why should Lucian be the only one to find some distraction these days? Aiden had instructed every bard in Tir Alainn to send him any information they might hear about witches or wiccanfae. The only things that had been passed to him were the songs he'd already heard, but they told the Fae nothing except that they had an enemy in the human world capable of destroying the Fair Land.

They had lost more Clans over the past few days. More pieces of their land were suddenly gone. And there was still no answers.

I am the Huntress, and I am helpless, Dianna ranted silently. *How can we fight something when we don't even know what it is? How can we find these wiccanfae if we don't know what they are or where to look? It's like trying to fight a shadow that sucks the life out of whatever it brushes against.*

So why shouldn't she spend a little time satisfying another curiosity. She *was* curious about Ari. And she was wondering why, if Lucian was finding Ari's bed so pleasurable, he seemed troubled by it.

As they passed a marking stone, the mare pricked her ears and quickened her pace. Dianna didn't rein her in. It was already midmorning. Having to wait until Lucian returned to Tir Alainn so that he wouldn't ask questions about where she was going—and why—and then riding to Ahern's farm and back to Bright-wood had wasted enough time.

Ari was working in the low-walled garden, wearing the same shabby clothes. She looked up when she heard the horse, then smiled and raised a hand in greeting.

"Do you live out here?" Dianna asked, guiding the mare to the wall.

"At this time of year, yes," Ari said. She petted the mare's nose. "It's planting time, and I've still got a lot of seeds and seedlings to get into the ground."

Dianna looked at the still-empty sections of the garden. "If it's so much work, why plant so much?"

A little puzzled, Ari replied, "To have enough food to last through the winter."

"But—" What had looked like a large plot of land a moment ago suddenly seemed smaller. "Can you harvest enough from this?"

Ari's smile now held a hint of worry. "Usually. Some years are better than others. I also pick apples, strawberries, and raspberries. Some blueberries, too, but I'm not fond of them, so I leave most of them for the birds and the Small Folk to harvest. I have a bee-hive as well, and they share their honey with me. And I trade some baking and honey to Ahern for eggs and milk . . . and a bit of meat. It gets me by."

All of that, and more, was there for the asking in Tir Alainn, Dianna thought. The Fae didn't wonder if there might be enough. There was always more than plenty.

"It was kind of you to stop by during your ride," Ari said. Her smile seemed a little forced, a touch impatient.

So much for my assuming she would be delighted to en-tertain a gentry lady coming for a visit, Dianna thought.

*Courtesy forbids her from saying out loud, "Go away
and let me do my work," but her eyes say it all the
same. In another minute, even courtesy won't keep her
standing at the wall. She'll phrase it more politely, but
she'll tell me to go away. She will. I haven't dealt with
many humans. I've never wanted to. But they've
crossed my path enough for me to know she's different.
Why is she different?*

"I'll help you plant the garden," Dianna said impul-
sively.

Ari's mouth fell open. "You— You're going to help
me *plant?* You're going to dig in the *dirt?*"

"Why not? You do it, and it doesn't seem to have
any ill effects."

"But . . . but . . . you're a *lady.*"

She already found the pretense of being a gentry
lady sufficiently tiresome to welcome shedding it. "I
may be a lady, but I'm also a woman." She smiled,
but she knew her eyes revealed a bit of the Huntress.
"I'm not as weak as you seem to think I am."

"Oh, I don't think you're weak," Ari said hurriedly.
"It's just—" She caught her lower lip between her
teeth. "Well," she said after a long pause, "the work
will go faster with an extra pair of hands."

"That's fine then. I'll—" *—find some way to get out
of this fiend-made saddle without falling on my face or
making a fool out of myself.*

Ari seemed to be considering the same problem.
"How do ladies dismount when a gentleman isn't
around to help?"

With no charm and little grace, Dianna thought
sourly, suddenly understanding Ahern's malicious
amusement when he saddled the mare for her that
morning. The other day she had simply scrambled out
of the saddle in order to reach Ari before the girl fell.
Today, dismounting didn't seem as easy.

"Maybe you could use the wall?" Ari said hesitantly. "Or the chopping block out back?"

Dianna frowned at the wall. It was high enough for
her to step onto it—as long as the mare cooperated.

She brought the mare around so that the animal stood next to the wall. "Hold her head."

When Ari had a firm grip on the reins, Dianna carefully dismounted, stepping onto the wall. Half turned to keep one hand on the saddle for balance, she wobbled on the wall, wishing the round, uneven stones offered better footing. She shifted one foot, planted it firmly on the hem of her riding habit, lost her balance, and, with a small scream, fell across the mare's back.

The mare swung her hind quarters away from the wall, taking Dianna with her.

"Oh, dear," Ari said in a choked voice.

Silently cursing Ahern, Dianna slid off the mare's back, then glared at her companion. "Don't you dare laugh."

"I wouldn't, Mistress. Truly I wouldn't." Ari clamped a hand over her mouth, her eyes dancing with suppressed laughter.

"Not Mistress, just Dianna." Brushing at her skirt, Dianna took the mare's reins in her other hand. "*Mistress* is a lady who has to remain dignified and polite even under these circumstances. Dianna does not. Since I'm not feeling dignified or polite at the moment . . ."

"Yes." Ari cleared her throat. "I understand. Why don't we take the mare around back and let her graze." She studied Dianna's riding habit. "And we should find something for you to wear so that you don't get your clothes dirty."

"Fine," Dianna said, looking at her clothes. As if that mattered now. Then she whispered in the mare's ear, "If you don't behave, I'll feed you to my shadow hounds."

After tying the mare outside the cow shed, Dianna followed Ari to a bedroom off the main living room.

"Isn't it unusual to have a bedroom in this part of a house?" Dianna asked, looking around. In a Clan house, none of the private suites were connected to the communal rooms. Perhaps human cottages were built differently because they were so much smaller?

"It's the crone's room," Ari replied. "At least . . .

it is when there are three," she finished quietly. She hurried through the arch that led to another room.

While Ari rummaged around in the other room, Dianna studied the bedroom—but slid her eyes quickly past the bed.

Tie the knots and fiddle them, Dianna thought crossly. Being Lucian's sister didn't make her less a woman, and any woman worthy of her gender would be curious about what was taking place in that bed, especially if she knew the man involved was the Lightbringer. Especially after spotting the gold filigree necklace set with amethysts that was on the dressing table. That was a trinket that was usually considered sufficient for a parting gift after a brief, pleasant affair. She didn't think Lucian was ready to part quite yet since there were still several days before the dark of the moon. Was he preparing the way to be able to continue the affair when his promised time was done?

"This will do . . . I think," Ari said, returning to the room with a pile of clothing.

Dianna turned away from the dressing table and the thoughts that were making her uneasy. The bards knew enough stories and songs about Fae males becoming ensnared by human females. The lesson in all those stories, which were always tragic, was to enjoy and move on—and not look back. To linger too long was to become trapped by feelings that were best left unfelt, to be lured into wanting things that were best left unwanted.

Pushing away the desire to rush back to Tir Alainn and demand that Lucian tell her his intentions, which would only make his refusal to discuss it a certainty, Dianna took the clothing Ari was holding.

"They were my mother's," Ari said. "She was taller than me, so I think her things will fit you better. I'll see to the mare while you change."

By the time Dianna exchanged her riding habit for the loose-fitting tunic and trousers, the mare was staked to a long lead in the meadow, contentedly grazing, and Ari was back in the garden.

"Your mother and I may have been the same height, but her figure was more . . . generous," Dianna said, pinching the fabric under her breasts and holding it out before releasing it.

"She was the mother of the three," Ari said, sadness shadowing her eyes for a moment. "She looked . . . ripe."

Dianna narrowed her eyes. That was the second time Ari had mentioned "the three." And there was something about the way she said it that made Dianna sure it wasn't a meaningless phrase. "Who is the third?"

"The maid," Ari said, busily digging a small hole. "There have always been three. Now only the maid is left."

Dianna knew she was prodding a bruise, if not an open heart wound, but she didn't stop. "What happened to the mother and the crone?"

"They died."

Dianna looked around, feeling as if the landscape had shifted on her somehow. The cottage wasn't a manor house, but it was considerably bigger than most of the cottages that were scattered around the countryside. "If you do the work in the garden, who tends the house and does the rest of the work?"

"I do." Ari planted a seedling in the hole she'd just dug. "Although the cottage is tended better in the winter than in summer."

"Then you're alone here. Truly alone."

Ari sat back on her heels. "The Great Mother is always here. And so are the ones who came before me. It is not our custom to set up markers, but when I take a walk around Brightwood, I can tell when I pass a place where one of us was laid to rest."

"But—" She'd seen human burial places. Of course there were markers, and land set aside for that purpose. "So parts of Brightwood are sacred ground?"

"Brightwood is one of the Old Places," Ari said gently. "All of it is sacred ground. To some people anyway." She took a breath and blew it out. "Would you like to plant some seeds?"

What a strange girl, Dianna thought a few minutes later as she followed Ari's instructions for planting peas. *She talks about "the three" and sacred ground and being able to tell where the dead rest even when there are no markers. I've never heard anyone talk this way. I'll have to ask Lyrra if she's ever heard anything like this. She spends more time among humans because of her gift as the Muse. The three. Why is that significant?*

"Dianna . . . you're planting them too close together. They can't grow that way."

Dianna glanced at Ari, then looked away to hide her rising temper. How dare the girl chastise her—*her!*—when she was willing to help? So a few wouldn't grow. What difference—

If she goes hungry this winter because I'm playing with her survival, will I still say "what difference?"

"I'm sorry," Dianna said. And she was sorry. But she wasn't sure if it was because she had been careless in the planting or because she cared about what could happen to Ari because of it. She unearthed the peas, then sat back on her heels. "My mind wandered, and I stopped paying attention to what I was doing."

"It's easy enough to do that," Ari said with a smile. "I do a fair amount of dreaming when I'm working in the garden." She hesitated. "You could do that row over. No harm's done."

Dianna shifted until she was sitting more comfortably. She shook her head. "I'll just keep you company for a while."

Watching Ari for a few minutes was soothing. She didn't hurry through the planting, but she had a rhythm to her movements that allowed her to accomplish more than Dianna would have thought possible in a short amount of time.

When soothing changed to boring, Dianna shifted restlessly. She was reluctant to help again because she didn't want to feel responsible if the harvest was poor, but she didn't want to just sit there. She should leave, and would have left already if she'd gotten the information she'd come for. Besides, she wanted the novelty of planting something.

"Would you like to plant the flowers?" Ari asked.

"Flowers?" Boredom vanished. Flowers were just prettiness, weren't they? They wouldn't be important. She could plant them, and it wouldn't make any difference if some of them didn't grow.

"I plant flowers around the cottage, but I won't be able to do that until the vegetable garden is in."

Dianna hesitated. "If some of them don't grow, it won't make the winter harder, will it?"

Ari shook her head and smiled. "I use some of them to dye my wool, but there's always plenty. Come on, I'll show you."

Dianna followed Ari out of the garden gate to the readied ground that formed a border around the cottage. At the front corner, she could see plants already growing.

"Those are perennials," Ari said. "They come back year after year. On this side of the cottage, I plant new every year."

"Why?"

Ari shrugged, looking a little embarrassed. "The perennials represent continuity and the pleasure of seeing the familiar renew itself. This bed represents the excitement and potential of the new and unknown." She picked up a small basket next to the flower bed and brushed a finger over the bundles of cloth inside. "These are the different seeds I collected last fall. You take a bundle and scatter the seeds over the flower bed. Some years I scatter them in clusters so that there are distinct areas that are all one flower, and other years I scatter them throughout the bed so everything is mixed together."

"Which way should I do it?" Dianna asked.

"Whichever way pleases you. There are three exceptions."

Naturally, Dianna thought a little sourly. *It couldn't just be easy and fun.*

Ari held up one bundle. "The marigolds need to be planted in the front because they're short." Dropping that bundle back in the basket, she picked up two more. One was tied with white thread, the other yellow. "These need to be planted in the back of the bed because they need to climb. It's easier if you plant them first."

Dianna looked at the trellis that ran across the whole side of the cottage. "What are they?" she asked, taking the bundles.

"Moonflowers and morning glories." Ari hesitated, then mumbled, "I plant the moonflowers to honor the Lady of the Moon."

"Really?" Delighted, Dianna studied the bundle with more interest. "I don't think I've ever seen them." She glanced slyly at Ari, and teased, "If the moonflowers are for the Lady, are the morning glories for the Lightbringer?"

Oh, how Ari blushed over *that* question. She stammered out the instructions for how deep and far apart to plant, then bolted back to the vegetable garden.

Amused by Ari's reaction, Dianna turned her attention to the important business of planting her moonflowers.

After several minutes of debating with herself about whether to plant moonflowers along half the wall and the morning glories along the other half or mix them, she decided to alternate. That way the whole wall would be filled with flowers morning and evening. And it would be a truthful representation of the way she and Lucian were with each other. One claimed the day, the other the night, but their lives were intertwined because they were twins.

"Is there a problem?" Ari called out.

"Just planning," Dianna said.

Ari smiled and returned to her work.

After carefully planting the moonflower and morning glory seeds, Dianna spent several minutes frowning at the rest of the flower bed, trying to picture how it should look. She'd been frustrated to discover the seeds in the other bundles didn't give her a clue about what the flowers would be, and Ari, who probably knew each one, hadn't labeled any of the bundles.

Clusters, she finally decided, then went to work.

She was finishing the row of marigolds in the front of the bed when she noticed Ari leaning against the garden wall, smiling at her.

"I'm going to move the mare so she can graze in a fresh piece of the meadow. Then I'll see what I can find for us to eat. I'm afraid it will be simple fare. I haven't spent time cooking these past few days."

"Simple sounds wonderful," Dianna said, getting to her feet. Noticing a gold chain around Ari's neck that disappeared under the tunic, she realized this was a good way to ask a few questions.

"Has your Fae Lord returned?" she asked.

Ari blushed. "Yes, he's been back to visit."

"Since he's Fae, they must be interesting visits."

"Y-yes. Yes, they are. I'll see to the mare."

The blushes and stammers were amusing, but the unhappiness in Ari's eyes was too much like the troubled look she'd seen in Lucian's for Dianna to let it go. Was the girl still fretting about the custom of gifting? If that was all, she might be able to do something about that.

As Ari turned away, Dianna reached out and hooked a finger under the gold chain just above where it disappeared under the tunic. "Are you wearing one of his gifts? May I see it?" Before Ari could answer, Dianna ran her finger along the chain to draw the pendant out.

It was a five-pointed star within a circle. Never having seen anything like it, Dianna was certain that this wasn't a gift from Lucian. Why *was* Ari wearing this instead of one of her lover's gifts? "What is it?"

"It's a pentagram," Ari said quietly.

Dianna felt a tremor go through the girl. She glanced

at Ari's face. The girl was almost as pale as when she'd seen the cloud dragon.

Dianna waited.

"It's a witch's symbol."

Dianna dropped the pendant and took a step back without being conscious of doing either of those things. "You— You're a witch?"

"Yes."

Dianna felt dizzy, but she wasn't sure if the cause was fear or rage. "You're one of the wiccanfae?"

"That was an old name for us. It hasn't been used for a long time."

It's being used now, Dianna thought bitterly. But . . .

Ari was a witch. *Ari.* How could this girl be one of the creatures who were destroying Tir Alainn?

Dianna licked her lips, which were suddenly painfully dry. "You have magic."

"I have magic."

Dianna studied her opponent. Ari was no longer a blushing, stammering girl. She was a young woman wrapping herself in a cloak of quiet pride and dignity.

"Would you like me to saddle your horse now?" Ari asked.

She expects me to leave, expects me to run. Which means I can do neither right now. "What does it mean?" She tipped her head to indicate the pentagram.

"The lower four points stand for the four branches of the Mother—earth, air, water, and fire. The fifth point is for the spirit." Ari paused. "My gifts come from the branches of earth and fire."

"Your gifts?" Dianna said slowly.

"My . . . magic."

"What can you do with it?"

"Well, I can light a fire without using flint and steel, and I can ready the land for planting without needing a plow."

Dianna moved away so that she could lean against the garden wall. "If you'll pardon me for saying it, it doesn't sound like much."

A small smile curved Ari's lips. "It is if you don't have flint and steel handy—or own a plow."

True enough, but that didn't explain what was happening to Tir Alainn. Since she was facing the cottage, Dianna frowned at the seeds she'd just planted. "Why do you plant flowers for the Lady of the Moon?"

"Because she's the Queen of the Witches."

"What?"

"We follow the turning of the moon, and the turning of the seasons. The moon is our guide. She is always constant and ever-changing. The Mother's wiser daughter, and our older sister."

I'm not that *much older than you,* Dianna thought crossly. "She isn't always called the Lady of the Moon."

Ari nodded. "There is the other side of her. When she rides as the Huntress, she isn't always kind. But she's supposed to be our protector, the one we can call on for help." Bitterness aged her face. "I don't think she cares about protecting anything or anyone anymore."

The Huntress cares very much about protecting something, Dianna thought fiercely. *And I will do whatever I must in order to save Tir Alainn.*

She had to get away now, had to have time to think. Either she was standing beside a dangerous enemy or someone who might, somehow, be able to help the Fae protect Tir Alainn.

"I do need to go now. I have a ways to travel."

Ari's smile was polite . . . and distant. "Yes, of course. I'll go saddle the mare."

Dianna hurried into the cottage to change clothes. As she stripped out of the garments Ari had given her, she noticed the amethyst necklace again. A chill went through her, biting as deep as a winter storm.

Did Lucian know that Ari was a witch? He couldn't. He would have said something. He *knew* what was at stake. He wouldn't have said *nothing.* Was he in as much danger as Tir Alainn? Why *had* he fixed his interest on this female? Had it really been his own choice, or was this a trap to somehow ensnare the Lightbringer? And how could she ask him without making him defensive and difficult? Surely . . . *surely* he wouldn't allow lust to cloud his mind to that extent.

In the normal way of things, no, he wouldn't, Dianna thought as she put on her riding habit. But if he was caught in a lust over which he had no control, that could explain why he was looking so troubled lately.

Dianna swept out of the bedroom, anxious to return to Tir Alainn. The answers the Fae were seeking could be right here—if they dared to ask the questions.

Something's wrong, Neall thought, urging Darcy into a canter as soon as he saw Ari. He knew her well enough to recognize, even at a distance, that she was distressed about something. And the way her face lit up when she saw him warmed his heart and made him anxious.

Except that, now that he was closer, she didn't look distressed. She looked like she was struggling to hold in a belly laugh that could be heard in Ridgeley.

He couldn't think about that right now. Darcy was gathering himself to jump the low wall—which would put the gelding and those big hooves smack in the middle of the newly planted garden. Which wouldn't earn endearments for either of them, no matter how pleased Ari was to see him.

Why was she so pleased?

He reined in hard enough to warn Darcy he meant it. The gelding responded so fast he almost went over the animal's head. Of course, Darcy was also standing right in front of Ari with his head already thrust over the wall for the petting he expected.

My horse and I are in love with the same female, Neall thought sourly as he dismounted on legs that were a little shaky. *And he doesn't even have the balls to get excited about it, which, I suppose, is a blessing. I wonder how Ari would react to an amorous horse. Mother's mercy.*

"Neall, I'm glad you came by," Ari said while she petted the gelding.

"What's wrong?" Neall demanded, feeling testy now that he could see there was nothing wrong with Ari.

Ari hesitated. "Behind the cottage—"

"What? A snake? A wolf?" Royce? That mysterious lover who still had a claim on her?

"No, a—"

Another woman's voice carried through the air quite clearly. "Stand still, you four-legged piece of misery!"

Neall took a step back and watched Ari cautiously.

"It's a gentry lady," Ari said.

At least she sounds apologetic about it, Neall thought, having a good idea of what was coming next. Being related to Odella, he had enough experience with gentry ladies to know they could be the meanest creatures alive, and this one sounded riled.

"She stopped to visit, and—"

A pungent curse filled the air.

"—she's having a little trouble mounting."

"She rode sidesaddle? Here?"

Her eyes dancing with laughter, Ari pressed her lips together and nodded.

"I'd rather face a snake. A big, venomous snake. Or a wolf."

"That's quite sensible of you, Neall. It would even be sensible if there were such creatures in this part of Sylvalan. But it won't help Mistress Dianna get mounted—and she has been trying for a while now. The mare's a bit sulky about being saddled up again and apparently decided the chopping block Dianna was going to use as a mounting block was something to avoid."

"Why didn't you offer to give her a leg up?"

"I did, but she said I wasn't strong enough to boost her into the saddle."

Neall snorted. The woman obviously didn't know Ari. "And I should go back there because . . . ?"

"You're a man and, therefore, stronger and braver than I am," Ari replied sweetly.

Neall just stared at her. "You owe me for this."

"I'll hold your horse."

"As if you're going to convince him to move anytime soon," he muttered, taking the longest way around the cottage that he possibly could. "If you petted me the way you pet him, I wouldn't move either." He hoped the day would come when she did exactly that. And come soon.

As he rounded the corner of the cottage, he saw the mare sidle away from the chopping block at the same moment the woman tried to put her left foot in the stirrup. Since she was holding on to the saddle, the woman got pulled off the block instead of landing on her face.

"You're dog meat," the woman snarled.

Neal winced. He recognized the mare as one of Ahern's, and knew well enough how the old man felt about anyone threatening an animal he had bred and trained. The mare wasn't one of the special horses Ahern raised, but all of his animals were prime stock.

The woman had her back to him so he couldn't see her face, but he knew she wasn't from one of the local families. And he hadn't heard of a lady named Dianna staying with any of the gentry families in the neighborhood. If one of her acquaintances had a guest, Odella would have already paid a call in order to pass judgment on the stranger's sense of fashion and family connections. So she probably wasn't a gentry lady, regardless of what she had told Ari. But she *had* gotten a horse from Ahern, which meant the man approved of her—at least to some extent.

"May I give you a leg up?" Neall asked.

She whipped around to face him.

Neall's vision blurred. Not everything. Not everywhere. Just her face blurred, as if he were seeing two faces, one beneath the other, the same and yet slightly different.

That used to happen to him all the time when he was

a small child and his mother's friend Ashk came to visit, but it rarely occurred after he'd come to live with Baron Felston. Well, it had happened that once, when a traveling minstrel stopped at Ridgeley and the baron had taken him and Royce to the tavern to hear the man play. And it still happened occasionally when he was at Ahern's farm, but only when he was so tired he wasn't thinking clearly. A crowded, smoky room or dusky light at the end of a hard day were easy explanations for a moment of blurred vision. But neither of those things explained why he was experiencing it *now*.

"You're staring at me," the woman said. "Do you find this amusing?" Her voice held the cool arrogance any gentry lady's would have when caught in an awkward situation, but there was a dangerous undercurrent that made him sure she would hurt him badly if she was seriously provoked.

Shivering, Neall rubbed his eyes, then blinked a couple of times. When he focused on her again, he saw an attractive stranger. He didn't know her, and he was equally certain he'd seen her before in a different place or under different circumstances that made her now seem unfamiliar. Like a lady's maid dressing up in one of her mistress's old gowns and trying to pass herself off as a lady to someone who didn't know her. Was that all this was? A lady's maid who could pretend well enough but still didn't get it quite right?

"Are you amused?" Her voice had gotten colder.

Neall shook his head to clear it, then walked over to her—and tried to shake the uneasiness that increased with every step he took toward her. *Get her out of here, away from Ari, and then think it through.* "My apologies, Mistress. I was dizzy for a moment. Here. Let me give you a leg up." He bent slightly and laced his fingers to receive her foot.

When she didn't respond, he looked up. She was staring at him as if he, too, seemed familiar but she couldn't quite place him.

Finally accepting his assistance, she was mounted before the mare could decide to play any more games.

"If you're going to ride alone, you should ride astride," he said, checking to make sure her foot was secure in the stirrup.

"It isn't ladylike," she replied coolly.

"Even gentry ladies are practical enough not to use a sidesaddle when they don't have an escort to help them mount and dismount."

"Indeed." She frowned a little, as if chewing over his statement.

Not a lady's maid, Neall decided. An upper servant would know it was acceptable for a lady to ride astride, if for no other reason than knowing different garments were worn for riding astride. And she wasn't gentry. He was certain of that. So what, exactly, was she? And why was she in Brightwood?

Neall stepped away from the mare. "Blessings of the day to you, Mistress."

He wasn't sure why he used his mother's—and Ari's—usual greeting. Maybe just to see if she recognized it as a witch's salute rather than a gentry one.

Her light brown eyes narrowed. The look she gave him was thoughtful—and a little puzzled. She tipped her head in acknowledgment, then commanded the mare to walk on.

He watched her, moving enough to keep her in sight while she crossed the road and rode across the fields to Ahern's farm.

Ashk, why does your face look blurry when you first come to our house?

She stared at him for so long and in such a way that, for the first time, he felt afraid to be alone with her.

"You can see through the clamor?" she asked.

Later, he had asked his father what "clamor" meant. When told it meant "noise," he'd puzzled for a while over why he could *see* through noise, then decided Ashk had been teasing him. Since it only happened when he saw her, he never mentioned it again.

So what was it about this stranger who was interested in Ari that made him think of Ashk after so many years?

Too edgy to sit, Dianna paced one of the smaller rooms in the Clan house until Lyrra and Aiden hurried to join her.

"Have you seen Lucian?" she asked.

"I'm surprised you didn't pass each other going through the Veil," Aiden said. "I guess he was feeling randy enough that he didn't want to wait until sunset."

Dianna stopped pacing. Couldn't move at all now. "He's already gone? How could he just leave?"

"He's been doing exactly that since the Summer Moon," Lyrra said, puzzled. She shifted her voice to a soothing tone. "I know you've been concerned about him becoming too . . . attached . . . to this female, but I'm sure it's nothing more than an indulgence in carnal pleasure. Besides, it will be the dark of the moon in a few more days, and then the affair will be over."

"It's what happens when it's over that concerns me," Dianna said.

"Why?" Aiden asked sharply.

Dianna took a deep breath to steady herself. "Because the woman who lives in the cottage, the woman Lucian has taken as a lover, is one of the wiccanfae. She is a witch."

Silence.

Aiden shook his head and began to swear, quietly and viciously.

"How— Are you sure, Dianna?" Lyrra asked, sinking down on the nearest bench.

"She told me. When I was there today, I saw a pendant she wears. A pentagram. A witch's symbol."

"Lucian has said nothing," Aiden said savagely. *"Nothing."*

"I don't think he knows," Dianna said. "I'm sure of it."

"That doesn't make it any better, does it?" Aiden snapped.

"Why would the wiccanfae want to hurt us?" Lyrra asked.

"Haven't you ever wanted to hurt a lover who had tired of you?" Aiden said so bitterly Dianna and Lyrra stared at him. "What better way to hurt a Fae lover than to destroy a piece of Tir Alainn and all the Fae within it."

"We don't know the Clans who are lost have been destroyed," Lyrra protested.

"We don't know *anything* about them. There's no word from them, no way to reach them." Aiden paced the room. "There are enough Fae males who indulge themselves in the human world, and if a pendant is the only way to distinguish a witch from any other human female, they wouldn't have known the difference. What if what's happening to Tir Alainn is nothing more than the vengeance of spurned lovers?"

"That's enough," Dianna said firmly. "The only thing we know about the witches is what is being sung or told in stories."

"And none of *that* is good," Aiden said.

"I recall that you found those songs so offensive you used your gift as the Bard to strip away the musical skills of anyone who played them."

Aiden glared at her but kept silent.

"I agree that the witches might have a kind of magic that could close a road through the Veil, and they may be the reason Tir Alainn is in danger." Dianna sat on the bench beside Lyrra, but kept her eyes on Aiden. "We've lost more Clans since the Summer Moon, and we're no closer to finding out why. Now we have a chance to get some answers."

"From a witch?" Lyrra asked, sounding skeptical.

"Yes, from a witch," Dianna replied, ignoring Aiden's succinct comments. "She's alone and she's young . . . and I think she's lonely. If we were to befriend her, she would have no reason to harm us, and might even be willing to help us."

"If we befriend her and then discover she *is* a dan-

ger to Tir Alainn, what do we do then, Huntress?"
Aiden said.

Dianna felt her throat tighten. She knew what
Aiden expected her to say. She knew what she *had* to
say, what she would have said without a second
thought even a day ago . . . before she had been told
she was called the Queen of the Witches and was considered their protector.

It makes no difference. It can't.

"If she is a danger to us," Dianna said quietly,
"then the Huntress will take care of it—and she won't
be a danger anymore."

Chapter Fourteen

Adolfo tied his weary horse securely to a tree before moving a little deeper into the Old Place. It would have been better if he could have hobbled the horse and let it graze in the meadow bordering the Old Place, but his nephew's ghost kept beckoning to him from the other side of the meadow. He was certain the ghost couldn't leave the meadow since the body was buried there, but he wasn't certain about how much of the meadow the ghost could walk—and he wasn't certain how much power Konrad's ghost might have. So the animal would have to wait until he was done with what he had come to do.

The witch who had lived here was dead—Konrad had achieved that much—and Adolfo could feel the magic bleeding out of the Old Place. But power still thrummed in the land, in the trees, in the very air of this place. It grated against his bones even as it filled him with exultation.

As he walked, he brushed his fingers against the trees until he touched one and felt a dryad's shriek of anger as a tingling in his fingertips. He smiled. Before she could gather her small magic to strike at him, he pressed his hand against the tree and poured his own power into it, binding her inside the trunk. Taking a step away from the tree, he sank to his knees. Placing his hands firmly on the ground, he used the witch magic that was his mother's legacy to make the connection between himself and the Old Place. Then he began drawing the power out of the land, filling himself with it until his heart pounded and his body ached with the effort to contain it. And still he took in more and more, all the while murmuring the words that would change benign power into something malicious.

When he felt full to bursting, he released it all, letting it flood out of him as twisted ropes of magic that flew toward the village and nearby farms.

He heard the dryad scream as one of those twisted ropes struck her tree and consumed her.

He felt the land shudder as he took in more of its magic and released it, changed.

Finally unable to do any more, he broke his connection with the Old Place and slumped to the ground, trembling with exhaustion.

Power no longer thrummed in the land. It was still there. Nothing could destroy it completely in an Old Place. But it was a pale shadow of what it had been an hour before, and it would never again be more than a pale shadow—unless another witch came to live in the Old Place. Or the Fae. But that would never happen. The Fae only amused themselves in this world before returning to their precious Fair Land, and by the time he was done, no female would be able to set foot on this land without being condemned as a witch, whether she had any magic or not.

"And no man shall suffer a witch to live," Adolfo whispered, rolling onto his back. "No man shall be at the mercy of any kind of female magic. We shall be the masters, the rulers, and what little power we grant we can also strip away. So shall it be."

With effort, he climbed to his feet and slowly returned to his horse. Opening a saddlebag, he pulled out a flask of brandy and drank deeply. He followed that with hunks of bread and cheese. His strength returned, slowly—far more slowly than it once did. But he was older now, and it took more out of him to strip power from the land.

Finishing the bread and cheese, he drank his fill from the water canteen, then poured water into his cupped hand for the horse.

"That's enough," Adolfo said, shaking the last drops

of water from his hand and tying the canteen to the saddle.

He walked the horse out of the woods.

His nephew's ghost now stood halfway between its grave and the border of the Old Place.

Adolfo suppressed a shudder, viciously controlling himself so that nothing would show on his face.

A twist of released magic must have struck the ghost, turning it into a nightmarish image, all the more dreadful because it could still be recognized as the young man it had been. In time, the villagers might have become used to a handsome ghost prowling the meadow. No one would be able to look on *this* without fear.

"They will pay for your death," Adolfo told the ghost. "That I promise you."

He turned away, aware that Konrad trailed after him. He didn't breathe easily until he was well beyond the meadow and Konrad could no longer follow him. Mounting, he settled the horse into an easy trot. He'd ridden hard to reach this place at the right time. Now he would stop at the first available inn to give the horse and himself a well-earned rest.

He couldn't control what the twisted ropes of magic would do. He'd never been able to control it to that extent. He simply released it and let each rope find its mark. Over the next few days, the villagers would suffer unexplainable troubles. Wells would collapse, cows would suddenly go dry, chickens would cease to lay, a dog would turn vicious and savage a child, a healthy woman would be taken to childbed before her time and die in agony birthing a corpse.

And those ropes of magic caused transformations, taking something from the natural world and twisting it into something else. The nighthunters were formed that way. A few were always created when he or one of his Inquisitors drained an Old Place of its magic. That didn't trouble him since they mostly preyed on the Small Folk—or people who were foolish enough to walk through deep woods at night.

The villagers would still be reeling from Harro's grisly death so soon after Konrad's, and all the other troubles that would suddenly plague them would shatter any doubts they may have had about the existence of the Evil One and leave them at the mercy of what he had to teach them.

And he would teach them. In a few days, the other Inquisitors he had summoned would arrive at this village, as well as a couple of minstrels who found their purses well filled now that they played to his tune. He would return here as the Master Inquisitor, the Witch's Hammer, and by the time he was done purging these people of all the Evil One's servants, those who survived would spread a story that would leave no doubt about how thoroughly the Evil One could devour people wherever an Inquisitor died.

Chapter Fifteen

The road through the Veil shone in the deepening twilight.

Morag hesitated. It looked safe; it *felt* strong. It was the first shining road she'd found in the handful of days since she'd killed the young man in the black coat and taken the witch up the road that led to the Shadowed Veil. And yet . . .

The dark horse stamped one foot, mouthed the bit impatiently.

"There's a storm coming," Morag said quietly. "The sky is clear and there's no wind, but this place feels hushed, the way a place does when everything has sought shelter to hide from whatever is going to happen."

She stretched her senses and the magic that was her gift. Death didn't whisper to her, didn't stir. Almost as if Death also waited.

Morag looked around, still uneasy.

The road through the Veil beckoned.

"Let's go to the Fair Land," she said.

The dark horse needed no urging.

They cantered along that shining road walled by mist.

Little tendrils of mist drifted across the road.

She'd never seen that before.

Was it taking longer than usual to reach the Veil that separated the human world from Tir Alainn? Shouldn't she have reached it by now?

A storm was coming. She could feel it.

Mist drifted across the road.

Where was the Veil?

There!

Morag looked at the dark gray wall of mist they were swiftly approaching and clenched the reins. She couldn't see beyond it. That wasn't right. The Veil was usually translucent, not opaque. What if it was like that when they were passing through it? Would the dark horse be able to stay on the road if he couldn't see it? If he misstepped and took them into the walls of mist on either side of the road, they would never find their way back. No one ever had.

The dark horse hesitated. Morag leaned forward, her eyes intent on the Veil. "Go."

He surged forward. And they were nowhere, surrounded by heavy, thick mist.

No one gathers the souls of those who have slipped into the mist, Morag thought, fighting against a growing fear as second after second passed and they were still riding through mist. *No one gathers the souls . . . because no one can find them. If I'm lost here, would I be able to find the other lost ones but not be able to guide them to the road that leads to the Shadowed Veil? Or could I find that particular road no matter where I am?*

The dark horse snorted, gathered himself for another burst of speed.

They exploded out of the mist. Gently rolling land bordered the road now. Ahead of her, she saw the Clan house rising up out of the land. Unlike the great houses the humans built, boxy and predictable, the Clan houses consisted of many buildings of various shapes and sizes connected by gardens and courtyards, a tumble of living areas for the families that made up a Clan.

Breathing easier, and suddenly exhausted, Morag reined the dark horse back to an easy canter. A minute later, they rode into the first large courtyard, where the stables were.

Dismounting, she looked around. Why had no one come out of the stables to meet her? The stable doors were open, so someone must have heard her arrive. Where *were* all the Fae?

There's a storm coming.

Shivering, despite it being a warm summer evening, Morag led the horse toward the open stable doors.

"I suppose you'll be wanting him rubbed down and fed." The surly voice came from the shadows inside the stable.

"Yes, I do want him rubbed down and fed," Morag replied.

A Fae male stepped out of the stables. He eyed her with dislike. " 'Tis suppertime, and I've a fine meal cooling on my plate."

"The quicker you attend to your duties, the sooner you can get back to it."

"A horse can't be expected to wait," he said. " 'Tis rude to be coming through the Veil when there's a fine meal cooling."

"I'll remember that," Morag said softly.

He finally looked at the horse. His eyes widened. "That's a dark horse." He wasn't referring to just its color.

"Yes."

He looked at her again, all the color washed from his face. "You're—"

"The Gatherer."

He just stared at her for a moment, growing paler. "I'll take good care of him," he whispered.

"I know you will. He's not just a horse, he's a friend." Turning away from the man, Morag untied the saddlebags and pulled them off the dark horse's back. There wasn't much in them—a change of clothes, a few gold coins, a comb and brush that she hadn't used in days.

She patted the dark horse's neck. "Rest well."

He turned his head and lipped her sleeve.

She stepped back, but waited until the Fae male came forward and led the dark horse into the stables. She smiled, and knew if the male had seen that smile

he would have been terrified by the bitterness and
fury it held.

With manners like that, you could be human, Morag
thought as she walked to the steps that led to the first
tier of the Clan house. There was another courtyard
there, this one splashed with flowers.

What would she do if the matriarchs of the Clan
greeted her the same way, forgetting Clan courtesy
because she had inconvenienced them during a meal?

Anger grew until it was powerful enough to sweep
away anything in its path.

She took a step toward the door leading into the
Clan house. A voice, filled with delight, stopped her
from taking another.

"Morag! Well met, sister!"

"Morphia!" Morag dropped the saddlebags and
rushed toward her sister. They hugged with less restraint than the Fae usually showed in public.

They stepped back at the same time. Morag looked
at her sister, younger by two years. The same black
hair and dark eyes, almost the same height. But Morphia's face was softer, fuller, just as her body was
rounder and more blatantly female.

She looks like who she is, Morag thought. *The Sleep
Sister, the Lady of Dreams. If I asked, would she grant
me a gentle night's sleep?*

"Well met, Morphia," Morag said.

Her eyes twinkling, Morphia wrinkled her nose.
"You need a bath."

"That isn't all I need," Morag said wearily.

The twinkle in Morphia's eyes disappeared so fast
it might never have been there. She glanced around.
"Morag, you're Fae and, therefore, welcome. But,
lately, everyone who has visited here has brought
nothing but tales of woe and trouble."

"Then I'll tell no tales since I have no better fare
to offer. But then, I never do."

"I do not envy you your gift, Morag," Morphia said
quietly. She took her sister's hand. "Come. We'll get
you settled into a guest room—and into a bath. Then

I'll bring up some plates and we'll have dinner. Cullan will have to do without me for an evening." The twinkle was back in her eyes, somewhat muted but still present.

"Cullan?" Morag grabbed her saddlebags as she and Morphia passed them. *You're home. This may not be your Clan house or your family, but you're back in Tir Alainn. Drop the burden for a little while.* With effort, she pushed away the uneasiness that wanted to settle its heavy weight on her shoulders and made her voice light and teasing. "So this visit has a purpose? Who is this Cullan?"

"He's a Lord of the Woods. Not the Hunter, although he's finely built as stag or man." Morphia's voice was much too casual.

You bait me, inviting me to laugh. May the Mother bless you, sister.

"He visited our Clan a few months back, and I decided to repay the visit."

"That was kind of you. Or is he really that finely built?"

"You may judge for yourself. Tomorrow. After you've had a bath."

Laughing, Morag followed Morphia into the Clan house.

"Did you sleep well?" Morphia asked the next morning while they strolled through one of the gardens.

Morag slanted a look at her sister. "You made sure I would."

Laughing, Morphia linked her arm with Morag's. "It was the least I could do for my favorite sister."

"Your *only* sister."

"Which is why you're my favorite."

Pleased with each other, they walked in silence for several minutes.

"Your Cullan seems like a fine man."

"Yes, he is," Morphia said, sounding a little troubled.

Picking up on the change in mood, Morag continued, "He also seems out of place here, not quite part of his Clan." She winced the moment the words were out. "I apologize. I had no right to speak of a man I met an hour ago."

"But you're right. You usually are in your judgment of people."

"I don't judge—"

"You do." Morphia looked straight ahead. "But it's not really a judgment the way someone else might use the word. It's just that you look into a person's eyes, even when those are already clouded by death, and you can *see* who they are, what's inside them. I've wondered if that's why you tend to keep your distance from most people. I've wondered if, sometimes, you see too much."

Morag said nothing. What was there to say? Morphia was the Sleep Sister, and her gift was welcomed. But the Gatherer's presence usually reminded people of mortality and an ending they didn't want to greet in the present. Only those who were ready to journey to the Summerland welcomed her. And Morphia was right: sometimes she did see too much of what dwelled beneath the mask of flesh.

"Cullan is thinking of coming with me when I return to my Clan."

"For an extended visit?" Morag asked, wondering if Morphia was thinking about having a child with this lover and wanted him to return with her for that reason.

Morphia shook her head. "To stay. He's a Lord of the Woods. He doesn't feel he has a place here." When Morag frowned, she huffed out a breath in frustration. "Tir Alainn is the Fair Land, beautiful and perfect. But we have no forests. Why don't we have forests, Morag? Have you ever wondered?"

"No, I've never wondered," Morag replied softly. "Forests have shadows. Death and Life walk hand in hand there. Forests are beautiful, but they are not perfect. They're too alive to be perfect."

"Everyone else in this Clan has all they need right here," Morphia said, looking at the luxurious garden and the green, rolling land beyond it. "They can use their gifts among themselves or when they visit nearby Clans. They have no need to go through the Veil and touch the human world. But Cullan can't use his gifts unless he walks in the Old Place, and every time he goes to the human world he feels less welcome when he returns."

Having a visitor who arrived by coming through the Veil didn't please the Fae here either, Morag thought. *Are they afraid I've been contaminated somehow from my contact with humans? That somehow I'm no longer truly Fae?*

"At least in our Clan, there are many of us who visit the human world and use our gifts as we can, so Cullan could spend time in the forests of the Old Place where our Clan's shining road is anchored and not feel like an outcast when he returns to Tir Alainn." Morphia smiled ruefully. "It seems we have been a bit too free in our mating with the western Clans of Sylvalan and we're a bit sullied because of it."

Morag stared at her sister for too long. "I hope," she finally said with deadly gentleness, "that no one will require the Gatherer's help while I'm here."

"Oh, Morag, no," Morphia said worriedly. "You take the words as a personal insult."

"Why shouldn't I, since that's how the words were meant?" Morag snapped. "What gives them the right to judge who among the Fae we mate with? If other Clans are considered inferior, who *does* this Clan mate with? Themselves?"

"Let's speak of something else," Morphia pleaded. "Let's not spoil the morning. Please."

They walked in silence again, but this time it was neither easy nor comfortable.

"You're different," Morphia said quietly.

"I've been Death's Mistress too many times lately. Too many deaths. Too much pain. Too many unanswered questions. And here are these fools, with their razor smiles, sitting here passing judgment on who is or isn't Fae by their exacting standards while Tir Alainn itself—"

Morag stopped, squeezed her eyes shut, then opened them. She took a slow breath to calm herself, to keep the uneasiness that swirled around her at bay. "Have you ever looked at a pond or a small lake when the water was perfectly still and seen the land reflected in the water? Sometimes the reflection is so clear and so perfect, you can't see any difference between the reflection and what is being reflected. But there are other times when the reflection is slightly smudged. The lines are soft, a little hazy. Not so much that you would notice it unless you took the time to really look, but enough for you to know that what you're seeing isn't real."

"Is that how you see the human world?" Morphia asked, puzzled.

"No," Morag said, dread making her heart pound too hard, too fast. "That's what I'm seeing now. Here."

Alarmed, Morphia looked around the garden. "You're wrong, Morag," she said after a minute. "It looks exactly as it is."

Morag shook her head. "No, it doesn't. The edges are becoming smudged, hazy."

"I don't see it."

"You wouldn't," Morag said. "You've been here for a while now. You see what you expect to see. You don't have any reason to look closely. Neither does anyone else who lives here. But it's been some time since I've been in Tir Alainn, and I've never visited this Clan before, so I look with no expectations of what I should see."

"This is foolish talk," Morphia snapped.

"Is it? How many years has it been since anyone has heard from *any* of the Clans who had used the shining roads in Arktos and Wolfram? Now the roads to Sylvalan are closing too. What if this is the warning, Morphia? What if this is how it starts?"

Morphia shook her head. "The matriarchs say it's

the Clans that mingle too much in the human world who have disappeared, that they brought something back with them that weakened the magic and that's why the roads closed and they were cut off from the rest of Tir Alainn." She huffed. "You're tired, Morag. You've been too long in the human world. That's why you're talking this way."

Perhaps. But there's a storm coming. I can feel it. Death is waiting. "Do you know where the Bard is residing now?"

Still troubled, and a little angry, Morphia said warily, "I heard he's staying with the Huntress's Clan."

"That's to the south, along the coast, isn't it?"

"Yes." Morphia hesitated. "That's also the Light-bringer's Clan."

Even the Huntress and the Lightbringer wouldn't dare dismiss the Gatherer. After all, the day will come when I'll extend my hand to them.

"You're going there, aren't you?" Morphia asked.

"Yes, I'm going there. To talk to them and the Bard."

"You're tired, Morag," Morphia said quietly, worriedly. "Won't you stay a few days more and rest?"

A shiver of something she didn't want to name brushed down Morag's spine as a shadow fell across her sister's face. It was a shadow she knew well. It wasn't so dark that it was a certainty, but it was a warning that couldn't be ignored.

"Yes, I'll stay a few more days."

Morphia squeezed her sister's arm. "You'll feel better after you've had some rest."

Nothing and no one could compel her to leave while she saw that shadow on Morphia's face. Perhaps by being here she could prevent the warning from becoming a certainty. So she would stay. But she doubted she would find any rest.

Morphia said, "If you'd like, we can find Cullan and talk to him. I think he's listened to more of the travelers' tales than the others did. He might be able to tell you something."

"Thank you," Morag said. She would listen to whatever Cullan had to tell her, but she was becoming more and more certain that the answers the Fae needed most would not be found in Tir Alainn.

Chapter Sixteen

Ari sat on the bench beside the kitchen door, her back resting against the cottage wall, a cup of tea cooling beside her. Birds fluttered a few feet away, snatching small pieces of bread she had tossed out to them, then flying back to their nests.

She would have to bake today. The garden needed watering. The bed linens needed to be changed, and washing needed to be done. There was no wind this morning, no breeze coming up from the sea to soften the heat she could already feel against her skin. Best to get the chores done early. Especially today.

She sat on the bench, drinking her tea and watching the birds.

There would be no child. She hadn't wanted one, had hoped she would be spared. Still, the intensity of her relief when she discovered her bleeding time had come had surprised her. Perhaps if her mother and grandmother were still alive, she would have welcomed a child by Lucian. He made her body weak with hunger for the pleasure she knew would come when he touched her, made it sizzle with need while he prepared her for the mounting. Wasn't that how a woman *should* feel when she took a lover's seed and transformed it into life? And where would a woman find a more splendid sire for her child than the Lightbringer?

And yet, she was relieved his seed hadn't taken root. Lucian was a wonderful lover, but . . .

"When that fire doesn't burn, it gives no warmth," she told a bold sparrow that had fluttered up to the bench, looking for more bread. "The only time he spends with me outside of bed is when I put out something to eat. He's polite. I'll grant him that. He asked about the garden, about the weaving he's seen on the looms, but he's only listening enough not to be caught out. He's not really interested in my life, and he never talks about his own. If there's any truth to the stories, he lives in a Clan with other Fae. But he doesn't mention them, either. The only part of his life he wants me to know about is the part I can wrap my hand around."

Ari sipped her tea. The sparrow, giving up, flew off to find its breakfast elsewhere.

"He gives me trinkets instead of any part of himself. Expensive trinkets, but they don't mean anything to him, which is why he gives them. Perhaps that's all Fae males ever give females who aren't of their kind. Or, perhaps, that's all they're capable of giving anyone."

Swallowing the rest of her tea, she got up to take care of the chores.

As she worked throughout the morning, two thoughts chased each other: How did women tell men about the bleeding time . . . and would Lucian be willing to spend time with her, just to be with her, now that he couldn't have the bed?

Not one of my better times, Ari thought later that afternoon while she sat on the bench and brushed her hair, which was still damp from the cool bath she'd taken. Every chore had taken her twice as long as usual; the heat had sapped her energy until she wanted to weep from fatigue, and even the special herb tea she'd made hadn't dulled the ache in her belly. On top of that, she had a fierce craving for meat, and dinner was going to be vegetable soup and bread. No, it wasn't one of her better days.

And here was Lucian riding out of the woods, and she still had no idea how women told a lover about private female things.

Her heart beat a little quicker as he approached, but her body didn't quicken in anticipation of being under him. Still, she made an effort to smile in order to cover her nerves and rose to meet him as he reined the horse in and quickly dismounted.

"Is he a friend?" she asked, nodding toward the horse.

Her question stopped him in mid-stride. "A friend?" he asked, puzzled. Then he looked at the horse and laughed. "No, he's just a horse. He needed some exercise."

As he reached for her, she took a small step back. "Lucian—"

"Later."

His arms were around her and he was kissing her in that deep, hungry way that usually made it impossible for her to think of anything but him. This time, his tongue felt cold and alien instead of pleasant, and the hands roaming over her body felt selfish and greedy instead of exciting.

Gripping his arms, she pushed at him, breaking the kiss. "Lucian, stop."

"Why?" He pulled her against him, roughly.

She turned her head to evade the next kiss. "No!"

His hands clamped on her waist tightly enough to hurt her. "Why not?"

What burned in his gray eyes was anger, not passion.

"I can't today." For the first time since she'd met him, he reminded her of Royce—a man who was only interested in what *he* wanted.

"Why not?" Lucian demanded.

"I—" Feeling her face heat, Ari pressed her lips together. "I don't know how to say this without being indelicate. I've never had to expla—"

"Just say it," he snapped.

There was a dangerous, feral quality to his voice that made her afraid. Would he actually demand the use of her body even after she'd indicated she wasn't willing? And if he did and *then* discovered . . .

"It's my bleeding time," she blurted out.

He went still. Then, releasing her, he stepped back.

Hugging herself, Ari watched him, no longer trusting what he might do next.

"I see," Lucian said quietly, his voice betraying nothing of what he might be feeling.

Stinging as much from the sudden absence of emotion as from his unexpected anger, Ari mumbled, "It started this morning."

"I see," he said again.

Was that disappointment she saw in his face? Maybe . . . "There's vegetable soup and fresh bread. You're welcome to stay if you'd like."

He hesitated, then shook his head. "I thank you, but no. I don't wish to intrude upon you at such a time." He cleared his throat quietly. "I apologize if my behavior distressed you in any way."

"Lucian . . ." In two days it would be the dark of the moon. The promise she had made on the Summer Moon would have been fulfilled then anyway. What was she supposed to say to him? That she had enjoyed knowing him? That she hoped he would visit again sometime? One sounded dismissive, and the other sounded like an invitation for more than she intended. *Would* she have welcomed him again as a lover? An hour ago, she would have said yes. Now she wasn't so sure.

She flinched when she saw him reach into his pocket. Another trinket. A Fae custom and obligation once again fulfilled. Well, she hadn't earned this one, had she?

When he lifted his hand from his pocket, it was empty. Resting his palm against her cheek, he leaned forward and gently kissed her. There was no emotion in that, either.

"Be well, Ari," he said softly.

"The Mother's blessings be with you, Lucian."

Turning away, he mounted the horse and galloped across the meadow, never looking back as he disappeared into the woods.

She went to her room and stared at her bed. Done
then. He had come for the carnal pleasure she had
been obliged to give him, and he had found nothing
more to interest him.

*He's a Fae Lord. What else is there here that would
interest him? But it doesn't seem fair that he can leave
without a backward glance, and yet he managed to tug
on my heart enough to leave it bruised. I care about
him. He never shared anything with me except his
body, but there was something about him that made
me care. It isn't fair.*

Stretching out on her bed, on clean linens that carried no scent of him, she began to cry.

Leaning against the stone wall, Lucian looked up at
the canopy of leaves that spread above his favorite,
private place in the Clan gardens.

It was over, and he hadn't been ready to see it end.
In two days, the promised time would have ended, but
he'd thought he'd have these last two days to be with
her, to sink into pleasure with her. He thought he'd
have that time to delicately persuade her to continue
being his lover—despite what Aiden had told him
that morning.

And then he'd spoiled all of it by not paying attention to her mood. No, that wasn't true. He'd known
there was something on her mind. He'd seen it in her
face. He hadn't wanted to hear it, and hoped that
whatever it was would go away if he could cloud her
mind with sex. He'd misjudged, badly.

Fae women cloistered during the bleeding time, pre-
ferring rest and quiet and privacy in order to tend to
things that were not a man's business. Fae men re-
spected that desire for privacy and stepped back so as
not to intrude. That was the way it was done, so he
had done the proper thing by retreating.

But she *had* invited him to stay—and he almost had.
He had no idea if she truly would have welcomed his
company or if the invitation had been made out of an
obligation to give him time and his presence would

have made her uncomfortable. That, as well as custom, was what made him leave.

He didn't know her customs. It hadn't seemed important to ask about them. But that was when he'd thought she was a human female who was just a little more appealing than most of her kind. That was before Aiden told him this morning about the symbol the wiccanfae wore.

He'd never asked her about the pendant she always wore. He'd been annoyed that she preferred it over the gifts he'd given her, but he'd never asked if it had meaning. Another misjudgment.

Even knowing she was a witch, and possibly a danger to Tir Alainn, he had gone to be her lover.

He'd given her no parting gift. What he'd brought wasn't sufficient for a parting gift. He'd said none of the pretty words that were supposed to be said. With passion and apprehension warring inside him, he'd felt oddly threatened because she suddenly wasn't interested in him as a lover. He'd let that war of feelings burn through him as anger, and he'd let that anger show. Another mistake. He'd made a lot of them this afternoon.

But it wasn't supposed to end today. He hadn't been ready.

And now he had to wonder if, by his clumsiness, he had made an enemy who could harm his Clan and Tir Alainn.

Dianna's smile of greeting faltered when Lyrra took her arm and hurried her out to the terrace, away from where the other Fae were gathering for the evening meal.

"Aiden just told me that Lucian is back."

Dianna frowned at Lyrra. "What do you mean, he's back? He hasn't come back once before dawn since—" Her throat tightened.

"I know," Lyrra said, keeping her voice low. "But he's back, and he went to that wild spot he likes to go to whenever he's brooding about something."

Mother's mercy. "Did he say anything to Aiden?"

Lyrra shook her head. "Aiden did tell him about the pendant this morning. If Lucian's seen it, he knows Ari is a witch. Maybe, knowing that, he changed his mind and just came back."

Or something might have gone very wrong, Dianna thought. *He isn't foolish. He wouldn't have confronted her about being wiccanfae when we have no idea what kind of threat she might be. Or even if she is a threat.* "It might be nothing. She might have been called away."

"To do what?"

They looked at each other, neither one wanting to answer that question.

Chapter Seventeen

Eight of his Inquisitors stood to one side, watching the two in the rowboat that floated in the center of the pond. Beside him, the village magistrate cringed as the woman was pulled up, again, from beneath the water. She gasped for breath, a harsh sound that carried clearly in the still morning air.

"Do you admit your guilt and confess your crimes against your neighbors?" the Inquisitor holding the rope asked in a loud voice.

"No!" the woman gasped. "No! I—"

The Inquisitor let the rope slide through his gloved hands. The woman disappeared beneath the water. Again.

She's been in that pond for close to an hour, and she's still fighting, Adolfo thought, sharply watching the way the rowboat rocked on the water. *But she won't last much longer. Very soon she'll understand there's only one way she can end her punishment. And then we can leave this place.*

"Master Adolfo," the magistrate said, casting an anxious eye toward the other villagers who had been summoned that morning to gather around the pond. "Master, my wife's cousin is a good woman. She *couldn't* have done such malicious things."

"Are you saying these people, who look to you as a leader in their community, are liars?" Adolfo asked quietly. "Are you saying that the women who freely confessed in order to unburden their spirits couldn't name the others who had been drawn into the dreadful snare of the witch's magic, and became witches themselves?"

"Witches?" The magistrate sweated. "No, no, Master Adolfo. They weren't *witches.*"

Adolfo looked at the man until fear did its duty and the man's will crumbled beneath it.

"I am the Witch's Hammer," Adolfo said. "I have spent my life studying these foul creatures, these whores of the Evil One. I know its stench—and theirs—when I smell it. Do you deny the troubles that have come to plague your village? Do you deny that *two* of my Inquisitors have died here in a matter of days? Two men trained and prepared to deal with the Evil One's servants were overwhelmed while staying in this place. The only way such a thing could happen is if the Evil One found vessels to give it roots here, vessels who had remained hidden from the good people of this community."

He paused long enough to nod to the Inquisitors in the boat. The one holding the rope pulled the woman up to the surface again.

"Perhaps," Adolfo continued softly, "you protest this cleansing of evil because you fear what we might be told during a confession. Perhaps you have had lustful thoughts about your wife's cousin. She is a beautiful woman and bold with her opinions. Perhaps you are close to being ensnared into the Evil One's service. Perhaps. It is not always as easy to tell with men when the Evil One's hold on them is still weak. Softening the flesh is the only way to discover such things. But you and I have not talked about such things in private, have we?"

The magistrate turned pale and swayed on his feet. "I didn't . . . I never . . . But . . . can't you simply let her die?"

Adolfo could almost smell the man's fear. It didn't matter if the magistrate had done nothing more than allow his thoughts to wander or had actually indulged in fornication with his wife's cousin. Now he simply wanted the woman silenced before the Master Inquisitor found a reason to look at him more closely.

"She must have a chance to redeem her spirit," Adolfo said gently. "Otherwise, the Evil One will have her in death as it had her in life, and she will endure unspeakable torment in the Fiery Pit."

The Inquisitor in the boat let the woman sink, then pulled her up quickly. After a couple more dunkings, when she didn't have quite enough time to draw a breath, he pulled her up, let her gasp for a moment, then said, "Do you—"

"Yes!" the woman screamed. "Yes! I confess. I did what you say I did. I confess!"

Adolfo nodded.

The Inquisitor released the rope. The woman sank to the bottom of the pond, weighed down by the sack of stones that had been tied to her legs under her dress.

Everyone waited. Finally, the oars were set and the Inquisitors began rowing back to the shore.

Adolfo raised his voice enough to reach the silent crowd. The persuasion magic flowed through him, turning his words into hooks that would capture these people and never quite let them go. "It is done. The Evil One's servants have been cleansed from this village. The foul magic they released on their neighbors may continue a little while longer. There is nothing we can do to prevent that. But it will cease, and then you will be free of it—as long as you men remain vigilant. Look around you carefully and take note of the other honest folk who came to witness the end of evil—and remember who stayed away. Keep watch over the women who are beholden to you. Do not shirk in your duty to discipline them. If you do not wield the strap with enough strength to help them remain modest and chaste, you do nothing less than thrust them into the Evil One's embrace. Beware the sharp-tongued woman and the one who is bold with her opinions. They weaken men. Beware the woman who enjoys the carnal duties of marriage too much.

She will be tempted too easily to enjoy a handsome stranger, and the Evil One's face is always handsome when he seduces such a woman. Once she has fornicated with evil, she will become the vessel that will be able to ensnare *you*. Stay vigilant, do your duty, and the Evil One will not be able to touch your families again."

The villagers shuffled their feet uneasily. There was fear in the women's eyes, which satisfied Adolfo.

He strode away from the pond, his Inquisitors following. He didn't stop until he reached the inn. His carriage was out front, already loaded with his trunks. The guardsman, who was his new coachman, nodded to indicate everything was ready for the Master Inquisitor's departure. A surly man who did not welcome conversation, Adolfo found him to be an adequate replacement for the previous coachman. The fool who had tried to trick him into being on the road during the Summer Moon was dead. One of those unfortunate accidents that could occur on an unfamiliar road in a strange country—especially when the accident was arranged.

"It will be good to leave this place," one of the younger Inquisitors said quietly, looking back toward the pond.

"Yes, it will," Adolfo replied.

The young man looked at Adolfo with troubled eyes. "Master Adolfo, we have lost four of our brothers in the past few days, and others have been injured badly enough during the time we've been in this land that they've had to give up our great work." He hesitated, then the rest of the words came out in a rush. "This isn't our land. These aren't our people, our families. Why do we have to be here?"

Adolfo had wondered when that question would be asked. "We are here *because* of our land, our people, our families. If we do not cleanse this foul witch magic from Sylvalan, it can creep over the border and root again in Wolfram. There are already indications that the cleansing was not as thorough in Arktos as we had thought. You've already seen that the power here is stronger than anything we've stood against. The Evil One embraces many here."

He studied his men. They were already tired, and they were frightened. The Small Folk didn't have more than what was considered mischief magic, but even that kind of magic could become deadly when the Small Folk banded together. They hadn't been able to stop the cleansing of the witches from the Old Places simply because they hadn't realized what was happening until it was too late. Even so, in Sylvalan they were a force to be reckoned with, and the Fae's presence was stronger here as well. He had no doubt that this land could be cleansed of the magic that kept men from their rightful place as master and ruler, but the work was proving to be more dangerous here.

"The safety of Wolfram rests on our shoulders. We cannot put down the task we have been given. However, from now on, you must work in pairs so that you can keep watch for each other. You will continue your search for the witches. But seek *only* the witches. Do not concern yourselves with the females who embrace the witch's ways and do not conduct themselves with proper chasteness and modesty. They have no true magic and can be dealt with later. Use the power of the Inquisitor's Gift to seek out the real witches. Crush their magic swiftly, and go on before anything has time to rally against you. At the end of the summer, we will all meet again at Rivercross—and we will go home for the cold months of winter. We will go home to rest and regain our strength so that we may continue our great battle against the Evil One and his whores."

He had said the right thing, Adolfo decided as he saw the determination in his Inquisitors' eyes. They would cleanse the eastern border of Sylvalan to keep Wolfram, their homeland, safe. Then they would go home. And he would never tell them that it wasn't consideration or concern for them that had decided him; it was the woman on the dark horse who had ridden out of the woods and snatched his nephew's spirit from his body. He knew the stories about the Fae who were called Death's Servants. They could guide a spirit that had already left the dead flesh, but they couldn't take it while the flesh still lived. But there was one who was Death's Mistress, one who could ride through a village and leave nothing but corpses in her wake. Having Death's Servants picking around like crows on a battlefield was one thing; having the Gatherer become curious about the deaths around the Old Places was another.

So his men would do their work until the seasons changed, and then they would go home to a land where magic had been choked back to a whisper. Hopefully, by the time they returned in the spring, the Gatherer would have moved on to some other part of Sylvalan.

Chapter Eighteen

"**I**t's not that I'm not grateful to have soup and bread to eat," Ari muttered as she stirred the vegetable soup without enthusiasm. "But it's *all* I've had to eat since yesterday."

Didn't matter. There wasn't quite enough flour to make a new loaf of bread. By tomorrow, this watery soup she'd put together from the dwindling supply of vegetables she had canned last harvest would be the only thing she could put on the table. There were enough greens in the garden to enjoy the taste of something fresh, but not enough to fill an empty belly. She had done her best last year when she'd faced doing all the work alone for the first time. This year she would simply have to do better.

This was the last evening before the dark of the moon, the last evening when she was bound to the promise she had made at the Summer Moon. That didn't matter either. She knew Lucian wouldn't come simply to visit. Just as well. Her heart was feeling a bit raw and tender. She didn't need to be told again in one way or another that men only found her interesting when she provided sex.

"Hullo the house!"

Hurrying to look out the open half of the kitchen door, Ari winced when she saw Neall check his stride as he noticed the wash that was still drying on the line. She knew she was blushing because he'd seen her underclothes, and she hoped he wouldn't know what the long rectangles of cloth were for.

"How are you feeling?" he asked as soon as he was close enough to speak without raising his voice.

He knew.

"I'm fine, Neall. And you?"

"I'm fine as well." He looked over her shoulder. "Are you alone?"

Pride nipped her. "No, I'm not—" She clamped her teeth. There was no reason to snap at Neall—or let wounded pride make her dishonest. "Yes, I'm alone." She hesitated, then added in a low voice, "I'm not expecting anyone."

He gave her a sweet, almost wistful smile. "Want some company? Besides my own charming self—and this idiotic beast," he grumbled as he put his shoulder against Darcy, who was trying to push past him, and shoved. "*Wait.* She'll pet you when she's ready to pet you."

The gelding backed up a couple of steps, making noises that sounded like muttering.

Neall let out an exasperated sigh. "You realize if the bottom half of this door wasn't latched, he'd be in the kitchen with you."

Ari bit her lip to keep from laughing.

"Besides our charming selves," Neall said, narrowing his eyes at the gelding when it snorted, "I brought these." He lifted a string and showed her two salmon she hadn't noticed because she was too busy feeling embarrassed.

Ari's heart pounded. Her palms were suddenly sweaty. "Neall . . ." she said weakly. "I know you're Baron Felston's relative, but poaching is a serious offense. And you've said yourself that the baron doesn't permit *anyone* to fish in the streams of his land. If you're brought before the magistrate . . ."

"Are you going to summon the magistrate?"

Ari frowned. He was her friend. How could he think she would betray him?

"I got these from a stream on your land," Neall said. "Since I'm giving them to you, that doesn't really count as poaching, does it?"

A heaviness that had been closing around her heart vanished. "Oh." The word was breathed out in a sigh of relief. "Oh, in that case . . ." She paused. "But Neall, shouldn't you be attending your work instead of spending so much time fishing in my stream? Won't the baron be angry?"

"The work isn't going anywhere. It can wait for a day. Besides, it didn't take long to catch these fellows. But they won't be worth much if we don't get them into some water."

"Of course." Ari opened the lower half of the door. "Come in and be welcome."

Neall slipped in, closing the door just quickly enough to prevent Darcy from joining them. "See what I mean?" he muttered. He pumped water into the large oval basin that served as the kitchen sink, then set the salmon in it. Revived by the water, they began to move in the basin.

Watching them, Ari's mouth watered. "Neall, they're wonderful. I haven't eaten salmon since the last one Mother caught."

"Why not?"

"In order to eat one, you have to catch it first. Water isn't one of my branches of the Great Mother."

A puzzled look came and went in his eyes. "Do you know what to do with it?" he asked.

It was foolish to let pride ruin a fine meal. "No. Mother always cooked the fish."

"Then I'll make you a bargain. If you're willing to share the smaller one, I'll clean it and cook it."

She held out her hand so fast to seal the bargain he jumped. When he clasped her hand, he held it for several seconds. His hand felt warm and strong, more callused than a gentleman's hands were supposed to be, but Neall had never shirked when work needed to be done.

Feeling confused and a bit too warm, she turned away. "I— We could have what's left of the bread drizzled with honey or jam."

"Sounds fine."

"And there's some early greens ready to be picked." She nibbled on her lower lip. "But there's nothing to dress them with. And there's no butter to cook the fish."

Neall said nothing.

Would he make some excuse and leave now? Ari wondered. Gathering her courage, she turned to face him. He was staring thoughtfully at the salmon.

"Fish doesn't keep well. How's the ice cellar?"

"There's enough ice left to keep most things from spoiling, but I don't think the fish would keep for more than a day."

He nodded as if he expected that answer. "We'll trade," he said decisively. "Ahern is fond of salmon, and he grumbles often enough that the streams on his land don't have fish worth the effort of catching them. If we wrap the big one in straw and cloth and wet it down well, I can ride over to his farm and see what he'll trade for it."

"All right." Ari hesitated. How much would a fish be worth? "Perhaps some butter and a little salt?"

Neall hesitated, then leaned forward and kissed her cheek. "Leave the bargaining to me."

A few minutes later, he had the salmon wrapped.

Ari stared at the remaining salmon. Now that it had some room to swim in, it was acting more lively. A bit *too* lively.

Neall stepped outside and latched the bottom of the kitchen door. "Ari," he called softly.

She didn't like the way he was grinning at her.

"If it jumps out of the basin, don't leave it flopping about on the floor. Catch it and toss it back in."

"Jumps?" Ari said, snapping her head around to stare at the too-lively fish. She knew salmon jumped. Of course she knew that. She had seen them leap to get past small waterfalls in the stream, but . . . "It's going to jump in my *kitchen*?"

Ari leaped for the kitchen door, reaching it just in time to see Neall, grinning gleefully, put his heels to Darcy's sides and take off around the cottage.

"Neall!"

Racing through the cottage, she scrabbled to get the front door unlatched and flung it open. Neall was already cresting the low rise on the other side of the road.

"*Neall!*"

The gelding went down the other side of the rise, and Neall was gone.

Latching the door, Ari returned to the kitchen. Grabbing a small frying pan from its hook on the wall, she approached the sink warily. "If you jump, I'll smack you." She held up the frying pan to show the fish she meant it.

The salmon thrashed in the basin. The tail lifted, flinging water right in Ari's face.

Slowly, Ari set the frying pan down. Moving as far away from the sink as she could, she gathered the jars of honey and jam, then sliced the bread she had left.

"He knew this would happen. He knew it. He's probably just sorry he wasn't here to see it." She glared at the salmon. "You know, if he takes his sweet time getting back from Ahern's, you're not the only one who's going to feel a frying pan."

Neall grinned as Darcy galloped toward Ahern's farm.

Ari's lover was a fool. A wonderful, wonderful fool. Imagine getting squeamish about something so natural. The man could have had the pleasure of spending time with her, could have enjoyed just being with her. But he'd walked away because he couldn't have the bed. Tomorrow the dark of the moon began, and Ari would no longer be obliged to open her door or her arms to this stranger she'd met somewhere at the Summer Moon.

May the Great Mother bless the man all the days of his life for being a wonderful, wonderful fool.

Neall's grin widened.

And may She bless Ari as well. He knew she'd been struggling and didn't have enough coins to buy meat very often. But he hadn't realized that she hadn't made use of what would have been freely given until she'd told him how long it had been since she'd had fresh fish to eat.

What he'd told her was true. He *hadn't* spent much time catching the salmon. He'd simply gone to the stream and quietly stood on the bank. When a few of the water sprites who lived in and around the stream had asked why the young Lord of the Woods was just standing there, he had told them he wanted a salmon for Ari. They disappeared into the stream, and a few minutes later two salmon were being herded toward him. He had thanked the water sprites and taken the salmon. As simple as that.

He had stopped trying to explain to the Small Folk that he wasn't a Lord of the Woods. True, his understanding of the woods and the creatures that lived there had always been keen—and might have come from the man who had sired his father. And there was no denying that there were times, when meat was truly needed, when a rabbit or a young buck seemed to offer itself to his bow. But having a Fae grandfather didn't make *him* Fae. However, that didn't stop him from accepting whatever fealty was offered when he needed it.

The gelding refused to check its speed when they reached Ahern's yard, causing a couple of men who worked for Ahern to fling themselves out of the way to avoid being knocked over. A few yards away from the old man, the horse sat on its haunches, stopping so fast Neall almost went flying.

"We're going to have to talk about this," Neall muttered. Swinging one leg over Darcy's neck, he jumped to the ground and held up the wet sack. "I've come to barter."

The stern disapproval in Ahern's eyes didn't change. "You ride in here like a pack of shadow hounds are on your heels just to *barter*?" He shook his head. "I have nothing to offer the baron—" He looked over Neall's shoulder.

Neall turned to see what had caught Ahern's attention. The gelding was now facing the way they had come, its ears pricked. It took two steps forward.

"Wait for me," Neall warned.

Darcy took one step back and snorted.

Ahern looked at the gelding, then at the land the animal was aiming for.

"You haven't come to barter for the baron's table," Ahern said.

"No, sir."

Nodding, Ahern pointed at the sack. "What have you to trade?"

Neall grinned. "A salmon. A big beauty that's still so fresh it will slap you with its tail."

"In that case, come inside and we'll talk."

"You robbed him," Ari said, sounding too relaxed to be upset.

"I bargained well," Neall corrected. They were sitting on the bench behind the cottage, enjoying a fine summer evening.

"You cleaned out Ahern's larder."

"Did not. I only took what my saddlebags could hold." He didn't want her chewing over that too much, so he said, "Did you have enough to eat?"

She let out a laughing groan in answer.

Smiling, Neall took her hand. When she didn't pull away, he leaned back against the cottage and closed his eyes, content.

The bargaining *had* been fierce, and it had taken every ounce of persuasion he'd had to convince Ahern that he could only take so much for one fish without Ari starting to wonder if it was a fair barter or charity. Mentioning charity had made Ahern so angry Neall had thought the old man would strike him. But they both knew Ari, they both knew she could be stubborn to the point of being foolish, and they both knew her pride was the only thing that made it possible for her to face the people of Ridgeley. And bruising pride with too much kindness wasn't kindness at all. So they haggled and argued until Neall had promised to bring

another salmon or two in a few days and pick up the
rest of the supplies Ahern insisted Ari should have.

"Will the baron be angry about your ignoring your
work?" Ari asked. "Will he wonder where you are?"

"He doesn't give a damn where I am. He never has
unless he wants something. As for the work, let Royce
take care of it. After all, the estate and all the tenant
farms will be his one day."

He felt her turn to face him. He kept his eyes
closed.

"What will you do when that day comes, Neall?"
Ari asked quietly. "Will you work for Royce and take
what handouts he chooses to give?"

Neall hesitated, then thought, *Plant the seed now.
Give it time to take root.* "I have some land of my own.
It's in the west, about a day's ride from the coast. It
belonged to my mother. When my parents died, it came
to me. Now that I've reached my majority, it's time for
me to go home."

That shook her enough to make her hand tremble
in his.

"Why—" Ari drew in a deep breath, then let it out
slowly. "Why have you never said anything about
this?"

"Because my gentry relatives are greedy. The baron
would have made my life even more miserable if he'd
known there was something that belonged to me that
he couldn't use while I was under his roof. Besides, I
don't own the land in that way." He paused. "I did
tell your grandmother about the land. She told me it
would be a secret between us until I was ready to
share it with someone else. That she thought I was
wise not to tell anyone was the main reason I've been
able to keep it a secret for so long."

"And now you've told me," Ari said softly. "Thank
you."

He opened his eyes and looked at her. She seemed
to be working hard to remain calm, and that gave him
hope. "I wanted you to know there was land waiting
to be cherished again, that there was a place to go."

"The anniversary of your birthing day was weeks ago. You should have left then so that you'd have time to put in your own crops."

"I had reason to stay."

She pressed her lips together. "When are you going?"

"That depends on you." He watched her eyes widen with shock. He gently squeezed her hand. "If you know in your heart that you will never think of me as anything more than a friend, I hope you'll be honest enough to tell me—and I'll go alone. But if there's a chance that you could care for me as a lover and a wife, I'll wait for you, Ari."

"Neall . . ."

He shook his head. "Don't say anything now."

Ari looked at the meadow and the forest beyond. "I care for you, Neall. I do. But my family has looked after Brightwood for generations. It's my duty to stay here."

"Perhaps it's time for someone else to take care of Brightwood," he said quietly. "Perhaps it's time to make a new life somewhere else. Think about it, Ari. Please."

Releasing her hand, he stood up. "I need to get back now. Can I help you with anything before I go?"

Ari shook her head.

"Then I'd better stir my four-legged friend and convince him it's time to leave." He took a few steps toward the part of the meadow where the gelding was grazing before Ari called him back.

She was wringing her hands and looked so distressed he regretted that he had spoiled her peace.

"Neall . . . Even if I could leave Brightwood, it's not our way to marry."

"Sometimes it is," he said hurriedly. "My mother married my father, and they were happy." When she looked puzzled, he thought, *I hadn't meant to say that, hadn't intended to tell her—at least, not yet—but now I have to tell her all of it. One way or the other, it might make the difference in the answer.* "My mother's branch was earth. There was nothing she touched that wouldn't grow."

Ari stared at him. "Your mother was a witch?"

"Yes. And my father was half Fae." There was bitterness in his smile. "From things the baron has said, I gather the family had been embarrassed to have to acknowledge a child sired by one of the Fae. So they had been quite willing to forget about my father when he came of age and headed west to make his own fortune. The only thing they knew about my mother was that my father had married her."

"Why are you telling me this?"

"Because I don't want any secrets between us. Because I want you to know who I came from." He leaned down and kissed her cheek. "And now I'll go. Blessings of the day to you, Ari."

"Blessings of the day to you, Neall," she whispered.

All the way back to the baron's estate, he wondered if he'd done the right thing, if he should have waited to tell her about his parents and the land. Since he couldn't take back the words, he hoped he'd made the right choice.

Chapter Nineteen

"**S**omething has to be done," Dianna said, pacing the length of the terrace that overlooked her favorite garden.

"What *can* be done?" Lyrra asked. "The new moon has begun its journey—and Lucian hasn't gone down the road through the Veil since the day he returned early."

"Has he said anything to Aiden about *why* he returned early that night?"

Lyrra shook her head. "He's still brooding, and there's a look in his eyes that helps one remember that he's the Lord of Fire."

"We can't just sit here." Dianna stopped pacing and squared her shoulders. "There's one way to find out if Ari has become an enemy."

Lyrra paled a little. "You're going down to the cottage?"

"She doesn't know I'm Fae. I can pay a visit without arousing suspicion."

"Be careful, Dianna."

"With Tir Alainn at stake, you can rest assured that I'll be careful."

Returning to her suite, Dianna pulled the riding habit from the wardrobe. She paused, considered. If that male who had shown up at Ari's the last time she had visited had been speaking the truth, she could save herself the trouble of riding sidesaddle. And it wasn't as if she was intending to go riding where the human gentry would see her.

She dropped the riding habit on her bed and chose

one of her usual riding outfits—a skirt as light as cobwebs that buttoned over slim trousers and a simple
blouse made of fine linen. That would do quite well.

A few minutes later, as she was heading for the
stables, she heard a quiet whine.

The bitch that used to be her favorite approached
hesitantly, the dark eyes pleading to be forgiven for
whatever it had done that had made its mistress turn
away from it. Beside the bitch were the three pups,
the two that showed no outward trace of the undesirable sire and the third, which she couldn't bear to
look at.

She turned away, then turned back and snatched the
third puppy. It cried as if it knew the person holding it
despised its existence.

The bitch whined.

"It will be well taken care of," Dianna said. She
hurried to the stables before she had too much time
to think . . . and change her mind.

Wanting to avoid Ahern's farm for this visit, and
gambling that Ari didn't know horses well enough to
be alarmed at seeing a "gentry" lady riding a Fae
horse, she had the grooms saddle her pale mare. The
pup was wrapped in a piece of blanket so that it
couldn't squirm around. With one arm holding the
pup, Dianna cantered down the road that led through
the Veil.

Reaching Brightwood, she followed the forest trails
until she came to the road and was riding toward Ari's
cottage from the same direction she'd come before.

Ari, naturally, was working in the garden.

"Dianna," Ari said, surprise and pleasure in her
voice.

*She didn't expect me to return after I learned she
was a witch.*

"Blessings of the day to you," Ari said.

"Blessings of the day to you," Dianna replied, chok-
ing a little on speaking a witch's greeting. *They think
you're the Queen of the Witches. Speaking their words
won't set your tongue on fire.*

"I see you've forsaken gentry fashion for practicality," Ari teased.

Dismounting easily, Dianna gave Ari a cool stare. "I would prefer to be thought a peasant than deal with an insolent man."

"Oh." Ari seemed to be working through several replies, but ended up shrugging. "Neall can be opinionated at times."

Neall. A name spoken with easy familiarity. "Do you know him well?"

"We're friends."

You say that as if you're not quite sure. I wonder if Lucian was aware he had a rival.

The puppy squirmed.

"What's that?" Ari asked.

"Something I brought for you." Dianna unwrapped the puppy and held it out.

Her eyes lighting, Ari reached for the puppy and held him up so that they were nose to nose. "You're adorable."

The puppy licked her nose, making her laugh.

Ari's delight made Dianna smile. "He seems to think the same about you."

Cradling the puppy, Ari said, "He's wonderful, Dianna, but I can't accept him. He's obviously a valuable animal, and—"

Dianna waved her hand dismissively. "He has no value. He's deformed." Seeing Ari's stricken look and the way her arms tightened protectively around the puppy, Dianna bit her tongue. What use was it to give something and then say it had no value? "You're correct that the bitch is a valuable animal, but the quality of the sire is . . . suspect. The coloring is wrong."

Ari looked down at the puppy. "Wrong? But he has a beautiful merle coat."

Dianna bit her tongue again to keep from saying something else that would make the pup completely worthless—or saying something that would clearly tell Ari that the pup had come from a shadow hound.

"Yes, it is, but the breeder is very particular about coloring. So the pup has no worth for the breeder. But there's nothing *wrong* with him, and I thought he would have a good home with you."

There was still hesitation there. Dianna choked back frustration. The girl obviously liked the puppy. Why couldn't she just accept it?

"I—I suppose he eats meat."

"He's a dog. Of course he eats—" Dianna stopped, suddenly remembering that Ari hadn't offered any meat with the meal she'd prepared the last time Dianna visited. "Don't you eat meat?"

"Yes, I do—when I can afford it."

Dianna looked away. With every turn, there was another obstacle.

Ari caressed the puppy. "We'll find a way."

Dianna narrowed her eyes as she looked at the forest. "Don't you hunt?"

Ari smiled ruefully. "Neall taught me how to shoot a bow, and I can hit the bulls-eye in a target, but I can't hit anything when it stands there and looks at me."

Neall again. Maybe this Neall could make himself useful and provide some meat.

"Thank you, Dianna. The puppy will be a good friend."

Uncomfortable, despite the fact that Ari's gratitude was exactly what she'd hoped to achieve when she'd brought the pup, Dianna turned away, then stopped when she noticed the bare cottage wall. "The flowers didn't bloom?"

"Bloom?" Ari laughed. "The seeds have all sprouted and the plants are growing well, but they don't grow *that* quickly. They'll have flowers by the Solstice."

Solstice? That long? In Tir Alainn, the plants would already be in full bloom. Diana studied the vegetable garden. Small green things covered the ground between the paths of flat stones, but there was nothing ready for the table. "How long do you have to wait?"

"Harvest will begin in a couple of months."

Dianna didn't know what to say. "Are you still planting?"

"No, the planting is done. I was doing a bit of weeding and watering before the day got too warm."

"I'll help you." Catching Ari's apprehensive look, she added with prickly arrogance, "I may not be able to plant, but surely I'm capable enough to pour water."

Ari tipped her head, her expression thoughtful. "Why do you want to help?"

"Because I can't work in a garden at home," she replied without thinking.

"You're troubled, aren't you?"

About many things I cannot speak of. Not to you. "I have some concerns."

Ari nodded. "Working in the earth doesn't provide solutions to problems, but it can ease the heart. The clothes you wore the last time are in the trunk in the dressing room."

Dianna smiled. "I'll find them."

"I'll look after the mare . . ." Ari's eyes widened when she finally took a good look at the pale mare.

Dianna tensed. Could Fae magic cloud a witch's mind?

"You should meet old Ahern someday," Ari said. "He has beautiful horses, too."

"We're acquainted," Dianna said tersely.

"Oh dear. Did he admire the mare too much or too little?" When Dianna didn't answer, Ari added, "I just wondered because he has a gray stallion that he might have wanted to mate with your mare."

Dianna choked. No. The girl *couldn't* know the gray stallion was the Lord of the Horse in his other form. Although . . . There *were* some unsavory legends that said such matings were how the Fae horses had been created in the first place.

"I'll change my clothes," Dianna said. Leaving Ari to deal with puppy and mare, she hurried to the kitchen door.

"Go in and be welcome," Ari called.

That constant welcoming must be a witch custom, Dianna decided. Did it have to be said every time a person visiting walked out of the cottage and wanted to go back in? It must be a tedious custom if that were true. She'd have to ask. It wouldn't seem strange to ask since she knew Ari was a witch. And the Fae needed to know as much as they could.

There was only one trunk in the dressing room, and the tunic and trousers, washed and neatly folded, were lying on top of the other garments. Taking the clothes, Dianna closed the trunk and looked around. One side of the room contained a wooden chest with drawers as well as two staggered rows of pegs that she suspected held all the clothes Ari owned. The other side of the room contained a small desk, a threadbare chair that, nonetheless, looked comfortable, and a table with an oil lamp. It also contained a bookcase with leaded glass doors.

The bookcase was the finest piece of furniture in the cottage, speaking of a time when Ari's family must have had more wealth than was apparent now. Peering through the glass, Dianna frowned. The books inside didn't look impressive. All about the same size and thickness, they were bound in leather and reminded her more of the journals she'd heard gentry women were fond of keeping than tomes that had any value. Opening the bookcase, she took out the last book and opened it to the first page.

I am Astra, now the Crone of the family. It is with sorrow that I have read the journals of the ones who came before me. We shouldered the burden and then were dismissed from thought—or were treated as paupers who should beg for scraps of affection. We have stayed because we loved the land, and we have stayed out of duty. But duty is a cold bedfellow, and it should no longer be enough to hold us to the land. I don't think my daughter will listen, but I hope I can find the words to tell Ari—

"What are you doing?"

Dianna jumped, surprised by Ari's sudden appear-

ance as well as the anger in the girl's voice. "I saw
the books and wanted to look—"

"Those are my family's *private* journals. They
weren't written as entertainment for the *gentry*."

"I—"

Words of apology and explanation died when Ari
snatched the journal from Dianna's hands, carefully
replaced it in the bookcase, and closed the leaded
glass door. Keeping her back to Dianna, she said,
"Even a friend should respect privacy."

"I meant no harm, Ari. Truly. I thought they were
just books, and I was curious." Dianna paused, wondering how badly her next question would offend.
"Have you read them?"

Ari shook her head. "Only the crone has the age
and the experience to read them, and she is the one
who records the next chapter in our history." She
turned to face Dianna. "I am in no hurry to read
them. I think they have some awful tales to tell."

"What could be so awful?"

"I don't know. But the year my grandmother's body
declared her fully a crone, she read the journals over
the winter. My mother and I watched her grow old
during that time, as if a heavy burden weighed on her
heart. She didn't live to see another winter. So I'm in
no hurry to find out what bent a strong woman until
she broke."

"I'm sorry." She looked at the tunic and trousers,
and felt a pang of regret that she wouldn't feel the
earth beneath her hands. "Perhaps it would be better
if I didn't stay today," she said, hoping Ari would
politely disagree.

"I think that would be for the best."

Dianna walked to the doorway, then looked over
her shoulder. "I meant no harm. I hope we can be
friends again on another day." *When your anger has
faded—or you become lonely enough to overlook what
was, after all, a mistake.*

"On another day," Ari agreed.

The mare was still saddled. A bucket of water stood

nearby, still cool to the touch. Ari must have drawn the water from the well and then realized she had sent a stranger into the room that held what her family prized the most.

When Dianna mounted, the puppy yapped at her as if he knew he no longer needed to fear what she thought of him.

I hope I did at least that much right, Dianna thought as she took the long way around to reach the shining road through the Veil. *And I hope she will greet me as a friend on another day—not just because we need to understand her kind, but also because I like her.*

"Falco!" Hurrying toward her quarry, Dianna ignored the startled looks of the other men standing with the Lord of the Hawks. She also ignored Falco's protest when she grabbed his arm and pulled him out of the room.

"Dianna! Is something wrong?"

"Yes. No. Not exactly." She'd thought this over on the ride home. Her gift would be enjoyed more if there was a way to feed it, and there *was* something she could do about *that.* "I want you to catch a rabbit."

Falco started to reply, then changed his mind—twice. "You want me to catch a rabbit," he finally repeated.

He was acting like it was an odd request—which it was, but that was beside the point. "Yes."

Falco smiled hesitantly, as if he would be willing to share the joke, even one at his expense, if she would just explain it to him.

"I want you to go down to the human world, shift to your other form, catch a rabbit, and take it to the cottage near the sea." When he still hesitated, she snapped, "Why is this so difficult? You *like* catching rabbits. You've said so."

"That's the witch's cottage," Falco said carefully. "The one the Lightbringer warned me to stay away from."

"And now, I, the Huntress, am giving you a new command."

"Why?" Falco asked, sounding a little frightened. "If I'm going to have his wrath come down on me, at least tell me why."

Dianna winced. She had hoped she wouldn't have to reveal that much. "I gave her a puppy."

"You—" Falco's mouth fell open. "You gave the witch a *shadow hound*?"

"It was one of the mongrels, of no value to us," Dianna said testily. "Not really a shadow hound at all."

"But—"

Chaining her own agitated feelings, Dianna rested her hands on Falco's shoulders, as much to give comfort as to keep him from bolting—possibly straight to Lucian.

"Falco, Aiden feels certain that the witches are involved in some way with what's happening to Tir Alainn. This one is young, and not against us." At least, she hoped not. "If we are her friends, she won't want to do us harm. She might even be able to help us understand what is happening, might even be able to help us stop it. The puppy needs to be fed, so she needs the extra meat." She studied his eyes and realized Lucian's temper wasn't the only reason he was wary of approaching the cottage. "You don't have to stay. Just leave the rabbit where it can be found easily."

"All right." He stepped back, bowed to indicate this was a formal discussion, then quickly walked away.

"Falco!" Dianna called before he turned a corner. "It might be best not to mention this to anyone for the time being."

He gave her a measuring look, the same look she imagined was in a man's eyes when he was ordered into a battle he knew he couldn't win.

"Huntress, there is no one I want to mention this to."

*   *   *

Yap. Yap yap yap.

Ari looked at the cow shed guiltily. She'd never had a puppy before, but it had only taken a few minutes to convince her that puppies and young gardens weren't a good match. Since she didn't want to let him out on his own until he got used to his new home, she'd spent a few minutes running around the meadow with him to tire him out, then put him in the cow shed with a pan of fresh water. She'd have to ask Neall if he had any ideas about how to teach a puppy not to squat in the house.

Yap. Yap yap yap.

A couple more chores, then she'd let him out and find something for both of them to eat for the midday—

"AAIIIEEEEE!"

Ari raced to the cow shed, pulled open the door, and just stood there, not certain if the puppy or the small man clinging to the top rail of the stall would be more offended if she laughed.

"Don't just stand there!" the small man shouted. "Get an ax and defend yourself!"

Oh dear.

Ari grabbed the puppy and held the indignant bundle of fur close. For something so small and young, he was certainly a fierce little creature.

"It's all right," Ari said.

Yap yap. Grrr.

"All right?" the small man shrieked. "I come in here to get a bit of rest and find this hulking great beast ready to tear off my limbs, and you think it's all right?"

"Hush!" Ari said to the puppy.

After one more *yap*, the puppy hushed. The small man glared.

"He's just a puppy," Ari said soothingly. "You probably startled him as much as he startled you."

"Not likely since he's got a meaner set of teeth."

"He's a puppy."

The small man made himself more comfortable on

the top rail. "Puppy," he said ominously. "You mean to say that hulking beast is going to get *bigger*? How much bigger?"

"I don't know. But he's bound to get a little bigger than he is now."

The small man looked at the puppy. His eyes narrowed. "A stray you found in the woods, was he?"

"No, a . . . friend . . . gave him to me."

"Friend."

"Yes, she—" Startled by a hawk's cry, Ari turned toward the door. She heard the small man scramble down the stall rails, felt him brush against her legs as he cautiously peered out of the door.

"You've got company," he said in an odd voice.

A hawk stood on the chopping block, a rabbit held securely in one taloned foot. He watched them in a way that made Ari uneasy.

"Do you suppose some of the gentry are out hunting, and one of their hawks strayed too far into Brightwood?"

"No jesses," the small man said. "That one belongs to no one but himself."

"Why would a wild hawk bring his kill so close to a cottage?"

"That's something you'll have to ask *him*." The small man paused. "Best to leave the hulking wee beast here. No use having him killed before you have a chance to be annoyed with him."

"But . . ." Ari looked at the hawk. "Surely it would just fly away if the puppy ran after it."

"If it was only a hawk, it might do just that."

A chill ran through her. It deepened when she saw the small man pull a sling and a couple of stones from his pockets. The Small Folk were as skilled at hunting with slings as they were with bows.

"You'd best go out and see what the Fae Lord wants. The sooner his business here is finished, the sooner he'll be gone."

"Fae? If he's . . . If he knows . . . Surely he can't mean me harm. I mean, the Fae Lord I've met was friendly." More than friendly. Just remembering Lucian's kisses made her knees weak. Or, perhaps, it was remembering his anger the last time she saw him that was producing that effect.

"Oh, they're always friendly when they get want they want. It's when they don't that you have to take care. The Fair Folk have a streak of meanness in them. They have that in common with humans." His smile was grim and malicious. "Go on out now. I'll see you come to no harm."

Setting the puppy down and hoping he would understand somehow what *stay* meant, she wiped her suddenly sweaty hands on her tunic and walked slowly toward the chopping block.

"Blessings of the day to you, brother hawk."

The hawk stared at her, looked down at the rabbit, then back at her.

"That's a fine rabbit you have."

The hawk ruffled its feathers. Waited.

What was it waiting for? Ari wondered. If this *was* a Fae Lord, what did he expect of her? He couldn't . . . Oh, Mother's mercy, he couldn't think she would open her arms to any of them simply because Lucian had been her lover. Could he?

After a long pause, when neither of them moved, the hawk released the rabbit. Waited.

"You brought the rabbit for me?" Ari asked. Why would he do that? Not that the meat wouldn't be welcome, especially with the pup.

Moving slowly, stretching her arm as far as she could to keep her face away from the beak and talons, Ari's hand gripped the rabbit. She stepped back, still holding the rabbit out, ready to drop it if the hawk seemed angry.

It just watched her.

Finally, when it lifted its wings, Ari said, "You did the work, so you should have part of the bounty. Wait a moment, if you please."

Hurrying into the kitchen, she pulled the largest knife she owned from the wood block, put the rabbit in the kitchen basin, and cut off a hind leg. Grabbing a towel to hold under the leg and catch the blood, she went back out and set the leg on the chopping block.

She almost thought she saw surprise in the hawk's eyes.

"Thank you for the rabbit."

Another pause. Then the hawk sank its talons into the rabbit leg and flew off.

Ari sank to the ground, her legs suddenly feeling too watery to hold her up.

The puppy barreled out of the cow shed, yapping frantically.

She looked at the small man walking toward her and wondered what magic he had used to keep the pup quiet and contained.

"You did well, Mistress Ari," the small man said.

"It could have been just a hawk."

"And I could be a giant." His expression was grim. "This friend who gave you the pup. What's she look like?"

"She's fair-haired, has light brown eyes, and," Ari added, attempting to smile, "she's fairly useless in the garden. I thought even gentry ladies knew plants wouldn't bloom in a handful of days. She does have some fine horses, though. Especially the gray mare she was riding this morning."

"She rides a pale mare."

Puzzled at the odd phrasing, Ari said, "Yes. At least she did today. Do you know her?"

"I've seen her." He didn't seem pleased about that.

As if it knew who they were talking about, the puppy whined and climbed into Ari's lap.

"I'd best be about my business," the small man said. "Take care, Mistress Ari."

Ari watched him walk across the meadow. Despite watching, she lost sight of him long before he reached the woods. But that was the way with the Small Folk. They were never seen unless they chose to be seen.

Had he been right about the hawk? *Had* it been a Fae Lord? Why would *any* Fae be showing themselves

now? They'd never done so before. At least not that
she could recall. Was it just curiosity because Lucian
had been with her, and his presence here had been
taken by some of the others as tacit permission to
make her aware of them? Or was it something more?
And if it *was* more, what did they suddenly want
from her?

And what *hadn't* the small man said about the pup
and Dianna?

Sighing, Ari rubbed her nose against the puppy's
head. "Come on. There's a rabbit waiting for us. A
stew for me and meat for you. And while the stew is
cooking, we have an important task— finding the right
name for you."

Neall leaned over, cupped his hands under the spill of
water, and drank. The last handful he splashed over
his face.

They could use a soft, soaking rain. The streams
and creeks were already running a bit low, and crops
weren't growing as well as they should. To make
things worse, the tenant farmers had chosen yesterday,
when he'd been with Ari, to bring their complaints
and concerns to Baron Felston's bailiff. The bailiff, in
turn, had brought them to the baron's attention. And
Felston had blamed Neall's "sloth" for fewer acres
being planted and the lack of rain to help what was
planted grow.

How many times had he told Baron Felston that
people would not starve through the winter in order
to plant full acres in the spring when the reward for
the hunger and hard work was to have more of it
taken in tithes. Being blamed, again, for the problems
caused by Felston's greed was the last wound in a
lifetime of such wounds. Today, while riding to all the
tenant farms to verify the complaints—as if he needed
to do again what he'd been doing since the spring—
he was trying to decide if he was going to head west
to his mother's land and come back later for Ari, or
if he was going to try to find a place nearby where he

could stay and work while she considered whether she was going with him or staying at Brightwood.

He filled his canteen and stepped away from the creek. "Come on," he told Darcy. "Let's get this finished."

A round stone hit his boot hard enough to sting.

He scanned the strip of woods that separated a couple of fields. Saw nothing.

"You would be wise to look to Brightwood, young Lord," said a gruff voice.

Nothing more. There was no use searching. There would be nothing to see, no one to find.

Neall threw himself into the saddle. The Small Folk didn't give idle warnings, which meant something had happened that they wanted him to know about.

"Brightwood," he said, letting the gelding choose its own speed. If Felston punished him for shirking his duties, so be it. What the baron wanted wasn't worth a pebble compared to Ari.

When he and Darcy reached the cottage, they were both sweating heavily from the hard, fast run.

"Ari!" Neall kicked out of the stirrups and leaped out of the saddle in a way that would probably get him killed with any other horse.

What could be wrong here? Had something happened to her? The only weapon he had was his work knife, and *that* wasn't going to help much. He drew it out of the sheath in his boot and promised himself that he wouldn't go out again without at least a bow and quiver.

"Neall?"

Her voice was faint. He turned, trying to catch the direction. The gelding figured it out faster and ambled toward the privy that stood a few feet from the cow shed.

Neall ran to the privy, reached for the door—and had enough sense left to hesitate. "Ari?"

"Neall?" she squeaked.

"Yes, it's Neall."

"Go away."

"Damn it, I will *not* go away!" He reached for the door again.

"Neall . . . go stand by the well for a minute or two. Please."

Starting to feel foolish, and angry because he did, he turned and strode to the well. "Walk," he told Darcy. "Go on, take a bit of a walk around the meadow to cool down. Then you can have some water."

Darcy snorted, looked at the privy, then began an easy walk around the meadow.

Neall watched for a few seconds to make sure the gelding would walk and not start to graze. May the Mother bless Ahern. He didn't know how the man managed to raise horses that had more brains than any others, but he was grateful the old man had been willing to sell the gelding to him.

Filling a bucket from the well, he stripped off his sweaty shirt, then used the dipper Ari kept on a hook to pour water over himself.

A bit of maliciousness? Was that all the warning had been?

Darcy paused, snuffled something in the grass, then shied and trotted back toward him.

Neall saw a gray body with black streaks rise out of the grass and felt his heart trip.

Yap. Yap yap yap.

The puppy raced toward him. The breath he'd been holding came out in a rush of relief when he saw the tan front legs.

A few feet away from him, the puppy tripped over its feet and somersaulted until it ended up nose to toes with his boot. It yapped fiercely at his boot until Darcy, curious now, came up behind it and snorted on its tail.

Yipping, the puppy tucked its tail between its legs and ran for the privy. Ari came out, picked up the puppy, and headed toward the well. She looked frustrated and annoyed—until she noticed that the gelding was lathered. Then worry filled her eyes.

"What's wrong?" she asked.

Feeling too many things that weren't comfortable, Neall splashed his face with water before replying. "You tell me."

"So," Ari said quietly after a long pause. "It bothered him that much."

Neall straightened slowly, wiping the water off his face. "Who?"

Ari hesitated. "One of the Small Folk was here when the hawk came. It brought a rabbit, and he"—she put a slight emphasis on the word to indicate the small man —"said the hawk was a Fae Lord."

Neall's chest tightened. "A Fae Lord brought you a rabbit. Did he say why?"

"He was in the form of a hawk, Neall. There wasn't any conversation."

"That doesn't explain—" Something shivered through him, making him hope he was wrong. He'd known the man who had claimed Ari at the Summer Moon wasn't local gentry, but he'd wondered if the lover might have been a well-to-do merchant who was staying in the area for a while. Now he had to consider that the man might have been one of the Fae. He, better than anyone, knew such meetings and matings were possible. "The . . . gentleman . . . you gave the fancy to. Could that have been him?"

"No."

"Ari, if he didn't tell you he was Fae—"

"It wasn't him. That's not his other form."

Neall leaned against the well, staggered. So she *had* known her lover was a Fae Lord. Not a man who had stayed in the area awhile and gone away, but someone who might still be around—and still be interested in Ari.

"There must be a Clan nearby," he said quietly. "The roads through the Veil are always connected to the Old Places. So there must be a road that leads to Brightwood."

"How do you know those roads connect to the Old

Places? None of the stories are that specific about where the shining roads are. And if that's true, why hasn't anyone around here seen them until now?"

Because they hadn't wanted to be seen. Neall shook his head. This wasn't the time to tell her he'd seen the Wild Hunt come out of the woods beyond the meadow. But he could tell her the other reason why he knew. "A friend of my mother's told me that when I was a small boy." He hesitated, gathered his courage, and wondered if he'd lost her before he'd tried to win her. "Do you know who he was? The one who . . ." He couldn't say it.

She didn't answer for a long time. Finally, "The Lightbringer."

"Mother's mercy."

"He was kind, Neall . . . and now it's done."

"Are you sure?" Was a rabbit any different from a salmon as a wooing gift?

There was enough of a hesitation before she nodded to make his heart sink. So. She was still drawn to the Lord of Fire. Enough to welcome him to her bed again?

Neall straightened, pulled on his shirt, and shook off feelings that could cripple him. *I haven't lost until she tells me to go without her.* But there was no question of him heading west and coming back for her. Not with a Fae Lord for a rival—especially *that* one.

"So," he said, holding out his hand for the puppy to sniff. "You're not going to give him an embarrassing name, are you? Women always give dogs names that make men cringe."

Ari narrowed her eyes. "Women aren't the only ones who sometimes choose odd names for animals. You named the gelding Dark Sea and ended up calling him Darcy."

"That's how it sounds when you say it fast," Neall muttered. Deciding not to continue a discussion he couldn't win, he studied the puppy. "Where did you get him?"

Ari's huff at the blatant change of subject turned into a smile. She set the puppy down. "Dianna gave him to me. I was going to name him Fleetfoot."

The puppy spotted a butterfly and gave chase until he tripped over his feet and went rolling.

"Then I thought of calling him Hunter."

The puppy found his tail and chased that, too.

"So what did you decide to name him?" Neall asked solemnly.

"Merle."

Neall nodded. "A good choice. At least it's a name he can live up to."

They looked at each other and laughed.

Dianna cursed silently as she watched Lyrra and Aiden stride toward her, probably coming to find out what had happened at the cottage today—which was something she didn't want to discuss with them yet. Falco would reach her first, but there wouldn't be enough time to talk before they had unwelcome company.

She gave Aiden a cool stare, knowing it was pointless to give a subtle command to Lyrra. She was, after all, another woman—and the Muse thrown into the bargain. She would see it, understand it, and ignore it if she chose.

Aiden, however, slowed his steps and caught Lyrra's arm, forcing her to match his pace.

"Well?" Dianna asked Falco. She'd been worried about him, although she'd never admit it, and it made her sharply impatient.

Falco shifted restlessly. "She gave me a hind leg."

Dianna wanted to shake her head vigorously to clear up whatever was wrong with her hearing. "She what?"

"From the rabbit. When she took the rabbit into the cottage, she cut off a hind leg and brought it back out to me since I had done the work of catching it."

Dianna's narrowed eyes snapped with temper.

"Why were you still there? I told you to leave the rabbit and go."

He blushed. "I wanted to see a witch. I'd seen her before, of course, but I hadn't known at the time she was one of *them*. So . . ." He hunched his shoulders. "She knew I was Fae."

Dianna sucked in a breath. "How could she know? You *didn't* reveal yourself, did you?"

"No!" he said quickly—and too loudly. He looked around to see if anyone had noticed, then lowered his voice. "One of the Small Folk was with her, and they *always* recognize us, no matter what form we wear."

What she muttered under her breath made Falco flinch. "What was one of those mischief-makers doing there?" If the Small Folk started causing trouble, would Ari feel any warmth for *any* other folk who were magic?

"She wasn't troubled by his being there. And—" He looked puzzled. "She seemed afraid of me. If these wiccanfae are so powerful, why was she afraid of *me*? What could the Lord of the Hawks do to *her*?"

"Maybe not all of them are powerful," Dianna said thoughtfully. "Maybe they're like us in that way, and there are stronger and weaker among them." If that were true, Ari might not have enough power to harm them, but she still might be able to help them understand what was happening to Tir Alainn. Noticing that Aiden and Lyrra were now only a few steps away, she smiled at Falco. "Thank you. You did well."

He studied her carefully. "One rabbit won't last very long, especially with a growing pup to feed. I could bring another in a day or two."

"I'll consider it."

Falco greeted Aiden and Lyrra, bid Dianna farewell, and left them.

"What was Falco up to today?" Lyrra demanded as soon as Falco was out of earshot.

"Nothing foolish, I hope," Aiden said.

"He was performing a small service for me," Dianna replied. "Aiden, you will play your harp for us tonight, won't you?"

Lyrra looked mutinous at the change of subject, but when Aiden unexpectedly yielded, the Muse considered him for a moment and didn't argue.

Dianna knew she shouldn't push them aside. They were both too aware of the dangers to Tir Alainn, and since she couldn't talk to Lucian right now without admitting that she'd been visiting Ari, these two were her best allies.

But she couldn't talk to them tonight. Not just yet. In a couple of days, she would go back to Brightwood and find out if the puppy was pleasing enough that she would be forgiven for not respecting privacy.

Then hopefully, she would have something to tell them.

Lucian stood at the edge of the terrace and watched the windows of the Clan house fill with lamplight, one by one, as the daylight gave way to dusk. Inside there was food and company. He wanted both and could stomach neither.

He missed her. He tried to believe that it was her body and her bed that he wanted, but the truth was, he missed *her*. Missed the sound of her voice, even though the things she spoke of usually bored him. Missed looking at her as she moved about the kitchen to feed the belly's hunger after the loins had been sated. He missed the quiet strength in her, and wondered what she would be like when she truly bloomed. And he missed touching her . . . and being touched.

He shouldn't have missed any of those things. Didn't *want* to miss them. He should have been able to walk away and not look back. Except it didn't feel finished. *That's* why he still thought of her, hungered for her. He hadn't given her the parting gift, so he didn't feel as if they'd parted. If he'd had those last two days to enjoy her, it would have been done, and he would have been the lover who had taught her what pleasure could be found in bed and she would have become a warm memory for him—and nothing more.

Instead, he thought about her and wondered if she was well, and if her garden was blooming, since it seemed so important to her. And he wondered, if he went back to visit, if she would open her arms and take him to her bed again.

Lucian's heart beat a little faster.

There was no reason why Ari wouldn't welcome him. He'd been a generous lover, in bed and out. There was no reason why she should turn away from a man who excited her. And he did excite her. He *knew* it. He could go to her cottage tomorrow evening and—

No. Not the evening. That would look too much as if he assumed his expectations would be met. Tomorrow morning, then. Just to spend time with her, be with her. Maybe it would help him understand her a little. And when he left, he would take nothing more than a kiss so that she would know it was more than her body that he wanted, if only for a little while longer.

He drew in air and was certain it was the first deep breath he'd taken in days.

Smiling as he heard the opening notes of a tune, Lucian went inside to join his kin.

There was still enough light to stop at one more tenant farm before returning to Felston's house.

It's not home anymore, Neall thought, letting Darcy do the work of keeping them safe on the road while his mind wandered through all the pieces of the day. *Never really was home.*

Each day he spent there chafed him more than the last. He wasn't a child anymore who was forced to feel grateful that someone in his father's family had taken him in. He was a man who had a future waiting for him, and it was time he reached for that future.

Would Ari choose to go with him? Or would the Lightbringer's presence be enticement enough for her

to stay at Brightwood? But how long would *he* stay?
And what would happen to Ari when the Fae Lord
tired of the affair and disappeared?

"Dianna gave him to me."

The pup had given him a scare until he saw the tan
legs. He'd thought it was a shadow hound.

Who was Dianna? She had enough arrogance to be
gentry, but she wasn't. He'd bet the meager wages
Felston grudgingly paid him on that. So who—

"You can see through the clamor?"

Suddenly dizzy, Neall dropped the reins and swayed
in the saddle. The gelding did its best to help him stay
in the saddle, so, rather than taking a hard spill, he
slid out of the saddle and onto the ground.

Ashk.

*He went into the woods to find the fox den his father
had shown him a couple of days before. He wanted to
see if the vixen had had her kits yet. His father was
busy, so he went into the woods alone, even though he
wasn't supposed to.*

*As he quietly approached the den, he saw Ashk sit-
ting on a log nearby. She didn't realize he was there
until he was almost beside her, and then . . .*

*Her face was the one he could glimpse through the
blurriness, the face beneath the one the eye usually saw.
It didn't occur to him that there was anything strange
about her ears being pointed or that the feral quality
in her face was something to fear. She was Ashk, his
mother's closest friend, the friend who sometimes
looked after him when his parents both had work that
couldn't be interrupted by a young child.*

*She stared at him for so long, he wondered if she
was going to scold him for coming into the woods
alone. Then she invited him to sit with her since it was
almost time for the birthing.*

*He heard nothing, but she did. He knew by the way
she smiled and squeezed his hand that the vixen had
birthed her kits and all of them were well.*

*Then she walked him back to his home. And the
only time her face had blurred again when he looked*

at her was the day she had taken him to the village to meet the stranger named Felston, the man who had agreed to burden himself with a family obligation.

Neall lowered his head until it rested on his raised knees. Darcy snuffled him worriedly, no doubt confused about why he was just sitting in the road.

Ashk, his mother's friend, was Fae.

"You can see through the clamor?"

He'd asked his father what "clamor" meant but had never explained why he'd wanted to know. So the answer had made no sense to him. But that wasn't what Ashk had said. She'd said *glamour*—the magic the Fae used to confuse the eye and make themselves appear to be human.

And he could see through it. *That's why his vision blurred at times. He was seeing through the mask for a moment before his eyes yielded to the magic.*

"Dianna gave him to me."

He *had* seen her before . . . on the night of the Summer Moon, riding a pale mare with her shadow hounds running ahead of her.

Mother's mercy, why was the *Huntress* spending time at Brightwood pretending to be human?

Darcy shoved him. He raised a hand and rested it on the gelding's muzzle—and felt another wave of dizziness sweep over him.

Ahern, who raised the finest horses in this part of Sylvalan—perhaps in *all* of Sylvalan. Ahern, whose face sometimes blurred for the first few seconds when Neall saw him. Ahern, the gruff old man who seemed to have a proprietary interest in the women who had lived at Brightwood—and the girl who still lived there.

Ahern, too, was Fae.

Slowly climbing to his feet, Neall leaned against Darcy for a few moments to get his balance before mounting.

It was tempting to turn around and ride to Ahern's farm, but he needed time to think and steady himself before he confronted the old man.

The Fae had been present all along. But why were

so many of them showing up now? And why had the Lightbringer and the Huntress, the two who could command all the others, suddenly becoming interested in Ari?

Chapter Twenty

Morag woke from an uneasy sleep. At first, she thought the light was so pale because it was just past dawn. Then she heard children playing outside and knew it was later than that.

There's a storm coming.

Shivering, she quickly dressed in black trousers and black overdress. Her *own* clothes. For the past few days, she'd worn garments loaned to her by other women in the Clan while her "corpse clothes" were cleaned and mended. The words had been teasingly said, but the women's eyes had conveyed something else. There was no one in *their* Clan who was one of Death's Servants, and in her own clothes, she looked too much like who she was. For Morphia's sake, she had yielded. But not today.

Picking up her brush, she turned to the mirror to work the sleep tangles out of her hair.

The brush slipped from her hand and clattered to the table beneath the mirror.

There were shadows on her face. The same shadows she'd been seeing on Morphia's face for the past few days.

Moving quickly, she packed her saddlebags and left the room. She hurried down one flight of stairs, almost tripping in her haste, and cursed the Clan elders who had given her sister a room on a different floor from hers.

She ran through the corridors until she reached her sister's room. She tried the door, found it locked, then pounded her fist against it.

There was annoyance on Cullan's face when he opened the door and saw her—and there were shadows. Morphia just looked at her with amused resignation when she brushed past Cullan and entered the room.

"We were just going down for the morning meal," Morphia said as she walked toward the door. "Will you join us?" Then she smiled, and added, "I told Cullan you wouldn't tolerate looking like a bouquet of spring flowers for very long, even if the colors *did* flatter you."

Black flatters me more, Morag thought, grabbing Morphia's arm to prevent her from leaving.

"Morag!" Morphia protested. "Let me go!"

Not if there's a way to prevent it.

She saw Cullan watching them, his mouth tightened in disapproval. Was he reconsidering his decision to go with Morphia now that he had met her sister? It was one thing to know the Gatherer was closely related to the Sleep Sister. It was quite another to see them together and realize they weren't always so far apart as others might think.

"I'll wait for you downstairs," Cullan said, sounding a bit too sulky for Morag's liking.

As soon as Cullan closed the door behind him, Morphia rounded on her sister. "What is the matter with you?"

"Stay close to me today," Morag said fiercely.

Morphia let out a huff of exasperation. "Enough is enough. I have listened to your vague complaints that something is wrong because I know you're troubled, but even I have limits."

"Then extend your limits and listen for a little while longer. If you love me at all, promise me you'll stay close to me today!"

Morphia studied Morag. Then she paled. "Is it my sister or the Gatherer who is asking?" She shook her head. "Don't answer. What do you want me to do?"

"Pack what you can in your saddlebags. If you brought more than that, leave it. See what you can bring in the way of food and drink, then meet me at the stables. I'll get the horses saddled."

"Horses! Where are we going?"

"Down the road through the Veil. We're leaving here. Now."

Morphia shook her head. "No. This isn't just a casual mating. I care about Cullan, and—"

"*Then bring him with you.* But don't delay, sister." Morag headed for the door.

"You say enough to frighten but not enough to illuminate," Morphia said angrily. "What is it you think is going to happen?"

Morag turned to look at her sister's shadowed face. "I don't know. But I don't think we have much time left."

As she left the Clan house and hurried toward the stables, she passed three children—a boy and girl ripening toward maturity, and a little girl.

"The fog's so thick beyond the gardens, if you hold out your arm, you can't see your hand," the boy said.

Morag stopped, turned, stared at the children. Their faces were shadowed. Death could never be cheated, but there were times when Death was willing to turn aside for a while.

"I don't believe you," the girl said. "I think you made it up."

The little girl tugged on the older one's sleeve and pointed. "Look! That part of the Clan house has a white veil."

Morag looked in that direction and shivered. One part of the Clan house *did* look as if it had been covered with a sheer gauze that paled the color of the stones.

"Come with me," Morag said, grabbing the hand of the little girl. "All of you, come with me."

She didn't wait to see if the other two would follow. When the little girl balked, she picked her up and moved toward the stables at a speed that left her breathless by the time she set the girl down to one side of the stable doors.

"Stay here," she ordered.

The little girl looked at her with wide eyes filled with fear.

Morag rushed into the stables. "Saddle the horses," she snapped at the men who had stopped whatever chores they were doing to stare at her.

"They haven't been fed yet," one of the men protested.

"Leave it. Get them saddled. Now."

The dark horse thrust his head over the bottom half of the stall door and watched her.

She opened the bottom half of the door, dropped her saddlebags over it, then turned to retrieve her tack. "Step out of there," she said over her shoulder. "We have to go."

When she came out of the tack room with her saddle and bridle, she saw the men still standing there, doing nothing.

"Saddle those horses, or it's the *last* thing you'll refuse to do," she snarled.

Coming from her, *that* threat they understood.

She saddled the dark horse, then hesitated when he lowered his head to accept the bridle. She stuffed the bridle in her saddlebags, tied them to the saddle, and hurried out of the stables, knowing he would follow her.

The fog was playing with the part of the Clan house that had been veiled a few minutes ago, obscuring part it for a moment, then lifting enough to reveal it again. But each time, more of it remained to shroud the walls.

She picked up the little girl and set her on the dark horse's back.

"My sister," the girl whimpered.

"You stay here with him," Morag said. "I'll find your sister." *And mine.*

As Morag ran toward the Clan house, the fog retreated, then swept in again. The most distant part of the Clan house disappeared—and didn't return.

"Mother's mercy," Morag whispered. "Morphia."

A thin layer of fog swiftly covered half of the Clan house.

Morag ran faster.

When she reached a terrace, she skidded to a stop. She couldn't see into the fog that formed a wall, cutting her off from the house. She hesitated, then thrust her arm inside the fog. The boy had been right. She could barely see her hand.

"Morphia!"

She thought she heard a muffled sound nearby. She swept her arm in that direction, hit something, grabbed it, and pulled.

The boy stumbled out of the fog, bringing the girl with him. They looked at her with terrified eyes.

"Y-you can't see in there," the girl stammered. "You can't see *anything*!"

"Go down to the stables." Morag gave them a push. "Hurry. *Go!*"

Thrusting her arm back into the fog, she walked the length of the terrace, grabbing at anyone who brushed against her.

"Morphia! *Morphia!*"

By the time she paced the terrace twice, she'd had to retreat until her leg was brushing against the terrace wall.

"Morphia!"

Morphia would have come out this way—unless she'd gone back to find Cullan and try to persuade him to come with them.

"Morphia!"

"Morag?"

Fog drifted over her. She could barely see her black sleeve—and couldn't see her hand. Keeping her leg pressed against the terrace wall, she turned far enough to see behind her. And saw nothing at all.

"Morag!"

"Morphia!"

Clamping one hand on the wall, Morag stretched as far as she could, shouting for her sister.

When she'd almost given up hope, a hand brushed

against her outstretched one. She lunged, losing her grip on the wall but finding that hand again. Her heart pounded as she groped for the wall—and her breath came out in a sob when she found it.

"Stay close to me," she said, inching her hand along the wall as fast as she dared.

"I promised that I would, didn't I?" Morphia replied, but she sounded like she was weeping.

One moment there was stone under her hand. The next, nothing. She moved her hand back, felt the comfort of stone.

"We must be at the terrace stairs," she said, shuffling her foot and wondering if there would be anything beneath her feet when she took the next step.

"Can you see?" Morphia asked.

"No, but—" Her foot dropped, pitching her forward. "I did find the stairs." But there was no stone railing, nothing to guide her hand. She tugged and guided until Morphia was standing beside her. "We get down these stairs and walk straight ahead."

Morphia said nothing, just squeezed her sister's hand. They felt their way down the stairs.

"That's the last of them—I think," Morphia said. "Ahead of us is grass, then a garden with a fountain."

"Then we go forward," Morag replied. She counted the paces. Ten. Twenty. Thirty. How much farther? How much time had she spent looking for Morphia? Were they already too late to escape?

The fog thinned suddenly, enough for her to make out shapes. To her left she could hear the fountain.

"I know the path through this garden," Morphia said. "I'll lead." She moved forward, guiding Morag.

Halfway through the garden, they stepped out of the fog and ran down the path until they reached another terrace.

Morphia turned back. "Mother's mercy."

Morag pulled on Morphia's arm. "We have to get to the stables. We have to get down the road through the Veil while we can."

Morphia pulled away. A couple of pieces of the

Clan house were still visible, but the ground around them was thick with fog. "Cullan is still in there."

"You don't know that. If he has any sense at all, he'll have run."

Morphia shook her head. "He cares about me, Morag. He would have tried to find me when he realized the danger. I can't leave him—"

"You *promised* me."

"*Morphia!*"

They looked up, saw Cullan leaning out of a tower window.

"Cullan!"

"Go!" he shouted. "Get away from here! I'll meet you."

Morphia hesitated, looked at the fog.

Morag gripped her sister's arm. "You can't go back into that."

"I'll meet you!" Cullan shouted, waving at them to move.

Fog danced at their feet.

"We're going through the Veil!" Morag shouted back.

Before Morphia could resist or do something foolish, Morag pulled her toward the stables. By the time they'd taken a dozen strides, they were running.

"I dropped the saddlebags and food sacks somewhere," Morphia panted, bracing one hand against a wall when they finally reached the stables.

"It doesn't matter now," Morag replied, looking around. The dark horse stood outside the stables. The little girl was on his back, and the boy and girl she'd pulled out of the fog were standing beside him.

There were no other horses.

She burst into the stables. A handful of horses were saddled. *"What have you been doing?"*

The men eyed her with dislike.

"What's the hurry?" one of them said. "Is the world about to end?"

"Yes," Morag snapped. "It is."

Their mouths fell open. One rushed outside, the others followed.

Morag slapped the rump of the first saddled horse. "Outside. Go!" Not waiting to see if the horse obeyed, she ran to the rest of the stalls, flinging the doors open, and shouting, "Outside! Go!"

At the far end of the stable, a horse trumpeted a challenge.

She ran to that stall, looked inside.

The stallion pawed the straw. It was a sun stallion, called that because of the golden hide and white mane and tail.

"We have to get down the road through the Veil before it's too late," Morag said. She flung the door open and stepped aside.

The stallion charged past her. The rest of the horses followed him.

She ran outside. The Clan house had completely disappeared. A few of the Fae were running toward the stables, but not many.

The girl was now mounted on the dark horse behind her little sister. The boy was mounted on another horse. Morphia was helping a couple more children mount the horses that were saddled. The grooms were simply staring at the fog in disbelief.

Morag turned her back on the Clan house. She had tried to talk to the elders, had tried to talk to anyone who would listen. Now there was nothing more to say—and no time to do anything but save what she could.

She went to the dark horse, pressed one hand against his cheek.

"I want you to go down the road through the Veil. I want you to lead the others. You know the way better than the rest of them. Take them down to the human world."

He laid his ears back, planted his feet.

"Lead the way," she said. "I'll follow behind you. I promise."

She felt him relax a little. And she knew that, if he

reached the human world and she didn't appear quickly, he would go back up the road to find her. She just hoped, if she couldn't keep her promise, the road would close fast enough to keep him in the human world.

"Go," she whispered, stepping aside.

He moved out at a fast walk. She wanted to shout at him to hurry, but the only horse that followed him was the one the boy was riding.

"Go!" she shouted.

The horses milled around until the sun stallion nipped one and sent it trotting after the dark horse. He nipped another, sending it on its way.

While the stallion got his mares and the geldings moving, Morag and Morphia helped anyone they could to mount the remaining horses. Mostly it was children too young or frightened to argue. The adults wouldn't listen to her.

Morag grabbed one of the younger grooms while Morphia lifted a small boy onto a mare's bare back.

"He's too small to ride by himself," Morag said. "Get up behind him and take him down the road through the Veil."

The groom looked at her with terrified eyes. "I've never been down the road. I don't know how."

"The dark horse knows the way. The others will follow. Now *go*!"

He mounted behind the boy and sent the horse galloping after the others.

The only horse left was the sun stallion. He took a step toward them.

Morag shook her head. She and Morphia changed shape at the same time.

The stallion whirled, racing after the last horse while a raven and an owl flew above him.

As they reached the beginning of the road, she heard shouts behind them, frightened cries. Too late, the Fae were finally understanding the danger and were trying to flee.

Great Mother, let my wings fly straight and true.

She could barely see the road, and what she could see had shrunk to a narrow corridor. One misplaced hoof and someone would be lost.

Morphia no longer flew beside her.

"Morphia!" The word came out in a caw.

An owl hooted behind her.

When they reached the Veil, she couldn't see anything, not even the sun stallion's golden hide.

She flew—and wondered if the road was still beneath her or if she had slipped to one side just enough that she would fly through this mist and fog forever.

Somewhere ahead of her, a horse neighed again and again. She followed the sound.

The mist thinned. She saw the sun stallion beneath her and a dark shape up ahead.

Stay there, she thought fiercely. *Stay there.*

The sun stallion disappeared.

Another wingstroke, two.

She flew over the dark horse's head close enough for her wings to brush his ears. She glided a few feet before landing and changing shape.

The road was fading.

She ran back to it, throwing herself to the ground as Morphia flew out of the mist. She placed her right hand on the road and her left on the ground, digging her fingers into the earth. There was power beneath her left hand, magic enough to hold the road open a little while longer. But she couldn't find the key to unlock that magic, so she poured what power she had of her own into the road. It gulped down her strength, sucking her dry.

"Cullan!" Morphia cried. She threw herself on the other side of the road, following Morag's example.

She heard some the Fae who were still on the road shouting, screaming. A hawk flew past her. Then a swan. She caught a glimpse of a stag leaping into the human world. And she heard Morphia cry out.

Then something clamped on her right arm, pulling her hand away from the road, cutting off the drain of her power.

Her chest cramped. She curled into the pain, fighting to breathe. That made it cramp more, so she rolled onto her back, forcing her muscles to stretch. That hurt, but at least she could breathe.

She opened her eyes—and stared at the dark face hovering over hers.

"I'm all right," she said weakly.

The dark horse raised his head and snorted.

"Morphia." Morag turned her head.

Morphia was on her feet, staggering toward Cullan, who stared at the road with shocked eyes. She wrapped her arms around him, holding him close. His arms came around her, but limply.

Morag struggled to sit up. She looked behind her.

The road was nothing more than a sparkle in the air, and even that was fading.

"Oh, Cullan," Morphia said. "You shouldn't have looked for me for so long. You could have been trapped there."

"I—"

Morphia had her face pressed against Cullan's chest, but Morag saw his eyes.

She is the Sleep Sister, Morag thought sadly. *The Lady of Dreams. But some dreams are found in the heart and not in sleep, and even some of the Fae are vulnerable when it comes to those kinds of dreams. He wasn't looking for you, Morphia. He waited because he didn't want to believe that what had happened to other Clans was happening to his own. He was leaving his Clan and going with you for his own reasons. Yes, he cared enough to tell you to go, but he wouldn't have risked himself. If you had been lost, he would have found another lover soon and not looked back. That is our way.* She wondered why the truth of that tasted so bitter.

Cullan looked around. "Is . . . this all of us? All that is left?"

"This is all who came through the Veil," Morag said, slowly getting to her feet. She gripped the dark horse's saddle for support.

"Why did this happen?" Cullan said. "Why was this done to us?"

"I don't know," Morag replied. "But the answer is here." This road had ended in a glade. She scanned the surrounding trees, drawing on her diminished power to find another spark of magic. She found one in a tree set a little apart from the others. "I think there's a dryad living in that tree. She might know something."

Near the trees was a mound of barren earth. The ghosts of a woman and a newborn babe sat on the mound, watching them sadly.

Cold filled Morag as she stared at the grave. She wasn't sure she wanted her questions answered, but she walked toward the tree, keeping her hand on the saddle for balance. The other Fae followed behind her.

"I am the Gatherer," she said when she reached the tree. "I wish to speak to you. Please."

Nothing stirred.

Cullan stepped forward and said in a commanding voice, "I am a Lord of the Woods. You *will* attend and speak."

Silence.

Then the dryad appeared from behind the tree. There was hatred in her smile.

"The Lord commands us to attend and speak," she said. "How grateful we are that the Lord notices us at all."

Cullan pointed toward where the road had been. "The road between the Veil has closed. Do you know why?"

"I know why," the dryad taunted. "All the Small Folk know why. Don't the powerful Fae know why?"

"You will remember to whom you speak and answer respectfully the questions put to you," Cullan said.

"Take care, Lordling," the dryad said. "I've killed one man, I can kill another." Before anyone could respond, she continued, "Why should we tell you anything? You *never* listen to us. *They* were the only ones who listened. *They* cared for someone and something besides themselves. And now they're gone." The dryad took a step back. "*That's* your answer, Lordling. We have nothing more to say to *you.*"

"Then talk to me," Morag said quietly. "Tell me what happened to the witches." She heard Morphia's quiet gasp, and several Fae muttering.

The dryad studied her. "You're not from this Clan."

"No, I am not."

"Are you truly the Gatherer?"

"I am the Gatherer."

The dryad hesitated. "If I answer your questions, will you promise to show them the way to the Summerland?"

"No." Morag watched hatred flood back into the dryad's eyes. "I will not use souls as markers on the bargaining table. I will guide them to the Shadowed Veil whether you speak to me or not. But I've guided too many witches lately, and I want to know why."

The dryad bowed her head. When she raised it, tears filled her eyes. "The Black Coats came. The . . . Inquisitors. They're witch killers. That's all they do. Warnings were whispered on the wind, and we all told the witches they should flee. And they were going to, but—" She looked at the grave. "Her time came early. They had to wait for the birthing. The other two, the Crone and the Elder, wouldn't leave her. The Black Coats came with other men while she labored in the childbed." She closed her eyes and shuddered. "They burned the Elder. They dragged *her* from the childbed and buried her alive, with her legs tied together. We could hear her screaming, but there was nothing the Small Folk could do to help her. Not against so many humans."

"And the Crone?" Morag asked softly. "What did they do to her?"

"They—" The dryad pressed her lips together and shook her head. After a long pause, she said, "We couldn't save the witches, but we made sure *those* Black Coats will never harm another." She looked up.

"One of them stood under my tree after they buried the witch. I asked the tree for a sacrifice, and it gave it willingly. See where the branch had been? It was big . . . and heavy. The tree sacrificed the branch so fast he didn't even have time to look up before it fell and crushed his head."

"And the other one?" Morag asked.

The dryad smiled. "Streams are dangerous. It's so easy to slip and hit your head on a stone and drown. Especially when a stone leaves the sling with enough force to stun and the water sprites hold you under the water. They're quite strong for their size."

"While we sympathize with you for the loss of your friends," Morphia said, "what does that have to do with the road closing?"

Morag ground her teeth and wished Morphia had held her tongue. These Small Folk had no liking for the Fae.

The hate-filled smile was back. "Everything," the dryad said. A chittering sound in a nearby dead tree caught her attention. "The Black Coats have some magic, too. They have the power to create *those*."

Something black spread its wings and flew toward them.

Morag shuddered with revulsion. It looked like a nightmarish cross between a squirrel and a bat. When it opened its mouth, she saw needle-sharp teeth.

The dryad raised her hand, made a hissing sound.

The creature screeched and returned to its tree.

"What *is* that?" Morphia said.

"We call them nighthunters," the dryad replied, watching the dead tree. "That tree was alive not so many days ago. But the nighthunters suck life out of things. And they devour souls." She looked at Morag and smiled. "It must be painful, having your soul torn into pieces and chewed. The Black Coat's ghost remained near my tree—and they found it. We heard him scream, too."

"Can they be destroyed?" Morag asked.

"They can die like anything else."

Hearing the message—that Fae could die as well—Morag thought it best to go back to something the dryad didn't hate. "So the witches know the key to using the power in the land, the power that anchors the roads to this world."

"The witches *are* the key." The dryad looked thoughtful. "The Fae can anchor the roads, too," she added grudgingly, "but it takes so *many* of you to do what one of *them* can do. You may be the Mother's Children, but *they* are the Daughters." She looked uneasy, as if she'd said too much. "I don't want to talk to you anymore." She pressed her hand against the tree and disappeared.

"That didn't tell us much," Cullan said.

"Didn't it?" Morag replied softly. "There are riddles within riddles here, but one thing is clear: The roads are closing because the witches are being killed."

"You only have the dryad's word for that," Cullan said.

Morphia gave Cullan a troubled look. She turned and hugged Morag, then whispered in her sister's ear, "I know he didn't stay because of me, even though I wished it for a moment. I also know who *did* stay in order to find me." She stepped back. "What do we do?"

"You're going to take these children to our Clan. Find the nearest road that looks safe and travel through Tir Alainn. Don't linger with any of the nearby Clans. If these Inquisitors are moving from place to place, there may be other roads closing soon. But warn those Clans about the fog. If they see it, they should go down the road as quickly as they can. And if there are witches still living in the Old Place that anchors their road, they should do what they can to protect them."

Morphia looked at her. They both knew the Fae might heed the warning about the fog, especially coming from someone who had seen it, but they wouldn't spend time in the human world protecting the witches.

Not until someone like the Huntress or the Light-bringer commanded them to.

"And what are you going to do?"

"I'm going to take the witches to the Shadowed Veil so that they can go on to the Summerland. Then I'm going to find the Bard to see what he can make of these riddles."

"I'll join you there as soon as I can."

Morag didn't ask Morphia if Cullan would be traveling with her. A sister didn't ask such things—especially when she was fairly sure of the answer.

Morag watched them sort out riders and horses. So few of them. She didn't know if the others were dead or lost in the fog, living but trapped. If they still lived, how long could they survive that way?

When they rode away from the glade, the sun stallion and a handful of mares were still there, grazing. She saw Morphia look back once, but none of the others did.

"Are you thirsty?" a quiet voice asked. The dryad's head appeared out of the trunk of her tree. "There's a stream nearby, and the water is clean."

"Yes, I am. Thank you."

The dryad stepped out of her tree. "I'll show you."

Morag glanced at the dead tree nearby. "Can you leave your tree unprotected?"

"For a little while."

The dryad headed into the woods. Morag and the dark horse followed.

When they reached the stream, she let the dark horse drink its fill before she knelt and drank. She sat back on her heels. "What will happen to the Old Place now that the witches are gone?"

The dryad smiled sadly. "The same thing that has happened in the other Old Places. The Small Folk aren't strong enough to hold it, so the magic will die."

Chapter Twenty-one

"Hello, Ari," Lucian said. It was barely midmorning, and she already looked sweaty and bedraggled. He liked seeing her that way when they were through with each other in bed, but it was less appealing when it was caused by work.

"Blessings of the day to you, Lucian," Ari replied, stepping out of the cow shed. She set two empty buckets beside it, a gesture that clearly indicated she was putting aside necessary work to entertain a guest.

There was uncertainty in her eyes, and a little wariness, but not the warm welcome he had hoped for, even expected.

"What brings you here?" Ari asked.

"I came to see you." When she seemed more troubled than pleased, he added with a suggestive smile, "I thought we might go for a ride."

She blushed, and he wondered if she was remembering the night she had ridden him as a stallion or one of the nights she had ridden him as a man. He'd been thinking of his other form and how one kind of ride could lead to another. He'd told himself he would act with restraint, but now that he was with her again, that wasn't going to be as easy as he'd thought.

"Did you send the Fae Lord?" Ari asked abruptly.

His eyebrows rose. "The Fae Lord?"

"The hawk who brought the rabbit."

He gave himself the pleasure of considering what fire could do to wings, but he decided he'd let Falco try to explain before reacting. It couldn't have been anyone else from the Clan. Not in that form. But it did no harm to let her think he'd had a part in it, so he shrugged, and said negligently, "It was nothing." Especially since he hadn't known about it. Then he thought of a reason for her wariness and the less-than-enthusiastic welcome. "Did he upset you?"

"He startled me a little, but the rabbit was most welcome." Ari smiled, humor lighting her eyes. "Especially since Merle doesn't eat vegetables."

"Merle." Jealousy burned in him along with lust.

Ari gestured toward the empty bench behind the cottage.

Wondering what game she played, it took him a moment to notice the puppy sleeping under the bench—not because the puppy was hidden but because it looked so at home his eyes had passed over it, as if it was something that had always been there. He'd seen that mongrel pup in Tir Alainn only a few days before and knew without a doubt how it had ended up with Ari. What he didn't know was why.

Falco he could deal with easily. He would have to take more care when confronting his sister. But both those discussions could wait.

Stepping up to Ari, he cupped her face in his hands, and bent to kiss her. "I've missed you." He'd intended it to be a friendly kiss, but hunger snuck in, and the kiss turned possessive, demanding, and hot. He felt her weaken and yield.

Then she pulled away, stumbling as she backed away from him.

"No," she said.

"Why not?" he demanded, the heat in his loins sparking his temper. "You want me. You can't deny that. And I want you. So why should we turn away from the pleasure we can give each other?"

She didn't argue, and she didn't yield. She just watched him too closely.

Frustrated, he raked his fingers through his hair. "Men get angry when they're denied." Before he could add that it was bluster edged by frustration and was nothing more than another form of persuasion,

Ari said, "The Fae also get angry when they're denied. When the man is Fae, does it become twice as dangerous to refuse him?"

He shifted, ready to take a step toward her.

She tensed, prepared to flee.

That shocked him enough to make him step back and regain some control—and to remember that she had little experience in the games between men and women. "If you're going to refuse me, at least tell me why."

"It's not the same now, Lucian, and I—"

"You didn't welcome me to your bed only out of obligation," he snapped. "You enjoyed what we did there are much as I did."

"I don't deny that, but there are other things that have to be considered."

"What things?" Then he knew. "You mean there's someone else who has to be considered. Who is he?"

She shook her head. "The point is, it wouldn't be right for me to dally with you while he's waiting for my answer."

Dally. *Dally.* It was one thing for him to consider this nothing more than a dalliance. It didn't sit well for *her* to call it so—especially when there was a rival waiting to take his place.

"You're considering having an affair with him?"

"I'm considering marrying him."

If she'd struck him, it wouldn't have stunned him more. "You'd actually give yourself to one of these . . . humans . . . instead of being with me?" It wouldn't do. It simply wouldn't do. "Ari, think about what you're doing, think about what you're turning away from." When she didn't seem convinced, he added, "I care about you," knowing it was the sharpest weapon that could be used against a woman's heart.

"I— I care about you, too, Lucian, but . . ." She looked troubled, torn. "I need to work." She hurried to the front of the cottage, disappeared around the corner.

Lucian walked over to the well and leaned against it.

When he'd come down the road through the Veil a short while ago, it had been with the intention of persuading Ari to continue a pleasant affair for a while longer. Now that he knew another man wanted to claim her in a way that would take her completely out of his life, he wanted more.

But how much more? Not marriage. The Fae didn't have such chains between men and women. There were some who remained with the same partners for years, but they never *promised* not to accept pleasure if it was offered elsewhere. Why should they?

He had to think carefully about what he wanted—and what he was willing to offer. Right now, though, he had to overcome any reluctance she might have about him.

He went to find Ari. Just as he reached the corner of the cottage, he heard Ari talking to someone. He stopped, staying out of sight.

"You *must* know *something* to deal with this," a woman said, her voice rising sharply.

"I'm sorry, Odella," Ari said, "but I know of no spell or potion that would help you."

"You must," the woman insisted. "*Your* kind know about these things."

"There may be witches who know how to do that kind of cleansing, but I don't." Ari hesitated. "Perhaps Granny Gwynn would know something?"

"*That* one." The woman sounded furious—and frightened. "Bonnie got a draught from her to take care of things and she's *still* in a sickbed. There's even talk that she might end up barren because of it. *That's* not going to happen to *me*. Because *you're* going to help me."

"I *can't*." Ari sounded frustrated. "There is nothing I know that would help you with this. Besides," she added quickly, "you may only be a bit late."

"I'm *never* late." A pause. Then the voice turned

ugly. "You'd find a cure fast enough if *you* were facing this."

Spurred by the ugliness in the woman's voice, Lucian swung around the corner. The woman had her whip raised, ready to lash Ari.

Seeing the movement, the woman glanced over at him. Her eyes widened. Her mouth fell open. She lowered the whip and stared at him.

He'd forgotten the glamour. He hadn't bothered with the magic that would create a human mask since the first night he'd come to the cottage. Ari knew who, and what, he was, so there was no reason to pretend he was human.

The woman recovered quickly enough from the shock, gave him a simpering smile that repulsed him, and said, "Good morning to you, Lord."

"Mistress," he replied curtly.

He noticed the alarm in Ari's eyes as she realized her guest was seeing one of the Fae. He would do whatever was necessary to placate her once this . . . creature . . . was gone. And he wanted her gone. He wasn't sure what it was about her that offended him so much, but he *did* find her presence offensive.

The woman gave Ari a razor smile. "Aren't you going to introduce us, Ari?"

"No, she is not," Lucian said before Ari could make any reply.

Embarrassment and a seed of hate filled the woman's face. She slashed a look at Ari. "You'll regret this." Wheeling her horse around, she galloped off down the road.

Lucian strode over to where Ari stood, watching the road. Grabbing her arms, he turned her to face him—and immediately gentled his touch.

She was worried . . . and frightened.

"Who is she?" Lucian asked. "What did she want?"

"It's private business between women," Ari said, trying to step back.

Her words almost made him yield, but since it

wasn't Ari's private business, courtesy crumbled under concern. "What did she want?" he repeated.

Ari shifted uncomfortably. "I don't think she wants to wed at the Midsummer Feast."

Lucian frowned. "So she doesn't want to wed." *And what man would want her?* "What does that have to do with her coming here?"

"Her family would expect her to wed at Midsummer if she's carrying a Summer Moon child."

"There's not much time between one and the other to be certain about such things."

"Certain, no. But enough time to suspect that it may be so. That's been sufficient for a good many marriages, especially when couples use it as the final persuasion to convince their families to accept their choice of life partners."

Partners for *life*. Lucian suppressed a shudder, finally beginning to understand some of the jests about shackles and being harnessed to the marriage plow that Aiden had told him human males often make when safely out of female hearing. That a man would have to stay with one female, enduring all of her moods, simply because he had sired a child on her was unthinkable. Not that the moods of female kin didn't have to be endured, but that was different than a lover. Lovers could be vindictive.

"Could you have helped her?" Lucian asked.

Ari shook her head. "I truly don't know anything that would have helped her."

"Then why are you worried?"

She hesitated. "Her family is very influential. They could make things . . . difficult."

Lucian drew her closer and wrapped his arms around her to offer comfort. As she relaxed against him, he looked around—and found no comfort for himself in what he saw.

He'd appreciated the cottage's isolation while he'd been visiting each evening. Now he saw just how alone she was out there, and he didn't like it. If someone *did* choose to cause trouble for her, there was no one close by who would notice, no one who might help her. That was something he would have to think about.

He eased back. "I should let you get on with your work."

"Thank you for stopping by, Lucian." She sounded distracted—too distracted to realize she had just dismissed him with no more thought than she would have had for an insignificant human male.

He kissed her cheek and walked around the side of the cottage. Shifting to his other form, he galloped over the meadow toward the forest trail that would take him to the road through the Veil. At the edge of the meadow, he stopped, looked back. He couldn't see her. Was she watching him? Or had she even noticed he was gone?

He trotted along the forest trail until he saw the shining road that led to Tir Alainn.

Nothing was as simple as it should have been where she was concerned. This wasn't even the challenge of seduction, which at least would have given spice to the frustration.

It stung that she would refuse him to spare a human male's feelings.

It also troubled him that he cared enough that he was getting tangled up in aspects of her life that had nothing to do with their pleasuring each other. Such things were dangerous for a Fae male when he indulged himself in the human world.

But even if he kept his distance, he could still find out what was happening at Brightwood.

He'd just send Falco out to catch another rabbit.

Ari fetched the buckets she'd left outside the cow shed, then filled them at the well. The garden needed watering, and after that there was plenty of work to do.

There was always work to do. And with every day that passed, it gave her less pleasure.

Already tired, she looked around, studying the cottage, the meadow, the woods.

She'd been born here, had grown up here, as had her mother and grandmother and generations of witches before her. Why had her family stayed at Brightwood? To provide a home for the Small Folk? To look after and cherish an Old Place? Were witches as much gentry as the other landowners, or were they nothing more than unpaid groundskeepers? And if that was so, who *really* had claim to the Old Places?

Neall was right. She had no chance of a life here. She couldn't sell her weaving in Ridgeley for anything near what it was worth. The last time she'd gone into the village for a few supplies, the only shopkeeper who would sell anything to her was Granny Gwynn, and Granny had tried to charge so much over the usual price, she had left the supplies on the counter and walked out—which is why her larder had been so empty of things like sugar and flour before Neall had bartered the salmon to Ahern.

The land was rich because it had always been cared for. Even so, she felt as if she were doing little more than surviving. When Neall left, it would be harder to do even that.

Neall.

She would have to give him an answer soon. After the Solstice. That would be enough time to hear what her heart had to tell her.

That decision made, she picked up the buckets and went to water the garden.

"Blessings of the day to you, Ari," Dianna said.

Ari looked up from the flower bed she was weeding. "If visitors are the blessings for the day, I could use fewer blessings."

Taken aback by the words, and the temper behind them, Dianna wasn't sure how to respond—and regretted her impatience. She should have waited a couple more days before coming back to the cottage.

"I—I just wanted to see how you and the pup were getting along."

Ari sat back on her heels and sighed. "I'm being rude. I'm sorry, Dianna. Merle is doing fine."

Dismounting but still uncertain of her welcome, Dianna said, "That sounds like a good name for a puppy."

At that moment, the puppy trotted around the cottage, saw Dianna, and started yapping.

"Hush, Merle," Ari said. The smile she gave Dianna was considerably warmer than the initial greeting. "He's my protector. He protects me from butterflies, bugs, twigs, leaves, and anything else that moves—as long as it's smaller than he is. Or close enough in size."

"And if it's bigger?" Dianna asked.

Laughing, Ari got to her feet and brushed dirt off her trousers. "Then he bravely stands behind me and tries to warn off the intruder."

In a few months, he won't stand behind you, Dianna thought, studying the puppy. *And any intruders will find out how savage an animal who's even part shadow hound can be.*

"I'm glad you're doing well with each other. I won't keep you from your work." She turned to mount her pale mare.

"Dianna . . ."

Dianna looked over her shoulder.

"I *am* sorry I was rude. And I could use a rest if you want to stay for a bit. I could offer you—" She huffed out a breath. "Well, there's water. Or tea, if you'd like something warm."

"Some water would be welcome." Following Ari to the back of the cottage, Dianna stopped long enough to slip off the mare's bridle to let her graze. She watched Ari fill a bucket and set it beside the well for the mare, then go into the cottage. Bringing out two mugs, Ari filled another bucket, poured water into both mugs, then poured the rest of the water back into the well.

"At this time of year, the water in the well is a bit

cooler than what I get from the pump in the kitchen," Ari explained, handing Dianna a mug.

Dianna sat on the bench. Ari remained standing, staring out at the meadow.

"What's troubling you?" Dianna asked.

"I've had my share of bullies for the day."

"In that case, *who* has been troubling you?" Dianna the Huntress asked.

"What makes men think they have the right to use anger to intimidate someone into giving them what they want?" Ari demanded, whirling around. "How can 'yes' have any meaning if you're afraid to say 'no'?"

"What did he want?"

"He wanted sex. What else could he want?" She was almost shouting now. "And then Odella shows up and wants a spell or potion because she's afraid she's with child and obviously doesn't like whoever she ended up with during the Summer Moon enough to consider wedding him. And when I told her I didn't know anything that would help her, she threatened me."

Dianna dismissed Odella as insignificant. But this male . . . What was his name? Ah, yes. "So this . . . Neall . . . threatened you because you wouldn't give him sex? What right does he have to expect such a thing from you?"

"Not Neall," Ari snapped. "Lucian."

Dianna choked. "A F—" She choked again.

"Drink some water," Ari said, coming over to give Dianna a couple hard thumps on the back.

Dianna drank some water, swallowed wrong, then coughed until her eyes watered and Ari thumped her back again.

"A *Fae Lord* threatened you because you refused him?"

Ari looked at her warily. "How did you know he was a Fae Lord?"

"Your conversation isn't sprinkled with male names," Dianna replied testily. "Since it wasn't this Neall, it was easy to figure out it was the Fae Lord."

"Yes, it was him."

Dianna watched Ari pace in front of the bench. *Lucian, you fool, what have you done?* "Sometimes men are stupid," she said, offering it as a sop to a bruised female ego.

"I'll drink to that." Ari raised her mug in a salute, not breaking stride.

Worried that Ari hadn't taken the words as they had been meant and shrugged off her annoyance with a smile of agreement, Dianna sipped the water. This was no girl who could be led. This was a young woman who was steaming mad. "Maybe he misunderstood something you said?"

"He greeted me, I returned the greeting. If *that's* all it takes to be misunderstood, I simply won't speak to him again."

Groping for something to say, Dianna blurted out the first thing that occurred to her. "I'm surprised you didn't turn him into a large stone or something."

"I couldn't do that even if I wanted to," Ari said. "My magic doesn't work that way." She paused, narrowed her eyes. "Although stuffing him down the privy is an appealing thought."

Dianna felt her jaw drop. *Mother's mercy.* She studied Ari more closely. Oh, there was plenty of anger there that belonged on Lucian's shoulders, but not *all* of it was because of him. He simply had become the focus for it. And that wasn't good.

"Perhaps if you started from the beginning and explained . . ."

Those words seemed to loosen the pebble that was holding up the dam. As all of Ari's pent-up anger and frustration and doubts about dealing with the villagers of Ridgeley, men in general, and Lucian in particular spilled out, Dianna thought over and over, *She isn't like us. She may not be like other humans, but she also isn't like us. And not even the Lightbringer can afford to forget that.*

Dianna paced her sitting room, waiting for Lyrra and Aiden to answer her summons. Lucian's blunder wasn't as bad as it had sounded, but she also knew that, as much as Ari had said, some things had been left out. It was clear that the girl's reasons for refusing Lucian had something to do with that Neall, but Ari hadn't said exactly *why* she'd refused. Still, there had been other things that had been said that had given her an idea of how to ease Ari toward thinking well of the Fae.

A quick rap on the door was the only warning before Lyrra and Aiden slipped into the room.

"Forgive the haste," Lyrra said, "but Lucian was heading for his suite, and we didn't think you wanted anyone to know we were meeting with you here."

"You both have plans for the Solstice," Dianna said abruptly.

They looked at each other, then at her.

"The Muse and the Bard usually do," Aiden said, amused. "It *is* one of our feast days."

"This year you're going to be absent from the feast in Tir Alainn. The three of us will be celebrating the Solstice at the cottage."

"With the witch," Aiden said, no longer amused.

"With *Ari*," Dianna said.

"Who is a witch," Lyrra said.

Looking at their grim faces, Dianna tried to find a way to explain without really explaining. "The humans also celebrate Midsummer. There's feasting and music and dancing. But Ari isn't welcome among them and will be alone. I thought . . ." She trailed off, not sure how to finish.

"You thought that bringing a couple of musicians and a bit of a feast would take the sting out of not being welcome elsewhere," Lyrra said.

"Yes."

Lyrra and Aiden looked at each other.

"Does she know you're Fae?" Aiden asked.

Dianna shook her head. "But I think I should tell her soon, so she won't feel that I've deceived her."

"We're both used to appearing as humans, so holding the glamour for an evening won't be a problem,"

Aiden said. "Slipping away from Tir Alainn unnoticed will be more of a challenge."

Dianna smiled. "We'll find a way. Besides, the only one we really have to avoid is Lucian."

"Aiden."

Lucian wondered why the Bard tensed so much before turning away from the stairs to speak with him, then dismissed it. He'd spent most of the afternoon prowling the gardens while trying to figure out how to placate Ari enough for her to overlook his blunder that morning. He needed to offer something that would please her more than his other gifts had—and Aiden was his answer.

"I'm going to need you on the Solstice."

Aiden paled. "Lucian . . . as much as I regret refusing you, I must. The Huntress has already requested my services for a special performance that evening."

Disappointment weighed heavily on his shoulders. "I see. Perhaps the Muse—"

Aiden shook his head. "She's also engaged that evening." He hesitated. "There are a couple of other bards here. Perhaps one of them could—"

"No." Needing air and open ground, Lucian quickly went down the stairs. Then, remembering courtesy, he turned and looked up at Aiden, who was still looking pale. "I thank you for the suggestion, but I wanted the best."

"Perhaps another night?" Aiden said faintly.

"Perhaps."

Lucian prowled the gardens until well after dark. Finally, weary enough to rest, he returned to the Clan house.

He had no voice for songs and no skill with an instrument, so there would be no music. And he didn't have the Muse's gift, either, but he could tell a story fairly well. Enough to amuse and provide a little pleasure.

It wouldn't be the entertainment he had wanted, but at least Ari wouldn't spend the Solstice alone.

Chapter Twenty-two

Adolfo dipped his pen in the ink pot and made another *X* on the map spread out on the desk. Two more witches would no longer foul the world with their magic. After glancing at his courier to make sure the young man was still too busy wolfing down the meal that had been ordered for him, Adolfo studied the map and smiled.

His Inquisitors were making good progress in this part of Sylvalan now that they weren't spending the time needed to convince the common people that witches were evil and simply could get on with the job of eliminating the vile creatures. The barons supported the purge since the witches' land came to them. For now, their support was enough. The minstrels he had hired to travel through the villages, singing the songs that revealed the witches' foul deeds, would prepare the ground for the ideas he would plant later, after those who had magic running through their veins—the Small Folk and the Fae—were driven off by the death of magic in the land. After it was safe to linger in one place long enough to teach men how to be the masters of their lives.

His Inquisitors also reported that several Old Places had been abandoned recently, and in each there had been signs that the women who had lived there had fled in haste. They had fled him in Wolfram and Arktos, too. It hadn't done them any good. He'd found them in the end.

He read the next letter the courier had brought him—and frowned. He hastily read the others, then stared at the courier. The young man, glancing over at that moment, abandoned his meal and hurried to stand beside the desk.

"Why are all of my Inquisitors asking me to replenish their purses?" Adolfo asked softly. "I gave each of you sufficient coin to cover ordinary expenses." He continued to stare at the courier, only now considering that the young man's hunger had been more than a day's riding would warrant. "Is your purse empty as well?"

The courier licked his dry lips and looked at the desk. "Yes, Master Adolfo," he whispered.

"What did you do with the money? Were you gambling? Drinking?" He paused, then added with rapier delicacy, "Whoring?"

"N-No, Master," the courier said, stammering in his haste to get the words out. "It's just—"

The courier bit his lip so hard Adolfo waited to see if it bled.

"The gentry have refused to pay for the food and lodging," he blurted out. "They said that since we hadn't been invited and had done nothing to prove our worth, there was no reason why *they* should pick up the tab at the inn."

"Did any of you explain that it was customary—and an honor—to provide for an Inquisitor's well-being while he is in a village?"

"They said it wasn't *their* custom!" The courier sounded outraged and shocked and so very young.

Adolfo sat back in his chair. Yes, most of the men he had brought with him *would* be shocked by such a lack of respect. They were used to the deference tinged with fear that they received in Wolfram and Arktos. They were too young to remember a time when that had not been so. But he had slept in many barns and had felt the keen edge of hunger many times when he'd first begun his quest to annihilate the witches.

"Master . . ." The courier hesitated. "Could these witches be different from the ones that were in Wolfram and Arktos? Could they be . . . *good* witches, and that's why the villagers don't want them caught?"

So very young, Adolfo thought sadly, *and just weak enough to listen to strangers, and wonder. And once one man begins to wonder if what we do is right, that doubt can spread like a plague through the others. Something will have to be done. But not just yet. He has the stamina for the courier work and will be needed for a little while longer.*

"There are no witches who are not the vessel of evil," Adolfo said. "There are only fools who believe they are something else."

"Yes, Master."

"There is a cot in my dressing room. You may sleep there for the night. You should turn in now. You'll have another long ride ahead of you tomorrow."

"Yes, Master. Goodnight."

Adolfo waited until the courier had retired before picking up the last letter. Expensive paper. A family crest pressed into the sealing wax. He opened it, scanned the evasive prose, and read between the lines.

Baron Prescott had made a deal to sell some fine timber, a deal that would replenish his family's dwindling funds. But the land upon which the timber stood did not belong to the baron. However, a man of Adolfo's skill would be able to rectify the matter quite easily.

Yes, Adolfo thought as he folded the letter, he could rectify the matter quite easily for two bags of gold paid in advance. The baron would protest the sum, but not for long. They never protested for long. All it usually took was explaining what a changeling child was and how witches often exchanged their own children for gentry children, sometimes for vengeance, sometimes simply to have their children raised in luxury. Gently suggesting that the children be examined to see if such a thing had befallen the family was usually sufficient persuasion for any gentleman.

So he would have the gold that would take care of his own expenses, the baron would have the timber that would more than make up for the price of services rendered, and the witch who now owned the land . . .

When the time came, he could decide what would be a fitting death for her.

Chapter Twenty-three

Hearing the mare's pathetic whinny, Morag's hands tightened on the dark horse's reins. He shook his head, but slowed his pace, as if waiting for her to decide if he really had to stop.

She drew back on the reins, then twisted in the saddle to look behind her. The other mares walked past her but didn't go far. The sun stallion turned, blocking the road.

The last mare kept coming toward them. She was sweating heavily from the effort to keep up. The dead hide around the nighthunters' bites kept sloughing off, leaving more open sores for the flies to find.

If it wasn't for the mare's tenacity, Morag would have summoned Death to end the suffering. But anything that fought so hard to live should be given the chance to fight until there was no hope—and the mare didn't know there was no hope.

The mare stopped before she was close enough for the sun stallion to lash out at her.

Morag faced forward, pressed her knees against the dark horse's sides, and said, "Let's go."

She still didn't understand why she had ended up with the sun stallion and his mares. After she had guided the witches' spirits to the Shadowed Veil, she had returned to that meadow just to check on the horses Morphia and the others had left behind. Then she had set off on her own journey since there was nothing she could do for them. She'd been surprised when the sun stallion had rounded up his mares and come after her. Perhaps the horses felt some comfort in being close to one of the Fae; perhaps they recognized her and the dark horse as the only familiar things in a world that had gone strange. All she knew for certain was she was now traveling with a stallion and five mares, as well as the dark horse.

The dark horse snorted, stopped, looked toward the woods beyond the roadside field.

"Water?" Morag asked quietly, noticing that all the horses had flared nostrils and were looking in the same direction. Whatever they scented didn't frighten them.

The dark horse pawed the road.

Water.

But was it safe to enter those trees in order to reach it?

Morag studied the land, looking for signs.

On the right-hand side of the woods was a cluster of dead trees.

She let her power drift over the land, feeling, listening.

Death whispered.

Death will whisper louder if we all don't get water soon, Morag thought. Urging the dark horse to head for the woods, she said quietly, "Stay watchful. Be careful. Those . . . *things* . . . are nearby."

The dark horse snorted softly. So did the sun stallion as he fell back far enough to guard the mare who had already been bitten by the nighthunters. Morag watched the trees as they approached the woods. There were no birds here, no squirrels. The small creatures had fled, another sign that the nighthunters had claimed this piece of land.

Mother's mercy, but those things grew and bred unnaturally fast. And when they fed, they devoured blood and magic and a little bit of the creature's spirit.

She lost track of the days since she and Morphia had parted company, each to give her own warnings. The traveling had been slow because she stopped whenever she came to an Old Place. She had found no witches. Sometimes the land simply felt abandoned; sometimes it felt like the magic was bleeding out of it. She had thought of going up the shining roads through the Veil to warn the Clans that their roads would soon be closing, but even the dark horse had refused to approach the roads, as if he sensed what was about to happen. And, in truth, she didn't want to change to her other form and go up those roads herself since she didn't know how fast those roads might close. She had been lucky once to have escaped before a shining road closed. She couldn't trust that she would be as lucky again.

Besides, Death had summoned her in each of those places.

The Small Folk were suffering from the nighthunters' attacks, and at each Old Place there were several who asked to be guided to the Shadowed Veil.

At first, she'd resisted because they didn't appear to be so terribly ill. Then the Small Folk explained that none who had been bitten had recovered. The ones who asked for her help were more afraid of having their spirits devoured before another of Death's Servants passed by than they were of giving up life prematurely.

So she had gathered them gently and taken them to the Shadowed Veil so that they could pass through and reach the Summerland beyond.

Even for the Gatherer, death had become too constant a companion.

As soon as they reached the stream, the mares hurried forward to drink their fill. Then the sun stallion took his turn, drinking quickly while the dark horse stood watch.

Morag untied her canteen from the saddle and dismounted. "Go on, drink," she told the dark horse. She watched the trees for any movement. The sun stallion guarded the mares.

When the dark horse finished, she filled her canteen and drank, gulping down the water, which had a slightly bitter taste. Another sign of the nighthunters' presence—or the loss of magic in the land.

As she bent down to refill the canteen, the sun stallion reared, screaming, and struck a mare's flank with his hoof.

As the mare bolted toward the field, a small black body fell off her flank. The nighthunter spread its wings and leaped toward the sun stallion, trying to sink its needle-sharp teeth into the sole of the up-raised hoof.

The sun stallion twisted its body. The nighthunter's teeth scraped the side of the hoof. Before it could attack again, the dark horse lashed out, knocking it to the ground. His hoof came down, pulping the body.

Then came the awful sound of nighthunter wings in flight.

"Run!" Morag yelled. The horses had to be away from here before she made her own kind of strike. The mares obeyed instantly, running for the field. The stallions moved to either side of her, prepared to fight.

Frustrated and scared, she swung her canteen by its straps, hitting the sun stallion's rump. He whirled, ears flat, teeth bared.

She swung the canteen again, hitting one of the nighthunters before it could reach the dark horse's neck. "Run so I can fight!"

That they understood. The horses ran, and, for a moment, she was alone, feeling as defenseless as any other creature against those spawns of twisted magic.

Then she gathered her power and released it in a short burst, hoping the horses were far enough away not to be touched by it. The nighthunters fell all around her, stunned. But they wouldn't stay stunned for long.

Morag ran.

The other horses had fled the length of the field and were gathered by the road. The dark horse, however, danced nervously a few yards away from the woods.

"You stayed too close," Morag said angrily.

The dark horse snorted, offered his left side.

Morag barely had time to get both feet in the stir-rups before he turned and galloped across the field to join the others.

Her power couldn't kill the nighthunters. She'd learned that the night the mare was attacked. They were bodies without spirit, and there was nothing for her to gather. But her power *could* leave them flopping on the ground for a few minutes. They weren't completely helpless—they could still bite and scratch—but they *could* then be killed by mundane methods.

When they reached the other horses, Morag dismounted and sank to her knees, shaking. Her skin crawled while she raked her fingers through her hair, almost expecting to dislodge a nighthunter from the tangles. After a minute or so, she got to her feet and examined the horses. One mare's flank was bleeding a little where the sun stallion's hoof had struck her, but none of the others had been injured. The sun stallion's hoof, where the nighthunter's teeth had scraped it, wasn't really damaged. Still, she poured the water she had left in the canteen over the stallion's hoof and the mare's flank to clean them as best she could.

She glanced at the woods. The nighthunters would be revived by now and were no doubt flying through the woods to reach the trees closest to this part of the field. But it was still daylight, and there was enough open ground between the trees and where she stood. The nighthunters kept to the woods and the shadows within it. They wouldn't cross this much open ground in daylight. However, once the sun set . . .

She would have been willing to stay a little longer to give the horses a chance to graze, but, although they sniffed at the grass in the field, none of them ate.

"Let's go," she said, moving toward the dark horse. "We'll find someplace else to rest."

Death whispered.

Morag turned in a slow circle, trying to find the reason for that whisper.

The sun stallion and the dark horse watched the road. The mares bunched together.

Moments later, a young man riding a floundering horse came into sight. When he saw them, he spurred his horse. It broke into a heavy-footed trot for a few paces, then dropped back to a walk, its head hanging down.

There was nothing exceptional about the young man that Morag could see. He had average looks, and his hair was adequately described as brown. He wore black trousers and a black coat, both dusty.

The sight of him repulsed her.

He swung out of the saddle, quickly stripped the bridle off his horse, and walked toward her, greedily eyeing the stallions before focusing on the mares.

"I require one of your horses," he said, approaching the mares.

That he thought he could take what he pleased with no more explanation than that, and that she would meekly yield to his command, infuriated her.

"They aren't for sale," Morag said coldly.

He gave her one quick, thorough glance, as if debating if she were another kind of mare he'd like to mount, then turned his attention back to the horses.

The mares trotted way from him—except the mare who had been bitten by the nighthunters. She laid her ears back and stood her ground.

As the man looked at the mare's wounds, Morag saw recognition—and satisfaction—in his eyes. Her own eyes narrowed as she studied him again.

"You're a Black Coat," she said. When he gave her a puzzled look, she added, "An . . . Inquisitor."

"Yes," he said impatiently. "I'm the personal courier for the Master Inquisitor. My horse is used up. I need one of these."

"So that you can deliver your Master's orders to kill more witches?" she asked, her eyes on the flat leather bag that rested at his hip.

"Of course." He looked proud and arrogant. "He is the Witch's Hammer."

"And I," Morag said softly, "am the Gatherer."

His face paled as he finally, really looked at her. "You killed Konrad," he whispered.

"I didn't ask his name."

As he turned to flee, the wounded mare lashed out with her hind feet, kicking him in the chest.

Morag heard bone snap.

The nighthunters flitted around the edge of the woods, darting out a few yards into the daylight before returning to the shadows. A fresh death would make them bold enough to come to the feast before anything else could feed, despite the sunlight.

"Move out to the road," Morag told the dark horse. He and the sun stallion obeyed. The mares followed.

Morag approached the young man, but not close enough for him to touch her. Bloody foam bubbled over his lips. She could sense the blood spilling inside him, filling him up.

"Help me," he gasped, trying to reach for her.

She smiled at him. "You want me to gather you?"

His eyes widened in fear as he struggled to breathe. "No! You'll send my spirit to the Fiery Pit, the Evil One's lair."

Morag tipped her head to one side, studying him. "I have never heard of the Fiery Pit, but it sounds like a fitting place for your kind. Perhaps your Master Inquisitor can show you the way." She looked at the woods. The nighthunters were becoming bolder, but weren't quite bold enough—yet. "Then again, perhaps his other servants will take care of you."

With effort, the young man turned his head, saw the black shapes darting out from among the trees.

"You can't leave me here with them," he gasped. Blood gushed from his mouth. "You can't leave me."

"You and the other Inquisitors created them, didn't you? They didn't exist here until your kind came to soil this land."

His eyes glazed. He made one more feeble attempt to reach her. "Please. You can't leave me."

The nighthunters left the shadows. Morag watched them fly across the field.

"Yes, I can."

Hurrying toward the dark horse, she made a sharp gesture with her hand. "Go!"

The mares cantered down the road, the sun stallion following to guard. The courier's horse trotted after them.

Morag mounted the dark horse, then looked at the courier's horse. If it tried to keep up with them, it would die soon. It might die anyway.

Let it try to stay with us, Morag thought, keeping the dark horse to a trot the courier's horse could manage. *There's nothing I would want to see die near that field. Almost nothing,* she amended as she heard the courier's ghost scream.

Exhausted, Morag snuggled into the straw to get a little more comfortable. Even with the summer days being so long now, they hadn't been able to travel as far as she'd hoped. But they had reached this farm. One of the small bags of silver she'd found in the courier's saddlebags when she'd stopped long enough to strip the saddle off the horse had been enough to buy grain for the horses, a meal for herself, and a place in the barn for her and the dark horse. The sun stallion and the mares were in a nearby pasture. They would be safe enough for the night.

The farmer thought the courier's horse might recover with proper care, so she'd given the animal to him to keep or sell. She couldn't take it with her. Fae horses had more strength and stamina than ordinary horses. Sooner or later, the poor beast would be left behind to fend for itself if the effort to keep up didn't kill it.

Tomorrow was the Solstice. She hadn't known that, had lost track of the days. The farmer and his wife had invited her to stay for the Midsummer celebration, but she had declined. This year, the only thing the Solstice meant to her was there would be more daylight during which it was safe to travel. And that was especially important because she finally had a name in the human world to mark her destination.

Ridgeley.

It had taken some effort to get her hosts to understand that she wanted to find a village on the southern coast of Sylvalan but didn't know its name. She really wasn't interested in a particular village; she just wanted to have a marker in the human world that would help her reach the southern Clans as swiftly as possible. Because of the horses, they'd told her the place she was looking for was a village called Ridgeley. An old man named Ahern lived near there—a man who bred the finest horses around. When the dark horse had pricked its ears at the sound of Ahern's name, she had a suspicion about who she would find there. But even if it wasn't the right place, the Lord of the Horse would surely know where to find the Lightbringer or the Huntress.

Three days more. Four at the most, depending on how swiftly they could travel. And then . . .

No. She wouldn't let her mind circle around what might be. She would find out soon enough what might be waiting for her in Ridgeley.

Chapter Twenty-four

"Today is the Summer Solstice," Ari told Merle as she brushed him. "The longest day of the year. A celebration day. And the only day in the summer when work gets set aside to simply enjoy the feel of the season. Well, there'll be a little work or else we won't have our feast this evening." She put the brush beside her on the bench and leaned back against the cottage wall. She grinned at the puppy, who seemed to be grinning back. "May the Mother bless Ahern. *Beef.* A lovely piece of beef that will make a wonderful roast. Not that the rabbits the hawk has brought haven't been welcome, but they aren't the same thing, are they?"

She stood up, stretched. "Come on. This morning we'll walk the land. Not all of it, of course, Brightwood is much too big for that. But I'll show you some of my favorite places. The hill my grandmother always favored because she said it was the best place for her to sit and listen to the messages the wind brought her. And the pond my mother favored."

She sobered. Merle, sensing the change, whined quietly.

"It's also the day to visit the dead," Ari said softly. "Because it may be the last time I'll take this walk on the Solstice. My grandmother died on that hill. She went to sleep in the autumn sunshine . . . and she never woke up. And my mother . . . Her body rests with the Great Mother near the pond. I wasn't sure she would want to be there after . . . There wasn't another place I thought she would prefer to be, except, perhaps, near that spot on the beach that she often went to. But it wouldn't have been a good resting place."

She shook off the mood before it had a chance to take root. "A long ramble, then I'll start preparing our feast. And after that, a long, deep bath." She laughed as Merle backed away. The puppy was having trouble learning what "no" meant, but, apparently, he'd learned "bath" quick enough. "For me. You've already had your bath. I don't know what you rolled in this morning, but you certainly smell better now."

Merle sneezed.

Laughing, Ari set off, with Merle bumbling along beside her, to walk the land and listen to whatever messages were there.

"Are we ready?" Dianna asked quietly.

"If the horses' hind legs don't sink into the ground from the weight of these saddlebags, then we're ready," Aiden teased. "I wouldn't be surprised to learn we didn't leave anything for the Clan feast."

"We aren't bringing *that* much," Dianna muttered.

"That's easy for you to say." Lyrra said it in a grumble, but her eyes danced with amusement. "You weren't the one who kept taking bits and pieces of the feast—or the jars to put them in. And you weren't the one who requested a plainly roasted chicken." She widened her eyes and shuddered. "*Plain* chicken?" she said in horror, her voice a high, scratchy, perfect imitation of the Lady of the Hearth, who ruled the kitchens that produced the meals for the Clan. "The Huntress *can't* be wanting *plain* chicken."

Dianna stared at Lyrra, not sure if she should laugh or run. "Did we get a plain chicken?"

Lyrra, continuing her imitation, sniffed haughtily. "It'll be basted with honey butter. That will be plain enough. Imagine. *Plain* chicken, No stuffings. No sauces." Sniff. "So, yes," Lyrra said in her own voice, "we got a plainly roasted chicken, and I'm sure between requesting that and snitching the rest I'll never get another morsel out of the kitchens no matter how many amusing stories I tell."

"Oh," Dianna said. She was very glad she hadn't braved the kitchens. The Lady of the Hearth would have been doubly offended if *she'd* asked for the chicken directly. At least with Lyrra, such a request, while unusual, wasn't too shocking. The Muse was known for moments of whimsy.

"Are you sure we can't bring a packhorse?" Aiden asked plaintively.

"That would be too obvious," Dianna said tartly. Then she looked at Aiden's harp and caught her lower lip between her teeth. "Unless *you* need one."

He smiled at her, and she knew she'd swallowed the bait and never saw the hook.

"I'm bringing my smallest harp," Aiden said. "It doesn't have as much range as the other, but it will do well enough for this evening. And Lyrra can manage her drum. It's not that long a ride."

"Then let's go while everyone else is preoccupied with dressing for the evening feast and festivities."

Except everyone *wasn't* preoccupied. Falco met them before they reached the stables.

"Take me with you," he said.

"This is a private celebration," Dianna said, giving him her best Huntress stare.

"You're going to the cottage, aren't you? That's what you've been whispering about these past few days, isn't it?"

"This is none of your concern," Dianna said sharply.

"You're taking Aiden and Lyrra, and *they've* never even been there before." He gave her a sly look. "I've been there several times."

"And you wouldn't be able to keep *that* to yourself," Dianna snapped. "She knows the hawk is a Fae Lord, but she doesn't know *I'm* Fae, and she's not going to. Not yet. But you'd give out so many hints about rabbits and hawks she'd have to be deaf and blind not to realize *you're* the hawk. And if you're with us, it would make her wonder about *us*."

Falco looked sulky. "If I can't go with you, I'll just have to spend the evening with Lucian."

Dianna's breath caught at the audacity of that threat. Lucian would find out about this evening sooner or later, but she'd prefer that it be later. Much later.

"If wanting to go is making him stupid enough to utter a statement like that, we'd better take him with us," Aiden said coolly. "At least that way we'll know what he's up to. But the Lord of Hawks would do well to remember just how sharply the Bard can hone words into a weapon."

"Especially when he has the Muse to inspire him," Lyrra added.

Falco looked nervous but didn't back down. "I'll behave. I just want to see how witches celebrate the Solstice."

Don't we all, Dianna thought, wondering just what they would find when they reached Brightwood.

Ari put on the long, sleeveless sea-blue vest, then looked down at herself. Her own brown skirt would stand for the earth. The ivory lawn tunic, which had belonged to her grandmother, would stand for air. Her mother's vest would stand for water.

"I doubt anyone would mistake me for a lady of fashion, but at least, in some way, the three of us will stand together for this celebration. Besides, no one but Merle is going to see me, and *he* won't care how I'm dressed. And *I* don't care what anyone would think about the way I'm dressed anyway. Well, perhaps Neall." She paused, then added softly, "But he would understand that the three of us together had held the four branches of the Mother, and this is the only way I can do that—and this is only a gesture to water and air at best. But I still need something for fire."

Opening a drawer in her dressing table, she took

out her grandmother's jewelry box. "Gran used to wear a garnet pin to stand for fire. That would—" She opened the box, frowned at the contents. Lucian's gifts were on top of the bits of jewelry the women in her family had collected over generations.

She took out a ruby pendant, held it up to the light.

"On this day, we give thanks to the Lightbringer, the Lord of the Sun, for the season of light and the warmth of that makes all things grow."

She didn't think she would be able to say those words this time. It had been different when he'd been nameless, faceless. When it had seemed that he did, indeed, hold the power of the sun in his grasp. When she'd thought he was a little different from the rest of the Fae, who seemed to use their gifts only when there was something in it for them. But he really wasn't different from the rest of them. In fact, he had much in common with the gentry men of her own world— except that he could turn into a horse.

No, it was the Mother who changed the seasons and made things grow. The Lightbringer might be one of Her most powerful servants, but he was no less a servant than the rest of them—and he didn't even acknowledge that much.

Do you ever give anything you value, Lucian? Do you ever give when the giving would inconvenience you?

It didn't matter what he did or didn't do. The pledge she'd made to him had been fulfilled. And there was Neall to think about now, Neall who was patiently waiting for an answer. But there was one way she could honor the Lightbringer and what he stood for.

She put on the ruby pendant. It nestled above the pentagram as if it belonged there.

It was the first time she had worn any of the jewelry he had given her. Since he was who he was, the pendant was a fitting choice to stand for fire.

Dianna wasn't sure if it was shock or just surprise that filled Ari's face when she looked out the open half of the kitchen door and saw them all standing there.

"I didn't want you celebrating the Solstice alone, so I decided to join you." Dianna hesitated, no longer certain this was a good idea since Ari looked so uncomfortable. "And I brought some friends," she finished lamely.

"Blessings of the day to you," Ari said.

Oh dear, Dianna thought when Ari didn't open the other half of the door and welcome them in. *Maybe she isn't alone. Maybe that Neall is with her, and that's why she isn't eager to have us here. If that's the case, that's all the more reason to stay. I'd like to get another look at Lucian's rival.* "This is Aiden, Lyrra, and Falco. Aiden is a minstrel, and Lyrra sometimes accompanies him."

"I'm his inspiration," Lyrra said, giving Ari a smile.

Aiden slanted a look at Lyrra and said nothing.

Looking more resigned than pleased, Ari opened the kitchen door. "Come in and be welcome."

It was the first time Dianna had seen Ari openly wear the pentagram. It was also the first time she'd seen Ari wear any jewelry that had come from Lucian. Oh, yes, she recognized that pendant and began to wonder—and worry—about why Ari chose to wear it tonight.

Out of the corner of her eye, she saw Falco's grimace as he made a quick appraisal of Ari's costume. And she saw the way Ari blushed and looked increasingly uncomfortable.

Before she could decide what to say, or how to move close enough to Falco to stomp on his foot without it being obvious, Lyrra stepped forward. Her expression was equally appraising.

"Is that a traditional Solstice costume?" Lyrra asked. "It reminds me of places where land and water meet." She laughed quietly. "Never mind me. Everyone says I can be a bit fanciful at times."

"Actually, you're right," Ari said. "I chose these clothes to stand for earth, water, air, and fire—the four branches of the Mother."

Dianna suppressed a sigh. Had Ari given any thought

at all to Lucian when she decided to wear that pendant or was the ruby being a red stone the sole reason for the decision?

"We didn't come empty-handed," Dianna said brightly.

Ari still hesitated. "Dianna, may I speak with you for a moment?" She turned and walked into the cottage's main room.

Glancing uneasily at her companions, Dianna followed.

"I appreciate your thoughtfulness," Ari said hurriedly, keeping her voice low so she wouldn't be overheard. "But the Solstice— Do they know what I am?"

"Yes, they know," Dianna replied.

"And they can accept that?"

"They wouldn't have come with me if they couldn't." Dianna waited. "Is there something you need to do this evening that can't be done while others are here?"

"There is something that needs to be done," Ari agreed slowly, "but it can be observed by others."

"I just wanted to bring you a little company and music. If that doesn't give pleasure, we can go."

"No," Ari said quickly. She finally gave Dianna a warm smile. "No, don't go. It *would* give me pleasure to celebrate with you."

"In that case, let's unpack the feast."

As she turned back toward the kitchen, she heard a soft whimper.

"Merle?" Ari said, walking over to the rocking chair in front of the hearth. She knelt beside it, frowning at the cowering puppy. "There's nothing to be afraid of, Merle. These are friends."

Not his friends, Dianna thought as she stared at the puppy. *And he knows it.*

Ari rose. "I guess he's intimidated by having so many people here. He's not used to it."

That explanation would serve well enough.

Not giving Ari any more time to wonder about the

puppy's behavior, Dianna linked her arm through Ari's and led the girl back to the kitchen.

Lyrra was emptying the saddlebags Aiden and Falco had brought in. A variety of pots and jars filled the worktable beside the sink. Apparently, they'd had no doubts about her ability to convince Ari to let them stay.

"Hold the saddlebag," Lyrra muttered at Aiden. "This one's stuck." When she finally tugged the covered dish out of the saddlebag, everyone stared at the bright-colored ribbons that were tied around it.

"Were you expecting it to fly away?" Aiden asked blandly.

"I didn't want the cover to fall off," Lyrra grumbled. A minute later, as the knots refused to yield, the grumbling turned to growls. "Do you have a knife?"

The Mother only knew what Ari was thinking while she sliced through the ribbons. Dianna wasn't sure what to think either. At least Aiden was deft enough about opening and pouring the wine, and Falco managed to put a sufficient number of plates and pieces of cutlery on the table for them, even if it looked like they'd been tossed on the table rather than deliberately set.

When everything was on the table, Falco carved the chicken while Aiden carved the beef roast. Ari put a small bowl with pieces of beef and chicken in front of the rocking chair for Merle. She looked sad when even that wasn't sufficient to entice the frightened pup.

They had just taken their seats when someone knocked on the kitchen door.

"Excuse me," Ari said, hurrying to answer.

Dianna watched her go. No one pretended to fill their plates. They were all too busy trying to catch the conversation, especially since the voice responding to Ari was pitched low enough to belong to a man.

That Neall. Who else would be showing up this evening? And *he* certainly hadn't been in *her* plans.

Except it wasn't Neall.

A few moments later, Ari returned, looking nervous.

Lucian didn't look nervous, and what burned in the back of his eyes wasn't surprise. But there was nothing he could do without distressing Ari—at least, Dianna hoped he would take that into consideration.

"What a pleasant surprise," Lucian said mildly.

"Blessings of the day to you," Lyrra said, smiling. Her smile faded when Dianna and Lucian just stared at her. "I'm sorry. Isn't that the proper greeting?"

"It is in this house," Ari replied. She made the introductions, then said, "I'll fetch a chair for you, Lucian."

"I'll get the chair," Aiden said. "Ari, you sit next to your guest. Falco, move over and sit beside Dianna."

While Ari hurried to get another place setting, Falco moved his chair and Aiden found another.

At first, Dianna wished she'd been the first to offer to move since sitting beside Lucian throughout the meal wasn't going to be comfortable. When Aiden set his chair at the other end of the table and sat down, she was glad she hadn't been the first to offer. At least she wouldn't be the one who would have to keep meeting the anger in Lucian's eyes—and if anyone could stand equal to the Lightbringer in a battle of wills, it was the Bard.

"We are well met," Dianna said, raising her glass.

"We are well met," Lucian echoed, following her example.

"May friendship warm us all the days of our lives," Ari added, smiling.

There was nothing to add to that, and, somehow, for Dianna, those words made her deception over the past few weeks a difficult meal to swallow.

Deception might be a hard meal to swallow, but, Dianna reasoned, honesty would have been harder, and a little more deception wouldn't hurt at this point. She pulled Ari aside as soon as she could after the meal ended, and whispered, "Is he the one?"

"Yes," Ari whispered back.

"He's certainly handsome."

"Yes, he is." Then Ari added with a touch of annoyance, "But he's usually more polite."

Dianna gave Ari a woman-to-woman smile. "I expect he was hoping to spend time with you alone."

Ari grabbed Dianna's hand, squeezed lightly, then let go. "I'm glad you came tonight," she said abruptly. Pushing up her sleeves, she pumped water into the basin to wash the dishes.

Not sure what to make of that statement, but certain that it didn't bode well, Dianna hurried back into the main room to help Lyrra finish clearing the table.

"We scraped through dinner all right," Lyrra said quietly. "Aiden can hold his own with Lucian, but Falco looks like he's going to try to change shape and fly away at any moment."

"Why don't you go outside with the men and try to keep things calm?"

"I'd rather stay inside and help Ari with these chores. Why don't you go out there?"

"I met her first. I get to stay inside. Besides, Lucian isn't angry with *you*."

"Oh, I think Lucian is angry enough right now for it to spill over on all of us. But nothing will happen until we get back to Tir Alainn." Lyrra picked up the wineglasses. "I must admit, tonight I don't look forward to going home."

Neither do I, Dianna thought, *unless Lucian stays here tonight. And I don't think he will.*

"How about a little music?" Aiden asked, taking his harp out of its case.

"Dance music," Dianna said brightly. "We have two fine gentlemen here who will sacrifice their toes in the spirit of a pleasant entertainment." To avoid seeing what Lucian might think of this, she turned to Ari. "Come on, Ari."

"Oh, I— I don't know how to dance," Ari said quickly.

"You don't dance?" Lyrra sounded scandalized.

"Not that kind of dance."

Dianna could feel curiosity swell the air around them, but none of them felt quite brazen enough to ask what kind of dances witches *did* know. "Well then, it's time you learned. Just a simple country dance. The steps aren't difficult. I'll show you." She grabbed Ari's arm and pulled until the girl was standing beside her. Then she looked expectantly at Lucian and Falco.

Falco gave Ari one hopeful look before wisely taking his place facing Dianna. Lucian took his place more slowly, his eyes watchful.

"It truly isn't difficult," Lucian said softly.

Lyrra set the beat with her drum.

Good, Dianna thought as Aiden and Lyrra began to sing. The dance had simple, repetitive steps. Even so, Ari was too self-conscious to relax into the music and follow its rhythm. Or maybe too conscious of Lucian. He did look wonderful when he danced. If only that was the reason Ari kept missing the cues in the music of what to do next.

The next dance was a little better, even if it wasn't a dance any of them knew.

Deciding to give Falco a warning that he was coming too close to acting like a fool, Dianna trod on his foot. Falco, exaggerating shamelessly, began hopping in a circle on one foot. Ari, thinking this was the next step, imitated him. There really wasn't anything for Lucian and Dianna to do but go along with it. Lyrra abandoned the words of the song and began singing silly dance steps.

By the time the tune was done, Ari was laughing, and Lucian almost looked as if he would forgive them for coming to Brightwood that evening.

"No more," Ari gasped, collapsing in one of the chairs that they had brought outside. She fanned her face with her hand.

Sinking into the chair beside Ari's, Dianna exchanged a look with Lyrra, who grinned. Yes, the evening was going well, despite its surprises.

"Why don't you play us a song, Aiden?" Lucian said.

"The Lover's Lament," Dianna said. A moment later, seeing the way Lyrra's eyes widened, she realized it might not have been the best song to request. Then again, maybe it would help Ari understand a man's feelings where the custom of gifting was concerned.

After a slight hesitation, Aiden began to play the introduction. He glanced at Lyrra, who nodded. She would sing the woman's responses to her lover.

> I gave my love a string of pearls
> As fine as they could be.
> She gave me back the string of pearls.
> "These aren't the jewels for me."
>
> I gave my love a sapphire fair,
> 'Twas bluer than the sea.
> She gave me back the sapphire fair.
> " 'Tis not the jewel for me."
>
> I gave my love a diamond rare,
> 'Twas beautiful to see.
> She gave me back the diamond rare.
> " 'Tis not the jewel for me.
> 'Tis not the jewel for me."

Dianna looked out of the corner of her eye at Ari. The girl didn't seem caught up in the feelings of a lover's sadness that his gifts were never sufficient; she seemed puzzled.

"Didn't you like it?" Aiden asked.

"It's lovely," Ari said, "and you both sing it very well. But—" She struggled for a moment, then added, "I wondered why you didn't sing the last two verses. The song is very sad this way."

Dianna stiffened. She looked anxiously at Aiden, whose eyes had changed to a piercing blue.

"You know other verses?" Aiden demanded.

Aiden, she's not an apprentice bard. Don't take that tone with her.

"Umm . . . well . . . yes," Ari stammered, then added hurriedly, "But it might be that it's not usually sung with the other verses. It's just the way I learned it."

"Then you can sing them?"

Lucian straightened up in his chair in response to the sharpness in Aiden's voice.

"Aiden," Lyrra said, giving him a gentle nudge, "sometimes you let your quest for songs ride rough-shod over your manners." She gave Ari her best smile. "Don't pay attention to him. *I* would like to hear the other verses."

"Oh . . . I don't sing very well."

"That doesn't matter," Aiden said. He huffed when the next nudge Lyrra gave him wasn't so gentle. "Please sing them. Start with the last verse we sang and go on."

He started playing the verse. Ari didn't sing. She just chewed on her lower lip and hunched in her chair.

Aiden took a deep breath—and let it out slowly. "What?"

"Well, it's not really two more verses. There's a . . . a . . . transition verse—"

"A bridge."

Ari nodded. "A bridge, and then the last verse."

"I think I can follow along," Aiden said dryly. When he started to play again and she still didn't sing, he stopped. "Something else?"

"The version I know isn't played quite so mournful."

Aiden played a verse through at a slightly increased tempo, then glanced at Ari. When she nodded, Dianna sighed in relief.

> I gave my love a diamond rare,
> 'Twas beautiful to see.
> She gave me back the diamond rare.
> " 'Tis not the jewel for me."

> I wandered through the days and nights
> And finally I did see

What jewels it was my lady fair
Was looking for from me.

I gave her kindness, courtesy,
Respect, and loyalty.
I strung them on the strands of love.
"These are the jewels for me.
These are the jewels for me."

Aiden finished the song with a repeat of the introduction. When he finished, there was silence.

An uncomfortable, almost painful, silence.

None of them dared look at Lucian.

Oh, Lucian, Dianna thought. *If that's what she's expecting from a lover, she's more of a starry-eyed romantic than any human I've met. No wonder your gifts meant so little.*

"That was lovely, Ari," Lyrra said.

Ari mumbled a "thank you" and looked out at the meadow.

A drum beat. Stopped.

They all turned toward the sound.

Six of the Small Folk were standing nearby. Three men and three women. They all wore surly, suspicious expressions. Two of the men carried drums.

"Blessings of the day to you," Ari said, smiling. "Come and be welcome."

One man came forward. "We came for the dance," he said gruffly, looking at Dianna. "We always come for the dance. 'Tis a custom."

"The dance?" Dianna asked quietly, leaning toward Ari.

"Yes, the dance," Ari said. She looked out at the meadow and the softening daylight. "It's time."

Dianna tensed when Ari stood up and walked to a spot in the meadow that was parallel to a brazier filled with kindling. When they'd come outside after dinner, she'd noticed the small circle of stones that formed the fire pit that held the brazier, but thought nothing of it.

For a full minute, Ari just stood there. When she took the first step, the small man began to beat the drum. The other drummer joined him. When she'd taken half a dozen steps, Ari made a quarter turn so that she faced the brazier. She raised her arms, her hands curling as if she were clasping two other dancers' hands on either side of her. Crossover step, crossover step, turn to face forward, step one, two, three, then turn back to face the center of the circle. Crossover step, crossover step, turn to face forward, step one, two, three, then turn back to face the center of the circle.

Not a circle, Dianna decided when Ari reached the point where she had started. *A spiral dance that will end right at that brazier. And then what will happen?*

Her feet tingled. At first, she ignored it. When she saw Lyrra jerk her feet off the ground, she pulled her attention away from Ari to look at the rest of the Fae. Lucian was pale and had his hands clenched. Aiden was holding his harp so tightly his knuckles were white. Falco looked scared. And Lyrra kept shifting around in her chair, as if she could no longer sit still.

The tingling got worse, as if her feet were in some odd kind of river.

It is a river, Dianna thought, focusing on the dance that spiraled closer and closer to its end. *A river of magic. She's drawing all the magic in Brightwood into that spiral.*

There was no wind, but the air seemed to be in motion—and she would swear that something in the air sparkled as it moved toward the dance.

She glanced at the Small Folk. They weren't alarmed by what was happening while Ari danced.

By the time Ari reached the brazier and stood quietly before it, everything felt like it was in motion.

Ari pointed at the brazier. The kindling inside it burst into flames. "We give thanks for the branch of fire. It is the Mother's heart, and like all passions, it can warm or it can burn." She picked up a goblet beside the fire pit and slowly poured the water inside it onto the ground. "We give thanks for the branch of water. It is the Mother's tears, shed in laughter and in pain." She raised her arms until they formed curves over her head. "We give thanks for the branch of air. It is the Mother's breath." She moved her arms closer until her fingertips touched. "We give thanks for the branch of earth. It is the Mother's body and gives us life. May Her blessings be bountiful."

As Ari slowly opened her arms, Dianna felt the surge of released power. It rose high in the air, arced, then flowed in ripples that spread and spread and spread until they would reach every stone, every tree, every nook and cranny within the boundaries of Brightwood.

The drumming stopped.

The Small Folk were smiling.

Looking weary but content, Ari smiled back at them. "May the Mother bless your days," she said.

"And yours, Mistress Ari," one of the small men said. Giving the Fae a wary glance, he and the others walked across the meadow and disappeared into the woods.

Dianna sat there, knowing she would have to say something—the *right* something—when Ari rejoined them. She had no idea what that might be. Only one thought kept circling in her head: she hadn't realized just how powerful the witches truly were, hadn't realized how much power *Ari* had. If the girl gathered that much magic and released it toward a target . . .

Was that what had happened to the roads through the Veil? That much power would certainly tear it away from whatever anchored it to the human world. They had known the witches were somehow connected to losing pieces of Tir Alainn. But Ari had seemed harmless, ineffective.

She wasn't harmless. Now they had proof of just how powerful a witch could be. Had Lucian known that?

Dianna slanted a look at her brother.

No, Lucian hadn't known.

Now, more than ever, they needed to make sure Ari was a friend to the Fae—or they needed to make sure she could do no harm.

She didn't want to think about that possibility. Not right now.

When Ari sank into the chair beside hers, Dianna still didn't know what to say.

"You probably want to start back now while there's still some daylight left," Ari said, not looking at any of them.

"Yes," Dianna said faintly, "that would be best."

"I'll saddle the horses," Falco said.

"I'll help him, if you'll pack the harp," Aiden said, glancing at Lyrra, who nodded.

Since the saddlebags had already been repacked, it didn't take much time before they were ready to leave.

"It was a lovely evening, Ari," Lyrra said. "Thank you for sharing it with us."

"Blessings of the day to you," Ari replied quietly.

Dianna reached for Ari's hand, gave it a light squeeze. "I'll see you again soon."

"Yes."

Dianna joined Lyrra, Aiden, and Falco by the horses. She looked back in time to see Lucian kiss Ari's hand. Was he being that circumspect because he had an audience or because he didn't dare do more?

With one hot glance at her, Lucian changed form and galloped across the meadow. Since the rest of them still had to pretend they'd come from somewhere in the human world and had to circle around out of sight in order to reach the shining road, he would be back in Tir Alainn well before the rest of them.

That was for the best. She might be able to slip by him and avoid any discussions until the morning.

As they rode away, Lyrra asked quietly, "Did we do harm or good here tonight?"

"I wish I knew," Dianna replied.

*   *   *

Ari poured the last of the pale-tasting wine Lucian had brought, drank it down in two swallows, then sat on the bench. Hearing a soft whine coming from the open kitchen door, she said, "It's all right. They're gone now."

Merle crept out of the cottage. He pressed himself against her leg, shivering.

Ari picked him up and set him on her lap.

"They don't know anything about witches," she told him. "If they did, they would have known their glamour magic wouldn't hide them during the dance. They must all know each other, maybe they're all from the same Clan, and yet they pretended Lucian was a stranger. I may be young, but I'm not blind." She laughed. There was a hint of bitterness in it. "Well, Dianna did tell me she had had dealings with the Fae. She'd just forgotten to mention that she was one herself. I wonder which one." She rubbed her nose against Merle's soft fur. "Perhaps that's a question best left unanswered." She studied the puppy's coloring. "You're a shadow hound, aren't you? But your mother mated with a less-than-desirable male, and that made you worthless in their eyes. No wonder you're so afraid of them. No wonder you can recognize them. But if you're undesirable because you're not a pure blood, what does that make me? I can't even claim that much of their world. What do they want? I'm certain now they want something. But they're keeping it hidden, just as they hide their real faces."

Setting Merle down, she walked over to the chopping block.

"Since you were hiding, you didn't see how often Falco looked at this chopping block and tried not to smile. I wonder if we'll be getting any more rabbits after today."

She walked over to the brazier and sat down. The kindling had burned quickly, but there were still a few hot embers. They never doused this fire. It always quietly burned out on its own. It had been a dry summer, so she would sit there for a while to make sure no puff of wind blew a spark into the meadow.

No, the Fae didn't know about witches, didn't understand the dance. Strong pockets and pools of magic would form over time. The cottage was one of them because that's where she lived. But there were other places around Brightwood that drew magic to them, making it harder for Small Folk who didn't live near one of those pockets or pools to keep their own magic balanced. And sometimes those pools became strong enough to trap a being who didn't have much magic. So the dance drew all the magic that came from the Mother's branches into one place so that it could flow through the witches and be sent out again to cover the Old Place.

It drew magic that came from the Mother's branches. But no other kind of magic. So the Small Folk always appeared as bright spots of magic standing in a world that looked a little pale. And she'd expected to see Lucian as another bright spot. She hadn't expected to see the rest of her guests shine as well.

"In one way, they did me a kindness tonight," Ari told Merle. "Now I have an answer to give Neall the next time I see him."

Lucian was waiting for her when she got to her rooms at the Clan house.

"As we live and breathe, Dianna, what were you thinking of?" he shouted.

Already worried, Dianna put spurs to her temper and let it run. As she slammed the door, she shouted back, "I could say the same about you!"

"*I* didn't know she was a witch when I accepted the promise she made at the Summer Moon. And if I remember right, *you* were the one who encouraged me to accept it."

"You *still* wouldn't have known if I hadn't been visiting and found out."

Lucian's voice got quiet and deadly. "But you knew

before tonight. You knew before the rest of us. Oh, yes, I figured out where Aiden got his information about the pentagram. So tell me, sister, just why have you been visiting Ari?"

"Because I was concerned about *you*!" Dianna stopped, paced, made some effort to rein in her temper. "You've never shown that much interest in a human female before. I wanted to see for myself what kind of person she was."

"That explains the first time you went there. It doesn't explain the rest."

"What rest?" Dianna snapped, feeling more and more cornered.

"You kept going back," Lucian said, his hands curling into fists. "Why? And why give her a useless puppy? Did you think I wouldn't recognize the little mongrel? Especially when I'd seen it right here in our own gardens?"

"It has no value to us, but it's not useless to her!" Dianna pressed her lips together.

"It's easy to give away something that has no meaning, isn't it?"

You should talk, Dianna thought furiously. And then realized that was exactly where some of Lucian's anger was coming from. "I did no harm."

"No harm?" Lucian stared at her. "*No harm?* She's a *witch*! You felt, and saw, the way she drew the magic out of the land. If she hadn't released it again, would we have had a home to come back to tonight?"

"You can't lay this all on my shoulders, Lucian. You *can't.*"

"*Why were you there tonight?*" he roared.

The truth burst out of her. "*Because I like her!*" She tried to stop . . . and couldn't. Tears filled her eyes, spilled over. "I like her. I didn't want to, had never intended to go there more than once. I went the first time because I was concerned about you. I went back the second time because I was curious about her. But I kept going back because I like her." She brushed the tears off her face. "Tonight I just wanted her to have a little fun. She told me there's a Midsummer celebration in the village, with music and dancing, but she's not welcome there because she's a witch. And we would be celebrating the Solstice here, with music and dancing and a feast. And she would have been alone. I didn't want her to be alone."

Lucian sat on the window seat. His shoulders sagged. He sighed. "I know. That's why I went to Brightwood tonight." He smiled wryly. "Poor Aiden. No wonder he was so tense when he told me you had already engaged him and Lyrra to perform at a special celebration."

Hopeful that the storm between them had passed, Dianna took a couple of steps toward her brother. "Aiden wasn't nearly as upset as Falco. He'd threatened to tell you we were going to Brightwood unless we took him with us—and then you showed up."

Lucian chuckled. "Served him right."

As amusement and anger faded, she saw the hurt and confusion underneath. "You care about her, don't you?"

He wouldn't look at her. "Yes, I care. I don't want to. At least, not this much. But I do care." He hesitated. "I did have another reason for going there tonight."

"I can think of one obvious one," Dianna said dryly.

He shook his head. "One of those louts from the village has asked her to marry him, and she's actually considering it. I couldn't see any reason why she would do that unless she couldn't stand being so lonely anymore. So I thought . . ." He raked his fingers through his hair. "I've visited most of the Clans here in Sylvalan—the eastern and midland ones, anyway. I even visited a couple of Clans in Arktos before they completely disappeared. And in learning how to deal with the human world, I've seen a good part of Sylvalan as well. The farthest she's ever gone is a coastal town a day's journey from Brightwood. She knows little of stories and music. She knows little of anything besides her weaving and her garden and her magic. I could show her the stories and the music, talk to her about other things."

"Be a mentor as well as a lover?" Dianna asked softly.

"What's wrong with that? Why should she settle for some rutting human who will roll on top of her, pump his hips a few times, then roll back off, when I can give her pleasure? Why should she grow old while she's still so young because she's always working?"

Dianna frowned. "Then why *weren't* you there tonight to be a lover?"

Lucian sprang up from the window seat. "Because she won't be with me until she's decided what to do about *him*. Only a dog should have that kind of loyalty."

The words hung in the air.

"If she chooses you, how long would this arrangement last?" Dianna asked cautiously.

"As long as it pleases both of us."

"What if she wants children?"

He shuddered—and she quietly sighed in relief.

"My children, when I have them, will be Fae," he said quietly. "I am the Lightbringer. I can accept no less." He took a deep breath, let it out slowly. "I want to be with her because I care. But we also need to keep Ari away from anyone who might turn her against us."

"Agreed. We need to protect her for her own sake as well as for ours." She had a name for that lout who wanted to marry Ari. But that wasn't something she was going to share with Lucian just yet. Not until she knew what Ari decided.

Chapter Twenty-five

After bedding down Darcy, Neall lingered in the stables.

Was there anything lonelier than being surrounded by people and still feeling alone? If he could have, he would have gone to Brightwood to celebrate the Solstice with Ari, to see the dance he vaguely remembered his mother performing, to feel the magic flowing to a living focal point and then spilling out over the land again.

It had been prudent to go with Baron Felston and the others to the village's Midsummer feast; tomorrow he would ride over to Brightwood and see if Ari had reached a decision. Then, one way or another, he had plans to make.

Not much longer, Neall assured himself as he walked to the house. He would never again have to celebrate the Solstice in Ridgeley. The village's Midsummer feast used to be a joyful time, a promising beginning for the young couples who chose to be wed that day. For the young men and women who willingly had clasped hands and pledged themselves to each other, it was still a golden day, and the way those women had looked at their new husbands had made him ache to hold Ari. But he'd noticed that none of the gentry couples had looked at their life partners with that same joy and anticipation. He suspected that, for them, the days between the full moon and the dark had been more than enough time for them to grow tired of each other. The ones who had pledged themselves in marriage had done so because a Summer

Moon child was on the way—but it was status and property settlements that were the real enticements in accepting the "yoke of marriage." Better to marry an heir than a second son you actually loved. Better to marry the daughter of a gentleman, even if she felt nothing but contempt for you because you were slightly beneath her own social status, than a merchant's daughter who admired you.

Neall opened the front door and stepped into the hallway. Odella had been acting vile for the past several days, but at least they'd been spared—

"You slut!" Royce's shout came from Baron Felston's study.

Neall didn't hesitate. He ran to the study and pushed the door open.

Baron Felston and Royce stood in front of the chair where Odella cringed yet still managed to look defiant. Felston's wife stood to one side, looking at her daughter with undisguised contempt.

"You shame your family because you think you're above custom and tradition?" Felston roared. "You had the chance to do what was proper. Even as late as this morning, something could have been arranged. A babe that comes early to a Midsummer marriage isn't considered early at all. No one counts the months on their fingers or smirks behind their hands. Neither family has its reputation smeared or loses any of its standing in the community. But a marriage that takes place even a week later is quite a different thing."

Odella's lips trembled, but her voice was sharp enough. "I told you. I *can't* marry him."

"You lifted your skirts for a married man?" Royce yelled. "Have you lost *all* decency? What are you going to be? Ridgeley's fancy whore?"

"Royce!" the baroness said sharply. "I won't have such things said."

"Why not?" Royce demanded, turning on his mother. "If that's what she is now, she should at least get paid for it."

"He isn't married!" Odella said, straightening in the chair.

"Then what is he?" Baron Felston said. "Did you go on your back for some ill-bred lout who shovels out the stables?"

"He wasn't ill-bred, he wasn't a lout, and he wasn't married!" Odella shouted. She paused, then said dramatically, "He was a Fae Lord."

Silence.

Neall heard the clock in the hallway strike the quarter hour.

"A Fae Lord," Baron Felston said heavily. He rubbed the back of his neck. "Are you telling me the truth, girl? You're not just saying this?"

"I saw his face," Odella said. "His *real* face."

"Then where are the gifts?" Royce said. "According to the stories, the Fae always give gifts when they bed a woman. Let's see them."

"I didn't get any gifts. He said a gift wasn't given for the night of the Summer Moon, but he would bring a gift the next night."

"So where are the gifts?"

"There aren't any gifts. He didn't come back."

Royce snorted. "Were you *that* much of a disappointment?"

Outraged, Odella shot to her feet. "He didn't come back because he was bewitched. He didn't come back because Ari saw him and wanted him. So he forgot about me and has been having his romp inside *her* drawers!"

"Liar!" Royce raised his fist.

"You think just because she refused you, she hasn't been lifting her skirts for someone else?"

"She wouldn't dare."

Odella laughed. It was a nasty sound. "Oh, she dared. I saw him there one morning, as bold as you please. *My* lover. The one who had promised me chests of gold and jewels." Her mood changed. Her face crumpled in unhappiness. "When I greeted him, he just laughed at me. He *laughed*. And he was already pulling up her skirt before I could ride out of sight."

"That bitch," Royce said quietly. "I warned her about lifting her skirts."

"When was this?" Neall asked. He knew the Light-bringer had been Ari's lover, but, somehow, the Fae Lord being at the cottage during the day seemed more intimate and threatening than the man spending the night in Ari's bed. That was just sex, a promise fulfilled because of that damned fancy. But during the day . . . that was *life*. The collection of small details that made up a shared day was what gave richness to what happened in the bed at night.

When they all turned to look at him, he realized he should have kept quiet, should have backed out of the room before they'd noticed him.

"Not long ago," Odella said, her eyes filled with delighted spite. "Well after the new moon, so it wasn't as if she was just fulfilling a pledge."

Neall closed his eyes as he tried to absorb the verbal blow. So. It hadn't ended. Was that why Ari hadn't given him an answer yet?

Wait. *Wait.* Something wasn't right here. What had Odella said about the morning she'd seen the Fae Lord? That he'd lifted—

Neall looked at Odella. "You're lying. You may have seen a Fae Lord there one morning, but you didn't see him lifting Ari's skirt." He smiled bitterly. "She only wears skirts when she has to come to Ridgeley. At Brightwood, she wears loose trousers because they're easier to work in." He took a step forward. "What else are you lying about, Odella?"

"I'm not lying," Odella spat. "He was mine! I should have had all the gold and jewels he's given to *her*!"

Neall shook his head. A kind of recklessness filled him, pushing aside any thought of caution. "You couldn't have met him on the Summer Moon. I'm not saying you didn't meet a Fae Lord. It's possible. But it wasn't him. Which means she didn't steal him away from you."

"I say she did!"

Recklessness shifted to grim anger. "You want to deny whoever it really was you've been with in order to avoid a bad marriage, that's fine. You want to say it was a Fae Lord who got you with child, that's fine too. That gives you a way out since everyone knows Fae men don't marry human women. But don't accuse Ari of something she didn't do. You might steal a man away from another woman simply because you wanted him, and you wouldn't give a damn what it might mean to her. You'd even use one of Granny Gwynn's potions to do it if you couldn't entice him any other way. But Ari would never do that. *Never.*"

"How dare you?" Baron Felston said. "How dare you say such things to my daughter? How dare you side with that *witch* against your family? Have you forgotten who's fed you, clothed you, given you a roof over your head for all these years?"

"I've forgotten nothing," Neall snapped. "I haven't forgotten that you've begrudged me every mouthful of food and every castoff piece of clothing."

"I've made allowances for you because your father was a gentleman in name only, but—"

"My father was more of a gentleman than you'll ever be," Neall said.

Baron Felston's face flushed to an ugly red. "Get out of my house. Get out and stay out. You set foot on my land again, I'll horsewhip you."

"It will be a pleasure to leave you," Neall said. He turned and walked out of the room. When he reached the staircase, he checked to make sure none of them were watching him. Then he raced up the stairs and ran down the corridor to his room. Let the servants think what they would; he needed to get out of here before Felston—or, more likely, Royce—thought about trying to keep the one thing he truly valued: Darcy. He hadn't paid Ahern anywhere near what the gelding was worth, but he'd paid the asking price out of his own money, from the paltry wage Felston had reluctantly paid him for all his work on the estate.

Within minutes, he had stuffed his saddlebags with a couple of changes of clothing and his grooming tools. He took his bow and the quiver of arrows, then looked around the room to see if there was anything he'd missed that he would regret leaving behind. He grabbed the threadbare winter coat from its hook on the wall and left the room.

Down the servants' staircase and out the kitchen door. Running to the stables as quietly as he could. Opening the doors for whatever light the moon would provide, then slipping inside and moving down the wide aisle.

Darcy's head appeared over the stall door.

"Shh," Neall said quietly before the horse could greet him. There was always one stableboy sleeping in the loft in case he was needed. He listened, heard a muted snore. Good.

Leaving his things beside Darcy's stall, he opened the door and motioned the animal to stay. Moving as quietly as he could, he got his saddle and bridle from the tack room.

Darcy didn't even shift his feet while Neall saddled him and arranged the saddlebags and the rest of his gear.

"Let's go," Neall whispered. He walked the gelding out of the stables. It was easier to close the doors that way.

As Neall turned to close the doors, Darcy snorted a warning. Neall spun around, swung into the saddle just as Royce ran toward the stables, shouting, "Thief! Thief! He's stealing our horse!"

Before Neall could collect the reins, Darcy charged straight at Royce. In the moonlight, Neall saw Royce's eyes widen with fear as he skidded to a stop and barely flung himself out of the gelding's path.

Darcy raced down the estate drive. When they reached the road, Neall tried to slow the animal, but the gelding had the bit between his teeth and refused to obey. They raced down a road full of moonlight and shadows—and Neall realized that they weren't running away from Baron Felston's estate and the village of Ridgeley; they were running toward something. And someone.

"We can't go there," Neall said firmly. Holding Darcy back wasn't easy, but he'd had enough time to consider what to do before they'd reached this point in the road. "Not tonight."

If he showed up at Ari's cottage tonight, she would let him stay. He couldn't do that. The choice to come with him had to be her own. It couldn't be made because *he* had to leave now. Tomorrow he would ride over to Brightwood.

"This way," Neall said, turning the gelding away from Brightwood. "We'll see Ari tomorrow." Darcy made one more try at heading where he wanted to go, then set off down the road in a heavy-footed, bone-jarring trot that made Neall grit his teeth to keep from biting his tongue.

There were still lights on at Ahern's farm. There was even a small bonfire between the house and stables.

Yes, Neall thought with grim amusement, Ahern and his men would still be celebrating the Solstice.

As he trotted into the light, the talk and laughter around the bonfire faded.

"You're out late tonight," Ahern said, stepping away from the fire to meet him.

Neall swung out of the saddle. Feeling Darcy's muscles bunch, he kept a firm grip on the reins. The last thing he needed was the gelding bolting for Brightwood.

Ahern's sharp eyes took in the bulging saddlebags, the bow and quiver, the winter coat tied behind the saddle. "You going on a journey?"

"Soon. Not tonight." Neall hesitated. That reckless feeling was pushing at him again. "The baron threw me out of his house tonight. I was wondering if I could stay here for a few days. I'll work for my keep."

For the first time that Neall could remember, Ahern looked uncomfortable. "I can put you up tonight, but it would be best if you made other arrangements in the morning."

"Why?" Neall said quietly. "Because you're Fae?"

He was aware of the men moving toward him. He was aware that some of them were holding pieces of burning wood, and it wasn't because they wanted more light. But he kept his eyes on Ahern's face and wondered if he'd misjudged the man.

"What makes you think I'm Fae?" Ahern finally asked.

"Fae blood runs through me too. I can see through the glamour."

A long silence. Then Ahern said, "Get your gear. We'll take it up to the house and then talk."

As soon as Neall let go of the reins to get the saddle bags, Darcy knocked him down and bolted.

"You!" Ahern said sternly.

Hooves clattered to a stop.

"Come back here and behave yourself."

With obvious reluctance, Darcy returned and stood quietly while Neall got his gear.

Ahern looked at two of his men. "Get him bedded down." He watched while the men led the gelding into the stables. Shaking his head, he led Neall up to the house. "When he was a foal, she used to pet him whenever she stopped by. Got to the point where we had to lock him up to keep him from following her home. I thought he would have forgotten by now."

"She still pets him, so he's not likely to forget," Neall said dryly. "But it does explain why he gets so stubborn whenever we're nearby and don't stop at Brightwood."

"She never took to riding. I made sure she knew how to sit a horse, but she didn't want one of her own. If she had, you'd never have gotten that one."

They said nothing more until Neall left his gear in a

small guest room and they were back outside, walking toward one of the paddocks.

Ahern rested his arms against the top rail of the paddock fence. "How long have you known?"

"I've been seeing it ever since I met you," Neall said. "But I just recently figured out what it was I was seeing." He hesitated, then decided a question left unspoken was a question that would never be answered. "Which one are you?"

Ahern made a sound that might have been a gruff laugh. "Can't you guess?"

"A Lord of the Horse," Neall said. When Ahern just looked at him, he felt a little chill run down his spine. "*The* Lord of the Horse."

Ahern nodded. "The Lord of the Horse. I command, they obey."

"Why are you living here? Why aren't you in Tir Alainn like the rest of them, coming down here whenever you want to amuse yourself?"

"There's a large dose of bitterness in those words, young Neall."

"Maybe I have reason to feel bitter. Or, at least, worried. The Fae seem to be taking a lot of interest in Brightwood these days. And in Ari."

Ahern stared at the land. "You're going to your mother's land, aren't you? That's where you're headed now that you've reached your majority and Felston doesn't hold the reins in any way. And you're taking Ari with you, aren't you?"

Neall just stared at him.

"Well then," Ahern continued, "it doesn't really matter whether the Fae are interested or not, does it?"

"How— How did you know about the land?"

"Astra, Ari's grandmother, told me about you." He made another gruff, amused sound. "Obviously, there were a few things she didn't mention. But she told me you would go back to your mother's land when you came of age—and she told me not to stand in your way if you tried to persuade Ari to go with you."

Neall studied the older man, saw strong emotion ruthlessly controlled. "Why would it matter to you?"

Ahern didn't say anything for a long time. Then, "When I was a young man, I did exactly what you said—I came to the human world for diversion and amusement of all kinds. Young human gentlemen call it getting some town bronze. The Fae don't have a name for it, but it amounts to the same thing. Seasoning. Experience. I was a randy young stallion. And I enjoyed myself.

"Then one day, I met a young woman who was quite unlike anyone else I'd ever met. She was forthright and bright—and not at all impressed that a Fae Lord found her interesting. A challenge for a young man who was impressed with himself. So I did my best to woo her. And I succeeded a little too well. She loved. I cared. Can you see the difference?"

"Yes," Neall said softly.

Ahern nodded. "Thought you would. I visited the Clan near where she lived for a couple of months, but I spent most of my nights with her. Then, one day, I got an itch for . . . a different experience. So I left. Traveled. Grew into my power and became the Lord of the Horse. But I never forgot her, compared every other woman to her. So I decided to go back, sure I would be welcomed with open arms. After all, I was a Fae Lord and she was just a human female.

"Except she wasn't just a human female. She was a witch. I knew that. As I said, she was forthright. I just didn't understand what it meant.

"When I trotted up to her cottage one evening, I saw a small child, a girl, playing outside. She was holding a bowl and was making the water inside it rise and fall. She had my dark hair and her mother's woodland eyes."

When Ahern didn't say anything more, Neall said, "What happened?"

"I wasn't welcome. And it hurt. I still cared, but she no longer loved. I had tossed that aside like a trinket when it had been new and shining. I never got it back. Even when we eventually became lovers again for a while, I never got it back. She cared. That was a pale emotion compared to what she'd once given me.

"I couldn't live with her family, and I couldn't go back to the way I had lived my life. I tried. So I made an agreement with the matriarch of the family to lease some of the land. I built a house, and I brought some fine Fae horses with me. I bought a stallion and some mares from this world, and I began to breed horses.

"And I watched that girl child grow up into a fine young woman. And I watched that young woman fall in love with a selkie man, a Lord of the Sea. And I watched her bring a daughter into the world, a little girl with the gifts of earth and fire.

"I watched from a distance what I might have shared in full."

Neall gripped the fence rail with both hands. "Does Ari know you're her grandfather?"

Ahern shook his head. "And she doesn't know her father was a selkie man, just that her mother had a love for the sea." He paused. "Tell me something. You must have gotten the Fae blood from your father. Do you know anything about him?"

"He had a quiet laugh. When we took walks, he would tell me stories. I didn't realize at the time how much he was teaching me about the woods with those stories. And I remember the way he and my mother would look at each other and just smile."

Ahern gave him a strange look. "He lived with you. She was a witch, and he lived in her house."

"Yes." Neall saw Ahern's face tighten with some strong emotion. "I want to have with Ari the same thing my mother and father had. I want to love . . . and be loved."

"You're going to Brightwood tomorrow?"

"Yes. I'll go over to see if she's made her decision yet."

"You can stay here until she does." Ahern closed his eyes. "Find the right word to convince her, young Neall. Find the right words."

Chapter Twenty-six

When Ari saw Aiden riding down the road early the next morning, she set the water buckets down by the garden wall and waited.

Did they use the glamour magic and ride down human roads because they didn't want to alarm any humans they might deal with? Or was it nothing more than a deceit that made it easier for them to get what they wanted, a deceit that would be maintained until they chose otherwise?

"Good morning, Mistress Ari," Aiden said.

"You must have been up at dawn to get to Brightwood so early," Ari said. "From what Dianna has said, I had gathered you have a ways to travel to get to . . . where you're staying."

She saw his puzzlement and caution. She hadn't given him the expected greeting. Hadn't actually responded to his.

"My apologies," Aiden said. "I'm disturbing you."

Ari relented. She didn't know why Aiden had come with Dianna last evening, but he'd done nothing except provide enjoyable music.

"The kettle is still hot. Would you like a cup of tea?"

"Thank you." When he dismounted, he noticed the buckets by the garden wall. "Can I carry those somewhere for you?"

Ari smiled. "I thank you for the offer, but they're right where they're supposed to be." Then she paused, and added, "Perhaps you should bring one to the back of the cottage. Your horse may want some water, and I've only the two buckets."

Aiden picked up one bucket and followed her around the cottage. While he set the bucket in a bit of shade and slipped off the horse's bridle so the animal could graze, Ari made tea and put some of the small cakes that were left over from the feast on a plate. She felt a prick of amusement when Aiden looked at the plate and quickly hid his disappointment—and she wondered if she should have offered slices of her bread instead. She'd noticed that her guests had all helped themselves to more of her food than all the dishes they had provided. She couldn't blame them. The beef roast had tasted wonderful while the chicken, like the rest of their food, had been like eating solid air—the teeth found something to chew, but the tongue found no flavor.

"I came this morning for a selfish reason," Aiden said, sitting on the bench with her, the plate of cakes between them.

Naturally, Ari thought. Would one of them have come for any other reason? "And what is that?"

"The song. It pricked my pride." He smiled. "I have an excellent memory, and I'd been sure I'd learned most of the songs that are sung. "But I'd never heard those verses of 'The Lover's Lament' before."

"As I said, it may be a variation of the song that's only known around here."

"No," Aiden said thoughtfully. "I don't think that's true. I have the feeling it's sung that way more often than anyone realized."

"Perhaps. Here, it's known as 'Love's Jewels,' so the different name may have caused confusion."

"I've never heard it by that name, either."

Ari didn't know what to say to him, so she said nothing.

Eventually, Aiden said, "It occurred to me that you may know some songs that have been forgotten elsewhere. There's one I've been trying to find for a while now."

"I'll answer your question if you'll answer mine."

"All right."

Ari turned on the bench so that she faced him. "Which one are you?"

"I'm Aiden," he said slowly. "The minstrel."

Ari turned away and huffed. "If you're nothing more than a minstrel, then I'm the finest gentry lady in Sylvalan. You're a Fae Lord. I want to know which one."

"What makes you think I'm Fae?" He didn't drop the glamour magic, but the grim expression made the human mask look more like his real face.

"Magic shines, Lord Aiden," Ari said. "Especially during the dance. It's something you should keep in mind the next time you want to deceive a witch."

"It wasn't meant to be a deceit," Aiden protested.

"It isn't what I call honesty," Ari said sharply. "Friendships that are founded on lies aren't friendships."

"The feelings can be true even if the surface isn't what you would call honest," Aiden replied, his voice equally sharp.

"Are there any feelings, Aiden?" Ari asked, her anger suddenly changing to sadness.

"I can't answer for someone else." He looked out at the meadow for a long time. Then he sighed. "I'm the Bard."

Ari almost asked about the others, then decided against it, knowing instinctively that he would answer questions about himself but would become protective about the others.

"What did you want to know?" she asked.

He hesitated, and she wondered what he thought would happen now if he asked the question.

"Do you know any song about the Pillars of the World?"

She thought for a moment, then shook her head.

Aiden sighed.

Pillars of the World. Why was that familiar?

"I remember," Ari said before she could bite back the words.

The air around Aiden filled with his intensity, and that intensity made her cautious. She had to tell him something—but not everything. Not until she figured out why the Fae had become so interested in Brightwood. It wasn't just because Lucian had been her lover for a little while. She felt sure of that.

"The day my grandmother died," Ari said, struggling to find a way to say just enough, "she went for a walk, up to her favorite hill. Before she left, she said, 'The Pillars of the World have been forgotten. It is time they also forgot.'"

"Did she say anything more?" Aiden demanded.

Ari shook her head, not daring to look at him in case he could sense the lie. "We— We went looking for her when the afternoon waned and she still hadn't come back. We found her on the hill. She had fallen asleep . . . and died."

"I'm sorry."

"So am I. I miss her." She stood up. "You'll have to excuse me, Aiden. I want to get the garden watered before the sun is too high."

"Yes, of course." He whistled to his horse. "Thank you for your time."

When he was mounted, she said, "Blessings of the day to you, Aiden."

She wondered why he looked so relieved to hear her say that.

"And to you, Mistress Ari."

"Why don't you save yourself some time on the journey back and simply go across the meadow," Ari said. "That's the way Lucian went when he left, so I assume it's the shortest way back to Tir Alainn."

His only response was to turn his horse and ride away.

Ari watched him until he disappeared into the woods. Then she returned to the chore of watering the garden. There was a great deal to do in the coming weeks—and more to do once the harvest began.

She hoped she hadn't told Aiden too much. But if anyone could put together the whole from bits and pieces, it was the Bard. She strongly suspected that what he didn't know, he would be able to guess. She didn't have a reason for not telling him all of it, only an instinctive hesitation.

The Pillars of the World have been forgotten. It is time they also forgot. It is time they tasted the richness of feelings instead of living on the scraps of affection thrown to them by people who no longer even remember why they throw the scraps.

That sounds like a sad way to live. Who are the Pillars of the World, Gran?

We are.

Yap yap yap.

Ari turned in time to see Merle bound away from the creek bank and head straight toward Neall, who was crouching to greet the pup.

"Be careful," Ari called. "His paws are—"

Merle bounded one step too far. His paws hit the target.

"—muddy," Ari finished.

Wincing a little, Neall stood up. "He's already gotten bigger." He looked down at Merle. "You're going to have to learn not to jump like that. You're getting too big."

Merle's entire rump wagged in greeting as he looked up at Neall.

"Are you all right?" Ari asked. "Should I try to wash the mud off?"

"Let it harden first," Neall said. He blushed. "The mud. Let the mud harden." He closed his eyes and muttered, "Mother's mercy."

Ari burst out laughing.

Neall gave her an exasperated look. "You think this is funny?"

"I'm sorry, Neall, but you've got two paw prints—"

"I know where they are," he said dryly.

"Yes, of course you do." She focused on a tree to

avoid looking at the paw prints. He was embarrassed.
She found that sweet. She could see herself teasing
him about it months from now.

"Ari . . ."

When she looked at him, concern drove away the
amusement. He looked like a man who expected to
be hurt.

"Do you have time to talk?" Neall asked quietly.

"Yes." She held out her hand, surprised by the way
his trembled when he took it. Strange to feel like she
was the one who was suddenly older, stronger, wiser.
But she had the answers; he only had the questions.

"I'm no longer staying at Baron Felston's house,"
Neall said abruptly. "I was asked to leave." He made
a sound that was both bitter and amused. "Thrown
out, if you want the truth."

"Why?"

He shook his head. "It doesn't matter. If it hadn't
been this, it would have been something else. It's a
relief to be away from them."

"This happened this morning?"

"Last night. I'm staying with Ahern for the time
being."

"It didn't occur to you to stay here?" She tried to
pull her hand from his. His fingers tightened, refusing
to let go.

"Yes, it occurred to me. Mother's mercy, of course
it occurred to me. But it wouldn't have been fair." He
took a deep breath, let it out slowly. "Ari, I've tried
to wait, I've tried to be patient. But now I need to
know. I'll be leaving soon. Will I be going alone?"

"Why have you never kissed me, Neall?"

"Because I was afraid I would want too much more,
and you wouldn't want the same."

"And now?" She saw his hesitation, saw the nerves.

"Is this a test?" he demanded. "Does my future
depend on how well I kiss?"

"No."

"Then will you at least tell me if this kiss is an
ending or a beginning?"

Kindness, courtesy, respect, loyalty. Love. What were Lucian's trinkets compared to jewels like that? She'd thought about it last night. If she never saw Lucian again, she would remember him fondly and have no regrets. If she never saw Neall again . . .

"It's a beginning," she said. Then she smiled. "We'll build a good life together, Neall."

His face lit with joy. He put his arms around her, and he kissed her.

There was honesty in his kiss. And there was heart. It didn't burn through her until she couldn't think. But it created a warmth deep inside her that swelled until it filled her. This wouldn't burn hot and fast, swiftly turning to ashes. With Neall, the fire would burn long and slow and sweet.

He broke the kiss, buried his face in her hair. "How long will it take you to pack what you want to take with you? I'm sure Ahern will loan us a wagon. He might even be willing to have a couple of his men ride with us so that they can bring the wagon back."

"Will Ahern let you stay with him until the harvest?"

His head shot up. "Harvest?" he said in a strangled voice.

"Be sensible, Neall. When we get to your land, there won't be time to plant a crop to see us through the winter. There won't be any seeds for next spring. If we wait until the harvest, I'll be able to can as much as possible from the garden here for us to take with us."

"But . . . Harvest?"

He sounded so plaintive, she fought not to smile. "Not everything has to wait until the harvest."

Desire filled his eyes. Then he shook his head. "We'll wait. If you end up with child, you might feel too poorly to enjoy the journey."

She almost told him that this was a safe time and that she knew how to prevent creating a babe. But, in a flash of insight, she realized he didn't want to be with her in the same bed that Lucian had claimed for a little while. He didn't want to be in a bed where she might compare lovers and find him wanting.

"All right." Now she smiled. "Come on. We both have work to do."

"What does that mean?" Dianna asked, looking from Aiden to Lyrra, then back to Aiden. "How can a pillar forget?"

"I can only tell you what I was told," Aiden said. He raked his fingers through his hair. "But she knows more than she said. I'm sure of that."

"The Pillars of the World have been forgotten," Lyrra said quietly. "Pillars of the World. Branches of the Mother."

Aiden nodded. "That's what I was thinking."

"What?" Dianna said impatiently.

Lyrra sighed. "What if those two things are somehow connected? What if it's the witches' magic that anchors the road through the Veil to the human world, even if they're not aware of it?"

Dianna jumped up, too edgy to sit anymore. "Why should it? The Fae created Tir Alainn."

"All the roads through the Veil are anchored to the Old Places," Aiden said. "We've never thought to look, but it wouldn't be difficult to find out if there are witches living at each one. And if they *are* living in the Old Places and that's what keeps the roads from closing, they might not be destroying Tir Alainn deliberately."

"All they would have to do is leave the Old Place. As their magic fades from the land—"

"The road would close," Dianna said softly. "If that's true, we'll just have to make sure the witches don't leave the Old Places."

"Blessings of the day to you, Ahern," Ari said. "Are you looking for your old gray stallion again?"

Ahern snorted. "No. And I'm not looking for that pony stud of yours either." When Ari looked puzzled, he smiled. "The boy said he'd work to earn his keep, so I put him to work."

Ari felt her cheeks heat. "He told you then."

"He told me. Well, he didn't *say* anything, but he was grinning like a fool when he came back." He turned toward the sound of a whimper. His face became grim. "When did you get the pup?"

"A few days ago." Ari stared at the puppy cowering under the bench, then at Ahern as he crouched in front of the bench and held out his hand. No. He *couldn't* be. "He's afraid of the Fae."

"Shows he has brains. Is he afraid of horses, too? He'll smell them on me."

"Not afraid, exactly. Neall's gelding likes to sneak up on him and snort on his tail."

Ahern chuckled. "That one. His sire was a dark horse."

"A dark horse?"

For the first time she could remember, Ahern looked disconcerted.

"A dark horse is a breed unto itself. They have brains and courage . . . and they can be fiercely loyal."

"Are those the special horses you breed? The ones you don't sell?"

Ahern nodded slowly. "Special horses for a special kind of person. When the right person comes along, the horse goes with her."

Merle crept forward enough to sniff Ahern's hand. Apparently he liked what he smelled. When he started to jump up, Ahern swiftly put his hand on the pup's head and pushed him to the ground. The pup cringed.

"Take care, little one," he said as he rubbed Merle's belly. "There's no sense in bashing your brains out before you're old enough to use them."

Ahern stood up. Merle rolled over, shook himself, and bumbled off to explore the meadow.

"He'll be a good animal when he grows into himself."

"He's already a good animal," Ari said defensively.

Ahern smiled in approval. "Will you accept a going-away gift?"

"You don't have to give us anything. Neall said you already offered the loan of a wagon."

"Not a gift for both of you. Just you."

"I—" What was she supposed to say to that? How was she supposed to interpret the look in his eyes?

"A horse," Ahern said. "I know you didn't want one before, and, considering some things that happened last year, I think I understand why."

"I don't know. I—"

"Neall was a small boy when he came to live here. He doesn't remember how far away the nearest village is from your land. You'll need a horse of your own, and I want to be sure you've got a good animal under you."

"I'm not sure."

"Ari." Catching her chin between his thumb and forefinger, he raised her head until she looked at him. "Let me do this for you. For my own sake."

She wrapped her arms around his neck, hugging hard. "I'll miss you."

He patted her back awkwardly before stepping away.

"Ahern, do you think I'm doing the right thing?"

"Do you have doubts about the boy?"

Ari shook her head. "No. Not about Neall."

"Then go with him and don't look back." He paused. "Your grandmother was hoping you'd go with him one day. She told me that."

Ari wiped her eyes before the tears could spill over. She sniffed, dabbed her nose with her sleeve. "You know the hill Gran favored?"

"I know it."

"Sometimes, when the ground is still soft after a rain, I've noticed there are hoofprints on the hill. I think that's where your gray horse goes when he goes wandering."

Ahern stared at the land for a long time. Then, in a voice she could barely hear, "I know he does."

*   *   *

Merle dove under the bench, knocking over a basket of yarn.

"You must regret having him a dozen times a day," Dianna said, walking over to the bench where Ari sat. She wasn't surprised by the coolness in Ari's eyes, but she *was* surprised to feel stung by it.

"I don't regret having him." Ari righted the basket and continued her task.

"What are you doing?"

"Sorting the yarn. I can't take all of it with me, so I want to be sure I take what I need for the weavings I have in mind."

"Take it?" Alarm made Dianna's heart race. "Where are you going?"

"I'm leaving Brightwood."

"You can't!"

"I'm not chattel, Dianna. I'm not bound to the land."

"But you *can't* leave." Dianna paced to the well, then back to the bench. "It's because of that . . . that *Neall,* isn't it?"

"Yes. We're getting married."

"That's no reason for you to leave. Let the lout live here with you if you're so determined to have him."

Ari shot to her feet. "He's not a lout, and what I do is none of your business."

"Oh, but it is my business," Dianna said sharply. "You don't understand." She took a deep breath, choked down her temper. "Ari, Tir Alainn is disappearing, piece by piece. We believe it's because the witches are leaving the Old Places. In some way, your magic anchors the road through the Veil."

"Well, I'm sorry, Dianna, but you'll have to find someone else to anchor your road. I'm leaving."

"How can you be so selfish?" Dianna shouted. "If you walk away from here, my home will cease to exist, my entire Clan will die. Will you have the deaths of that many people on your shoulders?"

"You can't lay that on me," Ari shouted back. "I

have nothing to do with Tir Alainn or the Fae. I'm a witch. My family has kept this land for generations. Now it's time for someone else to look after it. Let the Fae look after it."

"I thought we were friends."

Ari just stared at her. "How convenient that you decided to become friends at this particular time. Where were you before now? Where were you during all the years before now?"

"We didn't know—"

"That's right! You didn't know! You didn't know someone besides yourself might be important, might have wants, needs, dreams. I'm going to have my own life, and I'm going to have it with Neall."

"Why would you want someone like him when you can have a man like Lucian?"

"*Because I don't want worthless trinkets!* I want *my* daughter to have a father. *I* want to have a lover who will also be a partner."

"Ari—"

"I looked in my family's jewelry box today. And do you know what I saw, Dianna? Trinkets. Lots of trinkets. That's all we've ever been worth to anyone. Well, I'm *not* going to settle for *trinkets*."

"*You can't leave here.*"

"You can't stop me."

Oh, yes, I can. Furious, but not knowing what else to do for the moment, Dianna walked away.

Chapter Twenty-seven

Adolfo carefully refolded the letter.

Baron Prescott had gained the land and timber he'd craved easily enough. Too easily. The witch who had owned the land had been old and weak. He had barely taken her through the first level of cleansing torture before she broke and confessed to being the cause of all the village's ills.

Because she had confessed so quickly, the baron had not been quite as grateful as he should have been. So this new plea for assistance was most welcome—for two reasons.

His courier had disappeared and all the silver coins that the man had been charged to deliver to the other Inquisitors had disappeared as well. Two of his men, riding to their next assigned village, had found the courier's horse at a farm. The farmer swore that he'd been given the horse by a woman who wore a strange-looking black gown and rode a dark horse.

She had left the next morning, riding south.

He shivered at the memory. He couldn't tell if it was fear or rage that made him react so, and that infuriated him.

So he would accept Baron Felston's invitation, rid the baron's virtuous people of the foul stench of the witch, and refill his own purse.

And on the journey to Ridgeley, he would think of some way to deal with the Gatherer and teach her the penalty for stealing from the Master Inquisitor.

Chapter Twenty-eight

The dark horse stopped walking, snorted in surprise. Morag snapped out of a light doze. Seeing no obvious reason for the horse's reaction, she pushed her tangled hair away from her face and grimaced as she forced her body to straighten up in the saddle.

Something had been pushing her for the past two days, a feeling that if she didn't keep moving, she would be too late. For what, she couldn't say. But the feeling had been strong enough to keep her on the road, only stopping for a few hours each night to let the horses rest.

Those hours had held no rest for her. The same dream washed through her uneasy sleep, over and over again. She was standing as the Gatherer in front of someone. She couldn't see who it was because mist surrounded both of them. She held out her hand—and kept hoping the other person wouldn't take it. She didn't want to gather this spirit, but that decision wasn't hers. The person standing before her would make that choice. Then a hand slowly came out of the mist, reaching for hers . . . and she would wake up, shivering.

Driven out of sleep once again—and briefly wondering if Morphia was trying to send her a message through this dream—she had saddled the dark horse and continued the journey, traveling through the early hours of the morning. The sun was barely up now, and she had no idea where she was or how much farther she had to travel. She only knew she had to keep going until . . .

There was a cottage up ahead. She'd been looking at it without really seeing it. But all the horses' attention was focused on that place, even the wounded mare.

She took a deep breath, breathed out slowly. A sweetness in the air. A richness.

She had come to an Old Place.

"Let's see if there's anyone home," she said.

The dark horse pricked his ears and moved forward at a fast walk.

She turned him off the road before they reached a low-walled garden, going through the meadow to circle around to the back of the cottage.

A young woman stood at the well, warily watching her approach.

I should have used the glamour so she wouldn't be afraid of being approached by one of the Fae. Since the woman had already seen her, Morag dismissed the thought. Besides, she wasn't in the habit of hiding what she was.

"Blessings of the day to you," the woman said.

"And to you," Morag replied. So tired. So desperately tired. "Could you spare some water for the horses?"

"Yes, of course." The woman turned to fill the buckets on the ground beside the well. She paused. "Who are you?"

Morag grunted softly as she dismounted. "I'm Morag." Then she realized that wasn't actually the question. "I'm the Gatherer."

"Oh." The woman filled the buckets, then set them a couple of paces away from the well. Two mares hurried forward to drink. "I'm Ari."

No longer compelled to keep moving, Morag wanted nothing more than to lie down in the meadow and let the strength in the land flow into her weary body.

She no longer felt compelled to keep moving. She looked at the cottage, at the meadow, and, finally, at Ari. "You're a witch."

"Yes, I am."

"I've—" —*never met one of your kind alive.* Morag shivered, clutched the saddle to stay on her feet.

Ari hurried over to her. "Why don't you sit on the bench and rest." She wrapped one arm around Morag's waist and led her over to the bench. "Would you like some water?"

"Please." Morag leaned back against the cottage wall and closed her eyes. Some time later—seconds, minutes, hours, she couldn't tell—Ari said, "Here," and pressed a mug into her hands. With her eyes still closed, Morag raised the cup to her lips and drank. There was strength in the water, strength in the air, strength in the land. Strength that was still vibrant. Mother's mercy, it had been so long since she'd felt this.

After refilling the buckets for the next two horses, Ari stood in front of the bench, twisting interlocked fingers. "Will I have time to say goodbye to some people and find someone to take care of Merle?"

Morag opened her eyes and studied the woman in front of her. "I see no shadows in your face," she said quietly. When Ari only looked puzzled, she added, "I didn't come here to gather. I stopped to ask for water—and directions."

Ari's puzzlement took on a different quality. "I didn't think the Gatherer would need directions in order to . . . gather."

Morag smiled. "I have a guide for my work, and I hear the call quite well. When that's not the reason I'm looking for someone, I depend on a map or directions just like anyone else."

"Oh." Ari returned the smile. When the sun stallion bugled a demand for water, she rolled her eyes. "I'm coming." She hurried to refill the bucket for the sun stallion and the dark horse. Then her eyes lingered for a long time on the wounded mare. "What happened to her?" she asked when she returned to the bench.

"Nighthunters," Morag replied wearily. "They devour life."

Ari studied the mare a while longer. "Poor thing. Is there nothing that can be done for her?"

"I don't know. That's one of the things I want to find out once I find Ahern. And I have to find the Bard."

"Well," Ari said with a tartness that focused Morag's drifting attention, "neither will be difficult to find. You can reach Ahern's farm by crossing the road and going over the fields. And the road through the Veil is in the woods beyond the meadow."

"How do you know the Bard will be there?" Morag asked slowly.

"I don't know if he's still there, but he came to Brightwood with some . . . friends . . . for the Solstice."

"Brightwood? Yes, the name fits this place."

Ari went back to the well and filled the buckets again. Looking at the wounded mare, she picked up the buckets and walked over to the privy house. The wounded mare followed, each step an effort.

Her own muscles protesting, Morag rose from the bench and also followed.

Ari set one bucket down for the mare to drink. She crouched, placed her right hand in the other bucket, and closed her eyes.

Morag tensed as she felt power gather and flow. She could almost see it shining through Ari's skin.

"The cleansing heat of fire to burn out what is not welcome," Ari said quietly. "The strength of earth to heal." Rising, she picked up the bucket and poured some of the water over each of the mare's wounds.

Morag wasn't sure what she was expecting, but she felt a stab of disappointment when nothing happened. Ari, on the other hand, studied the wounds and nodded. Then she sighed. "That might help her enough until Ahern takes a look at her. Although I'm not sure there's anything even he can do."

Morag kept her eyes on the mare. *You know the Bard but don't recognize the Lord of the Horse? Yet you know him, too.*

"May I leave the horses here while I go to Ahern's?" Morag asked.

Ari hesitated. "You're tired. Why don't you rest for a while? I can walk over to Ahern's and ask him to come over here to see the horses."

Morag almost agreed, then decided against it. She wanted to talk to the Lord of the Horse on his own ground, where she wouldn't have to worry about revealing who he was. She shook her head. "Rest would be welcome, but there's no need for you to interrupt your own work." She tipped her head toward the horses, who were now eagerly grazing in the meadow. The dark horse looked at her longingly, waiting to be free of saddle and bridle before joining the others. "Talking to Ahern can wait for a few hours."

Ari picked up the buckets and smiled ruefully. "I do have plenty of work, especially since I have to decide what to pack and what needs to stay here."

Alarm surged through Morag. "Pack? You're leaving the Old Place?"

Ari's friendly expression turned wary. "I'm getting married. Neall and I are going to live in the west."

"But—"

Death whispered, *I'm coming to this place.*

Morag shivered and bit her tongue lightly to hold back the words. Death was coming to Brightwood. Not today. Perhaps not tomorrow. But Death was coming.

"In that case," she said, "that's all the more reason for you not to take time out of your day." *No matter what it means to the Clan who lives here, the sooner you're gone, the better. Although even the west of Sylvalan won't be far enough away if we don't do something to stop the Black Coats.*

She walked back to the well with Ari, who again refilled the buckets and left them for the horses.

"Would you like a bath?" Ari asked.

Morag groaned. "A bath. I could kill for a bath." Seeing the way Ari's eyes widened, she smiled. "I should phrase that differently, shouldn't I?"

"Definitely."

Morag laughed. "A bath would be most welcome. But let me get my horse settled first."

After the dark horse was unsaddled and the gear stored in the cow shed, Ari led Morag into the cottage.

"Come in and be welcome," Ari said.

Morag wasn't sure how Ari managed to heat so much water so quickly, nor did she care. The bathing tub was big enough for her to sink down and soak her torso in the well-heated water as long as she kept her knees bent. When the water began to cool, she washed herself, then used the two pitchers of water Ari had left beside the tub to wash and rinse her hair.

She hadn't been this clean since she and Morphia had fled down the road through the Veil. After drying off, she wrapped the towel around herself and grimaced at her clothes, not eager to put them back on.

A knock on the door was followed by Ari cautiously poking her head into the room. She held out some clothes. "These may not fit well, but they're clean."

"Thank you."

"I'll fill a washtub, and you can let your clothes soak for a bit."

Morag smiled. "There isn't anything I own that I would want to put on a clean body right now."

Ari returned the smile. "I have the same feeling after working in the garden all day."

Morag dressed quickly, then followed her nose to the kitchen.

"Would you like some soup? Or would you like to sleep for a while?" Ari asked.

Morag's stomach rumbled, answering the question.

Ari dished out two bowls of soup. Before she could take them to the table in the main room, Morag said, "May we eat outside? I'd like to keep an eye on the horses to make sure they're settled."

Ari folded some small towels into pads so they could hold the soup bowls without burning their hands. She brought out some cheese and lightly buttered bread and set the plate between them on the bench.

They ate in silence while they watched the horses graze.

Contentment seeped into Morag. The horses were relaxed, even the dark horse and the sun stallion. That was a good sign that there was nothing here that would harm them. They'd both been uneasy since the first meeting with the nighthunters.

"May I ask a favor?" Ari said.

"You may ask," Morag replied cautiously.

"You can see the spirits of the dead." Ari waited for Morag's nod before continuing. "I was wondering . . . I'd like to know before I leave Brightwood that my mother and grandmother have gone on to the Summerland."

"That I can do," Morag said. She started to set her bowl of soup aside, then stopped when Ari touched her arm lightly.

"There's time," Ari said.

When they finished the meal, Ari led her to a bedroom off the main room. "I'll make up a bed in one of the upstairs rooms for you, but for now, you can sleep here."

Unsettled by the strength of the relief she felt that Ari would allow her to stay for a day or two, Morag just nodded and sat down on the bed. She waited until Ari closed the door before stretching out on top of the covers.

Sleep didn't follow exhaustion. She lay awake for some time, listening to the quiet sounds of living. She was just starting to drift off when she heard a nervous snort followed by the sound of the window being pushed up by someone outside.

Opening her eyes just enough to see, she watched the window, tensed.

The dark horse's head poked into the room.

"See?" Morag heard Ari say in a low voice. "She's fine. She didn't leave you. She's just sleeping. Now get your hooves out of my flower bed, you big oaf."

The dark horse withdrew his head. Morag heard Ari scolding him to watch where he put his feet if he was going to keep poking his head through the window.

The dark horse snorted. Ari huffed.

Picturing the standoff made Morag smile. And smiling, she fell asleep.

The daylight had already softened by the time Morag woke up. At first, the silence was peaceful, soothing. Then she sat up and listened hard.

Should it be so silent? What if something terrible had happened and she'd slept so deeply she hadn't been aware of it? No. Surely if something had happened, she would have heard the dark horse. Surely.

Yap yap yap.

Turning toward the sound, she got out of bed, went through the arch that led to the adjoining dressing room, and looked out the window. What was a shadow hound puppy doing here?

Then she saw the tan front legs, which explained well enough why the pup had been abandoned in the human world. Not a responsible thing to do—and not a safe one. The shadow hounds had been bred to run with the Wild Hunt, and even an animal that wasn't a purebred shadow hound would grow into a large, fierce hunter.

Wondering if she should talk to Ari about the pup, she watched from the window for a minute before she realized the dark horse and the sun stallion were playing "tease the puppy."

The sun stallion pranced in front of the puppy, catching its attention. Yapping, the puppy did its own less-than-graceful prancing, daring the stallion to come closer. While the pup yapped at the sun stallion, the dark horse silently came up behind it, his head low to the ground. When his muzzle almost touched the puppy's hindquarters, he snorted. Loudly. Yipping, the pup dashed away.

"Stop it, both of you," Morag heard Ari say sternly.

"You shouldn't be teasing him. You're both so much bigger."

Smiling, Morag turned away from the window to join Ari outside. As she left the room, she noticed the glass-doored bookcase, but didn't stop to look at what was inside.

When Morag appeared at the open kitchen door, the dark horse trotted over, looking very pleased with himself.

"If he nips your nose, it's no less than you deserve," Morag said quietly. But she smiled and petted him to soften the scold. She knew he had a playful side—it was part of his breed—but he seldom had a chance to play.

Seeing Morag, Ari walked over to the kitchen door, the puppy sheltered in her arms.

"This is Merle?" Morag asked, remembering that Ari had been concerned about finding someone to take care of Merle when she'd thought Morag had come to gather her.

"Yes, this is Merle." Ari looked at the dark horse and huffed. "What is it about horses that color that they enjoy teasing puppies?"

Morag's hand froze against the dark horse's cheek. "Horses that color?"

"Dark, like yours. Neall's gelding does the same thing. He thinks it's funny. The gelding, that is." Ari frowned. "Neall probably thinks it's funny, too, but he's smart enough not to say so."

Morag stared at Ari. "Neall. The man you're going to marry. He rides a dark horse?"

"Well, his gelding is the same color as your horse, so I guess it could be called a dark horse," Ari said. She looked puzzled. "He bought it from Ahern, and Ahern told me the gelding was sired by a dark horse. One of his special horses."

One of Ahern's special horses? Oh, yes, they were special. So who—and what—was this Neall that Ahern would sell him an animal sired by a dark horse?

"There's still plenty of light left," Ari said. "Did you want to ride over to Ahern's?"

Morag stepped out of the kitchen. She didn't want to ride anywhere at the moment, didn't want to pass the borders of this place. She focused on the wounded mare, and her eyes widened in surprise.

"She looks a little better."

"Yes," Ari said thoughtfully. "I think, in her own way, she's been undoing the harm done to her so that she can heal." She pointed to a spot in the meadow that, to Morag's eyes, looked no different than the rest. "I've watched her today. She's stayed near that spot where I did the Solstice dance. And as she's grazing, she keeps moving widdershins to undo what has been done."

"She can't undo what the nighthunters' bites did just by moving in a certain direction," Morag protested. "If it were that simple, she would have done it before." Even as she said it, she knew why the mare hadn't done it before. "It's not that *she* knows. She's just instinctively following something that's *here*."

Ari looked uncomfortable. Rubbing her cheek against Merle's head and giving him one last pat, she set him down. He sat on her foot and stared at Morag. "Yes, I think so. My family has done a lot of dances in that meadow over the years. Even when it's quiet, the magic is strong there."

"If you're willing, I'd like to let the horses stay here tonight."

"Of course." Ari paused. "Is there something you would like to do? I have some stew cooking. It should be ready soon."

"I'd like to answer your question about your mother and grandmother." Morag looked at the dark horse and added a bit plaintively, "Do we have to ride?"

Ari chuckled. "No. It's a pleasant walk. This way."

When they reached the edge of the meadow, Morag looked back. The dark horse trotted up to her. The sun stallion was watching her, as if uncertain if he should round up his mares and follow.

Morag sighed. "We're just going for a walk," she
said, raising her voice enough for the sun stallion to
hear. "You can all stay in the meadow. You too," she
added quietly.

The dark horse shook his head. He knew why she
was taking this walk.

Merle yapped once at the dark horse, then trotted
ahead of Ari to see what interesting messages his nose
might pick up.

Ari led the little procession to a pond. A large oak
tree grew near it.

"My mother used to sit under that oak tree and
watch the pond," Ari said. "Her body is there."

Morag looked at the tree and all the surrounding
land. She shook her head. "She isn't here. I didn't
show her the road to the Shadowed Veil, but one of
the others who are Death's Servants must have done
so."

There was something about Ari's sigh of relief that
Morag found disturbing. "How did your mother die?"

Ari stared at the pond. "Lung sickness. We have a
small ice cellar to keep food cold and fresh. I had a
chill that day. She told me to stay home and keep
warm, and she went out to cut the ice by herself. She
fell into the pond, and—" Ari stopped. Closed her
eyes. "She didn't fall in. Water was her branch of the
Mother. When she commanded, water obeyed. She
could walk across that pond when there was only a
skin of ice and come to no harm."

Morag felt something wash through her. Something
dangerous and feral. "Do you know who pushed her
in? That *is* what happened, isn't it? Someone wanted
the witches gone from this place and attacked her
when she was alone, throwing her into the pond to
drown."

Ari shuddered. "Anyone else, weighed down by
heavy winter clothes, would have drowned. But the
water obeyed. And she got out of the pond and made
it home. But the lung sickness took hold, and there
was nothing I could do for her."

"Did she tell you who pushed her in?"

Ari shook her head. "She kept mumbling 'Ridgeley,' but that's the name of the village. She had a fever, so it's not surprising that she made no sense."

"What else did she say?"

Ari shrugged. "She talked about daughters, about how Gran was right—the daughters needed to go away."

Morag stared at the pond. "Why didn't she fight? She had magic. She had power. Why didn't she fight?" The depth of her anger surprised her. She had no right to aim it at Ari, who had shown her nothing but courtesy. *But there are things you do not ask of the dead that can be asked of the living.*

Ari looked at her warily. "It is our creed to do no harm with our magic. Besides," she added with a bit of temper, "what could she have done? Her gifts were water and a little earth."

"She could have broken the ice beneath the feet of whoever attacked her and drowned the bastards," Morag said fiercely.

Ari's eyes widened.

Struggling not to let the rage inside her escape, Morag took a deep breath, let it out slowly. "Ari, on most days your creed is a commendable way to live. But there is a great difference between doing no harm and defending yourself. I have shown too many young women the road to the Shadowed Veil because they followed your creed. For them, it was already too late to say anything. But you . . ."

"I—I'm not sure I could do that. I'm not sure I could use magic to harm someone, even if—"

"Do you love Neall?" Morag demanded.

"Y-yes."

"If someone was trying to hurt him, would you just stand by and let him suffer or would you *do* something?"

Ari didn't answer.

Morag sighed. "Where is your grandmother?"

"This way," Ari said in a subdued voice.

They didn't speak on the way to the hill. Even the animals were subdued, picking up the changed mood.

The moment Morag set foot on the bottom of the hill, she knew. But she said nothing.

When she reached the top of the hill, a light breeze played with her hair and made the wildflowers dance.

"Even on the stillest day, there's always a little wind on this hill. This was Gran's favorite spot."

"Her gift was air?" Morag asked.

Ari nodded, then looked at Morag anxiously.

The ghost of an older woman smiled at them, then pressed one finger against her lips.

"There is no one here," Morag lied.

"Thank you." Ari sighed in relief. Then she smiled. "We should get back to the cottage. I left the stew on the back of the stove where it would just simmer, but it will be done by now."

Morag followed Ari. Before leaving the crest of the hill, she looked back and whispered, "I will return."

Yes, the ghost replied. *There are things to be said.*

Chapter Twenty-nine

"That's all the messages said?" Dianna asked impatiently, her eyes raking Lyrra and Aiden, then skipping past Lucian. Ever since he'd learned of Ari's intended marriage, his brooding had taken on a surly quality.

"The bards from several Clans have all basically sent the same thing," Aiden replied, his own patience sounding strained. "Which makes sense since the Sleep Sister is the source of all of the messages. 'The witches know the key to keeping the roads through the Veil open, and they need to be protected.' "

"Well, it's a little hard to protect them when they blithely decide to run off with some . . . *human*."

"They aren't Fae," Lyrra said carefully. "They can't be expected to think like we do. Or care about the same things we do."

Dianna whirled around to face Lyrra. "But it's not too much to expect them to show a *little* heart. If Ari leaves, this part of Tir Alainn will be lost—and the Clan with it. *He* doesn't need her. *We* do. And one way or another, she's going to stay here."

"That explains what's threatening our part of Tir Alainn," Aiden said. "But that doesn't explain the rest. We need to find out why the witches are leaving the Old Places, and we need to find out how they're connected to the Pillars of the World. Because I'm sure there *is* some connection."

"I can't tell you about the Pillars of the World," said an unfamiliar voice, "but I can tell you why the witches are leaving the Old Places."

Dianna turned toward the intruder. "This is a private—" A chill went through her when she saw the black-haired woman standing in the doorway.

The woman entered the room, carefully closed the door, then walked toward them, her black gown fluttering around her in a way that made Dianna's skin crawl. Stopping before she was close enough to touch any of them, her dark eyes traveled over each of them.

"Who are you?" Dianna asked, knowing already . . . and hoping she was wrong.

"I am Morag," the stranger said. "The Gatherer."

Silence settled around the room.

"Why are you here?" Dianna said, not realizing that her voice had gone shrill until Lyrra gave her a sharp, warning look.

Something flashed in Morag's eyes so fast Dianna couldn't identify it.

"I came seeking the Bard, the Huntress, and the Lightbringer. I came seeking answers." Her eyes pinned Aiden to his chair, then swept over Lucian and Dianna. "And I came to give a warning. The Fae have to protect the Old Places and the ones who live there. If they don't, soon there will be nothing left of Tir Alainn."

"At the moment, it seems you have one more answer than we do," Aiden said. "Why are the witches leaving the Old Places?"

"Because," Morag said softly, "they're being slaughtered."

Dianna sat with her hands clenched in her lap, unable to think of anything to say. What could anyone say after listening to Morag's tale?

"Who are these Inquisitors?" Lyrra finally asked. "Where did they come from?"

"Arktos, maybe," Aiden said thoughtfully. He narrowed his eyes. "Or Wolfram. I think the roads through the Veil started closing there first."

"And then they spread like a plague against magic," Lyrra added, brushing her hair back wearily. "It certainly explains the songs and stories we've heard lately. It's so much easier to stand by and let someone suffer if you've been told they're evil."

Dianna sat up straight, excitement coursing through her. "But if some of the witches fled before the Inquisitors could capture them, all we would have to do is find them and bring them back to an Old Place. Then the road through the Veil would open again. There might still be Fae who survived." She slanted a look at Morag. "You did say you weren't sure what happened to the Clan when the mist covered that part of Tir Alainn."

"No, I don't know what happened to them," Morag replied too calmly. "But you've given no reason why any witches who have survived in Arktos or Wolfram—or even in the eastern part of Sylvalan—would want to return to an Old Place and let anyone know they still live."

"Why wouldn't they be willing to return if the Fae are willing to protect them?" Dianna asked.

"I must go," Morag said abruptly, rising from the bench. "I've done what I've come for."

Dianna and the others exchanged a startled look as Morag walked out of the room. Seeing the way her gown fluttered like tattered black shrouds made Dianna jump up and follow.

"Morag," Dianna called. She suppressed a shudder when the Gatherer turned to face her. *I am the Huntress. I am the female leader of the Fae. There's no reason why I should fear her. She, too, answers to me. And there is no one better suited to take care of this.* "There is something you can do that will save this part of Tir Alainn."

He fears the shining roads, Morag thought sadly, feeling the tension drain from the dark horse when he was back in the human world. *Has feared them ever since we barely escaped having one close around us. Even in a place like Brightwood, where the magic is so strong, he no longer trusts that the roads will be safe. And each time we've taken the road to the Shadowed Veil, it's been harder for him. The day will come when fear will rip something from his heart that can never be restored. But if I choose another dark horse and leave him, it would break his heart. There has to be a way to let him go without hurting him.*

Where two trails in the woods met, the dark horse firmly headed for the one that led to Ari's cottage.

"No," Morag said, turning him toward the other trail. "There's something we have to do first."

He didn't like it, but since they weren't returning to the shining road through the Veil, he obeyed.

I'll find a way to let him go. I'll find someone to take my place for him. He's too young to be given to Death simply because he's inconvenient. Just like . . .

Morag's lips thinned to a grim line. The dark horse was the least of her problems at the moment.

At least the Lightbringer and the Huntress were aware of the danger to Tir Alainn. At least they didn't scoff and refuse to listen. At least they'd said they wanted to protect the witches. But she'd sensed the undercurrents swirling in the room. She hadn't understood them . . . until Dianna had asked her to gather a particular spirit and show it the road to the Shadowed Veil.

Neall. The young man Ari loved. The man Dianna wanted eliminated so that Ari would stay at Brightwood. The man who had bought a dark horse from Ahern.

Very soon she would have to make a decision about Neall. But there was a visit to be made first.

When she got to the hill where the wind always blew, she left the dark horse at the bottom of the hill and climbed to the top. She walked over to the ghost, sat down beside her.

They sat in comfortable silence for several minutes. Then the ghost said, "The wind from the north carries much sorrow."

"Yes," Morag said softly.

"There are warnings whispered. A violent storm has

come to Sylvalan, a storm that rejoices in the Daughters' pain. They must flee the Old Places and hide before it strikes them."

Daughters? Morag wondered. But she asked a different question. "Did none of Death's Servants come to show you the road to the Shadowed Veil and the Summerland beyond it?"

"One rode this way," the ghost said. "She took my daughter with her. I chose to stay for a while."

"Why?"

"Because of Ari. I wanted to know that she was going with Neall, that she had the strength to leave duty and choose a life that would nourish her heart."

Morag shifted uneasily. "You want her to leave with him? You approve of Neall?"

"Oh, yes." The ghost smiled. "He's a fine young man. With him, my granddaughter will have a richer life than she could ever have here."

"If she leaves here," Morag said carefully, "the road through the Veil will close and a piece of Tir Alainn will be lost. The Fae need her to stay."

The ghost's smile turned brittle and bitter. "The Fae are very good at knowing what they want. They're also very good at having someone else shoulder the burden in order for them to have what they want. They may *want* Ari to stay, but they don't *need* her to stay. The Fae can hold the shining road."

"Then why haven't we?"

"Because you had us to do it for you." She paused for a long time. Then, "Tir Alainn was meant to be a sanctuary, a place to rest and renew body and spirit. But the Fae found life in a land that required little toil was more to their liking than a world where the rose and beetle both reside. They lived above the world like creatures who live in the branches of a tree and touch the ground only to play—or when they see something they want. But they forgot that without the roots the tree cannot survive."

"And you are the roots?"

The ghost looked out over the land. "The Fae are

the Mother's Children. But we are the Daughters. We
are the Pillars of the World."

Morag shook her head. "I don't understand."

"Don't you? The answers are in plain sight, if you
choose to look for them."

*This is why I never converse with the ghosts of old
women,* Morag thought irritably. *They no longer need
plain speaking, so they adore riddles.*

"What makes Neall so special that you would have
Ari leave the land and home your family has held for
generations?" Morag asked.

"He can give her more than trinkets," the ghost
replied sharply. She was silent for a moment. "If the
Fae here did persuade Ari to stay in order to keep
hold of their part of Tir Alainn, would they live here
with her, day after day, from season to season? Would
they accept the disappointments as well as the joys of
living in this world? Or would they fawn over her until
Neall finally left without her? And once he left, how
long would it be before they stopped visiting because
it was no longer necessary?"

Morag brushed some dirt off her boot. "You're very
bitter about us, aren't you?"

"I have read my family's history. I have reason to
feel bitter." The ghost sighed. "And I know that the
fault doesn't lie just with the Fae. The women in my
family chose trinkets of affection. But I want Ari to
have the richer jewels of love."

Morag stood up. "When she's gone, I'll come back
and show you the road to the Shadowed Veil."

"When she's gone, I, too, will be ready to go."

Morag walked over to the point where the hill
sloped downward. Then she turned back. "What is
your name?"

"I am Astra."

Nodding to acknowledge that she'd heard, Morag
walked down the hill to where the dark horse waited.

"What do you think of her?" Ahern asked, resting his
arms against the top rail of the paddock.

Neall grinned as he brought the dark mare to a halt and dismounted. "She's light on her feet, responsive to commands, and smart enough to compensate for the most inept rider. She's a beauty, Ahern." He stroked the mare's neck. "I hope you won't have to let her go to someone who won't appreciate her."

"The dark horses go where I will," Ahern replied. He paused, then added, "She's for Ari."

Neall's hand froze on the mare's neck as he stared at Ahern. "For— For Ari?"

"As you said, the mare can take care of a green rider. You'll need another horse for the journey, so I'll see that Ari's mounted as it suits me."

"But—"

"You have some objection?"

One look at Ahern's stern face had Neall turning his attention back to the mare. *He needs to do this because he cares about her. He's watched her from a distance all her life, and when we leave, he won't have even that. But every day he'll think of Ari and the mare and take some comfort in it.*

"No, sir," Neall said. "It's a very generous gift— and a welcome one."

"That's settled then." Ahern opened the paddock gate. "Get her settled in her stall before you head over to—"

The *clip-clop* of a horse's hooves, immediately followed by silence, made them turn.

A chill went down Neall's spine when he saw the woman on the dark horse riding toward them. A Fae woman on a Fae stallion. The dark horse had deliberately made that sound to alert them to its presence.

The woman dismounted and joined them at the paddock. Neall wished she'd just go away. Something about her unnerved him.

"You are Ahern?" When Ahern nodded, she said, "I am Morag." Then she looked at Neall and her interest sharpened.

"Blessings of the day to you, Mistress," Neall said. She smiled warmly, and whatever it was about her that unnerved him vanished in that warmth. "You must be Neall."

Out of the corner of his eye, he saw the way Ahern tensed. Fear spiked through him, although he couldn't have said why. The woman certainly hadn't done anything to cause it. "How did you know?"

"I'm staying with Ari, and your name has come up a time or two." The way she said it made it plain that it had been more than "a time or two." He felt his cheeks heat with pleasure. He hadn't been certain that Ari was pleased with her decision, but if she was actually talking about him—about *them*—surely that was a good sign.

"And I've heard that you're a fine young man who rides a dark horse," Morag added, looking at the mare. "So it wasn't difficult to figure out."

Ahern opened the paddock gate wider. "Take care of the mare," he said gruffly.

The abrupt dismissal surprised Neall. Ahern could be blunt to the point of rudeness, but, somehow, while the bluntness had been directed at him, the rudeness had been aimed at the woman.

He doesn't want me around her, Neall realized as he led the mare to the stable. *No. He doesn't want her around me. Why?*

He stopped just inside the stable, where he wouldn't be easily seen. As he turned to study the two Fae, he heard Ahern say, "Now what brings the Gatherer to Brightwood?"

"Horses," Morag said. Before she could say anything more, Neall and the dark mare burst out of the stables, galloping toward Brightwood. "Is something wrong?"

"I imagine he's going to see if his heart is still at Brightwood," Ahern replied. "Is she?"

"Ari? I imagine so. I haven't seen her since early this morning, so where else—" Morag's heart leaped. She clutched the paddock railing for balance. "She wouldn't go into the village by herself, would she? She wouldn't go alone.'

Ahern's frown turned to puzzlement. "She might. She's been doing just that since her mother died. Although lately—"

"She mustn't go by herself," Morag said urgently. "She *mustn't*." She told Ahern everything she knew about the witches dying at the Inquisitors' hands. She told him about the nighthunters and about her escape down a shining road just before it closed. She felt a keen satisfaction in the brutal grimness that filled Ahern's face.

"You think they're coming here," Ahern said. "To Brightwood."

Morag closed her eyes. "I'm not sure, but . . . Death is whispering. Death is coming here. Soon."

Ahern nodded. "Ari wants to wait to bring in the harvest so that they can take it with them. But that won't be for another few weeks—and that's too long, isn't it?"

"If the Inquisitors come here, even a day may be too long," Morag said wearily. "It doesn't take much time for someone to die a hard death, Ahern. It doesn't take much time at all. It was hard enough with the others, but I didn't know them. I've talked with Ari, eaten with her, come to know her a little. I don't want to show her the road to the Shadowed Veil. Not now. Not because of *them*."

"Then we'll have to convince her to leave without the harvest."

"*Can* you convince her?"

"Between us, Neall and I will convince her," Ahern said. "And if we can't, we'll tie her to the horse so that he can take her away." He shook himself, as if he could shake off the grimness for the time being. "Now what's this about horses?"

It will be all right, Morag thought a short while later as she and Ahern rode to Brightwood to look at the sun stallion and the mares. She'd been startled by his fierce determination to, as he'd phrased it, "put the

whole of Sylvalan between Ari and the Inquisitors,"
but she'd welcomed that determination. He, too, was
Fae. He knew as well as any of them what Ari's leaving would mean to the Clan who used the shining road
anchored to Brightwood. He still wanted her to go,
wanted her to be safe. Knowing he would do everything he could to make sure Ari and Neall were on
their way to their new home heartened her—and
made it easier to think about tomorrow morning,
when she would go back to Tir Alainn and tell the
Huntress her decision about Neall.

Stepping out of his carriage, Adolfo noticed the way
the baron's smile faltered as the man took note of the
other two Inquisitors and the guards who rode behind
the carriage.

"Baron Felston?" he said, taking a step forward to
reclaim the man's attention. "I am Adolfo, the Master
Inquisitor, the Witch's Hammer."

"I'm pleased—grateful—that you could put aside
your other duties and attend to my little problem so
quickly," Felston said.

*And you will express your gratitude with more than
words,* Adolfo thought. *In advance. Or you will find
yourself bargaining for more than the witch you wish
to be rid of.*

Felston flicked an uneasy glance at the other Inquisitors. He leaned toward Adolfo. "Are all these men
really necessary?" he asked in a low voice. "There's
only one witch at the Old Place, and she's not very
powerful."

Adolfo stared at the baron in a way that had wilted
stronger-willed men. "Many of your associates have
also assured me that the witches who are plaguing
their people weren't all that powerful. So I sent fully
trained Inquisitors to deal with the creatures. In the
few weeks I have been in Sylvalan using my skills to
help the people here rid themselves of the Evil One's
foul servants, I have lost more Inquisitors than I've
lost in *years* in Arktos and Wolfram." He shook his

head. "Do not tell me my business, Baron Felston. I know far better than you what kind of creature lives outside the village of Ridgeley, and I know what is required to deal with her. Besides," he added when Felston seemed about to argue again, "there is evidence that the Fae are also nearby. They, too, can be dangerous."

Bright spots of color appeared on Felston's cheeks, making Adolfo wonder if the man had already had an encounter with the Fair Folk.

"Come, Master Adolfo," Felston said after a moment, gesturing toward the front door of his house. "Let's get you and your men settled in. Then I think you should have a talk with my daughter, Odella."

Adolfo replied gravely, "If she has had the misfortune to have any dealings with the witch, I think that would be wise."

"Ari? Ari!" Neall vaulted out of the saddle, his heart pounding wildly when he didn't immediately see her. *"Ari!"*

A golden stallion galloped toward him, cutting him off from the cottage before he could take a step toward the half-open kitchen door.

Neall took a step forward. The stallion laid his ears back.

The dark mare nipped his sleeve and pulled him back.

Wondering how the warding spells would react if he tried to climb in through a window—and wondering if he could get in fast enough to avoid the stallion's hooves coming down on his back, Neall cupped his hands around his mouth and yelled, "Ari!"

An upstairs window opened. Ari leaned out. A delighted smile lit her face when she saw him. "Neall! Wait there. I'll be right down."

"Doesn't look like I'm going anywhere," Neall muttered, eyeing the stallion. He felt a flicker of amusement when Ari reached the kitchen door and found herself peering around a golden rump.

"Move," Ari said, giving that golden rump a timid smack.

The stallion kicked the bottom half of the door in response.

Ari disappeared. A few moments later, she appeared from around the side of the cottage. Before the stallion could charge toward her, she pointed a finger at him, and said sternly, "No matter what you seem to think, I am *not* one of your mares. I'm *his* mare." She frowned. "I didn't say that right, but you know what I mean."

Neall grinned, the relief of seeing her safe and well making him a little silly. "I think you said it just fine. And I promise you I have more finesse in certain areas than *he* does."

The stallion snorted.

Ari dashed over to Neall. "I was taking a look through the linen cupboard upstairs to see what we could use, and—" The light went out of her face when she noticed the dark mare. "What happened to Darcy? Is he hurt?"

Neall put his arm around her, needing the contact. "No, he's fine. He's probably mad at me for leaving him, but I wanted—" No, that wasn't why he'd come. He'd ridden the mare because she was already saddled and handy. But he'd have to take care how he said other things if he didn't want to end up battering at Ari's stubborn streak. "I wanted you to see her."

Ari held out her hand, palm up. The mare approached, quite willing to be introduced. While Ari and the mare were getting to know each other, Neall kept an eye on the stallion—who seemed to be keeping an eye on him. Then the wind shifted enough for the horse to catch his scent. The stallion suddenly relaxed and trotted off to join his mares.

"That's strange," Neall said quietly.

"Maybe he senses the Fae in you, and that told him you were all right." Ari patted the mare's neck, fingercombed the mane.

"What difference would that make?" Neall asked—

and then knew. The horse's hooves had made no sound. "He's a Fae horse."

Ari nodded. "Morag ended up with the sun stallion and the mares, so she decided to bring them to Ahern since she can't keep traveling with a herd of horses following her."

Neall leaped at the opening Ari's words provided. "She showed up at Ahern's a short while ago. Ari . . . You do know who she is, don't you?"

Giving the mare a final pat, Ari turned to face him. "Yes, I know. And while she's a guest in my house, I expect her to be treated with courtesy, Neall." She looked away. "I know what it's like to feel unwelcome."

There was nothing he could say that wouldn't make Ari defensive.

"All right," Neall said. "Since I'm here, is there anything I can help you with?"

Before Ari could answer, the dark mare pricked her ears and whinnied a greeting.

Neall tensed, turned to face whoever was coming.

Ahern and Morag rode around the cottage. When the Gatherer looked at him, her dark eyes were filled with too much understanding.

Ari's right. I doubt she ever feels welcome.

"Blessings of the day to you, Ahern," Ari said. She smiled at Morag. "I see you found him."

Morag returned the smile. "Yes, I found him."

When they dismounted, Ahern studied the sun stallion, who was nervously pawing the ground as he watched them.

"He's a fine one," Ahern said. "So are the mares." His gaze swung to the wounded mare, grazing by herself. He winced.

"She's better than she was," Ari said hurriedly. "I think she'll heal."

Ahern nodded, but Neall didn't think the movement was expressing assurance or confirmation of Ari's opinion.

"Will you take them back to your farm?" Ari asked.

The sun stallion, who had been moving closer to them, suddenly reared and laid his ears back.

Ahern snorted, sounding very much like a horse. "You can walk them over in the morning," he said dryly. "Then I'll deal with them. And I think a little more time here will do that mare more good than I can do her." When he turned toward Ari, his expression was grim.

Neall felt Ari press against him for support. When he glanced at Morag, he saw that her expression was equally grim.

"Now, girl," Ahern said. "There are things happening in Sylvalan that make it necessary for you and Neall to leave as soon as you can. Tomorrow would be good."

"Tomorrow?" Ari's mouth fell open. "We can't possibly leave tomorrow. There are all the things to pack—"

"You need to get as far away from here as fast as you can," Ahern said bluntly. "The two of you can travel fastest on horseback, so that's the way you'll go. You can make a list of what you want from the cottage. Neall can tell me where to find you. I'll see that a wagon is packed, and I'll have a couple of my men bring it to your new place."

"But—" Ari stammered. "But there's the harvest—"

"May the Mother blight the harvest," Morag said fiercely.

Neall felt the shock run through Ari that anyone would say anything that . . . obscene.

"The men who created the creatures that harmed that mare may be coming here soon," Morag said. "You have to be gone before they arrive."

Ari stared at Morag. "If they're coming to harm Brightwood, then I should stay to protect the land."

"They aren't coming here for the land. They're coming to kill *you*. Just like they've killed the others who are like you."

Ari paled, and Neall wondered what Morag had told

her. It didn't matter. Morag had just said enough to convince him not to delay.

"Ari—"

Ari shook her head.

Mother's mercy, Neall thought. This was no time for her to get stubborn.

"Your grandmother wants you to go," Morag said.

Ari's knees gave out so suddenly Neall grabbed her to keep her from falling.

"But— But you said she was gone," Ari whispered.

"I lied. She didn't want me to tell you she was still here."

"My . . . mother?"

"She has gone on to the Summerland." Morag gentled her voice. "Your grandmother wanted to wait until you and Neall left Brightwood. She wanted you to go, Ari. She still wants you to go. And . . . the Inquisitors aren't the only reason you should leave Brightwood as soon as you can." She flicked a glance at Neall.

Ari stiffened as if she were braced to fight—or defend. Then she sagged again, and asked hesitantly, "What about Merle?"

"The pup can stay with me for a few weeks," Ahern said impatiently. "He'll come along with the wagon— and the harvest."

"Ari . . ." Morag took a step toward them, her eyes so full of emotion Neall had to look away. "Ari, please go. Death is coming. I want you gone before it arrives."

Ari closed her eyes. When she opened them again, they were filled with bleak resignation.

Neall's heart ached for her. This wasn't the way she wanted to leave Brightwood. This wasn't the way he wanted her to leave. "Ari . . ."

Her hand closed over his arm, held on tight. "I need tomorrow to take care of things. Then, if Ahern doesn't mind, I could stay there tomorrow night and we could leave first thing in the morning the day after."

Looking at Morag and Ahern, Neall held his breath.

Ahern appeared to be doing the same thing, his attention focused on the black-haired woman beside him. She seemed to be listening to something only she could hear.

"All right," Morag finally said. "The day after tomorrow should be soon enough."

Chapter Thirty

Ari looked doubtfully at the pile of clothing on her bed, then at the saddlebags Morag had given her. "I've never been anywhere before. Except to Seahaven once, but I was only gone for a couple of days. How can I know what I'll need?"

Morag picked up the comb, brush, and handmirror from the dressing table and brought them over to the bed. After wrapping a camisole around the mirror, she put it in the still-empty saddlebags. "You pack clothing, since that's what you'll need immediately, toiletries—and whatever you use for personal needs."

Ari puzzled over that last part until Morag added pointedly, "a woman's needs." She dashed to the bathing room, opened the small chest that held those supplies, then hesitated.

"You're going to be living with the man," she told herself sternly. "And it's not like he doesn't already know what these cloths are for." Still, she felt her cheeks heat as she took some of the rolled cloths. Well, she would just have to get used to it. But looking at the cloths reminded her of something else.

Dashing for the kitchen, she took out the jar of herbs she used during her fertile days. That reminded her to take the "recipe" book that contained the notes for the various simples and teas that she and the other witches in her family had made. Of course, she couldn't be certain she would find the same plants in the western part of Sylvalan, but these were things she *couldn't* leave behind. And the small jar of healing ointment would be handy to have as well.

By the time she got back to the bedroom, Morag had one saddlebag filled to bulging.

"Give me those," Morag said. Unfolding the tunic, she had just folded, she wrapped the jars and book.

Ari jammed the rolled cloths in the bottom of the second saddlebag. The jars and book went in next. While Ari folded another tunic and a pair of trousers, Morag opened the dressing table drawers. She pulled out the jewelry box.

"You'll want to take this."

Ari shook her head. "They're just trinkets." If Lucian had truly cared, would she be leaving Brightwood today?

Yes, I would. He just made it easier for me to decide. Lucian was like a powerful storm, intense and overwhelming, impressive in its moment. But Neall is soft rain, the kind of quiet rain that sinks deep into the earth. Storms may be exciting for a while, but it's the soft rain that I love and want to embrace for a lifetime.

Morag opened the jewelry box. "These may be trinkets in one respect, but they do have value. Keep a couple of pieces for sentimental reasons and sell the rest." She held up one piece. "A pin like this will buy you the best room at an inn, a good meal, stabling and feed for the horses, and a hot bath. After a few days on the road, you'll welcome all of those things."

"Why should I feel sentimental about any of those things?" Ari said a little defiantly. She was surprised to see Morag wince.

"I was thinking of your mother and grandmother," Morag said gently. "If they had a favorite piece or two, you might want to keep those."

"Oh. Yes, there are a couple of pieces like that."

Bringing the jewelry box over to the bed, Morag wrapped it in a wool vest, then worked it into the saddlebag, shoving it down the side as far as she could. She fastened the buckles on the saddlebags and stepped back. "That's it, then." She brushed her hair back from her face. "What are you going to do now?"

Ari blinked back tears. Leaving Brightwood would

have been easier if they'd been able to wait until the harvest. It would have been easier if she could have packed her own things, spent a little time picking and choosing the yarns and the looms she wanted to take with her, the bedding, the pots and pans, her collection of drawings that she used to inspire the weaving. It felt too much like she was being torn away instead of leaving on her own. But she understood why the cottage had to be empty when these Inquisitor men arrived in Ridgeley. *If* they were going to arrive at all.

Let it go. Don't look back. Someone else will feel the way the land here sings and will call it home. Maybe they'll need all the things you leave behind. Maybe they'll stay, and another family will write about Brightwood in their journals.

Ari gasped. The journals. She couldn't leave them here in an empty cottage.

"Ari?" Morag asked sharply. "What's wrong?"

"Oh." Wanting to ease the concern in Morag's eyes, Ari made an effort to smile. "I just remembered something else. When I take the sun stallion and the mares over to Ahern's, I want to ask him if he would bring the journals over to his house. I don't want them left here."

Morag frowned. "Journals?"

"My family's history. Brightwood's history, really."

Morag nodded. "What are you going to do now?"

"Finish making the list of things I'd like to take in the wagon so I can bring that to Ahern too." Ari made a face. "In case I have to explain what any of the things are. I doubt Ahern has paid much attention to anything that deals with spinning and weaving."

Morag smiled. "I'd guess that if a horse doesn't need it or can't do it, he hasn't paid any attention to it. So you might want to draw rough sketches of things while you finish that list. It'll save you both frustration."

Ari laughed. "That's a good thought." She paused, and asked shyly, "What are you going to do now?"

Some subtle shift of expression altered Morag's

face, making Ari shiver. This was not the Gatherer who would gently release a spirit from a suffering, dying body. This was the face Ari imagined men would see when Morag rode for vengeance.

"I have to go to Tir Alainn for a little while."

Adolfo finished his cup of tea and dabbed his lips with a napkin that had Felston's family crest embroidered in one corner. He looked at the teapot, as if debating having another cup. In truth, he was simply enjoying the way Baron Felston squirmed with impatience—a captive host chained to his own breakfast table by a show of good manners.

And he also wanted a little more time to consider what he'd been told yesterday.

Felston's daughter, Odella, had needed no persuasion to spew her story about the witch who had stolen the Fae lover who had gotten her with child. He didn't believe for one moment that a Fae Lord had pleasured himself with a girl as repulsive as Odella. Oh, she was pretty enough, but the moment she opened her mouth, any man with sense would have realized the pretty face and comely body weren't worth enduring the girl herself.

But the story about the Fae Lord had been a sharp reminder that the Fae *were* in evidence around here. If one of them *had* been enjoying himself with the witch, he might cause some trouble. *If* he found out what happened to her. But it would be simple enough to focus his attention elsewhere.

Out of the corner of his eye, Adolfo studied Royce, the baron's son. A thwarted lover, perhaps? Whatever the reason for Royce's sullen anger, the young man could be easily persuaded to create a diversion while the witch was brought back to the baron's estate to be dealt with. Not that he would explain it that way to Royce.

"You say this man, Ahern, takes an interest in the witch?" Adolfo asked.

"He tends to know what's happening at Bright-wood," Felston replied sourly.

Adolfo pushed his chair back and rose. "In that case, I think it would be wise to take a look at this man and determine how much trouble he might be."

"And how are you planning to do that?"

Adolfo smiled gently. "I'm going to buy a horse."

Dianna looked at Morag expectantly. "It's done?"

"No," Morag said quietly. "Nor will it be done. Neall is a young man with a full life ahead of him. I will not gather his spirit before his time."

Anger rushed through Dianna, swelling until it filled her. "Ari has to stay. *He* has to be eliminated. For the good of Tir Alainn—and for the good of the Fae."

"The Fae can hold the shining road through the Veil."

"We've never tried. You don't know that for sure." Dianna paced, turned back to face Morag. "Even if we can, how many of us will it take? How many would have to stay in the . . . human . . . world, sacrificing themselves?"

"You won't give *anything* but you're willing to sacrifice two young people's lives?"

"They're not Fae! Besides, we wouldn't be sacrificing Ari. We'll take care of her."

Morag stared at her until Dianna had to resist the urge to squirm.

"As what?" Morag asked softly. "A favorite pet? Someone whose life is contained so that it fits what *we* want? Is that what it comes down to, Dianna? We are the Fae, and the humans, the witches, the Small Folk, the *world* are there for our amusement and our pleasure?"

"We are the Fae," Dianna insisted. "We are the Mother's Children."

She wasn't sure what to think when Morag suddenly shivered and wrapped her arms around herself.

"Where is your loyalty, Morag?"

Oh, the change in that face, in those eyes.

"That is not a question you should ask me, Huntress," Morag said.

"He *has* to be eliminated."

"The Fae can hold the roads."

"How many of us?" Dianna demanded. "Do you know?"

"No, I don't. So you would be wise to pack food and whatever else you value the most and bring it down to the human world. You would be wise to have the Clan come down to Brightwood in case the road *does* close. Then the Clan will be safe, and you'll have time to find out how many are needed."

"And if you're wrong and it doesn't work, we lose this part of Tir Alainn."

"But not the Clan. Not your family."

"It's not *your* Clan who's being forced out of their home," Dianna said bitterly. "It's not *your* family who is at risk."

"Even if this *was* my Clan, my answer would be the same."

"That's so easy to say when it isn't."

Dianna clenched her fists, seething with frustration. For Morag to ignore the needs of the Fae because of one insignificant human . . .

"I command you to gather this . . . Neall's . . . spirit."

"I refuse."

Dianna pounded her fist on the table. "You forget who I am."

Morag's eyes flashed. "And you forget who *I* am. I don't just gather human spirits, Dianna."

Dianna's breath whooshed out of her. "Y-you're threatening me, the Lady of the Moon, in order to spare a *human*?"

Morag's smile was sharp and mocking. "Would you accept it easier if I was warning you in order to spare another of the Fae?"

"We're not talking about another of the Fae. *We* are the Mother's Children. We have no equals."

Morag's smile faded. "That's what we've chosen to

believe. I wonder if it's true." She walked out of the room.

Dianna stumbled over to a bench, sank down on it. Morag couldn't be trusted. That much was clear. Which meant there was only one thing to do if they were going to save their piece of Tir Alainn.

Dianna stood up, waited a moment to be sure her shaking legs would support her, then went to find Lucian.

"Morag!" a tired voice called. "Well met, sister."

Morag slipped her foot out of the stirrup and turned toward the voice.

Looking unbearably weary, Morphia rode up to her.

Morag knew her smile didn't reflect the warmth in her heart. There was still too much anger stirring from her meeting with Dianna. And something else that was just out of reach but kept sending a shiver through her.

So she did the only thing she could think of. She opened her arms in welcome.

"You're tired," Morag said, hugging her sister.

"In body and heart," Morphia replied, returning the hug before stepping back.

"The Bard has heard the warning you sent," Morag said, wanting to offer some comfort. "He'll make sure the bards carry the message to all the Clans."

Morphia looked at her sadly. "Yes, the bards I met listened and promised to send on the warning. A few of the Clans I talked to are angry about what is happening in the human world and intend to make themselves known to the witches who live in the Old Places so that they can be present and keep watch for these Inquisitors. But more of the Clans are blaming the witches for fleeing the Old Places and causing the roads to close before there's any danger." She sighed. "Were we always such fools, Morag? You don't need to answer. I already know. I've had to learn in these past weeks what you've known for so long because of who you are. Sometimes I used to send sleep and gentle dreams to someone in the human world who was troubled or hurting in order to give them rest from the pain. But just as often I would snatch sleep from someone simply because I could. I never thought about how that person would feel after a restless night or what difference it would make the next day. I used my gift to indulge my whims. I feel ashamed of that now. We are the Mother's Children. The *children.* I think, perhaps, we were aptly named."

"Perhaps," Morag agreed. "But now that you see things differently, you can choose to act differently." She gave Morphia's arm a comforting squeeze. "Have you just ridden in? You should make your duty call to the matriarchs of the Clan and then get some rest."

"What are you going to do?"

Morag mounted the dark horse. "I'm going back to Brightwood to keep watch—and to do what I can to protect."

"Neall," Ahern said quietly. "We're about to have company. Get out of sight. And take the mare and gelding with you."

Glancing over toward the lane that led to Ahern's farm, Neall spotted the riders. He didn't recognize most of them—or the horses they rode—but he recognized Royce and Baron Felston. Quickly turning his back and hoping Royce especially didn't spot him, he murmured, "Come on," to Darcy while he led the dark mare to the stables.

When they got inside, the mare calmly walked to her stall and went in. Darcy, however, immediately turned, crowding up against Neall.

"Step back," Neall hissed as he shut the stables door, leaving just enough of an opening to peer through. "And keep quiet. We don't want Ahern to have trouble with the baron. Especially now."

Darcy snorted but stopped shoving against him.

Neall watched the riders approach. Some were obviously guards. They carried themselves like men who had been trained to fight. Two younger men wore black coats. But it was the older man riding beside

Felston who made Neall's belly twist. A lean-faced, balding, strong-bodied man whose dark-gray clothing made him look severe.

No, Neall decided. It wasn't just the clothes that made the man look severe. It was the face, the way he carried himself. Just seeing him made Neall shiver.

Take care, Ahern. Whoever he is, take care.

Adolfo gave the farm a casual, sweeping look before he dismounted. The place stank of magic so strong it almost overwhelmed his ability to sense the men who now gathered to meet his group of riders. All the men working here were Fae—or at least had some Fae or witch blood in them. He knew the feel of those kind of men well, had trained himself to sense them. It was what he looked for in his apprentice Inquisitors. Magic had to be fought with magic, and those who had been forsaken were always the keenest to even the scales.

But having so many here who had the potential for magic meant the older man who stood waiting for them knew what they were and had let them stay. Which meant he was probably just like them, probably the strongest among them. And that meant he had to be dealt with carefully—until he could be dealt with completely.

"A good morning to you," Adolfo said pleasantly. "I am addressing Master Ahern, am I not?"

"What do you want?" Ahern replied.

"I understand you have some of the finest horses in this part of Sylvalan. I have a need for good mounts for myself and my men."

"There's nothing here that would suit you."

"Now see here," Baron Felston sputtered. "Master Adolfo is an important man."

"If he's with you, I know exactly how important he must be. So let me rephrase what I said: There's nothing here for the likes of you."

"I don't believe you understand who I am," Adolfo said, his voice quietly menacing. Then he stopped. As much as he would like to give the man a reason to fear him, it was better to wait for the right moment. It would come soon enough.

Ahern smiled, giving his face a feral quality. An icy fist curled around Adolfo's spine—and squeezed.

"I understand well enough what you are," Ahern said.

"And what is that?"

"The face of evil."

Adolfo felt the blood drain from his face. "How dare you say that to me?"

Ahern took a step forward, leaned toward Adolfo. "You're a killer. A butcher. A destroyer of all that is good in the world. Oh, yes, I understand well enough what you are."

Hearing the uneasy shifting of feet of the men who had come with him, Adolfo stiffened. "You will regret those words."

Ahern smiled grimly. "Go while you can."

As Adolfo mounted his horse, he began to summon his power. He would twist some of the magic here into a few nighthunters. Let that bastard see how well he could deal—

"Go!" Ahern shouted.

The horses wheeled and galloped down the lane, refusing to yield to spur or bit until they were back on the main road. During that ride, Adolfo hung on grimly. So did the other men.

When the horses finally slowed of their own accord, Adolfo reined in.

"What happened?" Felston said, puffing as if he'd been the one galloping.

What *had* happened? That shouted order could have startled the horses, but it shouldn't have made them unmanageable for all the time it had taken to get off Ahern's land. Magic didn't work on animals unless . . .

"Of course," Adolfo said softly.

"What?" Felston snapped. "Do you have an explanation for why well-trained animals would suddenly go mad?"

"He's a horse Lord," Adolfo said.

"What are you talking about?" Felston sputtered. "That surly bastard has been living at that farm for years, and there has never been a whisper that he'd come from any kind of gentry family."

"He isn't gentry," Adolfo said impatiently. "He's Fae. A horse Lord. That's the only explanation for the way he controlled these animals. For all these years, you've had a Fae Lord living among you, pretending to be human."

"Fae?" Felston paled. "Ahern is one of the *Fae*?"

"Oh, yes," Adolfo said. "I am certain your horse farmer is one of the Fae."

"Then what do we do?"

"First we ride to Ridgeley to have a restorative glass of something potent and a light meal. Then we'll take care of the witch before the Fae Lord decides to interfere."

"In that case, shouldn't we go to Brightwood now?" Felston said.

Adolfo shook his head. "There's time. He's Fae. No matter what he thinks, he won't believe there's really *that* much urgency. They never do."

Neall slipped out of the barn and joined Ahern.

"Who were those men?" he asked.

Ahern didn't answer. He watched the lane long after the men had disappeared. Finally, "I think they were the Black Coats Morag told me about. The Inquisitors. The witch killers."

"Ari." Neall spun around until he was staring in the direction of Brightwood.

Ahern nodded grimly. "Yes. Ari." He took a deep breath, let it out in an explosive huff. "She'll be here soon with the horses. Then, young Neall, I think we need to discuss a change of plans."

Ari took the biscuits out of the oven. Bread would have been better, but there wasn't time to bake bread today. Besides, the biscuits would be easier to carry.

She'd have to ask Morag if there was a practical way to carry a bit of food when riding on horseback. And she needed to remember her canteens.

Right now, she had to take the sun stallion and the mares over to Ahern's.

Giving the soup simmering on the back of the stove one last stir, she stepped to the kitchen doorway and pressed her hands against the frame. She felt the tingle of the warding spells.

"Those who have been welcomed before are welcome again. As I will it, so mote it be."

The warding spells shifted, formed a new pattern. If Morag got back before she did, the warding spells would allow the Fae woman to enter the house. After all, what was the point of leaving the soup simmering if Morag couldn't get inside to have something to eat?

"Come on, Merle," Ari called, stepping outside and closing the kitchen door.

When the puppy bounced over to her, she picked him up and hugged him.

"I hope you're not so young that you'll forget me in a few weeks' time. And that's all it will be. Then we'll both have a new home. And you'll have Neall to play with, too."

She put the puppy down and walked over to the sun stallion, patted his neck cautiously. "It's time to go."

The stallion pawed the ground.

"Come on, now. Come on. Ahern will look after you."

The sun stallion shook his head. When Ari walked away and kept going, he and his mares followed. Except the wounded mare. She remained in the meadow, near the spot where the witches of Brightwood had danced year after year.

Ari let her stay. The mare was doing better, and it would be a shame to take her away before the magic in Brightwood had a chance to heal her.

"I'll let Ahern know she's here," Ari told Merle as they crossed the road and headed for Ahern's farm. "He'll keep an eye on her." As she reached the top of the rise, she looked over her shoulder at the horses trailing behind them. "I wonder if a mother duck feels this way when all her ducklings waddle after her."

The image of a duck being followed by horses who thought they belonged to her made Ari smile. It was best to think of silly things today. It was best not to think at all.

Lucian watched the canopy of leaves over his head play with the sunlight and shadows. This little spot in the garden was always a peaceful place, but today he found no peace there. He kept thinking about the version of "The Lover's Lament" that Ari had sung on the Solstice.

A song like that was more than folly; it was cruel. Yes, cruel, since it filled a young woman's head with dreamy-eyed, unreasonable expectations. That wasn't the way of the world. That wasn't the way of *men*.

Is it cruel? something inside him asked. *Are those expectations really so unreasonable?*

Lucian shifted uneasily.

Kindness? Courtesy? Well, those things weren't so unreasonable for someone like Ari to want. And he'd already given her those. But respect? She was barely more than a girl. If a man showed her too much deference, she would never have the incentive to improve herself and become more interesting. After all, how much respect could any woman command when the only things she could speak intelligently about were weaving and gardens?

Loyalty? If that was so important to her, he could promise her a kind of loyalty. He could certainly pledge that he would never seek another human female's company. What he did when he visited other Clans—and he would since he was the Lightbringer—was none of the girl's business. And since she wouldn't know what took place in Tir Alainn, it would never trouble her.

Love? A bard's word to pretty up the truth between men and women. Passion burned bright and hot, but it never burned long. Affection truly was a kinder emotion than this . . . love.

Ari might grieve for a little while once she realized she had to give up her girlhood notion about love, but once she was over it, she would come to appreciate the companionship—and pleasure—he offered.

Lucian headed for the entrance to that little garden.

Soon it would be settled. Ari would stay at Brightwood—and stay with him. And Neall . . . Lucian thought about the Gatherer and smiled. And Neall would be gone.

As soon as Neall spotted the sun stallion, he ran to meet Ari.

"Are you all right?" he asked anxiously, pulling her into his arms and holding on tight.

"I'm fine, Neall," Ari said, rubbing his back to comfort him. "Truly."

"When it took you so long to get here, we thought—" He couldn't say it. He couldn't put into words what he'd feared because, somehow, that might make it come true.

"It wasn't long. I had to wait for the biscuits."

Neall stiffened. He leaned back and stared at her in disbelief. "Biscuits?"

"I thought they would be more practical than bread and stay fresher so that we could—"

"You baked *biscuits*?"

Ari's mouth began to set in that stubborn line he knew well. Ignoring it, he grabbed her hand and pulled her toward Ahern's house. "Let's just see what Ahern has to say about this."

"Neall!"

The sun stallion snorted, stamped one foot in warning.

"Back off," Neall snapped. "If she was one of *your* mares, you'd nip her for this."

Ahern was pacing the yard, looking grim enough to subdue even the stubbornest witch.

"She was baking biscuits," Neall said as soon as he

was close enough he didn't have to shout. Although he *was* shouting loud enough to have several of the men peer around the buildings to see what was going on.

"Neall!" Ari pulled back, digging in her heels.

As Neall turned, the sun stallion butted him hard enough to break his hold on Ari's wrist. He and Ari ended up sitting in the dirt, staring at each other between the legs of an angry horse.

Another horse snorted. The sun stallion bolted a short distance, then reared.

Neall looked over his shoulder. Not another horse, but someone no horse would disobey.

"That one must have a bit of the dark horse bloodline in him," Ahern said. "They aren't cowed by anything." He walked over to Ari and held out a hand to help her up. "Biscuits are a fine idea. With some cheese and some of that jam you make, it'll do for a midday meal tomorrow."

"That's exactly what *I* thought," Ari grumbled, brushing herself off.

"But the boy's been worried about you—and he has reason. The Black Coats have arrived in Ridgeley."

Ari paled.

Neall scrambled to his feet. It hurt to see her eyes so full of fear, but he couldn't afford to make it sound like something they could dismiss.

"Now," Ahern said, sounding calm but implacable. "You're going to stay here. Neall will go to Brightwood for your things. When he returns, the two of you are leaving. The horses are fresh, and that will give you hours of daylight to put some distance between you and the Black Coats."

"I can't leave yet," Ari protested. Her eyes filled with tears. "I *can't*. I'm not ready. I haven't said goodbye."

"Ari, there's no time," Neall snapped.

She looked at both of them, her hands spread in appeal. "I'll run back. It won't take long. But I need to do this."

Neall wanted to scream. She hadn't seen those men. She hadn't *felt* those men. How could he make her understand? "By the Mother's tits, Ari—"

"Don't you speak of the Mother that way!"

"—who is there to say goodbye to?" Neall demanded. "Morag? If she's there when I get there, I'll tell her. If not, when you don't return, like as not she'll come here and Ahern can tell her."

Ari looked at him with eyes that were suddenly far too old. "I would like to say goodbye to Morag," she said quietly, "but that's not the reason I have to go back." Ari reached for his hand. Her fingers curled around his and held on. "I have to say goodbye to Brightwood, Neall. I have to let go of the land. If I don't, it will always feel unfinished."

Neall sagged, defeated. If Ari always looked back on this day with regret, what kind of future would they have? Brightwood would always stand between them. He looked at Ahern, hoping the older man would have some argument against this, but Ahern just stared at the distant hills.

"All right," Ahern said reluctantly. "You go back. You say your goodbyes. But you do it quick—and then you get in the cottage and stay inside until Neall comes for you. The warding spells around the cottage will protect you, but they won't help if you go beyond the cottage walls."

Ari seemed about to protest, but she caught herself and simply nodded. She picked up Merle, handed him to Neall, and said, "You'd better shut him up somewhere so he doesn't follow me ho—" She pressed her lips together for a moment. "Back to Brightwood." She gave the puppy one last caress, then turned and ran.

"Come on," Ahern said. "We'll shut him up in the gelding's stall. He'll be fine there for now."

Neall hugged the squirming puppy, but it was the man he looked at. "I'll miss you."

Ahern shook his head. "Don't look back, young Neall. You go and don't look back."

"That philosophy the Fae live by makes it very easy not to take responsibility for anything."

Ahern didn't speak for a long time. Then, "There are times when it's an arrogant fool's excuse. But there are other times when it's simply the wise thing to do."

Chapter Thirty-one

Adolfo drained his wineglass. The tavern didn't offer the same quality of wine as Felston's wine cellar, but it was sufficient. "We have fortified ourselves for the difficult tasks to come." *And at the baron's expense.* "Let us go to Brightwood and capture the foul creature who lives there so that we can bring her back to the baron's estate for questioning."

"Questioning?" Felston glanced around the inn and lowered his voice. "There's no need for questioning. You have my daughter's statement and the confession you got from the Gwynn woman yesterday."

"I have those confessions," Adolfo agreed, watching the baron pale at the significance of those words. Yes, the baron was going to be most generous when it came to settling his account. "But the witch must confess to her crimes. She must admit her guilt. She must have time to regret the harm she has done. Therefore, she will be taken to the room at your estate my Inquisitors prepared for such questioning, and she will confess." *And then she will die.*

Morag paused at the edge of the meadow, watching the wounded mare graze. Ari must have taken the other horses to Ahern's. She looked to the west, wondering if she should go to that hill where the wind always blew and tell Astra that Ari was leaving.

Astra.

Something had been nagging at her, trying to catch her attention. But meeting Morphia and then trying to persuade the dark horse to gather his courage and go down the shining road again had pushed it aside. Now . . .

Astra. What was it about Astra?

The Fae are the Mother's Children. But we are the Daughters. We are the Pillars of the World.

Aiden had mentioned something about the Pillars of the World.

The answers are in plain sight, if you choose to look for them.

I want to ask him if he would bring the journals over to his house. I don't want them left here. . . . My family's history. Brightwood's history, really.

"Hurry," Morag said, pressing her legs against the dark horse's sides. He galloped across the meadow, right to the kitchen door.

Sliding off his back, Morag threw the kitchen door open. "Ari?" When she got no answer, she closed the door and hurried to the dressing room adjoining Ari's bedroom. She'd seen the glass-doored bookcase the other day when the sun stallion and the dark horse had played "tease the puppy," but she hadn't thought of it since.

She opened the glass doors and pulled out the last journal on the right.

I am Astra, now the Crone of the family. It is with sorrow that I have read the journals of the ones who came before me. We shouldered the burden and then were dismissed from thought—or were treated as paupers who should beg for scraps of affection. We have stayed because we loved the land, and we have stayed out of duty. But duty is a cold bedfellow, and it should no longer be enough to hold us to the land.

Morag read a little further, but there was nothing Astra hadn't already said to her. She replaced that journal, skipped over several, then pulled out another.

We are the Pillars of the World. The Fae no longer remember what that means. Or else they no longer care and just expect us to continue as we have done for generations. I know why they forgot us. I am old now, but I remember my Fae lover well, the father of my daughter. I remember his charm—and I remember his arrogance. The Fae, he had said, have no equal. And that may be true. It also explains why they don't want to remember the ones who had been more powerful— and still are, in our own way, more powerful. They do not want to remember that it was the Daughters who had the magic needed to create Tir Alainn, to shape the Otherland out of dreams and the branches of the Mother—and will. As we will it, so mote it be. And so it was. The Fair Land.

They can't abide that, can't admit that. If they do, they will have to give up their arrogance, their supreme belief that there is nothing to compare with them. And they do not want to see that they are fading, that they are so much less than they once had been.

Shaken, Morag replaced the journal, selected another. The *witches* had created Tir Alainn? If that was true, that certainly explained why their disappearance from the Old Places was causing pieces of Tir Alainn to disappear as well.

We are the wiccanfae, the wise Fae. We are the Mother's Daughters, the living vessels of Her power. We are the wellsprings. All the magic in this world flows through us, from us. Without us, it will die.

Morag leafed through a few more pages, then closed the journal in frustration. Ari would be back soon, and she didn't think the girl would appreciate someone reading her family's history without permission. But the answers were here, if only there was time enough to find the right one.

"Why are you the wellsprings? Why are you the Daughters? Why? *Why?*"

She pulled out another journal, close to the beginning. The book was so old the binding cracked when she opened it. Trying to peer at the pages without opening the book too far, she swore in frustration. The writing was spindly, and the ink had faded so much it was barely legible.

She walked over to the window, where she would

have the most light, and carefully opened the journal to the first page. She stared at the words.

I am Jillian, of the House of Gaian.

She closed her eyes, counted to ten, opened her eyes.

The words didn't change.

I am Jillian, of the House of Gaian.

The House of Gaian. The Clan that had disappeared so long ago. The ones who had been Fae— and more than Fae. Not the Mother's Children. The Mother's Daughters. Her branches. The living vessels of Her strength.

"Mother's mercy," Morag whispered. Tears filled her eyes. She closed the journal before any could fall and ruin the ink.

The House of Gaian hadn't been lost. They'd been forgotten because they were the Pillars of the World, and the rest of the Fae hadn't wanted to remember that *they* had not created Tir Alainn.

Rubbing her face against her sleeve, Morag gently replaced the journal, then ran out of the cottage. She swung up on the dark horse's back.

"We have to go back to Tir Alainn. We have to—" Her voice broke. "We have to tell the Lightbringer and the Huntress about the Daughters."

The dark horse planted his feet, refusing to move.

"We have to go back one more time—for Ari's sake."

He hesitated, then leaped forward. She let him have his head, let him race through meadow and woods, let him charge up the shining road to Tir Alainn. She had to get there before Dianna and Lucian did something foolish. She had to make them understand.

Or stop them if there was no other choice.

"Lucian!" Dianna hurried to meet Lucian as he walked out of that private place in the gardens.

Lucian raised his head, reminding her of her shadow hounds when they scent prey. "Have you heard from Morag?"

"Yes, I heard from her." It was easier now to feel angry when she wasn't close enough to the Gatherer to feel afraid. "She refuses to help us!"

Lucian stared at her. "She can't refuse. She's Fae. And even the Gatherer yields to the Huntress and the Lightbringer."

"Not according to the Gatherer," Dianna said bitterly. "Not only did she refuse to help, she threatened me. *Me*."

"She'll regret that," he said softly.

"Yes, she will." Dianna felt something inside her slowly untwist. Not even the Gatherer would stand against *both* leaders of the Fae. Not even the Gatherer would dare. "What do we do about that . . . that *Neall*?"

"What we should have done in the first place. Take care of the problem ourselves." He strode toward the stables. "You get your shadow hounds. I'll get your horse. Meet me at the stables and—" He abruptly stopped speaking and pulled Dianna behind a hedge.

"What?" Dianna said impatiently.

"Morag. Riding toward the Clan house."

"She's the *last* person we want to meet right now."

"Agreed." Lucian looked at her, a strange excitement shining in his eyes. "So we'll avoid her."

They parted, Lucian slipping through the gardens to go the long way around to the stables, and she running to the kennels where her shadow hounds were kept.

Yes, Dianna thought. They would take care of that Neall, and then Ari would have no excuse to leave Brightwood.

Ari stood in the spot where the spiral dance ended— and, in ending, began another kind of dance.

She raised her arms, breathed deep as she began to draw the strength of Brightwood into herself.

The land beneath her feet rolled, spun, swirled, pushed at her as if it were trying to hold in something terrible that was fighting to burst free.

Ari staggered, her arms dropping to help her keep

her balance. Stunned, she just stared at the ground that looked no different but felt so strange.

The land doesn't want me, no longer wants to know me. Can the magic that breathes through Brightwood somehow sense that I'm going away? Is that why I can't focus it, can't keep it from shifting and scattering? It tingles beneath my feet the way it does when a bad storm is coming. But the sky is clear.

Shivering despite the warm day, and suddenly uneasy about standing in the meadow, Ari ran to the cottage. As soon as she stepped into the kitchen and closed the door, the fear that made her run like a deer before the hounds disappeared.

She studied the meadow. It looked no different, but something had happened there. The wounded mare had felt it, too, and she was still standing there, watchful.

Maybe the land *hadn't* rejected her. Maybe, like Neall and Ahern, it had pushed her toward the place where she was the most protected.

Ari smiled.

Great Mother, I leave this place to those who will come after me. May the land I go to be as generous in its bounty to those who care for it—and are in its care.

Best to make use of the time. Neall would be here soon, and there were still some things to be done.

She took the soup off the stove and placed it on a metal trivet on the worktable. Then she banked the fire in the stove. If Morag returned soon, the soup might still be hot enough to eat. If not, it wouldn't be difficult to rekindle the fire.

She looked at her biscuits and frowned. She needed some kind of sack. Remembering her small pack, she rummaged in the storage cupboard until she found it. She wrapped the biscuits in a towel, leaving two of them for Morag, wrapped the cheese she had left in another towel, and a jar of berry jam in another. She filled the two canteens, then slipped them back into their places on the pack.

"Saddlebags," she muttered, hurrying to the bedroom.

As she walked back to the kitchen, she heard the mare scream.

Dropping the saddlebags on the table, she flung open the top half of the kitchen door.

The mare was lying in the meadow. She kept struggling to rise, but something was wrong with her legs and she couldn't get to her feet. She screamed, struggled, screamed again.

Ari opened the bottom half of the kitchen door. The air thickened in front of her—the warding spells' reaction when there was something nearby that shouldn't be allowed to enter.

Moving from one side of the doorway to the other, she tried to see if there was anything out there.

Nothing.

But the mare kept screaming, and . . . Was that white pus pushing out of one foreleg?

She had to do something. She *had* to. She could run out to the mare and see what was wrong. She couldn't just stand there and let the animal suffer. It would only take a minute. Just a minute to run out to where the mare struggled.

She took a deep breath—and ran.

She skidded to a stop a few feet away from the mare. It wasn't pus. It was bone sticking through the skin.

Something had broken the mare's legs. Broken them so fast the animal hadn't had time to try to run.

"Mother's mercy," Ari whispered. She whirled to run back to the cottage—and saw the men coming around the sides of the cottage, saw more men vaulting over the low garden wall where they must have hidden. She saw the two who wore black coats. And she saw the tall, lean-faced man who now stood between her and the open kitchen door.

The woods. If she could make it to the woods, she might be able to hide from them. She knew every path through Brightwood. If she could just reach the woods . . .

Neall.

If she ran and all of them didn't follow, what would happen when Neall came?

In that moment of hesitation, someone hit her from behind, landing on top of her when she fell to the ground.

"I told you not to lift your skirts for any other man," Royce said. "Now you're going to pay for it."

She fought, squirming, twisting, kicking, scratching. She raked his cheek with her nails, drawing blood.

He hit her hard enough to daze her, and kept hitting her until someone pulled him away.

She couldn't think, couldn't focus, couldn't get her legs to obey so that she could run.

A rope was lashed around her wrists. A piece of metal was forced into her mouth, holding down her tongue. More metal was strapped around her head, pressing against the places where Royce had struck her, making them throb unmercifully. Hands grabbed her arms, yanking her to her feet. Dazed and frightened, she was led to the tall man who stood waiting.

"I am Adolfo," he said in a gentle voice. "I am the Master Inquisitor, the Witch's Hammer. You will come with me now so that you will have a chance to unburden your troubled spirit and confess to the crimes you have committed against the good people of Ridgeley."

But I've done nothing! She couldn't talk, couldn't form words with her tongue held down like that. If they would just let her speak, she could tell them she was leaving.

Then she looked into the tall man's eyes and knew he didn't care about the people in Ridgeley. He only cared about being the Witch's Hammer.

And there was only one way he was going to let her leave Brightwood.

*   *   *

"Tuck this in your saddlebag," Ahern said, handing Neall a small bag.

As the contents of the bag shifted, Neall heard the clink of coins. "Ahern—"

"Don't argue." Ahern's face was set in stubborn lines that made Neall wonder if Ari had inherited her stubborn streak from the old man. "You're going to need provisions on the way, and you'll need something to tide you over when you get to your land. I won't be going hungry for lack of a few coins if that's what's bothering you."

Neall tucked the bag of coins into his saddlebag, then busied himself with tying down the flap securely. "Thank you."

"You take good care of the girl. That's all the thanks I want or need."

Neall nodded. He took a moment to steady his feelings, knowing the old man wouldn't want any maudlin displays. He held out his hand. "May the Mother bless you all of your days, Ahern."

Ahern grasped Neall's hand, then stepped back. "Go on with you. You're wasting daylight."

Neall mounted Darcy, then watched Ahern check the girth on the dark mare's saddle. He would have felt better if he could have taken the mare's reins and led her, but Ahern had said she would follow and there was no reason to doubt that she would.

Raising one hand in farewell, he pressed his legs against Darcy's sides. The gelding needed no further urging to canter toward Brightwood. The mare ran beside them, tossing her head in annoyance. He wondered if that was because she was going with them or because she was envious that the gelding had a rider.

You'll have a rider soon, Neall thought as they crested the rise and the cottage came into sight. It looked more shut-up and abandoned than he'd expected it would. As if Ari was already gone.

As they rounded the cottage to reach the kitchen door, both horses stopped abruptly and laid their ears back.

Neall stared at the mare lying so still in the meadow. Then he glanced at the open kitchen door, vaulted out of the saddle, and ran inside.

"Ari!" He didn't need to search. He could sense she wasn't there.

"The Black Coats took her," said a gruff voice.

Neall turned toward the open door and saw the small man standing just beyond the threshold. He couldn't speak. One thought filled his head until there was nothing else: *They took Ari. The witch killers took Ari.*

"Nothing the Small Folk could have done," the small man said. "There were too many men. And those Black Coats—" His face twisted up in disgust and fear. "They have some kind of magic, but it's nothing clean, nothing like what we feel coming from the Mother. So you'd best beware, young Lord, when you go to fetch the witch and get her away from those . . . *creatures.*"

"Fetch her?"

"They were riding toward the baron's estate."

His heart began beating again. He hadn't been aware that it had stopped. "She's— She's still alive?"

The small man nodded grimly. "Go fetch the witch, young Lord. Fetch her and take her far away from here to some place where the Black Coats won't find her."

When Neall took a step forward, the small man shifted. At another time, it would have been amusing to see one of the Small Folk trying to block a doorway. If Ari died, he didn't think there would ever come a day when he would feel amused by anything again.

"You'd best take what the witch will need," the small man said, nodding toward the pack on the table. "I'm thinking you won't have time to come back this way."

Desperate to leave, Neall glanced around, ready to deny that there was any time to waste on *anything.* But he saw the saddlebags and the long cape on the table in the main room, and the small pack with the canteens on the kitchen worktable. If— No, *when* he got her away from the Inquisitors, she would need those things. He grabbed them and ran out to the horses.

The mare was fidgeting and blowing, but she stood still while he fastened the saddlebags, rolled the cape and tied it to the back of the saddle, then tied the small pack to one of the rings on the front of the saddle. Ahern must have chosen that particular saddle because it was made for a traveler.

The small man watched him, then nodded in approval. "The mare came from the Lord of the Horse?"

"Yes," Neall said, hastily checking things one last time. Then he realized what the small man had said. "You've always known about him?"

"We've known. Just as we've always known about you, young Lord. Just as we've always known about the Daughters," he added quietly. "But some things are not meant to be spoken."

Neall shook his head. There wasn't time to ask what the small man meant.

"There are the five of us who were nearby when we felt something evil touch the land." He gestured to the other four small men who slipped out of the cow shed. "If you'll take up two of us, the mare can carry the other three. We'll do what we can to help."

"I'll take what help you can give."

After lifting three of the men onto the mare's saddle, he set another on Darcy's saddle, mounted, then lifted the last man up behind him.

As they galloped toward the baron's estate, he fretted about the minutes that had passed. But surely nothing terrible could happen to Ari in so short a time.

Surely not.

When Morag burst into the room where she'd last met Dianna, the Huntress wasn't there. But Aiden, Lyrra, and Morphia were.

She rushed toward them, stumbling in her haste.

Aiden grabbed her arms to steady her at the same time Morphia and Lyrra hurried to stand beside her.

"What's wrong?" Morphia said.

"Where . . . the Huntress? The Lightbringer?" A dam inside her had burst during the ride back to Tir Alainn. Now too many feelings were clamoring to be heard. The fierce need to speak made her mute for several seconds.

"What is it, Morag?" Aiden asked gently. "What has happened?"

Morag looked into his eyes and saw passion that had not been diluted from living in Tir Alainn because he, too, often walked in the human world. His gift had demanded that from him. If there was anyone who could understand—and make others understand—it was the Bard.

"The witches. The wiccanfae."

Aiden nodded encouragingly while Lyrra and Morphia made soothing noises.

"Wiccanfae is an old name for the witches," Aiden said.

Morag shook her head. "They're the wiccanfae. The wise Fae. The Daughters. We forgot them."

"Morag . . ." Aiden said worriedly.

The words rose from her in a keen. "They're the Mother's Daughters. They weren't lost. They were never lost. We chose to forget them. *We* did that."

"*Morag.*"

"They're the Pillars of the World. They created Tir Alainn. That's why pieces of it disappear when they leave the Old Places. 'As we will it, so mote it be.' "

"How could the witches have created Tir Alainn?" Aiden demanded.

She looked into stormy blue eyes that appeared so dark in his now-pale face. Painful knowledge filled those eyes as he began to put together bits and pieces. Seeing pain that matched her own filled her with strength. She wasn't alone now. At least in this, she wasn't alone.

"The witches . . . are the House of Gaian."

She felt the words shudder through him, felt his body tense from the emotional blow.

Lyrra made a keening sound, then clamped one hand over her mouth and turned away.

Morphia sagged against her for a moment before she, too, turned away.

Aiden faced her, his hand still holding her arms.

"The House of Gaian?" he whispered.

Morag nodded. "The witch killers will be coming to Brightwood soon. If we stand aside now, if we do nothing here, we have no one but ourselves to blame when Tir Alainn is completely lost." She stepped back. Something began to fill her, flow through her. She had never stepped onto a battlefield, but she instinctively knew this was what it felt like to be the Gatherer when she rode among screaming, fighting men, sparing some and taking others. When the Gatherer rode in *this* way, she was not always merciful—and she was not always kind.

"I'm going back to Brightwood. The witch killers aren't going to take Ari."

"We'll come with you," Lyrra said.

Morag shook her head. "You and Aiden find the Huntress and the Lightbringer. Tell them what you know. And rouse anyone else among the Fae who has the courage to stand and fight."

"I'm coming with you," Morphia said.

"There's—"

"Don't argue, Morag. I don't know what I can do, but I'm coming with you."

Lyrra looked at the two sisters. "If the witch killers do come to Brightwood, there won't be much the two of you can do to stop them."

The power hummed through Morag, making her smile. "Yes, there is. I have a weapon even the witch killers can't defy. I have Death."

Ari couldn't stop shivering. It wasn't caused just by being in a small, cool, dark room in Baron Felston's cellar. Mostly, it was fear trembling through her as she stared at the tall man who watched her.

"Why are your kind so resistant?" he asked sadly. "Why can't you admit to your crimes? You've committed no crimes. I know. You all say that. And yet . . ." He picked up a piece of paper from the long, stained table that dominated the room. He held it out in front of her. "Quite a list of grievances against someone who claims to have done no harm."

Her head hurt, and trying to focus on the words in the dim light of a single oil lamp made her stomach churn.

Mistress Brigston claiming that she had been bewitched into paying several gold coins for a piece of tapestry that Ari had delivered and then magicked away again. Granny Gwynn claiming that Ari had added something foul to a good, wholesome simple that Granny had sold to Squire Kenton to strengthen his wife's fragile health, making the woman more ill. Odella claiming that Ari had tricked her into taking the fancy she had then been forced to give a man in order to avoid the dire consequences of a thwarted love spell.

Poor crops, a lack of game, a dry well. Anything and everything that had gone wrong in Ridgeley had been blamed on her.

I've done none of that!

The Master Inquisitor sighed as if she'd actually spoken, then placed the paper on the table. Bending over, he pressed his hand gently against Ari's cheek.

"You have no choice. You must confess. You must admit to what you have done to the good people of Ridgeley. Don't force me to hurt you. Don't force me to make you suffer. I will hurt you if that is the only way, but I hope you won't require pain to help you do what you must."

He straightened up, went over to a chest that was pushed against the wall and removed something. He set the object on the table, next to the paper filled with her crimes. It was a metal device that looked a

bit like a bridle that would fit tightly over a person's
head—except there were three spikes attached to the
inside of it that would pierce the tongue and cheeks
when the bridle was strapped on.

Adolfo brushed his fingers over the spiked bridle.
"I will give you a little time to decide if you will allow
me to make this as quick and merciful as possible, or
if you'll force me to be the instrument of your suffering."

He lowered the wick in the oil lamp until there was
barely enough light to see by. Then he walked out of
the room, locking the door behind him.

Ari stared at the spiked bridle—and shivered.

Adolfo walked up the stairs, glad to be away from the
damp cellar for a while. He would have liked more
time to work with this one. Younger witches could
become quite malleable given enough assistance, and
their confessions were always so tearfully dramatic.
And he would have liked more time to question her
about the Fae and their noticeable interest in this
Old Place.

But it was the Fae and their interest that made it
imperative to wring a confession out of this witch and
dispose of her quickly. However, if the diversion
Royce created was successful, the Fae would have no
reason to look for the girl.

Still there was that Fae Lord at the horse farm to
consider. *He* might think to look beyond the borders
of the Old Place.

Adolfo sighed. No, he couldn't take the time required
to soften the girl to the humility that was proper and
becoming in a female. But she would give him the op-
portunity to work with the two younger Inquisitors
and teach them how to refine their skills.

Dianna gave the dead mare in the meadow a wide
berth. The shadow hounds sniffed the carcass, then
backed away, growling softly.

Lucian, in his other form, laid his ears back and

galloped to the cottage. Dianna followed, feeling her heart thump against her chest when she noticed the open kitchen door.

Lucian reached the cottage, changed to his human form, and went inside before Dianna and her hounds crossed the meadow. By the time she stepped into the kitchen, he was striding out of the bedroom.

"She's gone," he said, his voice filled with fury and bitterness. "She's already slunk away with that *lout*."

Dianna looked at the soup kettle on the worktable and the biscuits beside it. She gingerly touched the kettle. Still a bit of warmth. And the biscuits were fresh.

"I don't think she left with him," Dianna said softly. She remembered what Morag had said about the Black Coats, and a chill went through her.

"What are you talking about?" Lucian snapped. "There's signs of packing in every room."

Dianna walked to the kitchen door, stared at the dead mare in the meadow, then turned back to her brother. "Oh, she intended to leave with him, but I don't think that's the reason she isn't here." When he started to argue, her own temper sharpened. "If she was leaving for good, she wouldn't have left food out to spoil."

"Someone else would have taken care of it," Lucian said, pacing the main room. Then he stopped abruptly at the same time Dianna asked, "Who?"

They looked at each other.

Dianna licked her lips, which were suddenly, painfully dry. "Maybe she's just gone to Ahern's to ask what to do about the mare."

"Maybe." Lucian hesitated. "We'll wait here a while. If she doesn't return soon, I'll go to Ahern's to find out if he's seen her."

Relief flowed through Dianna. Whatever had happened to that mare looked bad, but it had nothing to do with Ari.

"While we're waiting, we might as well have some

of the soup," she said. "There's no sense letting it go to waste."

As she dished out the soup, she suddenly wondered why Morag had returned to Tir Alainn in such a hurry.

"Was the mare dead when you left?" Morphia asked.

"No," Morag replied. Hidden in the shadows of the woods, she studied the meadow—and shivered. *There's a storm coming.*

She had been gone less than an hour. She had been gone far, far too long. *I shouldn't have left her. If I'd been thinking, I wouldn't have left her.*

"The Huntress is obviously here," Morphia said, lifting her chin in the direction of the shadow hounds, who were gathered near the kitchen door. "Perhaps the Lightbringer as well. So at least we'll have some help."

Morag's heart had gone numb. That was the only way to explain this odd sensation of her mind seeing things with painful clarity while she felt nothing.

"No," she said. "We'll get no help from them."

"But isn't that why you came back to Tir Alainn?"

Morag shook her head slowly. "I went back to tell them about the witches, so that they would understand that Ari wasn't someone to manipulate for the Fae's pleasure. And to tell them why it was so important to protect her kind."

"All the more reason for them to help us now."

"Oh, they would help us protect Ari. But they're also interested in eliminating Neall because she wants to marry him and leave Brightwood. So we'll get help from someone who wants to protect both of them. We'll go to Ahern."

Something shivered through the air. Adolfo set his wineglass on the table, walked over to the window, and pulled the curtain aside. Nothing looked different, but *something* was different.

Maybe it was nothing. Even locked in the cellar, the

witch made this whole place stink of magic. It wouldn't feel right again until she was dead.

He turned to retrieve his wine, then stopped.

It *was* magic he was sensing, but there was too much of it to be coming from just *her*.

He opened the drawing room. The guard standing on duty immediately straightened.

"Get the horses saddled," Adolfo said. "Then wait for further orders." He closed the door, retrieved his wine, and drained the glass.

His hand shook. It hadn't done that in a long, long time. He always feared the witches, never felt easy until they—and their magic—died. That fear was his mother's legacy. Keeping them alive long enough to break them down was a test of his own strength.

This one was hardly more than a girl—and still his hands shook. Because of the Fae. Before now, he'd been able to dismiss them. They came and went, paying little attention to the human world beyond their immediate pleasures, and he'd never had to be concerned about them becoming adversaries. But there was the Gatherer to consider. She was already aware of the Inquisitors, already seemed to be taking an interest in the witches in this land. *She* could not be dismissed. Neither could the Fae Lord who had hidden his true nature from the people of this village for so many years.

There hadn't been time to get the feel of this witch, to know which branches of the Mother were her strength. No matter. They would take her somewhere on the estate far enough away that the ladies of the house wouldn't be distressed. And they would hang her from a tree and open up her belly. A crude method, but effective.

"I shall not suffer a witch to live," he whispered. He would make sure nothing and no one spared *this* one.

He walked out of the room and gave his orders.

The dark horse slid to a stop, his hooves bare inches from Ahern's boots.

"Where's Ari?" Morag demanded.

Ahern crossed his arms and lifted his chin. "Gone by now. She and Neall. The Black Coats came here today. When she came a little later to bring the horses that had come with you, I told her she and the boy had to go."

"Neall went with her?"

Ahern shook his head, his expression turning grim. "She ran back to make her peace with Brightwood. He followed as soon as he got the horses saddled. Couldn't have been more than a quarter hour behind her, half at the most."

Morag closed her eyes. "He didn't reach her in time. The Black Coats must have her. If Neall isn't careful, they'll have him too."

"How can you be so sure?" Ahern demanded.

Morag opened her eyes. "Death is whispering. Death is nearby."

Ahern lowered his arms, clenched his fists. "They'll have taken her to Baron Felston's estate. That's the only place the Black Coats could go to do . . . what you said they do."

"How do I get there?"

"I'll take you." Ahern turned, summoned one of the men who had been lingering nearby. "Glenn. You remember what I told you? All of it?" He waited for the man to nod. "No matter what happens today, you do what I told you."

"Yes, sir."

A few moments later, Morag and Morphia followed a gray stallion over the fields, racing toward Baron Felston's estate.

Neall rode close enough to the estate to see the house and stables. Too much activity. Why were so many horses being saddled?

"Best to leave us here," the small man said. "We'll make our own way to the house." He paused. "Do you know where they'd likely be keeping the witch?"

"There's a small room in the cellar. A cold, dark

room." He knew it well. He'd spent enough time there in his childhood as punishment for things Royce had done but for which he'd been blamed.

The small man nodded. "You give us a few minutes, then you ride up easy."

"I'm not welcome here."

The small man made an odd sound and gestured toward the dark mare. "You're bringing a gift, aren't you? Never seen a human who would turn down a gift." He turned his head and studied some nearby bushes. Then he smiled. "May the Mother watch over you, young Lord."

After Neall helped the Small Fork dismount, the small man studied him, then said, "The Fae have lived outside the world for too long, and they've forgotten much. You have as much power as they do. The real difference between you is that you have one face, and it's a honest one. Remember that when next you deal with the Fair Folk . . . young Lord of the Woods."

The small man turned and walked toward the house, his companions spreading out and following.

As Neall mounted Darcy, he saw a flash of red burst out from beneath the bushes.

The fox ran across the field, paused when it reached the small men, then continued toward the kennels where Baron Felston kept his hounds.

"Well," Neall said, gathering Darcy's reins. "Once those hounds get a whiff of fox, that should create enough noise to clear some of the men from the yard."

He scanned the field. There was no sign of the Small Folk. He counted to one hundred, clenching his teeth until his jaw ached. Then he gave Darcy the signal to move forward, holding the horse to an easy trot as if he had all the time in the world.

Ari stared at the spiked bridle and kept shivering, shivering. The one encasing her head hurt badly enough. She could imagine what that other one would feel like. But, somehow, the face she kept seeing being pierced by those spikes wasn't hers. It was Neall's.

Neall.

He would know where they'd taken her. He would be coming here. And they would be waiting for him.

Morag, if I knew what to do, I would use whatever power the Mother granted me to do whatever was needed to help him. But if they do catch him, if they do harm him, please, Morag, please be kind to him when you show him the road to the Summerland.

Her hands and feet were so cold. If only there was a little fire in this room to take away the chill.

Fire warmed. And fire burned.

She looked at the rope binding her hands together. If it was done carefully . . .

She slowly drew the branch of fire into herself, feeling its warmth flow through her. She channeled it down her arms to her wrists, let the heat build. She focused on the rope, drawing the heat to one spot until it was ready to burn. She twisted her wrists a little. A tiny puff of smoke rose from the rope.

A small flame inside the rope, burning upward.

More smoke. And heat. Then flame burst from the center of the rope, still small, still controlled. Must control it.

She watched the flame, kept twisting her wrists to help fray the rope, even though it rubbed her skin raw.

She winced as the flame brushed against her hand. One more pull and the rope snapped. Moving awkwardly, but as quickly as she could, she freed her hands and tossed the rope on the dirt floor.

She reached up to free herself from the metal bridle, then paused. Having her feet free was more important.

It was easier this time. She knew how to guide the fire into the rope, and she could use her hands to tug at it to make it break faster.

Once her feet were free, she fumbled with the straps that held the bridle. When she finally got it off, she studied it for a moment. It was a slightly more benign version of the spiked bridle sitting on the table, but that didn't make it any less cruel. Only someone with a withered soul would use this on another person.

Setting the bridle on the floor, she rubbed her legs, gritting her teeth against the fierce tingling as blood began flowing through her limbs again. When the tingling changed from unbearable to tolerable, she used the wall to help her stand up.

She stumbled over to the table and braced her hands against it. She was sure she didn't want to know what had produced the fresh stains on its surface, and she was suddenly grateful for the dim light.

She picked up the confession, held it out. Fire flowed from her fingers. The paper burst into flames. She dropped it, watched it burn.

She was free, and she could move. Now all she had to do was figure out how to get out of this room and away from these awful men.

One of the shadow hounds snarled a soft warning.

"Someone's coming," Dianna said.

A queer light came into Lucian's eyes as he unlocked the front door and stepped outside to meet their visitor.

Dianna went out the kitchen door, intending to come around the side of the cottage. She paused long enough to order the pack of shadow hounds to stay, then snuck to a spot where she could peer around a corner.

Several young men dismounted, handed their horses' reins to other companions, then strode toward the cottage. Four of those men paused long enough to light torches.

One man, who seemed to be their leader, stepped forward. He looked at Lucian and sneered. "If it isn't the witch's fancy Lord. You'd best be on your way. We have business here. And the witch won't be back to lift her skirts for you anymore."

"Where is she?" Lucian growled.

"Well, I'll tell you," the man said. "The Master Inquisitor is questioning her about the terrible crimes she's committed against the good people of Ridgeley." He let out a nasty laugh. "They call him the Witch's

Hammer. By the time he's done persuading her to confess, I don't think any man will be interested in lifting her skirts. Even a fancy Lord like you."

Mother's mercy, Dianna thought. Ari was in the hands of the witch killers. Morag had been right. Some of the Fae should have stayed here to keep watch and to protect. But . . . *Morag* had been here. *She* was the one who should have stayed instead of tearing off to Tir Alainn to embroil them all in what was most likely another silly argument about letting Ari leave Brightwood in order to marry that Neall. Now, because of *Morag,* this part of Tir Alainn was more at risk than ever.

"What is your business here?" Lucian said.

The man sneered again. "It's daylight. What do you *think* we need torches for?" He paused. "You *do* know about fire, don't you?"

Dianna shuddered. She was glad she couldn't see Lucian's face.

"Yes," Lucian said softly. He looked at the cottage. "Fire warms." He looked back at the men. "And. It. *Burns.*"

At that moment, the torches became balls of fire that engulfed the men holding them.

The other men stared at their companions for a moment, then turned and ran for the horses.

Screaming, the burning men tried to run after their friends, but only managed a few steps before they fell. One of them rolled back and forth on the road, trying to smother the flames.

It will do you no good, Dianna thought with fierce satisfaction. *That fire will burn as long as he commands it to burn.*

The horses' reins burst into flames, burning the hands of the men who held them. The terrified animals reared. The reins snapped, and the horses bolted before the other men could reach them.

A black stallion suddenly stood in the road where Lucian had been. Flames flickered through his mane and tail. Sparks leaped from his hooves. He charged down the road, straight toward the men who were now watching him with terrified eyes.

They threw themselves to the ground, rolling to escape his hooves.

He kept galloping down the road, heading for the village.

The men just stayed where they had fallen, watching him.

Dianna smiled viciously. It wasn't over yet. She ran to the back of the cottage, mounted her pale mare, and signaled her shadow hounds to go around the other side of the cottage. She trotted out to the road just as the men were getting to their feet.

"You want a hunt?" she taunted. "Then we'll hunt."

Some of the men turned toward Brightwood, as if intending to flee into the woods. But the shadow hounds flowed around the cottage at that moment, and the men turned and ran in the other direction.

That was good. She didn't want them touching Brightwood. And they wouldn't. Not ever again.

She went back around the cottage so the mare wouldn't have to walk between the burned bodies. She watched the fleeing men and smiled. Fear made feet swift. But not swift enough.

"Catch them," she said.

The shadow hounds raced after the men. And the Huntress raced with them.

"Fetch the witch," Adolfo told two of his guards. "It's time to take care of Baron Felston's problem."

As Neall rode up to the manor house's kitchen door, one of the men standing near the stables hurried to meet him.

"You'd best be gone, Neall," he said. "You know you're not welcome here."

Neall dismounted, then looked at the man. The words had been sharp, but there was concern beneath them.

He smiled. "I'm going for good, Winn. I just wanted to leave a peace offering." He tipped his head toward the mare.

Winn's eyes widened. "How'd you manage to get one of Ahern's special horses?"

"Let's just say I bargained well."

"She's a beauty. I guess the baron won't run you off until he's got her locked in the stables." The man looked at the saddlebags.

Neall tensed.

"The baron has guests," Winn said slowly. "Not the sort of men you want looking in your direction, if you get my meaning."

"I get your meaning."

"When you leave here, you'd better ride fast."

"I intend to."

The man started to say something more but the frenzied barking coming from the kennels silenced him. Then, "Mother's tits! What's wrong with *them*?" He hurried away.

"Stay here," Neall told the horses.

He opened the kitchen door.

Ari leaned against the stone wall, next to the door. In one hand she held the spiked bridle. She had looked through the Master Inquisitor's chest and had found other things that could be used as a weapon, but she couldn't bear to touch them. She could barely stand holding the spiked bridle. The metal was filled with the pain of the ones who had worn it.

If only she had a stone that size that she could throw at whoever opened the door. If it hit him in the face or chest, it might knock him down long enough for her to get away.

Could she use her magic to will the spiked bridle to feel like stone? She closed her eyes, picturing it clearly. A man opening the door. Stones flying to strike him. Knocking him down.

As I will it, so mote it be.

The wall she leaned against shifted slightly, making a quiet grinding sound.

Her eyes snapped open. Before she could wonder if she'd actually felt something, she heard the scrape of a key in the lock.

Her heart pounding, Ari gripped the spiked bridle, ready to swing it at whoever walked through the door.

Stones flying. Stones flying. As I will it . . .

The door started to open.

The wall beside her exploded outward, the stones striking flesh.

Stunned, Ari stared through the hole in the wall at the two guards lying on the floor, their heads buried under stone.

She tossed the spiked bridle into the room, gingerly stepped over the man nearest the door, then stopped. She wasn't the first person who had felt fear and pain in that small, dark room. From the moment the Black Coats had dragged her into that room, she had sensed the misery that had soaked into the stones over the years.

Pressing her hands against the stone wall on the other side of the door, she called the strength of the earth into her, let it flow through her to the stones.

"Bury this place," she whispered, focusing her will on the room as she drew more and more of the earth's strength into herself then channeled it into the stones. "Bury it deep so that no one will feel fear and pain here again. As I will it, so mote it be."

The stones trembled beneath her hands.

Ari turned and ran for the stairs.

The shadow hounds pulled another man down. He squealed like a rabbit as one of the bitches sank her teeth into his neck and tore out his throat.

Dianna raced after the next one. Some of the hounds were ahead of her, keeping their quarry running across open land.

The leader, the one who had dared sneer at the Lightbringer, was still up ahead. She let him stay ahead. He couldn't outrun her hounds. But she also couldn't let him reach the farmhouse she could see in the near distance.

He wouldn't. But being close to safety when she brought him down would hurt him even more.

As Neall entered the kitchen, the manor house shuddered, rumbled. He felt the kitchen floor drop beneath his feet, giving him the strange sense that he was being flung into the air.

Mother's mercy, was the whole place going to cave in?

"Ari," he whispered. If the house was collapsing for some reason, she would be buried alive.

He ran across the kitchen, yanked open the door that led to the cellar—and caught Ari before she could fall. With one arm around her waist, he hurried her across the kitchen and outside.

He hesitated, then led her to Darcy and gave her a boost into the saddle. There wasn't time to adjust the stirrups, so he placed her hands firmly on the saddle. "You just concentrate on staying with him. Let him do the rest. He'll take care of you."

"Neall . . ."

"Get her away from here."

Darcy spun, almost tossing Ari from the saddle. She regained her balance, and the gelding cantered away from the house.

Too slow, Neall thought as he swung up on the mare. *Too slow.*

As he urged the mare to follow Darcy, he heard shouts from the stables, saw some of the guards who had accompanied the Master Inquisitor running toward him.

And he heard glass breaking.

The manor house shuddered again.

Adolfo stumbled into a table, his heart pounding fiercely.

That *witch.* He should have gone to work on her as

soon as he'd brought her here instead of giving her a little time alone to let fear soften her.

Well, he could rectify *that* right now. Better yet, he would just slit her throat here and now and be done with it.

The window behind him shattered, spraying glass across the room.

As he stepped into the hall, Felston rushed to meet him.

"That young bastard Neall is escaping with the witch!" Felston shouted. "He's been trouble since the first day I allowed him to live here."

Adolfo ran to the front door, flung it open, then ran to the stables, Felston puffing along behind him.

He skidded to a stop. A wild fury filled him as he watched two dark horses running across the fields.

"Mount up," Adolfo shouted. He pointed a finger at Felston. "If they're riding in that direction, where are they heading?"

"That way will take them to Ahern's farm."

Adolfo swung around, pointed a finger at his Inquisitors. "You take half the guards and ride to the Old Place. They're more likely to head for the woods where they can hide rather than being chased over open land. Get ahead of them. We'll follow them. And they'll be trapped between us. The rest of you men come with me." He gave Felston a hard stare. "When we catch them, I'll take care of both your problems."

Mounting his horse, he galloped after the witch and her foolish lover.

Behind him, the manor house shook.

The man wasn't sneering now that her hounds stood in a snarling circle around him.

"You can't hurt me," he said, his voice coming close to a whine. "I'm Royce, Baron Felston's heir."

"I don't care who you are," ·Dianna said. "Where is Ari?"

A nasty, but pouting, expression came over his face.

"The Witch's Hammer took care of her, just like he's going to take care of you if you don't let me go."

"Where is she?"

"Dead! Dead dead dead. And he'll kill you too. You'll see."

"But you won't."

She watched impassively while her hounds tore him apart. When she finally called them to her, she looked away from what remained of Baron Felston's heir— and saw the dark smoke of a strong fire.

"Lucian," she whispered.

She dug her heels into her mare's sides and galloped toward the smoke, her hounds racing beside her.

The good people of Ridgeley had been introduced to the Lightbringer's wrath. Now let them meet the Huntress.

Neall brought the dark mare to a stop that sat her back on her haunches. He vaulted off her back and ran to Darcy.

"Neall, what are you doing?" Ari said, anxiously looking behind her. "They're catching up."

He adjusted the left stirrup, then shoved her foot into it. "I know," he said, ducking under Darcy's head to adjust the right stirrup. "But you're not a strong rider, and you need the stirrups to stay in the saddle at the speed we need to go."

"Neall . . . Maybe—"

"Don't say it." He gave her such a sharp look, she flinched. "We're in this together."

"Will we make it to Ahern's?" Ari asked.

Neall mounted the mare and shook his head. "Too much open land that way. We'll head for Brightwood. We can lose them in the deeper part of the woods." *The Small Folk will see to that,* he added silently, gathering the reins. "Just hang on, Ari. We'll make it."

He glanced back. The riders coming from Felston's estate were gaining too fast. "Let's ride."

The mare and gelding leaped forward, racing for Brightwood.

*   *   *

As they crested a low, rolling hill, Morag spotted the two dark horses racing back toward Brightwood. And she saw the other riders who weren't that far behind.

The gray stallion stamped one foot and tossed his head.

The dark horse danced, too fretful about not moving to stand still.

"Can we reach them before those other riders do?" Morphia asked, curbing her own horse.

"We'll reach them," Morag said. She gave the dark horse his head, letting him tear down the hill in pursuit of Ari and Neall. Morphia raced beside her.

But the gray stallion veered away from them and headed straight for the other riders.

May the Mother protect you, Ahern, Morag thought. Then she thought of nothing else but the two young people she desperately wanted to stay among the living.

Adolfo clenched his hands, dragging on the reins enough to slow his horse. The guards passed him, heading straight for that gray stallion.

Two black-haired women. One riding a dark horse. He had wanted to punish her for stealing from him, for killing his men. Now, seeing her, even at a distance, was more than enough. She reeked of magic. She reeked of death.

The Gatherer.

Despite the fear that had shivered through him every time he'd thought of her, he hadn't really believed until now that she could do to him what she'd done to his nephew and courier. He'd been certain that he was powerful enough to stand against any of the Fae and win.

But not against her. Who *could* stand against Death's Mistress?

A shout from one of the guards brought his attention back to the problem standing directly in their path.

No ordinary horse would have run toward his guards instead of staying with the women and their horses. Which meant the gray was no ordinary horse. There was only one man at Ahern's farm who was fully Fae and could shift into another shape, and that was Ahern himself.

Adolfo chided himself for allowing the sight of the Gatherer to distract him and make him doubt his own strength, even for a moment. Despite her power, she was still only a female, still only a creature that had to be taught to submit to the masters of the world. He would find her weakness and use it to crush her. In the meantime, the horse Lord standing in his way needed to be taught a lesson.

Before he could issue his orders, the gray stallion reared, bugling a challenge. Or, perhaps, a command.

The other horses turned away, fighting bit and spur. When the stallion bugled again, they reared.

Two of the guards, who were reaching for their crossbows, were thrown. One scrambled to his feet and grabbed his fallen crossbow. The other didn't move.

As his horse's forelegs touched the ground again, Adolfo kicked out of the stirrups and half fell out of the saddle, just managing to stagger out of reach before his horse's back feet lashed out.

Two more of the guards managed to grab their crossbows and get free of their saddles.

"Kill him!" Adolfo shouted.

The gray stallion reared.

The guards took aim.

A horse charged one of the guards, knocking against him at the same moment the quarrel left the crossbow. That spoiled the aim enough that the quarrel hit the stallion's shoulder instead of his chest.

But the other two guards hit the stallion's exposed belly, and the quarrels sank deep.

Screaming, the stallion whirled and galloped back toward the hill it had raced down a short while before.

Adolfo shouted in triumph. Fae or not, no matter

what his form, a belly wound was a fatal one. He watched the stallion struggle to reach the top of the hill.

It doesn't matter if you reach your farm or not, old man. You're still going to die.

For a moment, there was no sound but the harsh breathing of men and animals.

Then the horses went mad.

The glint of shoes in the sunlight as hooves lashed out. The thud of bodies hitting the earth.

The horses galloped up the hill, following the dying gray stallion.

Adolfo looked at the guards' bodies. He sank to his knees. This shouldn't have happened. *He* was the Witch's Hammer. *He* was the powerful one. This shouldn't have happened.

"Master Adolfo?"

One guard staggered to his feet, blood streaming from a wound in his head.

"Are you hurt, Master Adolfo?"

Adolfo started to shake. Couldn't stop. This shouldn't have happened. What were the Fae—*any* of the Fae—that they could thwart the will of men by controlling the four-legged beasts men used? But if men couldn't command the beasts, how could they rid the world of magic and be the masters as they were meant to be?

"Master Adolfo?"

Adolfo forced himself to get to his feet. He mustn't show weakness. If he did, they would never rid the world of the witches . . . and the Fae.

"When the witch is gone, the magic will die," Adolfo said carefully. "The magic will die, and there will be nothing that will make us afraid. We will be the masters."

"Yes, Master."

Adolfo looked at the bleeding guard, and his brown eyes burned with a queer light. "Good men were lost today, but not in vain. No, not in vain. We drove the witch and her foul lover into the trap, and the other

Inquisitors will see that she pays for the pain she has brought."

The guard didn't seem to be listening, wasn't even looking at him. He wouldn't allow other men to turn away from him, dismiss him. Not again. Never again. *No* man was going to turn away from him as his father had done. And any man who did would pay for it—as his father had done.

Adolfo took a few steps to the side, bent to pick up one of the crossbows.

Then the guard pointed. "Look! Smoke! Something's burning."

Adolfo sighed, as another man might after being satisfied by a woman. "It's the witch's cottage. Royce and his friends went to burn it down so there would be no trace of her left to foul the land."

The guard slowly shook his head. "There's too much smoke to be one cottage, master. And that's coming from the direction of—" The guard turned and stared at him. "Ridgeley. It's the *village* that's burning."

Morag reined the dark horse to a stop.

"Mother's mercy, Neall," she muttered as she scanned the woods. "How could you disappear so fast?"

"Will we find them?" Morphia asked.

"We'll find them," Morag replied grimly.

They *had* to find Neall and Ari.

Because Death was no longer whispering. Now, Death howled.

Neall followed the broadest trail through the woods. They needed to go deeper into Brightwood, away from the trails where someone could easily track them. But he was worried about Ari. She knew these woods better than anyone, but she wasn't a skilled rider and could be swept out of the saddle if she misjudged a low-hanging branch.

Distance. Distance. They needed to put enough distance between themselves and their pursuers to catch their breath and decide where the best place would be to lay low for a little while.

He cursed silently as he went down into a slight dip and saw the tree that had fallen across the trail. Not much room on the other side of it for a horse to land before the trail climbed again. He could have done it on Darcy, but he didn't know the mare well enough to have that kind of confidence in her—and Ari certainly couldn't make that jump.

As he reined in and turned the mare, he heard Darcy's angry challenge—and realized Ari was no longer right behind him.

The mare charged back up to level ground just in time for Neall to see the men wearing black coats step onto the trail, blocking the gelding's retreat.

Movement just beyond the edge of the trail. Guards raising their crossbows. Aiming at Ari!

"Look out!" Neall shouted.

Darcy pivoted on his hind legs, half rearing as he turned. Most of the crossbow quarrels hit him in the chest and neck, but two of them found their intended target.

Ari and Darcy both screamed as the gelding fell, throwing Ari out of the saddle. Blood reddened her tunic and trousers. When she tried to move, she cried out in pain.

Neall threw himself off the mare's back and ran toward Ari. "Leave her alone, you bastards!"

Two guards took aim at him. Before they could fire, a look of stunned surprise came over their faces. They fell to the ground. So did the rest of the guards. And the black-coated Inquisitors.

Neall stared at them for a moment, not sure that he believed what he saw.

He stumbled over to Ari, knelt beside her.

She raised her head, her eyes filled with pain. "Neall . . ."

He pressed a hand gently to her shoulder to keep her from moving. The quarrels had gone through her, so at least he wouldn't have to try to remove them here or have her endure riding with them still in her until he could get her to some kind of safety.

Darcy's labored breathing suddenly stopped.

In that silence, Neall heard the quiet sound of a hoof against earth. He looked beyond the fallen men to the two women who watched him.

"Morag," he breathed. Watching them dismount, he thought about snatching up one of the crossbows, but he knew he couldn't move fast enough to stop her. The dead men around him were proof of that.

Leaping to his feet, he took a few steps forward, then planted himself in the middle of the trail, standing between her and Ari.

"Morag," Ari said. Her voice sounded so terribly weak.

Neall tensed as the Gatherer approached him, but his eyes never left hers.

"Step aside, Neall," she said.

He shook his head. "Death can't be cheated, but sometimes a bargain can be struck." He saw her surprise before she could mask it. "The others who are Death's Servants have no choice about who they guide to the Shadowed Veil, but the Gatherer *does*. She can transfer one person's strength to another. At least, that's what the stories say."

"And if the stories are true?" Morag asked quietly.

"Then take me. Give my life strength to Ari, and take me."

She gave him a queer look. "You would do that?"

"No, Neall," Ari pleaded. "Don't give up your life."

He turned slowly and looked at her. "You are my life." When he turned back to face Morag, she was watching Ari intently. Fear spiked through him, roughening his voice. "Will you trade? My life for hers."

She gave him another queer look, then held out her hand.

He grabbed it, curled his fingers around it so she couldn't let go.

She gave him a tug that pulled him to one side of the path at the same moment the other woman slipped around him and hurried toward Ari.

He tried to pull away from her—and discovered she was stronger than he'd thought. So he just stood there, watching helplessly, as the other woman knelt beside Ari and gently brushed one hand over Ari's head.

Ari's eyes closed. Her head sank to the ground.

"You agreed to trade!" Neall said, feeling grief mingle with fury.

"I made no bargain, Neall," Morag said quietly. "Nor would I have. I see no shadows in her face. Let my sister do what she can."

"Sister?" He stared at the other black-haired woman, who was carefully lifting Ari's tunic.

"Morphia is the Sleep Sister, the Lady of Dreams."

How fitting that the Gatherer and the Sleep Sister were actually sisters.

Morag released his hand and walked toward Ari. "She is hurt, and she is in pain, but Death is not waiting here for her, Neall."

"If Death *had* been waiting, would you have agreed to the bargain?" Neall asked, keeping pace with her.

Morag was silent for a moment. Then she said, "I don't know. No one has asked that of me until now."

"Then what's happened to Ari?"

Morphia looked up at him. "I gave her sleep so she would feel no pain."

Sinking to his knees, Neall forced himself to look at the wounds.

"She bleeds, but the quarrels cut through nothing more than flesh." She looked questioningly at Morag, who held one hand over Ari's body.

Morag nodded. "I don't sense any damage inside her. Did you bring her saddlebags before the two of you ran?"

"Yes," Neall said.

"Then bring them here, and some water as well."

As Neall stood up to do her bidding, he glanced at

the dead men. Right now, it was better not to think too much about who Morag was.

He would have traded, Morag thought as she waited for Neall to bring the saddlebags. *Even without knowing whether it was truly needed, he would have traded his life for hers.*

Would any Fae male have cared so much that he would have tried to make that bargain? If necessary, he would fight for Clan and kin—and, perhaps, die in the fighting. But he wouldn't go into that fight *expecting* to die. He would expect to live and benefit from his courage in the fight. But for a man to hand over his life, knowing he wouldn't share in whatever would come after?

You did just make a bargain, Neall, although it's one you're not aware of. One I hope you'll never be aware of.

When Neall hurried back to them, Morphia used the water to wash the wound in Ari's side and the graze in her thigh. Morag rummaged through the saddlebags until she found the rolled cloths and the small jar of healing ointment.

"But those are—" Neall started to protest.

"Clean and made to absorb blood," Morag replied. She and Morphia smeared the ointment on the wounds and dealt with the makeshift bandages. Neall protested again when they tore up Ari's long nightgown to make strips long enough to wrap around Ari and hold the dressings. They ignored him.

"Now," Morag said as she put the supplies back in Ari's saddlebags, "lift her carefully and take her out of the way. We'll try to shift the gelding enough to get your saddlebags free."

"No," Neall said. "I don't need—"

Morag gave him a look that silenced him. "If you didn't need what you'd brought, you wouldn't have brought it."

It took effort, but between them, she and Morphia managed to pull the saddlebags free.

Morag rested one hand on the gelding's flank in a silent farewell. This one had had the courage of his breed, and she knew he would be sorely missed.

That reminded her of another problem. Neall and Ari couldn't travel however far they would have to go riding double on the mare. They needed another horse.

Handing the saddlebags to Morphia, she walked over to where the dark horse waited for her. She pressed her hand against his cheek and looked into his dark, trusting eyes.

"I want you to go with Neall and Ari. I know you like her, and I think you'll like him, too." When he started to take a step back, she shook her head. "They need you. They need your strength and your speed and your courage. They need you to look after them and take care of them. They're going to need that for a long time. So we'll say goodbye now, my friend. You'll have a good life with them. This much I know."

Giving him a last caress, she walked the dark horse over to where Neall stood, holding Ari in his arms.

"He'll go with you," she said quietly. "You'll need to ride double until Ari is strong enough to ride by herself. The mare couldn't do that. He can."

Neall stared at her. "I—I can't take your horse."

"Yes, you can. For Ari's sake." *And for the sake of a good horse who now fears what I would have to ask of him.*

"I'll wake her enough that she can help you get her mounted," Morphia said. "I won't send her back into a deep sleep since that will make it harder for you both to ride, but she'll doze enough to dull the pain."

Taking the saddlebags from her sister, Morag tied them to the dark horse's saddle. While Neall and Morphia helped Ari mount, she secured Ari's saddlebags and canteen to the mare's saddle.

When they were ready to go, Morag gave Ari one more long, searching look—and felt relieved. There were still no shadows in the girl's face. Ari would heal—and she would have the life Astra and Ahern had wanted for her.

"May the Mother bless both of you for all of your days," Neall said.

"Blessings of the day to you," Morag said.

Neall smiled oddly. " 'Merry meet, and merry part, and merry meet again.' That's another saying among witches." He murmured to the dark horse, who pricked his ears, considered the trail before them, then turned into the trees to find another path.

Morag smiled at the way Neall's eyes widened at having the decision made for him, but Neall was used to dealing with an animal that sometimes held an opinion that was different from his own. He and the dark horse would get along well together—once they got to know each other.

Merry meet, and merry part, and merry meet again.

A warm feeling filled Morag. Did that saying express a hope that she would visit them in their new home?

The warm feeling froze, began to shrivel. Or did that saying have more than one meaning, especially when it was said to the Gatherer? Was Neall trying to tell her he hoped they would meet again in this world—or that he hoped they wouldn't see her again until they were all in the Summerland, after their spirits had left their bodies to the Mother's keeping?

Foolish to want acceptance from anyone who lived in the human world, foolish to yearn to be welcomed as a friend when even her own kind drew back from her. She was Death's Mistress. That was her gift—and her burden. What did she truly know of life?

She pushed away her feelings before they could bruise her heart. Turning, she saw Morphia watching her.

"What do we do about them?" Morphia asked softly.

Morag looked at the ghosts who all glared at her— especially the Inquisitors. They would have to be dealt with, taken away from Brightwood. Whether she

would guide them all the way to the Shadowed Veil
was something she hadn't decided yet.

"Leave them," she said. "The Small Folk can do
what they choose with the bodies."

Morphia looked at the Inquisitors' ghosts and shuddered. "In that case, let's get away from here."

They mounted Morphia's horse, Morag riding behind her sister, then headed in the direction of the
cottage.

As they crossed the meadow, they saw the black smoke,
could smell the burning.

"It would appear the Lightbringer has passed judgment on the people there," Morphia said.

"Yes," Morag said softly. "They shouldn't have forgotten he is the Lord of Fire."

Morphia hesitated. "You're tired, Morag. Can't you
rest a little while before you gather the people there?"

I'll rest a long while before I ride into that village,
Morag thought. "Let another of Death's Servants
guide them to the Shadowed Veil. I am tired, and—"

Death called.

Morag listened carefully, looked in the direction
from which that call had come.

"And there's someplace else I have to be," she finished, her voice full of regret.

Abandoning the wounded guard, Adolfo ran toward
the group of people clustered around the stable.
Reaching them, he stared at the mound of debris-filled
earth that filled the place where Baron Felston's
manor house had stood a short while ago.

"What happened here?" he gasped.

One of the grooms gave him a hostile look. "The
earth swallowed it, then spewed up enough of itself
to cover it. I guess that was the Mother's way of saying
you Inquisitors should have let the witches be."

Adolfo looked at them, saw the same grim expression and hard eyes in all their faces. "But *she* was the
one who did this. The *witch* did this!"

"She never did any harm until *you* came!" one of the female servants shouted.

The groom nodded his head in agreement. "The ladies of Brightwood always had a lot more courtesy for the common folk than the gentry did. Even the villagers looked down on those who worked the land." He looked in the direction of the black smoke filling the sky. "Guess they're not going to be looking down on anyone for a long time to come."

"The witch—"

The groom shook his head, then gestured toward another man. "Russell said he saw a black horse racing toward Ridgeley. A black horse with flames in his mane and tail. Anything he passed that a man had made . . . burned. Guess the Lord of Fire was letting us all know *his* opinion about you taking the witch."

They were all against him. That, too, was the witch's fault. She should have accepted her fate, should have yielded to the need to have her spirit cleansed of its foulness. *She* had brought about this disdain for authority in servants who, a day ago, had been sufficiently meek.

"Where is Baron Felston? There are things I must discuss with him."

The groom tipped his head toward the mound of earth. "You can dig for him then. He never came out. There was plenty of time before the house started to cave in, but he never came out. Neither did the baroness nor Odella."

Adolfo's legs trembled. He forced himself to stand tall and show no weakness. These people were like a pack of feral dogs now. If he showed any weakness, they would attack.

"If you want answers," the groom said, "you could always try to ask the Small Folk. I saw a few of them heading away from the manor house just before it all caved in. I reckon they could tell you what happened to the baron and the others."

The Small Folk. The Fae. The witch. There was too much power here—power that should have been approached carefully instead of with haste. That had been his error. Felston had lured him here with the conviction that there was only one young witch to deal with. He should have proceeded with his usual caution instead of listening to the baron's reassurances. And there was still the not-insignificant matter of his fee.

"Where is Royce?" Adolfo asked.

The groom shrugged. "He left earlier today to ride out with some of his friends. Haven't seen him since."

He didn't want to know what happened to Royce, but it *was* possible the young man was still alive. It was possible.

"Saddle a horse for me. I'll find Royce. He needs to be informed that he is the baron now."

No one moved.

Then a shadow passed over them.

The groom looked up, watched the hawk for a moment, then turned to another man. "Winn, saddle a horse for him. The sooner he's gone, the better. No point having the Fae or the Small Folk angry with *us* because *he's* standing here."

Adolfo watched the hawk slowly circle, as if it were taking a good look at the destruction. Suppressing a shiver, he said, "It's just a hawk."

The groom made a harsh sound. "And that black horse that burned Ridgeley was just a horse. Get away from us, Master Inquisitor. You brought nothing but ill with you."

Winn came out of the stables, leading a saddled horse.

Not the best horse Felston had, Adolfo thought as he eyed the animal. An adequate beast and nothing more. But he mounted without comment, and rode away.

Once he was out of sight, he turned the horse away from the direction of the main road and cut across the fields so that he could pick up the road again on the other side of Ridgeley. He didn't want to ride through the village. He didn't want to be the scapegoat people accused of causing their pain and suffering.

He could reach the next village by late evening, even riding this inadequate animal. Once there, he would summon the other Inquisitors he'd brought with him to Sylvalan. Then he would return here and deal with the Fae.

Morag stood beside Ahern's bed, watching the shadows deepen in his face. His housekeeper and one of his men kept the bedside vigil.

"Ahern," Morag said softly. The Mother only knew how he'd made it back to the farm wounded as he was. She wanted to release him from the suffering, but wouldn't gather him without his consent.

"Go outside, Morag," Ahern said, his gruff voice now weak and gasping. "Go outside for a bit."

She did as he asked. As she walked toward the stables, she realized the place already felt empty and there was no sign of the men and horses.

Another of Ahern's men met her halfway.

"Where is everyone?" she asked.

"Going . . . or already gone," he replied. "Ahern had told us he was leaving, going back to the Clan he'd come from." Tears filled his eyes. He blinked them away. "He said he wanted to remember Brightwood as it was. He'd settled our wages and given us our pick of the horses. Except the special horses. He said they would find the place where they belonged." He hesitated. "I guess Ahern will be staying after all."

"His body will rest here within the Mother, but his spirit will go to the Summerland," Morag said gently. "That I can promise you."

The man nodded, wiped his eyes with the back of his hand. "He said you would need a horse and gear. He chose them, early this morning, before . . ."

Morag stared at the man. How had Ahern known she would need another dark horse? He couldn't have known what would happen today.

But as the Lord of the Horse, he would have sensed the dark horse's fear of the shining roads through the Veil, and he must have guessed that she would look for a way to let the animal go rather than continue to endure that fear.

"If you need help saddling him, I'll be nearby," the man said, brushing his fingers against the brim of his cap before he walked away.

Morag continued toward the stables. As if that was the awaited signal, a dark horse stepped out of the shadows, his ears pricked.

"You are a fine lad, aren't you?" she said softly, holding out her hand.

He came forward to get acquainted.

Yes, he was a fine horse, she decided as she petted him. Fine and strong, with the courage of his breed. Since Ahern had chosen him for her—and had chosen her for him—she had no doubt they would forge a strong partnership.

"Let's see how your saddle fits," Morag said.

As she stepped into the stables, she heard the whimpering. Following the sound, she opened a stall door.

"Ah, Merle," she said softly.

The puppy looked at her with heartbroken eyes.

Morag held out her hand for him to sniff. He crept toward her. The tip of his tail began to wag as he sniffed her.

He smells Ari, she thought sadly, petting the puppy. She picked him up and cuddled him, not sure which of them found it the most comforting.

"I don't know where she's going, Merle. I don't know where to find her. And it's better that way—for now." She set him down, then slipped out of the stall, closing the door behind her.

He immediately began whimpering again.

She looked at him over the stall door. "Quiet, little one. There's a journey I have to make, and it's on a road that you can't travel. But I'll come back for you. You won't be left behind. You won't be alone. That I promise."

She saddled the dark horse, then checked to see that Merle had food and water. She would come back

for him in the morning. It would be better not to take
him to the cottage and then take him away again.

This time, when she returned to the bedroom,
Ahern was ready. She gathered him gently. His body
took its last breath as his spirit stepped away from it.

The housekeeper, sitting beside the bed, covered
her face with her hands and wept. The man on the
other side of the bed bowed his head to hide his
own tears.

Ahern's ghost frowned.

You were cared for, Ahern, Morag thought. *Let
them grieve.*

She guided him out of the house.

"You approve?" he asked as they walked toward
the dark horse.

"I approve," she replied quietly. After she mounted,
Ahern floated up to sit behind her.

She didn't immediately seek the road to the Shadowed Veil. Instead, she went back to Brightwood,
back to the hill where the wind always blew, and
Astra, as well as Ahern, made the journey with her.

She left them standing before the Shadowed Veil.
When she looked back, she saw Ahern hold out his
hand . . . and she saw Astra take it. Together, they
walked through the Shadowed Veil to the Summerland beyond.

Merry meet, and merry part, and merry meet again.

She wasn't sure about the partings, but she hoped
that, when their spirits had rested and were reborn in
the world, Astra and Ahern would find each other
again. Perhaps, the next time, they would be able to
build a life together.

It was growing dark by the time she returned to
Ari's cottage, where Morphia waited for her.

Chapter Thirty-two

In the early dawn light, Dianna's pale mare trotted wearily beside Lucian, heading for Brightwood.

It was pointless trying to talk to him yet. He hadn't changed back to his human form once since those men showed up yesterday, intending to burn down Ari's cottage.

Perhaps it was better that she couldn't talk to him. She wasn't sure she would want to hear what he had to say—not after she'd seen what he'd done to the village of Ridgeley. The Lightbringer had been a vengeful Lord of Fire, and nothing had been spared. If humans had built it, he had burned it—and anyone who hadn't had the sense to flee.

Of course, the fact that he wouldn't talk to her right now meant she didn't have to tell him how many of those he'd allowed to flee had died anyway when they were confronted by the Huntress and her shadow hounds.

And she didn't have to ask if he knew for certain that Ari hadn't been in the village, held prisoner, before he burned it down.

So she urged the mare to keep pace with her brother, all the while hoping that what they would find at Brightwood would justify what they had done.

Lucian snorted, pricked his ears, and lengthened his pace.

Dianna let the mare fall behind—until she saw the two horses grazing in the meadow. "A little farther," she told the mare, urging her on. "Then you can rest."

The mare tried, but when her pace faltered, Dianna

dismounted and ran the rest of the way to the cottage. Ari was back. Ari was safe. And so was the Clan and their home territory in Tir Alainn.

Lucian changed form and strode toward the cottage. He looked at the half-open kitchen door and stopped suddenly, giving Dianna time to catch up to him.

Oh, Lucian, try to act like a joyous lover instead of an angry man. We won and—

Morag opened the other half of the kitchen door and stepped out of the cottage.

Dianna felt as if she were falling off a steep cliff, waiting for the pain of hitting the ground.

"Where is Ari?" Lucian demanded, looking past Morag to see inside the kitchen.

"She's gone, Lucian," Morag said quietly.

"Gone?" Dianna echoed. "How could she be gone when she'd been captured by—" She felt the blood drain from her head, making her dizzy.

"The Black Coats," Morag said, finishing the sentence Dianna had started. "And now she's gone."

"Bring her back," Lucian said, his voice calm and deadly. "The Gatherer can summon a spirit back from the Summerland if it hasn't been there very long." The calm broke, turning to fury. "How could you have taken her without consulting us first?"

"Why should I have consulted you?" Morag asked. "It was not your decision to make."

"Bring her back. She belongs here in Brightwood, with us."

"Even if I could do that, where would her spirit go? Do you know where her body lies right now? I don't."

"Her spirit could reside as a part of Brightwood," Dianna said.

"To feel the bite of every ax when wood was needed? To feel the cut of the spade when land was turned? Or would you have me bring back her ghost and leave it in the meadow? If her spirit doesn't reside in flesh, would she be able to do what you want of her?"

"Then we'll find another body for her to inhabit."

"Whose?" Morag asked softly. "A spirit doesn't leave a healthy body."

"You could gather another person's spirit and give the body to Ari," Dianna insisted.

"Whose?" Morag asked again, looking so pointedly at her that Dianna broke into a sweat.

"*You're* the one who took her without our consent. You're the one who should make it right."

Morag said nothing, but the coldness that crept into her dark eyes chilled Dianna.

"*Bring her back,*" Lucian said.

"Why?" Morag asked.

"Because she's needed here. And because I care for her."

Morag gave him an odd look. "Death can't be cheated, but, sometimes, a bargain can be struck. Are you willing to bargain with me?"

"I'm in no mood for games, Gatherer," Lucian warned.

"And I do not play games, Lightbringer. But, here and now, I will make a bargain." Morag held out her hand. "Your life for Ari's. If you go to the Summerland now, I'll find a way to bring her back to Brightwood."

"Fine," Lucian snapped. "Bring her back, and I'll consider it."

Morag lowered her hand and shook her head. "That's not the bargain."

Shocked speechless for a moment, Dianna regained her voice—and her fury. "He's the *Lightbringer*. How dare you demand such a thing from him!"

"That is the bargain," Morag said implacably. "Lucian's life in exchange for Ari's. Either agree to it or accept that she's gone and prepare to bring your Clan down to Brightwood to live."

"No man would agree to a bargain like that when you're standing there ready to accept it," Dianna said bitterly.

"That would depend on how much the man cared." A thought occurred to Dianna. "Then why don't you take that Neall in exchange for Ari? Surely, he's a worthy enough sacrifice."

"He is already gone."

Dianna wanted to scream in frustration. Why couldn't the man have lived a little longer so that his death could at least be useful?

Morag looked at Lucian. She held out her hand. "You were willing to destroy others for her sake. Are you willing to give yourself for her as well?"

The conflict showed clearly on his face, and Dianna felt it as keenly as if she were the one forced to make the choice. When he started to raise his hand, she wanted to cry out, wanted to tell him to stop. But she bit her tongue and kept silent.

His hand slowly rose toward Morag's. It began to shake. Before his fingers touched hers, his hand froze, then fell back to his side. He looked away.

"Ari is gone, Lucian," Morag said gently. "Accept it."

Bitterness swelled in Dianna until there was nothing else. "In that case, since we have no choice but to live here, Brightwood now belongs to the Clan. And *you* are no longer welcome on our land. Nor will you ever be. And by the time I finish telling the rest of the Clans about how you betrayed the Fae, *no* Clan will be willing to receive you—including your own. Tir Alainn will be as closed to you as it is to us."

Morag just turned and walked into the cottage.

Dianna stared at the open kitchen door. A few minutes later, Morphia came out and saddled the horses. As soon as she was done, Morag left the cottage. She tied her saddlebags to her dark horse, mounted, and she and Morphia rode away.

A sob rose in Dianna's throat. She turned away from the cottage that would soon become her home.

And saw Lucian disappear into the woods, heading for the place where the shining road anchored itself in the strength of Brightwood.

For a moment, she was stunned. How could he just leave her here alone?

Then she shook her head. Someone had to tell the Clan what had happened and rouse them to prepare to leave Tir Alainn. She just hoped they would have enough time before the road through the Veil began to close.

Morag filled another sack with grain. At least the horses would have some feed besides the grazing, and there was no reason to let it rot.

The house and the stables had been empty when she and Morphia returned to Ahern's farm. The housekeeper's little cottage also stood abandoned. No one here would begrudge her taking what was needed simply because she had done what needed to be done.

Banish her from Tir Alainn? Have her own Clan shun her? The Huntress had enough influence among the Fae to do exactly that. She had expected something like that from Dianna—and Dianna's solution for getting Ari back, while *unexpected,* hadn't been surprising. There were stories about such exchanges, and she knew the power to exchange spirits between two bodies resided within her, just as she had the power to gather someone's life strength and give it to another. That Dianna wanted *her* to relinquish her body so that Ari's spirit could inhabit it wasn't surprising either. Astra had been right: the Fae were very good at expecting someone else to shoulder the burden for them.

What *had* surprised her was how close Lucian had come to accepting her bargain. Perhaps he had cared more deeply than she'd suspected. But still not enough, may the Mother be thanked. If he had accepted the bargain, she would have fulfilled her part of it. She would have gone after Ari and brought the girl back to Brightwood, no matter what Neall thought or said. Now they were both safe, and, hopefully, no word of them would ever reach Lucian or Dianna.

"Blessings of the day to you," a male voice said softly.

Morag turned toward the voice, not sure what to

think when Aiden stepped inside the stables. "Blessings of the day to you."

"Dianna's very upset," Aiden said, slowly walking toward her. "And Lucian as well. Understandably so." He hesitated. "Was there nothing you could have done, Morag? Did we have to lose another Daughter from the House of Gaian?"

Morag studied him. He was a clever man with words, and that made her wary.

"Did you tell Dianna and Lucian about the Pillars of the World?"

Aiden nodded.

"If they had known before now who the witches were—and are—do you think they still would have expected Ari to oblige them, living a sterile life for their convenience and pleasure?"

He didn't answer for a long time. "They would have expected that whatever they offered would be enough, regardless of whether or not it truly was. And they would have resented her as much as they would have needed her to maintain Tir Alainn once she was old enough to no longer bend to their wishes."

Morag finished filling the grain sack and tied the opening securely. "Then things have worked out for the best."

"Not for Ari."

She heard the grief in his voice—and realized he wasn't grieving for a lost piece of Tir Alainn. But he *was* a clever man with words. "She's gone, Aiden."

"So you told Dianna. And the young man, the one who loved her, is gone, too."

"Yes."

Aiden rubbed the back of his neck. "You took them to the Shadowed Veil yourself?"

"Yesterday I took a man and a woman to the Shadowed Veil. I saw them cross through it and go on to the Summerland. Together."

He started to nod, then he frowned. "What happened to Ahern's spirit? You didn't leave him here, did you?"

She didn't ask how he'd heard about Ahern. The
Bard was sometimes capable of hearing far too many
things. "I took him and Astra to the Shadowed Veil."

"Astra? Who is—" He stopped. "You took Ahern
and Astra to the Shadowed Veil."

"Yes."

"And Ari . . ."

"Is gone."

Aiden sifted through the words. Morag knew the
moment when he understood what she was saying.

"The bargain you asked Lucian to make wasn't a
fair one, Morag," he said, looking extremely uncomfortable. "No man would have agreed to it while you
were standing in front of him."

"One man did." She paused, and then added, "I
didn't need to take what was willingly offered, but it
was offered, Aiden, not asked for."

His eyes widened. Then he said, more to himself
than to her, "So she did go with a man who could
give her love's jewels."

Morag frowned at him. He just smiled and shook
his head.

As he turned to leave, Morag said, "What will you
tell Lucian and Dianna?"

"What can I tell them that is different from what
you've already said? Ari is gone." He raised his hand
in farewell. "May you find firm roads and soft beds
on your travels. And may the House of Gaian pros-
per," he added softly, "wherever it may be."

By the time Morag left the stables with the grain
sacks, Aiden was already gone. Morphia was outside,
trying to find the best way to tie food sacks to the
saddles.

She looked at Morag, then shrugged. "They look
clumsy now, but they'll empty quick enough." She
fiddled with the saddle, not actually doing anything to
it. "If you don't mind, I'll ride with you for a while."

"What about your Lord of the Woods? Isn't he
waiting for you to return?"

A long pause. Then Morphia said, "I'll ride with you for a while."

Morag didn't ask any more questions. She walked back into the stables, opened one of the stall doors, and picked up Merle. "Come on, little one. It's time to go."

She mounted her dark horse and adjusted the pup so that she could hold on to him comfortably. When she and Morphia rode away from Ahern's farm—and Brightwood—she didn't look back.

Chapter Thirty-three

They were gone, Adolfo thought numbly as he packed his meager belongings in a cloth traveling bag. During the slow journey back to Rivercross, he'd kept telling himself that his messages had gone astray, that *that* was the reason he'd had no replies, that his men would meet him here as intended. But they weren't going to meet him here. They were gone. All the fine men, all the Inquisitors he had brought with him a few months before to rid this land of the stench of magic were gone. He hadn't been able to find out what happened to them. Every time he asked about his men, he got the same response: The person would spit on the ground and make a sign against evil.

He'd like to meet the man who wrote that song about the Inquisitors, calling them the Black Coats, magicians of dark magic who were the Evil One's servants, accusing them of creating the nighthunters that were plaguing several villages where Inquisitors had been.

The Inquisitors were the warriors *against* evil, the Evil One's *foe.* And everyone was supposed to believe the *witches* had created the nighthunters to harm the good villagers. The creatures had been a necessary weapon in the fight to free the world of the foul stink of magic.

But the song haunted, and it had spread like fire from village to village along the border of Sylvalan.

Yes, he'd like to meet the man who wrote that song. He'd like the chance to cleanse that man's spirit of the Evil One's influence.

But first he would go home and rest. Rest and gather his strength and his other Inquisitors. Then, over the winter months, he would decide what to do.

Adolfo straightened his coat, picked up the traveling bag, and left the inn. The ferry that took people and goods across the river that separated Sylvalan from Wolfram would be leaving soon, and he didn't want to miss it.

As he walked to the ferry station, he drew in a deep breath—and exhaled quickly, wrinkling his nose. The air smelled of dirty water, but underneath that was the first touch of autumn.

He would be glad to leave this hateful land and return to his home country where there was order and men were the masters. He would be glad to return to a place that treated Inquisitors with the respect and deference due them.

As he turned the corner of the short, cobblestoned street that led to the ferry station, he saw the black-haired woman on a dark horse blocking the way to the dock.

He trembled, but he forced himself to walk toward her.

"Get out of my way," he said in a commanding voice that, nonetheless, shook a little.

"I have a message for you," she said.

"Then deliver it and be gone."

She looked at him a long time. "The Fae are returning to the Old Places. We are reclaiming the land that has always been ours. As long as we are left in peace, the humans have no reason to fear us. If we are not left in peace . . ."

The warning hung in the air between them.

"It was you, wasn't it?" Adolfo said, his breathing becoming harsh, ragged. "*You* killed my men."

"It was the only way to stop them from doing more harm," she said quietly.

"Harm!" Adolfo stared at her. "*Harm!* We came here to free men from the chains of magic that keep them servants instead of the rightful masters of their world. We did no *harm*."

"You slaughtered the witches, who are our kin. *We* consider that harm."

"The witches." Adolfo's lips curled back in a snarl. It always came back to the witches. Females with magic who men had to placate in order to survive. Just like the foul creature standing in his way.

Except *he* wasn't some sniveling, powerless man. *He* was the Master Inquisitor, the Witch's Hammer. He had cleansed the world of *hundreds* of witches. And here was this creature just staring at him as if he was something she could brush aside and forget.

One blow to the head. That's all it would take to stun her enough so that she couldn't use her power against him. That's all it would take to change something dangerous into something helpless, something that was at *his* mercy. One blow. That's all it would take. And the other blows that would follow would soften her for the cleansing.

He would pull her from that horse and throw her on the cobblestones. He would smash her head against the stones, smash her face against them—one time for every man she had taken from him. Then he would find a quiet room, a dark room where he could work with her. He would break her fingers, break her feet. He would make a new bridle with witch stingers that would not only pierce the tongue and cheeks but eyes and ears as well. And when he was through with her, when she was humbled and obedient to his every command, he would take her out to some lonely road and leave her there, blind, deaf, mute, and crippled. *Then* let her see how much power she had.

With a cry of rage, he threw himself at her.

The dark horse pivoted.

Adolfo stumbled, thrown off balance. His left hand brushed against the woman's leg. He tried to grab her, tried to hold on, but his left arm suddenly went numb from fingertips to shoulder. Unable to regain his balance, he fell.

He lay there, breathing harshly.

"Remember what I said," she said softly.

He rolled to his side and watched her ride away. Her dark horse made no sound on the cobblestones.

A bell on the dock began to ring, alerting passengers that the ferry was leaving in a few minutes.

People hurried past him. A couple of them hesitated when they reached him, but when he looked at them, whatever they saw in his face made them leave without offering to help him.

Slowly, painfully, Adolfo got to his feet. His left arm hung at his side, useless.

Leaving his traveling bag on the street, he stumbled to the dock, fumbled one-handed for the coins to pay for his passage. When he finally boarded the ferry, he went to the bow and stared straight ahead at the Wolfram shore.

He stared at his homeland's shore for the entire journey—and never once looked back.

Chapter Thirty-four

Flustered and furious, Dianna galloped down the shining road through the Veil to Brightwood.

She'd settle this with Lyrra once and for all. Just see if she didn't. The *gall* of the woman! If one of the Fae staying at Brightwood hadn't come up the road to tell her about Lyrra's betrayal, when would she have known? When the road started to *close*?

She burst out of the trees that bordered the meadow. A low stone wall was in front of her, one she hadn't seen before. She jumped the pale mare over the wall, ignoring the shouts of the Fae working nearby as the mare trampled the young green plants growing in the turned earth. She jumped the wall near the cottage, then brought the mare to a scrambling halt just outside the kitchen door.

She pushed her way through the kitchen crowded with Fae, strode through the main room, and threw open the bedroom door.

Lyrra stared at her for a moment, then resumed packing her saddlebags.

"So it's true," Dianna said. "You're really doing this."

"Yes," Lyrra replied calmly, "I'm leaving."

Dianna slammed the door shut, and shouted, "How can you be so selfish? Don't you realize what this means?"

Lyrra threw down the tunic she'd just finished folding and turned to face Dianna. "It means you're going to have to keep your promise. It means you're going to have to stay at Brightwood to be the anchor that helps the rest of the Fae here keep the shining road open."

"*You're* the anchor. *You're* the one who has some trace of the House of Gaian in you, which we need to hold the road."

"And *you're* the one who has the moon magic that will *also* hold the road. We tested that, remember?"

Dianna's hands curled into fists. Of course she remembered, but that had nothing to do with anything. "You promised to stay!"

"I promised to stay a few days while you went back to Tir Alainn to pack the things you wanted to bring down to Brightwood. *You* promised to be back *in a few days,* Dianna. That was in the autumn. Now it's spring. And now I'm leaving."

"You're needed here!"

Lyrra pointed toward the window that looked out onto the road. "I'm needed out there. My *work* is out there. Most of the Clans *still* don't believe they need to do *anything* to keep Tir Alainn safe. I have to tell them. I have to convince them. Aiden's doing everything he can, but he can't do it alone."

"Your work," Dianna sneered. "Your *work*. You don't need to be wandering around in the human world to do your *work*. This isn't about your *work*, it's about *Aiden*. You just can't stand knowing he's spending his time between other women's thighs and not giving you a second thought."

Lyrra's eyes were blank and cold. "What he does is his own business. But he's the Bard, and I'm the Muse. We have to get the Fae to understand that they can't expect the House of Gaian to continue to shoulder the burden of Tir Alainn's existence while they do nothing."

"*They're only witches!*" Dianna shouted.

Lyrra's eyes turned colder. "Yes," she said softly. "I imagine that's how we justified it all those generations ago. They were Fae, but they weren't *really* Fae. They weren't like the rest of us. And they weren't. They were the Daughters, the wellsprings through which

the Mother's power flowed, the Pillars of the World."
She closed her eyes, turned away. "They owe us nothing.
But we owe them. It's time we paid that debt with
something more than trinkets and stud service to
breed the next generation."

Lyrra took a deep breath, let it out slowly, then
continued her packing. "I read the journals."

"You had no right to look at them," Dianna snapped.
"Those were private journals that belong to Ari's
family."

"Ari and her family are gone. There's no one left
to read them. Except us." She fastened her saddlebags, then turned to look at Dianna. "A couple of
journals seem to be missing. There were gaps in her
family's story."

Why should I care about the journals? Dianna
thought. *They're not important now. If Lyrra doesn't
stay . . .*

"If you're so determined to leave," Dianna said,
"wait another day or two so that I—"

"Can make another promise you have no intention
of keeping?" Lyrra shook her head. "Whether you
leave or stay is up to you." She started to say something else, then stopped and picked up her saddlebags.
"Aiden has the horses saddled by now. He's waiting
for me."

"Oh, yes," Dianna said bitterly. "When Aiden snaps
his fingers, you dance to his tune."

Lyrra stared at her for a moment, then brushed past
her, opened the door, and left the room.

Dianna waited until she heard the front door open
and close before she walked out of the bedroom.

The main room was filled with Fae. Friends. Family.
All looking at her with eyes that silently pleaded.

She walked back into the bedroom and shut the
door. She stood there for a few minutes, doing nothing, seeing nothing. Then she walked into the dressing
room and stared out the window.

A hawk flew low across the meadow, a rabbit in his
talons. Falco, bringing meat for the evening meal.

Tears filled Dianna's eyes. She pressed a hand against her mouth to keep from sobbing.

If she left now and the shining road closed, her Clan wouldn't remember that it was really Lyrra's fault. They would blame *her.*

So she was trapped here. She would live here in the cottage, confined to the boundaries of the Old Place, while she watched the families of her Clan come and go to a place she would never see again.

She swallowed against the bitterness that welled up inside her. And she wondered, briefly, if this was how the witches had felt when the Fae had gone to Tir Alainn and had left them to anchor the world they had created and never got to see.

Chapter Thirty-five

Early summer.

Morag looked at the generous dish of stew and the thick slices of bread smeared with honey butter and could have wept with gratitude. The past months had been bitter ones for her. The Huntress and the Lightbringer had made good on their threat. She was shunned by all the Clans, including her own, for her "betrayal" of the Fae. No one prevented her from traveling up one of the shining roads or entering a Clan house, but they all acted as if she didn't exist. She had endured it over the winter months, traveling from one Clan to another, because the season had been fiercer than previous years and finding adequate shelter in the human world for herself and her companions had proved too precarious. But as soon as she could, she had returned to the human world, traveling west, always west.

"Why do you not eat?" Ashk said, taking a seat across from Morag at the outdoor table.

Morag hesitated. When she had ridden into this Old Place earlier in the day and met Ashk walking through the woods, the woman had invited her to return to the Clan house for a meal. Ashk claimed to be merely a Lady of the Woods, but there had been sharp amusement in her eyes when she'd said it. And seeing how swiftly the other Fae reacted to her orders to make their guests comfortable, Morag suspected that Ashk was far more than "merely" anything.

"You know who I am?" Morag asked.

Ashk looked Morag in the eyes, her lips curving in

a gentle, but feral, smile. "You are the Gatherer. Have you come here for a reason?"

Morag shook her head. "I'm just traveling. But you should know . . . I've been shunned by the Clans."

Ashk twiddled her fingers in a dismissive gesture. "The Clans in the west of Sylvalan have always been thought to be inferior because we chose to maintain our connection with the Mother and not live entirely in Tir Alainn. Our males are looked down upon as inadequate sires for the children of other Clans, and the males from those other Clans have little desire, or ability, to be adequate mates for our females." The smile now held a dangerous quality. "It is their loss. They have no idea what bloodlines run through our veins."

A shiver ran through Morag, though she couldn't say why. Perhaps it was the feeling of more magic here, more power here, than she'd felt in any other Clan.

"If the Lightbringer or the Huntress find out you've offered me hospitality, they won't be pleased," Morag said.

"There is no reason for them to find out, and even if they did, it is of no matter. The Lightbringer and the Huntress are children who have had their noses bloodied for the first time and are howling to all who will listen about being treated unfairly. We do not listen to the poutings of children."

Morag stared at Ashk, stunned by such a scathing assessment, even if it was cuttingly accurate.

"So," Ashk said. "Now that you know how *this* Clan feels about the things that are being said, eat while the food is still warm."

This Clan? Morag wondered, obediently giving her attention to her meal. Or Ashk? Or was that the same thing?

"Besides," Ashk said, helping herself to a slice of bread, "there is plenty and more to share. The Mother shows her joy with her bounty."

"I'm glad to hear someone has a reason to celebrate."

Ashk nodded. Her eyes shone. "The young Lord of the Woods finally came home late last summer. He brought some fine horses with him, including two stallions. But best of all, he brought a wife."

Morag set her spoon carefully in her dish. "A wife?"

"A young woman as fine and strong as his mother, who had been a dear friend of mine . . . as well as a distant cousin. Oh, yes, that's why the Mother celebrates." Ashk opened her arms and looked up at the trees above them. "A Daughter of the House of Gaian once more walks this land."

"What?" Morag said faintly, not daring to hope . . . and not able to stop herself from hoping.

Ashk smiled at her. "A witch. The young Lord's wife is a witch."

The raven watched the man from her perch in a nearby tree. Beneath her, her companion whined softly but remained hidden.

The man stripped off his shirt, laying it over the low stone wall that formed the boundary for the large kitchen garden. He retrieved the narrow hoe to weed the next row of vegetables. He looked fit and well . . . and content.

So did the dark stallion grazing in the meadow alongside a dark mare. In a pasture beyond the home yard, she caught a glint of golden skin among the other horses and wondered if the sun stallion had found his own way here. Perhaps he'd had help, she decided as another man emerged from a fine-looking stable—the groom who had waited for her the day she'd taken Ahern to the Shadowed Veil.

It warmed her to know that all the males had found a good life. Still, she ruffled her feathers restlessly, waiting to see one other person.

Her wait was rewarded a short time later when the

woman walked out of the cottage and headed for the kitchen garden.

"Neall," Ari scolded. "You've your own work to do. I can weed the garden."

Neall mopped his face with his shirt and gave her a stern look. "You're supposed to be resting."

"I've rested. Now I can hoe. I'll stop if I get tired."

"You always say that, and you never do."

The raven watched their brief tug-of-war for the hoe end in a kiss that she thought should lead to more interesting things than deciding who would weed the garden.

Her companion whined again.

She fluttered to the ground, landing where the trees would hide her as she changed to her human form.

"Stay here," Morag said quietly.

She hesitated, not wanting to spoil their peace or their pleasure.

Merry meet, and merry part, and merry meet again.

She hoped so.

She stepped out of the trees and walked toward them.

Ari's eyes widened. Neall spun around, defensive. He vaulted over the garden wall and strode to meet her, much as he'd done once before.

"Morag," he said warily.

"Neall," she replied quietly. She knew what she'd hoped for. His expression told her it could never be.

Then Ari stepped up beside Neall, her eyes questioning but her smile warm. "Blessings of the day to you, Morag."

Morag returned the smile, even though it felt bittersweet.

"What brings you here?" Neall asked, still wary . . . and defensive.

Ari glanced at Neall, then gave Morag a worried look. "Morag . . . Do you see something?" Her hands moved protectively to cover her rounded belly.

Following that movement, Morag stared for a moment. Then she looked at both of them, delighted. "A babe?" And suddenly understood Ari's question. "May I?" When Ari nodded, she held her hand above Ari's still-protective ones. This time, there was nothing but warmth in her smile. "Life. Strong, healthy life." Then she added softly, "I see no shadows here."

They both relaxed . . . and it hurt her.

She looked into Ari's woodland eyes and saw too much understanding, as well as knowledge that hadn't been there the year before.

She knows who she is now. She knows she is a Daughter of the House of Gaian. She is no longer the girl Lucian and Dianna tried to hold onto for their own reasons.

"I was hoping we would meet again," Morag said. "I brought someone who has been waiting to see you."

She saw the apprehension in Ari's face and the tension in Neall's before she turned toward the woods and gestured.

Neall let out a strangled cry as a shadow hound burst out of the woods, racing straight for Ari. But Ari opened her arms and shouted, "Merle!"

Neall shouted, "Don't jump!"

Merle slid to a stop, tucked his tail between his legs, and cowered next to Morag, looking at the man with eyes that had never lost their sadness.

Neall dropped to one knee and held out his hand for Merle to sniff.

"Neall," Ari said, "don't scold him so. He's still a puppy."

"He's not a puppy," Neall said, petting Merle until the hound relaxed and began to wag his tail. "You've grown into a fine, strong, big lad, haven't you? And you're not really a puppy anymore. You're a young hound." The tail wagged harder. "And that's why you can't jump on Ari."

Merle looked at Ari and whined.

Ari knelt beside Neall and wrapped her arms around Merle.

Neall looked up at Morag, and said quietly, "Thank

you. We had wondered what happened to him after Ahern . . ." He cleared his throat. "Glenn did remember him and went back after leaving the farm, but the pup was already gone."

When Merle calmed down enough to let Ari get to her feet, Morag said, "I also brought three of the journals that belonged to your family. Perhaps I shouldn't have taken them, but I thought you would like to have your grandmother's journal and a couple of the others that would trace some of your family's history."

"Thank you, Morag. I would like to have them."

"Where are you staying?" Neall asked, some change in his eyes making Morag wonder just what the young Lord of the Woods was seeing.

"Oh . . . I'm staying with Ashk for a few days."

"You could stay with us," Ari said quietly.

"But if you do," Neall added, "you'll have to hoe your share of the garden."

"Neall," Ari hissed. "You don't make a guest work for her supper."

"She's not a guest," he replied. "She's Clan."

Something jolted through Morag, as if something painful inside her had broken and had to hurt before it could heal.

Will you walk away from this, Morag? The Clans shun you now, and you've made enemies among your own kind. And this was why you made those choices. So that they could be here in this place, with the rich life ahead of them. And now they're offering to share that life. They're offering to be family in a way your own ceased to be since you became the Gatherer. Will you walk away?

"I don't know how to weed a garden," Morag said.

Neall grinned. "Not to worry. I'll teach you."

Ari poked Neall in the ribs. "Behave." She held out her hand.

Morag hesitated a moment before slipping her hand into Ari's.

Ari smiled at her. "Come in and be welcome, Morag."

THE
TIR ALAINN
TRILOGY
by
Anne Bishop

The Pillars of the World
"Bishop only adds luster to her reputation for
fine fantasy." —*Booklist*

Shadows and Light
"Plenty of thrills, faerie magic, human nastiness,
and romance." —*Locus*

The House of Gaian
"A vivid fantasy world....Beautiful." —*BookBrowser*

Available wherever books are sold or at
penguin.com

The Black Jewels
Novels
by Anne Bishop

"Darkly mesmerizing...fascinatingly different."
—Locus

This is the story of the heir to a dark throne, a magic more powerful than that of the High Lord of Hell, and an ancient prophecy. These books tell of a ruthless game of politics and intrigue, magic and betrayal, love and sacrifice, destiny and fulfillment, as the Princess Jaenelle struggles to become that which she was meant to be.

Daughter of the Blood

Heir to the Shadows

Queen of the Darkness

Tangled Webs

The Invisible Ring

Available wherever books are sold or at
penguin.com